THE
KING'S
PAWN

A Sarah Black Spy Novel

By Lucy Hooft

Burning Chair Limited, Trading As Burning Chair Publishing
61 Bridge Street, Kington HR5 3DJ

www.burningchairpublishing.com

By Lucy Hooft
Edited by Simon Finnie and Peter Oxley
Cover by Burning Chair Publishing

First published by Burning Chair Publishing, 2022

ISBN: 978-1-912946-30-3

Also by Lucy Hooft

The Head of the Snake – Book 2 in the Sarah Black Series
(coming soon from Burning Chair Publishing)

For Caroline Malamba

PROLOGUE

'Why are we here?' Chris steps a polished brogue over a sheet of twisted metal.

'To play a game of chess.' The set of Michael's face gives nothing away, his immaculate appearance untroubled by the scene of destruction.

The thin light of dawn shows a landscape colourless and flat. An expanse of dust and rock stretches in all directions, broken only by the parallel lines of the tracks. Against this bare canvas, the devastation of the crash site jumps out in hard focus. The front and back of the train still stand—four perfect carriages, all but untouched by the impact, bookending a space stripped bare. The missing carriages have been obliterated by the force of the explosion.

'Why would he feed us something like this? Azerbaijan is strictly their turf.' Chris pulls a camera from a leather holster to record the damage.

'It is.' Keeping Chris a step behind, Michael walks on with the bearing of a silent hunter in a three-piece suit. 'The only thing you can be sure of from a KGB officer of Kuznetsov's vintage, is that it will be more than it seems. The question is: what move does he want us to make?'

Michael studies a group of workers sitting on the bank above the tracks; waiting, watching. Their faces register curiosity. The figure closest to him draws heavily on a cigarette, dark eyes fixed on Michael. They wear no uniform, carry no distinguishing marks. Kuznetsov's men, or just the work crew come to clear away the chaos?

'What if he's brought us here just because he can? To show that he calls and we jump?'

Michael raises a hand, instructing Chris to lower his voice. 'Perhaps. But I'd be surprised if there wasn't more. There will be something he wants us to know, and he needs to be the one to tell us.' Michael's voice is calm, playing through the moves with the sang-froid of an old hand. He side-steps a body lying next to the track, shrouded in a brightly-coloured blanket—only the top of the head and two bare forearms can be seen, as if the cover is nothing more than shade from an overbearing sun. The air hangs thick with ash and the smell of burning plastic and foam.

Michael scans the debris strewn across the bank—window frames twisted and contorted by the impact, a door panel still surprisingly intact, but opening now onto a cluster of stones. A pair of red-covered cushions lie face up as if thrust from the train by a twin ejector seat. He sees him. Kuznetsov—for many years a grim rival, now an awkward ally; at least when it suits him.

Kuznetsov stands framed by a ruptured cabin, both hands outstretched in greeting. He grips Michael's hand tightly and pulls him in close, pressing Michael's face into his shiny cauliflower ear. A brief nod of acknowledgement to Chris.

'You know, I was up very early this morning.' Kuznetsov is still holding Michael's hand. 'And you know what I saw? Mushrooms! Here, in this wasteland. Good enough to eat. A perfect little ring.'

'Extraordinary.' Michael catches Chris's eye.

'It is. You never know what you might find when you get up early, and if you remember to look.'

'I shall keep my eyes peeled.'

'Here, I have someone I want you to meet.' A hint of mischief lifts Kuznetzov's double-lidded eyes. Or is it something else? It is hard to tell in one so practised at keeping his own secrets. He scrambles down the embankment, gesturing for Michael to follow. With a magician's flourish, he whips off an orange polyester blanket that was covering another body. The figure beneath is lying face down, but the front of his chest gapes upwards. As Michael bends closer, trying to understand the contorted physiognomy, Kuznetsov rolls the head away with the toe of his highly polished boot. The head, no longer attached to its body, rolls to a stop, open mouth gawping at the sky.

Chris heaves deeply into his sleeve. Michael stares at the severed head, unblinking. The dead man's face has a waxy sheen, his eyes flung open in a final moment of shock. Michael is just as surprised to see him again.

'I'm told you might know who this is.' Kuznetsov tilts back his head, addressing Michael down the length of his oversized nose.

Michael lifts his chin. Of course Kuznetsov would know how deeply this face was written into his memory. Michael hasn't seen him since the sting, the moment that changed everything. But he'd never forget the face.

'It's a funny thing, you know, seeing him here.' Kuznetsov traces circles with his toe in the dusty ground. 'Because just last week he was in my office.'

'Oh?'

'He came to spill the beans on a weapons transfer into Azerbaijan. We'd picked it up, of course, but didn't know where it was going.' Kuznetsov swings forward on his toes.

'And he told you?' Michael tries to keep the impatience out of his voice.

'You know who he's connected to?'

'No. I only met him once.'

'You didn't know he was one of Ibragimov's guys?' Kuznetsov stops rocking, observing Michael with genuine surprise.

'Ibragimov…' Michael nods, his neutral expression clamped

3

in place is not enough to hide his glee. He's always known, or at least suspected, that Ibragimov—that creature of the shadows—was the one who set him up. But he's never had the proof to pin it to him. Until now.

'Huh.' Kuznetsov is smiling, shaking his large head. 'I always thought you knew.'

'That's the problem with secrets,' Michael's face opens into a lop-sided smile, revealing a top lip softened by a childhood scar. 'You never know who to tell them to.'

So that's Kuznetsov's game—offering Michael his chance for revenge, knowing he'd never be able to refuse.

'So our friend here squealed on his boss,' Michael continues, 'and a week later ends up dead. No accident, then?'

'An improvised explosive device in the toilets. He was lucky he only lost his head.' Kuznetsov gives a fat laugh.

'How many casualties?'

'Six. Only he was known.'

Chris raises his camera to the dead man, in both the spots where he now lies.

'Do you mind if my colleague checks over the other victims?' Michael asks.

'Be my guest.'

Chris moves away to photograph the remaining bodies under their colourful wrappings, leaving the two old spies to continue their game of chess.

*

'It's good to see you, Michael,' Kuznetsov says as Chris reappears, looking ashen. He lays a hand on Michael's shoulder before turning back to the work crew, still watching, awaiting his signal.

'What did you talk about?' Chris asks when Kuznetsov was out of earshot.

'Mushrooms.' Michael scratches his chin with the back of his thumbnail.

'Really?'

'No, not really.'

'If I'd known what this morning was going to be about, I'd have skipped those greasy sausages at breakfast.' Chris still looks pale. 'It's funny, the corpses smell different here.'

'Different how?'

'I don't know. Less meaty somehow, with a whiff of pickled vegetables. Must be the dry air.'

Michael pulls the blanket back over the dead agent's body. He was only the middleman, carrying out Ibragimov's orders, but there is a certain satisfaction in knowing that his disloyalty to Ibragimov would finally allow Michael to right a decade-old wrong.

A beam of sunlight breaks through the underside of the ruined carriage, revealing unexpected brightness where the roof has been ripped away. They walk in silence, Michael pondering what might be in it for Kuznetsov to hand him this ammunition. What does Kuznetsov stand to gain by setting Michael after Ibragimov?

'Those weapons?' Michael says to Chris. 'Kuznetsov thinks they're headed to Ibragimov in Azerbaijan. We're going to have to send someone in.'

'I can go,' Chris says.

'No, you can't. It's too risky. Besides, you don't speak Russian. You'd be no use to me.'

'So, off the books then?' Chris asks, his voice low.

'It has to be. I have someone in mind. I'd hoped to have more time with her, bring her up to scratch. But we're going to have to throw in a line. She'll do for now as bait.'

CHAPTER 1

d4 Nf6

She is going to tell him this time. She'll get in early. The moment she lets him take control of the conversation, it's too late.

Sarah strides through the restaurant, Michael's choice, as always, her jaw set. She spots him immediately—immaculate silver hair, finely-tailored suit showing no hint of the horizontal rain she has battled through on her bike. The restaurant is soulless but conveniently busy. Reliably full, nobody's regular, booking never required. This evening's venue has at least the aspiration of elegance: dark wood and shiny chrome echoing with office workers released for the week, theatregoers gobbling down the cut-price early-bird specials and the neat clack of the waitresses' lacquered heels. Sarah ignores her own bedraggled appearance reflected in the mirrored panelling, the squelch of soggy insoles in her leather boots, her hair clinging to her scalp in damp channels.

'You're wet,' Michael says as he pulls out her chair.

'It's raining. I came on my bike.' She lifts a damp clump of hair from her cheekbone and unsticks her blouse from her skin with a gummy smack.

'How very brave of you.' Michael sits back on the bench, fingertips tapping gently on the table. Taxi dry. 'That seems to be the current fad of your generation: endless moving and activity. In my day we were always quite happy taking the bus.'

'I like the exercise,' Sarah says, too sharply. He is trying to unsettle her. A surprising opening to knock her off balance. She mustn't rise to it and yet she does. It's his preferred style of play: sometimes charming, sometimes provocative, often both.

'I can't help but wonder,' Michael's expert eye probes over Sarah's shoulder at the next table. Their neighbour, a portly man with delicate hands, chews methodically, like a buffalo. 'If the modern obsession with activity and fitness is not just a way of hiding the inability of young people today to sit still, to reflect and engage in careful slow thought.' His eyes return to Sarah's, his face set in a half smile.

She's glad he's in a prickly mood. It's easier to stick to her resolve.

'I like the rush of adrenaline that comes from cycling in London,' Sarah replies. 'There's nothing like a quick brush with death to make you feel alert.'

'Well, we all like to set our hearts racing from time to time. And it suits you. The rain brings out the green in your eyes.' He delivers the compliment while turning away from her, his attention fixed on the menu, disarming her eyeroll. He handles the card as if it might crumble in his hands. His fingernails, cut blunt and short, strike Sarah as unnaturally shiny. The tightly curved arches rise at odds with his otherwise overtly masculine appearance.

'Remind me,' he asks. 'Do you prefer your wine fruity or dry?'

'I thought it was your job to remember these things.'

'It is. I also know that it's wise to allow a woman to change

7

her mind.' His smile over the top of the menu card is less point-scoring than she expects, almost gentle. His eyes are distant, preoccupied perhaps with another problem, but when focused on her they are startlingly blue.

'I'd like something dry please.'

'Of course. In that case, I think we should have the Sancerre. Happy?'

'Perfect.' Sarah takes a breath; he's ahead but the board is still wide open. She needs to tell him now.

Michael signals to the waitress, who appears instantly at his side. Her hair is held in a superbly slick ponytail, her uniform elegant black, but Sarah can't take her eyes off the quiver of the improbable eyelashes. She pictures them at the end of the evening, two upturned centipedes discarded on the nightstand.

Michael waits until the waitress is out of earshot. 'I am pleased to say that your vetting report has come back. Other than one or two,' he pauses mid-sentence and separates his lips with the tip of his tongue, 'interesting points, I have the go-ahead to take this forward.'

The waitress brings the wine and opens it with a considerable show, leaning low over Michael to pour a glass to taste. At his nod of satisfaction, her poised expression opens into a fawning smile, centipedes fluttering eagerly. Sarah wants to tell her not to bother, he's not worth the hard work, but she resists. The girl is only doing her job. The waitress fills both glasses, her attention focused fully on sealing Michael's approval. Near Michael's right elbow, Sarah notices an unmarked manila folder, the glossy corners of a stack of photos just visible beneath the cover. Michael must have set it there deliberately, to rouse and bait her curiosity. She won't look.

She stares at the folder as the waitress continues her performance, polished fingertips flashing as she adjusts Michael's napkin.

The waitress is dismissed with another nod and Michael raises his glass. 'So. To your future?'

This is the moment to make her move. To apologise to Michael for having wasted his time and leave. She needs to withdraw before being enticed into another of Michael's games. But she hesitates.

She has always enjoyed their debates. Michael probing her views on political issues of the day, arguing against whichever position she takes. Watching how she reacts under pressure, how her brain works, where her opinions are fixed and where there is wiggle room. She enjoys turning the table on him—making him justify clearly outrageous opinions dropped as if everyone is a secret fascist and would agree with him. She's never met anyone who could talk so entirely without scruple while giving away so little about what they really thought. Their battles intrigue her, challenge her to up her game, to pin him into the intellectual corner he always manages to swerve.

But their last meeting brushed closer to the real nature of intelligence work, posing questions designed to test not just her intellect but also her moral fibre. He twisted deeper into what it meant to work in his world, and suddenly it was real. Their relationship was not just a surreptitious set of coffee dates with a suave silver-haired spook, a bit of fun while her friends were filing graduate job applications and poring over the punctuation of their résumés. He was testing her for a career, a life choice, a step into his world of secrets and shadows. He needed to know if she could take it.

At the end of the last meeting, he left her with a question. Consider the case of a useful agent who is a committed alcoholic. He spills his best secrets as the evening descends into the depths of a whiskey bottle. But his wife is threatening to leave him if he doesn't quit the drink. What, Michael wanted to know, would Sarah do? Ever the philosopher, with an instinct of following every problem through to its natural conclusions, Sarah reached the only logical answer: kill the wife.

Immediately, she wanted out. She is not cut out for the grittier side of Michael's world. An entertaining side track to avoid the soul-crushing reality of job fairs and the "milkround" and empty corporate jobs with their promises of fat salaries in return for your pound of flesh was one thing. But it's no easier to sell her soul for the greater good, to rein in her sense of justice and equality to Queen and country first. Even the constraints of secrecy feel like a trap. She wants to talk it through, to thrash it out with her best friend over a bottle of cheap wine, to rant about the options round a kitchen table. But her friends don't know Michael exists.

She has to tell Michael she wants out before he has the chance to reel her any further in.

Michael's waiting, his glass raised, studying her hesitation. Disembodied piano music clatters over the cold echo of cutlery and glass. Sarah's hands are fixed in her lap. Why is it so difficult to say: *I want out?* The phrase that gave such blissful relief when she realised it was still an option. Sarah tries to dry the sweat on her palms, but the over-starched napkin slides about on the surface of her clammy skin. She takes a gulp of water and stalls. 'I've been thinking a lot since our last meeting.'

'You have?' Michael pauses, his glass hanging mid-air.

'Yes. I've been turning over some of the questions we discussed.' Sarah pictures the bumped-off wife, the inconsolable husband. 'And the more I think about it, the more I realise that this line of work really isn't for me.' Her voice breaks mid-sentence, but she keeps her gaze fixed on Michael's penetrating eyes.

He watches her, his face immobile. Sips his wine but says nothing.

'The question you gave me last time we met,' Sarah continues. 'I haven't been able to get it out of my head and I'm not comfortable with any of my answers.'

'And what would you do?'

'Well, kill the wife of course.'

Michael laughs, his eyes crease into warm lines Sarah has never seen before. 'You'd kill the wife? That's a bit extreme, isn't it?'

'That's my point.'

The warmth fades from Michael's face. He's waiting for more, but she won't give it. Waiting. Reading. He straightens the cutlery on the table. 'Well of course I'm disappointed. But you have also proved me right.'

'Right?'

'I very much hoped you would be able to get through this. I think the scruples are something you could get over with a bit of effort, we all do. But I have always worried that you weren't cut out for this work.'

'What do you mean?' Sarah is thrown. She expected disappointment, she had steeled herself for efforts to change her mind. He is not supposed to be agreeing with her.

'You're young, Sarah, and bright, but I rather feel you still see the world in the way that you think it ought to be, not the way it is. It's normal at your age to be idealistic, in fact it's enviable, but it's a difficult trait to satisfy in our line of work.'

'Isn't a strong sense of right and wrong a prerequisite for doing what you do?'

'Don't get me wrong; it is. But knowing where right lies is not always as straightforward as you might think.' He sits back, leaning casually onto one manicured hand. 'In this business we have to convince people to tell us things they are not supposed to tell. We have to understand what makes people tick, what gets them excited, what they would be willing to risk their lives for. And it is often not the good and noble causes that really drive people.' Michael pauses. 'We have to know what people are afraid of, find their weaknesses, the vices that keep them awake at night. Then we have to use them.' He takes another mouthful of wine, eyes fixed on Sarah. 'What I'm asking, Sarah, is whether you really think that your conscience would allow you to use all available means in order to convince someone to tell you what you needed to know?'

The noises in the restaurant grow louder, the piano music

11

jarring and discordant. 'All available means?'

'Yes, Sarah. Don't be coy; you know what I mean.'

'Well I just told you I'd bump off a man's wife for wanting to help her husband? Not tough enough for you?'

'No, you told me you didn't want this job because you thought I'd want you to kill the wife.'

'I never said I didn't want this job.' It's out before she realises what she's saying. Turning down Michael's proposition seemed a straightforward choice when she was certain a job would be offered. Now that he is questioning whether she is up to it, she is compelled to defend herself.

'Oh? That's what it sounded like to me.'

'I suppose the wife wouldn't have to die. You could sabotage her efforts for a while, maintain the status quo while making it look as if he's trying?'

'Good. You're starting to think through the layers of complexity.'

Sarah's stomach gives a warm purr. She knows she shouldn't care, but she can't help but feel pleased with his nod of approval.

'Okay, how about one final scenario?' He opens the manila folder at his elbow and spreads it across the table. The photo on top shows the mangled metal and shattered glass of a train crash. A body lies on the ground, chest up—its severed head staring at the sky from several feet away.

Sarah's world expands. Until this moment, the other people in the crowded restaurant were background noise, blending in with the cocktail music and occasional shouts from the kitchen. As Michael reveals the photo, the room grows eyes and ears.

She checks the next-door table, where the buffalo is still chewing ponderously over his partner's valiant attempts at conversation. The partner looks resigned to filling the gaps between her unanswered questions with another swig of chardonnay. On the other side, an older couple are having the sort of fun that could only be illicit—her painted grin stretches wide over shiny back teeth, an expensive shoe paws at his shin.

No one is paying the least attention to the silver fox in the well-cut suit showing photos of graphic violence to a dishevelled blonde.

'You're going to have to learn to look a lot less suspicious,' Michael says without looking up. 'Pretend I'm showing you some rather boring holiday snaps if that would make you feel better. I'm fairly certain no one in here would be particularly interested in my tour of Greek temples.'

'What happened?' Sarah's voice comes out as little more than a whisper.

'That's what we'd like to find out. A train was derailed in Azerbaijan, following an explosion. Someone had planted a makeshift bomb in the toilets—although the major damage seems to have come from the military-grade shaped charge device carried in a briefcase. Half a dozen killed. One of the dead was a known agent—looks like he was carrying the briefcase. But at the moment that's all we've got.'

Sarah's head spins faster with each detail Michael tosses out. Is this for real? Have they really slipped from theoretical drunks to real-life severed heads in the course of a glass of wine? 'But who…?' she stammers.

'We've taken our eye off the ball in the Caucasus. For years we've focused all our efforts towards the threat of Islamic extremism. Then something like this happens and it turns out we have no reliable agents to tell us anything.'

The waitress appears at Michael's shoulder, reaching across his arm to refill his glass. Sarah hardly dares look. Should she try and cover up the photo? She could fling her wine across the chair to distract the waitress's attention, make her look anywhere but at the incriminating picture.

'Is everything to your satisfaction, sir?' the waitress flashes her improbable eyelashes at Michael. 'Could I bring you another bottle?'

'Thank you, it was delicious, but I'm not sure we have time to properly enjoy another.' He looks up appreciatively, his pupils

13

dilating as he matches the waitress' smile.

'And would you like to order anything to eat? I can bring you the menu or let you know the specials we have this evening?' She drops her voice, responding to Michael's expertly calibrated flirtation.

'I'm sure your specials are all sumptuous,' Michael looks at Sarah and gives a suggestion of a wink, 'but I'm afraid we are rather pressed for time this evening. Perhaps I could trouble you to bring the bill when you have a moment?'

How can he be so relaxed, so casual, talking to a stranger over a table of secret material? But the waitress is only interested in his suggestive eyes. He has her full attention focused exactly where he wants it.

Michael watches the waitress sashay away, then turns back to Sarah as if nothing happened.

'We're in the dark here, Sarah. There's too much that we don't know, and we need people on the ground. Good people, who are willing to take risks, to get their hands dirty and help us understand what is going on before it is too late.'

He raises his glass and pauses, the rim close to his lips. 'People who value achieving good, rather than just philosophising about it.'

Sarah's blood rises.

'Do you want to be one of those people, Sarah? Or would you rather go back to that internship programme at McKinsey, or whatever other option it was that you were pursuing?'

The waitress is not the only one to have been successfully manoeuvred to exactly where Michael wants her. Sarah doesn't need to play through the final moves, she's ready to topple her king. There's no need to stretch the humiliation by arguing against herself any further. Is she that easy to play? She starts to reply but Michael interrupts.

'Don't answer now. I think you should sleep on it. These are big decisions, and not to be taken lightly.'

He stands, giving her a swift kiss on the cheek. His cheekbone

14

brushes hers, hard and cold. He smells of ruthlessness: sandalwood and soap, with a trace of alcohol.

'I'll call you in the morning. Do enjoy your cycle home.'

CHAPTER 2

THE RECRUIT

'And you're sure you're up for this?' The Castle leans back into the booth, tapping his cigarette into an ashtray on the round mirrored table. 'I don't even need to tell you how big this is. That's obvious, right?' He tilts his head to one side and squints at the Pawn through a cloud of smoke. 'But we'll need you to stay on target, to keep focus. We need complete trust in you.' He stabs a finger into the shiny surface of the table in time with his words.

'Sure,' the Pawn shrugs. 'Of course,' he adds, a little late. Focus is easy. He does not suffer from nerves anyway, at least not in the way other people do. What's the point? He knows what he's doing. Only other people can screw things up. He sits back, leaning onto his hand to mirror the Castle's confident swagger. The dark velvet of the booth is slimy to the touch, ancient grease and sweat congealed on the viscose fibres. He whips his hand back to his lap.

'And blood. Can you deal with blood?' The Castle is trying

to look serious, but his lips twist with dark delight. 'We can't have someone who's going to pull a whitey at the first sign of bloodshed.'

The Pawn nods; he's fine with blood. So long as it's not his own.

The Castle stubs out his cigarette and looks at the Pawn as if for the first time. His body language suggests brash confidence, unapologetic about the space he takes up. But there are cracks. His top lip is wet with sweat. Is he having doubts about the plan or about the Pawn's ability to pull it off? 'Have you done anything like this before?' he asks.

What's the right answer? Yes, show confidence, experience, offer reassurance that he knows what he's doing? Or no, of course not. No one has ever done anything like this before? The Pawn chooses a nod, holding the Castle's eye for longer than he'd like. He needs to say something.

'And I'll be alone?' the Pawn asks, to fill the void in the conversation.

'What was that?' The Castle's attention is strutting away across the dancefloor.

'I'll be acting alone?' the Pawn leans in closer to be heard over the thump of the nightclub music. Uncomfortably close. He can smell the meaty sweat radiating off the Castle's collar, even over the powerful aftershave.

'We'll be there watching, from a distance. And of course we'll get you out. But the less contact the better in the run-up. Keeps things clean.'

The Castle wasn't like the others. For one thing he only recently started coming to the meetings. Most of the others have been committed for almost as long as the Pawn himself. He turns up late, looks bored, doesn't say much. But they seem to want the same things. The Pawn's eyes sit uneasily on the string of sweaty beads lined up against the dark stubble of the Castle's top lip, magnifying the pores in the sallow skin beneath. He'd rather not have anything to do with this guy. But he'd never be able to pull off something like this on his own. He needs the Castle's connections. And his cash.

'At the meeting you mentioned money? Can I get some of it up front?'

'What, like a goodwill payment?'

The Pawn struggles to read the Castle's frog-like grin. 'Yes, like a goodwill payment. To seal the deal.'

The Castle laughs and slams the table so hard it shudders. 'No you can't get a goodwill payment—are you crazy?'

The Pawn waits for the laughter to stop. 'There might be expenses—'

'We'll cover them. But full payment comes on successful completion of the job. Don't worry,' the Castle's oversized hand lands hard on the Pawn's shoulder. 'It will be more than you can even imagine.'

'How will—'

'We'll be in touch,' The Castle says as he edges out of the booth and away into the crowded dance floor.

CHAPTER 3

c4 g6

'Pass me the socket set, would you?' Sarah's father steadies his hands on the miniature back door. 'I think some of these hinges need adjusting before we can get to work on the insignia.' He is wearing his "work" clothes—a red flannel shirt and filthy corduroy trousers in dark beige. Rogue eyebrows explore over the top of oversized safety glasses.

Sarah searches through the piles of tools, spread across the worktable as if catapulted from across the room. She finds the case and hands it to her father. The veins on the back of his hands are more prominent and the skin looks paper thin, but his grasp is still strong.

'It's looking pretty good, Dad. Am I allowed to ask what you're going to do with it when it's finished?' The model Land Rover has kept him busy all winter. A perfect replica Series II in mint green, large enough to seat a pair of four-year-olds. Except her father does not know any.

'You're allowed to ask so long as you don't smirk. Anyway, it's not really about what you do with it. Here, have you seen the windscreen wipers?' he reaches behind the windscreen and two tiny blades begin to whir across the glass.

'I hope they work better than on the real thing.' Sarah leans in to get a better look. 'Do you remember that storm in the Brecon Beacons? I had to hang out the window, yanking them with a clothes hanger.'

'Well it worked, didn't it?'

'I don't think I've ever been so wet.'

'Your mother was furious when we got home. At least she tried to be. I'm pretty sure she saw the funny side, even with the muddy scuffs up the stair carpet.'

Sarah watches him closely as he prises the grill from the front of the vehicle. The nuts fall one by one into a pile on the floor. His concentration seems intact. Sarah never knows how he will react when her mother comes up in the conversation. And she is never far away.

'You said you had something you wanted to ask me?' he says, wiping his hands on a large slimy square of fabric.

Sarah picks up the fallen nuts and hands them to her father one at a time. 'I'm thinking of accepting a job.'

'That consulting one? Who was it again? McKinseys or Accenture?'

'No, not that one.' She holds out another nut.

'Oh?' he lets his glasses slip down and looks at her over the top of the frames, his Roman nose strangely magnified by the curved lenses. 'Who then?'

'The Foreign Office.'

'You didn't tell me you were doing that? Have you done the Final Selection Board?'

'Yes, it was fine. All went well.' Sarah hopes her father will not ask for details. After a life-long career in the Civil Service, he is far better placed than her to know what an entrance to the real Foreign Office would entail.

'Didn't give you too much of a hard time, did they? I'm told they can be quite vicious.'

Sarah laughs, some of her meetings with Michael did feel like being sniffed out by an angry dog. 'Nothing I couldn't handle.'

'Well, I'm not surprised they were impressed with you.'

'That's because you are my father.'

'Perhaps. But I'm sure you could convince most people to give you a job. So why the hesitation? I would have thought this was right up your street.'

'It is. Well, I think it is.'

'It's still government work, but they get their pick of the Civil Service intake. You should find plenty of worthy intellectual opponents.'

'I'm just not sure if it's my world.' Sarah passes her father the final nut. He rolls it between his fingers, examining his daughter over his plastic specs, trying to read what is behind her hesitation. It is unlike her not to come straight to the point.

Sarah wants to come clean. Her father has enough experience in that world to offer clear advice. The simple act of unloading her doubts would make the dilemma more manageable. And help release the anxiety that Michael's "holiday snaps" only helped to inflate. But Michael was clear that she is not to discuss the offer with anyone, including close family. She smiles weakly at her father, willing him to guess what she is trying to ask.

He puts his hand across her shoulder. 'Shall we go and get cleaned up then?'

Sarah takes his arm. How small it feels angled in the crook of her elbow. Her father has always been of sturdy build. In the eyes of a young girl, his strength seemed limitless. But recently he seems to have shrunk, his muscles dropped, his body turned in on itself. For the first time in Sarah's life, he looks fragile.

They close up the garage, once her mother's studio filled with scroll-like tubes of paint and strange smelling solvents, now slowly being taken over as a workshop for the tinkering that keeps her father's hands and mind occupied.

'Ah, Jeff, I think I've got you this time,' a voice calls over the fence. The deep voice rises in an unexpected squeak, old windpipes cracked through overuse.

A man in a blazer, a handkerchief tied at his neck, leans over the front gate, his eyes lit with triumph. When he sees Sarah, the look of glee begins to wane.

'Oh. Well, you could have told me your secret weapon was here,' he looks put out. 'Maybe I'll tell you later.'

'Don't worry, I won't let Sarah look. I'm perfectly capable of beating you myself.'

'You're not still on that same game, are you?' Sarah asks the neighbour with a conciliatory smile, unsure if his sulk is genuine.

'Your father can be terribly slow,' the neighbour squeaks, puffing his chest over the gate. His enormous ears seem to ride up the side of his head.

'Well, come on then, out with it.' Sarah's father plucks the head off a dead rose growing up the pink brick of the front wall.

'Knight to g4,' the neighbour whispers with a conspiratorial wink. 'And mind you don't let her help you,' he raises his chin towards Sarah. 'Yes my lovely, I know, you're impatient. We'll be off now.' Sarah thinks for a moment he is talking to her, but he walks off, led by an imperious spaniel in a tartan coat.

'Knight to g4…' Sarah's father mutters as he lets them in through the front door, opening it with his elbow to protect the shiny brass knocker from his oily hands.

Sarah follows him through the hall to the drawing room. A marble chess set carved in white and pale pink sits on a custom-made table under the French windows, the pieces out in mid-game. Sarah's father picks up the pink knight. He lingers a moment, taking in the positions of the other pieces, tapping the knight against his lips before placing it down in the fourth rank. Sarah studies the board, quickly noting the strengths and weaknesses of both sides.

'Is that really the same game you were playing last time I was here?' she asks. 'You've been easy on him. You were just about to win, weren't you?'

'Of course I go easy on him.' Her father shoos her away from the table. 'It's no fun if you win every time. Surely I don't need to tell you that? Now get away from there, he'll know if you've been meddling.'

Sarah resists the urge to point out how to block the advancing knight with a counterattack. Her father is hardly in need of her help. At least not when it comes to chess.

She picks her way through the piles of magazines and carefully stacked newspapers that line the corridor. The cleaner has learnt to create pathways through the chaos, but no one dares touch her father's stacks. He's washing his hands at the kitchen sink, working methodically, pushing the pale green soap that smells of bitter eucalyptus into his nails and cuticles. He dries his hands on the tea towel hanging over the red Aga and looks around the kitchen, suddenly lost. Sarah fills the kettle and takes two cups down from the hooks above her head.

'I do know how to make a cup of tea, you know.' He takes the cups out of her hands and goes back to staring absently out of the window. Her mother's teapot collection still lines the wide windowsill, meticulously dusted but no longer expanding to all available surfaces.

'When do you need to let them know?' He fishes a jug of milk out of the back of the fridge and gives it a quick sniff.

'Let who know?' Sarah asks.

'The Foreign Office.'

'Oh yes, um. I think quite soon.' She takes the cup of tea and perches at the large oak table, fitting her knees in between the long refectory bench and the sturdy table legs. 'And I may have to go overseas.' Her voice raises at the end, making her sentence half a question, half a statement gently seeking his approval.

'Of course you would, that is what they do.'

'But, would you,' Sarah takes a mouthful of tea, 'would you, be all right with me leaving?'

It feels a betrayal even to ask.

'All right? Of course I'll be all right. I'm perfectly capable of looking after myself. And I have Angus here.'

Sarah checks to see if her younger brother is with them at the table. He has a habit of blending into a room. His demeanour so placid, his body language so docile, she has often not noticed his presence.

Her father laughs. 'He's down the road helping the vicar with the horse chestnut in front of the church.' Angus is certainly more in touch with trees than with people. He trained as a tree surgeon but finds the term too clinical, too suggestive of harm. He prefers Arboreal Protector. People know where to find him when they need advice, but he doesn't like to advertise. He is helpful with her father to a certain extent, but not able to provide the emotional support he needs. He tends to ghost out of a room just as imperceptibly as he enters, especially when souls are bared.

'He should be back for lunch,' her father says. 'Will you stay?'

'Not today. I'm meeting Jenny.' Sarah likes to keep her visits short. It helps her maintain control. She is more useful to her father when she can hold it together. Her mother is everywhere in the house. Her music book still lies open on the piano as if she were just about to sit down to play a piece of Debussy. Her artwork fills every wall—favourite pieces prominently hung and framed, but every last serviceable vertical space has been made home to something. The cushions that she chose that no one has ever liked but will now never dare to change. The longer Sarah spends around the house, the harder it becomes to block out. Away from the constant sensory reminders of her mother, Sarah has learned to make her grief a manageable size. A constant companion, but no longer one that dominates every scene. But in her family home, she feels it swell, always threatening to spill over her carefully constructed barriers. She knows why Angus seeks solace in trees.

'How do you know when something is right?' she asks, hoping to prompt an answer to the questions she cannot ask.

'I'm hardly the person to know. I stayed in the same job for forty years.'

'But you must have known that was the place for you. How do you choose where you fit?'

Her father sits heavily opposite her, stretching his legs out into the room. 'Your problem is a glut of choice. You could turn your hand to anything, you could make anywhere into your world. I've always thought you'd be better off in the private sector. Make a bit of money for a change. But it seems none of my nudges to put you off the Civil Service have worked. I'm sure you'll do what's best.'

'And what if I choose wrong?'

'Then have another go. You're not selling your soul; you can always change your mind afterwards.'

Sarah flinches at the unintended sting. Of course he is right, but there is something in Michael's offer that seems irreversible. Once you enter his world, how easy is it to escape?

'I might even run into you in Whitehall,' her father says, grappling with the lid of the biscuit tin. 'Would you like one?'

'I didn't think you ever had much need to be up there now.' Sarah's teeth crumble into a stale shortbread.

'They've asked me to come back. Only an advisory role, one or two days a week. High-level guidance stuff for the Cabinet Office.'

Sarah pauses. She doesn't want to show another betrayal of confidence, but it feels too soon. 'Are you sure that's a good idea?'

'You can't kick around for forty years without picking up a few useful ideas about what not to do.'

'I mean, are you sure you're up for it?'

He looks down at his hands. 'I know it didn't end well. But it's different now. It's been two years since your mother passed; I've had time to adjust.'

Sarah hates the sound of the euphemism in his mouth. It is so unlike him. It's an expression he would have laughed at before her mother's death. Passed where? Passed the window? But somehow he still seems incapable of acknowledging that she's dead, her life cut off by a ruptured aneurism in her brain, her body left defunct on the floral sofa.

'Have you spoken to Jack about this?' Sarah's older brother, a newly qualified surgeon in a busy London hospital, can always be relied on for sensible advice; if you can track him down. He was the pin that held the family together after their mother died. Where Angus is charming but happiest sticking to the superficial, Jack can be prickly and distant, but he can jump straight into the essential when needed.

'Not yet,' her father says. 'He's been on night shifts this week. But he's coming down for Sunday lunch next weekend, so I'll tell him then.'

'Trouble with Vanessa again?'

Sarah's father touches his fingertips together and beams beatifically. 'Why don't you join us?'

'Yeah, I'll see.' A week from now she could be anywhere if she took up Michael's offer. 'I'm still not sure it's a good idea to go back just yet. Didn't the doctor say to avoid any unnecessary stress?'

'It's only a couple of days a week. I've insisted that no meetings can start before ten o'clock, so that I can get there on my free travel pass.'

'But you're not even old enough for one yet?'

'I will be soon. It always pays to think one step ahead, Sarah.'

Sarah takes her cup to the sink. 'I need to be getting back.'

'I'll give you a lift to the station.'

He puts his arm around her, the angle a little awkward as if he's expecting her to be four foot tall. Sarah buries her head in the crook of his shoulder.

'Let me know what you decide about that job. I'm sure you'll make the right call. And please don't let your thinking be swayed by worrying about me.'

If only it were that simple.

CHAPTER 4

Nc3 Bg7

The rain has started up again. By the time she's at her flat, a one-bedroomed shoebox within earshot of Big Ben, Sarah is drenched. Still she pauses to enjoy the silence that greets her. A place that is just hers, where other people's mess and lives and piles and grief didn't need to mingle with her own.

She kicks off her shoes, peeling off her wet clothes while reading a text message from Jenny.

Jenny: Are we still on for lunch? You'd better tell me who you were having dinner with last night. Otherwise I'll have to make it up. x

How long is she going to be able to hold out under Jenny's scrutiny? Since bonding at university over a shared love of philosophy and talking nonsense, and supporting each other through oddly parallel family tragedies, Jenny has shared in most of the intimate details of Sarah's life. Until now. So far it has been easy enough to cover her meetings with Michael as a string of dates with a mystery man. But Jenny is hungry for details to feed her wicked imagination. And she can call Sarah out in a lie better than anyone.

There is something like an illicit romance about her meetings with Michael. But more than courtship, it reminds her of the feeling before a major chess competition - her body becomes tense and coiled, her mind sharp and aroused. She half expects to find her father waiting for her outside, reading Herodotus in his ancient Land Rover and pretending he wasn't interested in whether or not she won.

Leaving the restaurant last night had exactly the same cocktail of disappointment muddled with begrudging humiliation that came from being beaten by a stronger opponent. There was a rare kind of player she enjoyed being beaten by. Those who won with good grace, or at least swagger. Those she could learn from; she could study their play and strengthen her game. Michael reminded her more of the very worst kind to lose to. The ones who would watch her sit down and visibly roil with glee - whose eyes said this would be easy, she's just a girl. They were also the most fun to beat, to watch the glee sour and bite. But when they got the better of her, they were unbearable. And she was too annoyed to even look for what she could learn.

Michael played her perfectly. He diffused her rejection and provoked her into fighting for something she is not even sure she wants. It was intensely irritating, and yet she has to admit a grudging respect. He knew exactly how to get a rise out of her.

Leaving her soggy clothes in a pile by the front door she pulls on her dressing gown and slippers to warm up.

The doorbell rings, her pulse surges like a revving engine. She finds her skittishness ridiculous, but she's too concerned about who it could be to laugh at herself. Only since Michael entered her life has she jumped at the doorbell. She steadies her breath before lifting the intercom.

'Delivery for you, Miss.'

She presses the buzzer and waits for the unexpected visitor to climb the four flights to her flat, tying her dressing gown tighter around her waist.

A man bounds up the stairs and presses a large holdall into Sarah's hands. She accepts the bag without thinking, mesmerised by his razorblade cheekbones.

'For your trip, Miss.' He delivers the line like a Hollywood actor playing a cameo role—his silky voice milking the four words for all they had with a sideways glance to camera. Then he's back down the stairs before she has the chance to ask who he is.

Sarah drops the bag as if it's scalding her skin. She circles it, reluctant to touch it again, examining the tags and fastenings from a safe distance. Could she just leave it there? Could she call the delivery man back to return it? She is compelled to at least look. Steeling her nerve, she pulls back the zip. On top, a new passport in her name, complete with stamps from places she has recently visited, as well as multi-entry visas for Georgia and Azerbaijan dated ten days ago. Is she really that predictable? A laptop, a compact camera and an outdated mobile phone, a guidebook to the South Caucasus and a selection of clothes.

Sarah checks the bag for secret pockets or hidden compartments. That's it? No tech? No gun? No poisoned dart to slip into an umbrella?

She pulls out an evening dress in red embroidered silk. The fine weight of the cloth, the liquid run of the fabric through her fingers tell her it's far more expensive than anything she has ever owned. She tries it on: the silk feels cool against her skin but the fit is perfect. Her reflection in the full-length mirror inside the wardrobe door is faintly ridiculous with furry slippers, unmade face and rained-on hair—but the dress is a knock-out. Falling to just above her knee, redder and revealing more bare back than she would have dared choose, but more elegant than showy. The colour brings out her pale, almost translucent skin.

Feeling immediately at home in the dress, she continues her excavation of the bag: a pair of military-issue hiking boots in her size, a bag of cosmetics—curious, she rips it open. Mascara in brown-black from her favourite brand, Clarins face cream for sensitive skin, another favourite, a perfume she's never heard of. *L'Artisan Parfumeur: Safran Troublant.* Well, at least Michael hasn't got everything right. She pops open the lid and sprays a mist on her pulse. The click of recognition is immediate. Offerings in white carved marble temples in the hot sun, heady, exotic, and enticing. She's never smelt a perfume like it, but it's exactly something she would have chosen for herself. She sprays a cloud into the air and walks through it.

The phone rings. Michael.

She's tempted not to answer, at least not until she's had time to compose herself. She focuses on the dress in the mirror and picks up.

'I trust the delivery arrived safely.'

A cold chill runs over her naked back; she slams the wardrobe door shut to chase away the image of herself in evening dress and slippers.

'If you mean the bag, yes, it's just arrived. But what is this? What trip? I haven't even said yes yet.'

'Don't be alarmed. You don't have to accept it.' His tone is confident, as if he can see her down the phone.

'And what am I supposed to do with all this?'

'Anything you like, try it on for size.'

Sarah's cheeks burn as red as the dress.

'Let's talk in person. Can you make it to St. James' Park by one?'

Sarah remembers her lunch date with Jenny. 'Yes, I think so.'

'Excellent, I'll be over by the pelicans.' He rings off, leaving Sarah wondering whether this might be some sort of code she does not yet understand.

She has an hour to decide what to tell him and still no idea what she wants to do. Is this Michael's final attack? Will she have another chance to waver before his offer is withdrawn?

She steps out of the perfect dress and folds it carefully back into the bag. The unwanted gift captures all her competing feelings about the job. It makes her uncomfortable, as if her life is not her own, someone else taking presumptuous and personal decisions about every detail of her identity and appearance. Its very presence on her bedroom floor leaves her paranoid. Yet she can't deny its allure—it's exciting, it speaks of a life of adventure and intrigue in a part of the world she knows nothing about.

She remembers when she first received Michael's letter—an unremarkable envelope slotted into her pigeonhole in the Porter's Lodge in College, lying unobtrusively beside a bank statement forwarded by her mother and a note about Philosophy Society drinks. She tore it open then and there and almost sent it straight to the bin. It seemed to be a mistake. An invitation to an interview for a job she had never applied for. An appointment to meet with a recruitment officer at an address in St James'. But something caught her eye in the elegantly but opaquely worded letter, a sniff of something hidden between the lines.

She remembers her first meeting with Michael. He swept her from the front door the moment she arrived and out onto the cold London street. They talked as they strode at his long-legged speed through the park, Sarah forced into a trot to keep up. He told her just enough to confirm her suspicions and met most of her questions with more of his own.

At the time, none of it seemed real. But she loved it. The thrill of having something out of the ordinary, something that set her apart from the others. The quiet smugness in the pub in the weeks after their exams had ended, watching her grey-faced friends trudge in late from corporate jobs making rich people richer. I'm courting a spook. The thrill was only heightened by the imperative of secrecy.

But now it's real. Lives are at stake and hers is about to take a dive in an entirely new direction. Is this really what she wants?

She flicks through the passport. The name is correct—Sarah Black, no middle name—and the date of birth is her own. She hoped they might give her a few years for added gravitas. No one takes you seriously at twenty-two. She inspects the visa stamps, half expecting to see signs of forgery or fake. Georgia, Azerbaijan—Sarah's mental map for this part of the world is blank. She can scarcely even picture where they are. They are just words that still belong to Michael, peopled only with gruesome images of headless bodies and mangled train carriages.

She calls Jenny, hoping to catch her before she leaves home.

'No. Don't tell me you're pulling out on me now. Is it him? Are you still with him?' Jenny's voice jumps an octave in excitement.

'No. Luckily not or he would certainly have heard you. I'm really sorry. It's my dad. He asked me to stay for lunch and looked so disappointed when I said no. I hate letting him down.' Sarah knows the father card will work. Jenny's mother walked out on them at around the same time as Sarah's mother died. Supporting grieving fathers is something both of them understand only too well, and navigating its emotional pitfalls helped to cement their friendship.

'Of course you should stay.'

Sarah is heavy with guilt.

'But you're not off the hook. I still want details. Otherwise, I'm spreading the rumour that he's covered in fur and that's the only reason you can't meet out in public.'

'I'm really sorry to bail on you. I'll make it up to you soon, I promise.'

The words feel weak in Sarah's mouth. She hates lying to her best friend and hates even more how easy it was.

But she has to see him one more time.

CHAPTER 5

THE WAREHOUSE

The Castle stops in front of the low concrete warehouse, glad to see Timur waiting for him out front. He hates hanging around. And it is fucking cold.

He walks up the driveway, following the muddy tyre tracks through the snow that still cover the ground, frozen weeds crunching under his boots.

'Timur!' The Castle greets him with a nod and a slap on the shoulder. 'Been growing that beard again? They'll take you for a proper fundy soon.'

Timur nods in reply, a nervous hand reaching to the thick beard worn like a strap across his chin with no moustache. He never was big on small talk.

The paint on the outside walls of the warehouse peels in dark damp scabs, the lower set of windows has been bricked up with breeze blocks and orange stains ooze from the upper windows. The drainpipes from the roof stop halfway down the dirty cream walls, dripping icicles over the scrub bushes below.

'It's fucking freezing up here,' The Castle says, rubbing his hands together and giving them a quick blow. 'When does it start to warm up?'

'It's good in the cold,' Timur says, leading the Castle in through the heavily bolted door. 'No one comes looking.'

Inside is no warmer than out. If anything, the chill of the damp is more pervasive. The Castle reaches for a light switch to illuminate the gloom, but Timur shakes his head. He points to a spot halfway up the wall where a crucified bat hangs welded to a naked electric wire, poking out of the damp plaster.

'He fused the whole system,' Timur mumbles.

Several large wooden boxes and crates stand stacked against the walls, propped up on more grey breeze blocks.

'Can I have a look?' The Castle asks, approaching the biggest box, rubbing his hands again.

'Sure.' Timur cracks open the crate.

Poking his head inside, the Castle pulls out some of the newspaper and straw wrapped around the equipment, just enough to make one barrel clearly visible. He places his hand against the cold metal. 'Good work, Timur.'

CHAPTER 6

e4 d6

Michael is standing by the lake in St James' Park, watching the pelicans huddle for warmth on a landscaped rock. Sarah watches him from a distance, trying to put her finger on what it is that sets him apart from the other civil servants hurrying back from their lunch break. He wears the same Whitehall uniform—dark suit and leather briefcase—but his bearing is different, his posture both rigid and relaxed. His suit is perfectly cut but he wears it as if he hasn't even noticed.

Timed precisely to match her approach, he turns away from the pelicans to greet her.

'Sarah,' a kiss on both cheeks. 'Well, this is a good sign.'

'What is?'

'You came.' He gives a warm smile. 'From which I think I can deduce that you are in a rather more positive frame of mind than last night.'

Is he right? Sarah herself is still unsure.

'What makes you think that?' she asks, jutting her chin

forward. She can't make this too easy for him.

'Well if you were going to turn me down, you would have done it over the phone—quicker, cleaner, easier not to be swayed by my powers of persuasion.' Another broad smile with a suggestion of a wink. Winking men normally make her gag, but Michael pulls it off with an elegance that makes it more playful than pervert.

'I'm still undecided. This just all feels as if it is moving too fast.'

'This is real life. Whoever was behind that train crash is not going to sit and wait for you to make up your mind before planning their next move. We need people there now and I think you're the perfect fit.'

'But why me?'

Michael links his arm through hers and gently steers her towards a quieter path. His voice is gentle and relaxed. Old friends, enjoying a lunchtime stroll through the park.

'We have information from a proven source in the North Caucasus that a significant quantity of weapons and explosives are being moved out of Russia.' He crosses the path to avoid a large puddle still standing from the morning's rain. 'According to the agent on the train, the destination is Azerbaijan. It is quite an arsenal—three hundred PKM machine guns, all metal belts, high tracer count, almost six thousand standard stamped and riveted AKM Kalashnikovs. Thousand-to-one proportion of ammo to tooling, so either they already have a stash of AKs, or they really like dolloping the lead around. All the ammo is anti-corrosion, all designed for maximum yaw.'

'Yaw?' Sarah asks, struggling to keep up with Michael's list. Is he trying to baffle her or is it just second nature to him? She fits her mind to the new language she needs to learn.

'Designed to do a lot of damage to the poor sod it ends up in. Reams of RPG-7. No Simonov rifles, no Dragunov snipers, no RGD grenades or any of the other weapons of choice we normally find in the ex-Soviet space. Sounds like classic light offensive guerrilla kit to me—but a hell of a lot of it.'

By force of habit, she's committing Michael's arsenal to memory, storing it to look into later. But there's a voice in her head telling her this is just too weird. Can he be for real? Is she being filmed by a hidden camera? Is this a test as part of her application process? Sarah wonders if she is supposed to go along with it or report him.

'The source on the train had just squealed on his boss to tell us about these weapons and their destination the week before he was killed.' Michael pauses as they pass a large group of tourists. 'Of course, it's possible that these weapons are destined to reignite one of the frozen conflicts—the Azeris wanting another pop at Nagorno Karabakh, the Georgians seeking to regain Abkhazia. But it's highly unlikely the Russians would facilitate.'

Sarah unloops her arm from Michael's and draws her raincoat tighter around her waist, creating her own space. 'So, who's it for then?'

'The UK's biggest interest in Azerbaijan is oil and British Oil and Gas—BOG. The new BTC pipeline will link Baku through Georgia to a port in Turkey, providing oil and gas to the West that doesn't pass through Russia or the Middle East. This pipeline will be operated by BOG and was something of a British brainchild, so we have a great deal riding on its success. Unfortunately, it is also a rather obvious target for anyone seeking instability in the region.'

Sarah remembers the passing tourists. She tries not to gawp, adopting the look of someone used to discussing weapon specifications and geopolitics in the park. Michael continues as casually as before. 'In short, it matters to us a lot more now to know what is going on over there, but we don't have the contacts on the ground to find out.'

'And that is where I come in?'

The question knocks him off his stride, but he's pleased. 'That is certainly what I was hoping. The Grand Opening of the pipeline is planned for May the fifteenth. Anyone planning an attack would no doubt want to strike either the opening or the run up. You have a month.'

Sarah looks at her watch. 'Not even that.'

Michael shrugs. 'Close enough.'

A pair of mallards stalk across the path—the brown feathered female leading, the magnificent green plumage of the male in close pursuit.

'But why me? I don't know anything about that part of the world. Don't you have someone with a bit more training? Someone who knows what they're doing?'

'We've identified a way in, and you fit the profile we need to make the approach. You're a fluent Russian speaker—it's impossible to get anywhere in the former Soviet world without that.'

Sarah wonders whether this is the moment to admit that her schoolgirl Russian is far from fluent, but chickens out. 'Surely you have other Russian speakers?'

'Of course we have stacks of Cold Warriors, but you're young, you're attractive, you have done various do-gooder things and have a…' Michael pauses to look for the right word. 'A freshness that would help you blend in with the cover we have in mind.'

Sarah is unsure what to make of Michael's list—is she supposed to be flattered or insulted? 'So what is the cover?'

'And besides,' Michael continues blithely, 'knowing what you're doing is never that clear-cut in our game. It's mostly instincts, and I think yours are right.' Michael holds out his arm to move Sarah onto the side of the path as a large group of sightseers amble past them. His touch is presumptuous, patronising. She pushes his arm away.

'The agent believed that the weapons were destined for Mikhail Ibragimov, a member of the ruling elite in Baku.' Michael speaks the name with evident distaste. 'He was closely associated with Heydar Aliyev, the former President of Azerbaijan and the current president's father. Ibragimov stuck closely to Aliyev's coattails and followed his rise through the ranks of the Soviet system, carried out a lot of his dirty work and was rewarded with a healthy share of the kickbacks. After the fall of the USSR, when Aliyev was made president, Ibragimov had his finger in every pie in Azerbaijan—the State Shipping company, Azeri Rail, the Haulers Association, the Aviation Authority. You name it, Ibragimov had a controlling interest. But he seems to have fallen out of favour with the new generation.'

Again, Sarah is categorising, setting her memory to absorb as many of the details as she can. Everything is new: the names, the history, the gritty world of everyone on the take. How long would it take before all of this seems normal?

'These families are notoriously difficult to infiltrate,' Michael continues in his matter-of-fact tone. 'They tend to trust no one. But we've come up with an elegant way in. Ibragimov has a nephew, Viktor Skarparov, who may well be our weakest link. Typical Baku elite—spoilt, bored, vain, capricious—the type we can sometimes use. Mid-forties, lives off papa's oil money. Has dabbled in setting up casinos in various parts of the world but his business interests never amounted to much. This is him.'

Michael fishes a photograph out of his inner jacket pocket and hands it to Sarah while keeping up his leisurely stroll. The photo shows a middle-aged man in a shiny grey suit, jacket button pulling tightly around a considerable paunch. His dark hair flecked with grey is slicked back to show his prominent widow's peak. He has skin the colour of deeply polished walnut and his round eyes are surprisingly pale. He is smiling at someone or something behind the camera with a face quick to laugh.

'He doesn't look too bad,' Sarah says, handing back the photo.

'Jaded playboys your type then, are they?'

'No, I just thought he'd look meaner. He's more Winnie the Pooh gone to seed.'

'Sorry, I'll try harder to get you a proper baddy next time.' Michael links his arm back through Sarah's, angling his head towards her ear. 'So your friend Viktor has recently reinvented himself as a philanthropist, which struck us as rather out of keeping with his previous business ventures. The Skarparov Foundation launched to much fanfare in New York in September. He seems to be trying to present himself as the saviour of the down-trodden of the Caucasus. Interestingly, he's put in Irakli Makmudov to run it—a Georgian who happens to be very closely connected to Ibragimov. So there is your cover.'

'Cover?'

'He recently wrote to the Minister for International Development suggesting cooperation with the Skarparov Foundation. The Department for International Development has agreed to let us use them as cover. I think you are just the type who could blend in with the socks and sandals brigade.'

'So that's why you picked me?'

'A convincing cover is essential. We don't have many people who could seamlessly slip into that world, let alone those who speak Russian and look like prime Civil Service fodder but who are actually far too dogged to ever make it through the Civil Service personality test.' Another questionable compliment. 'You're the perfect candidate.'

'So I would be working for DFID?'

'Only for appearances' sake. He approached them, so it allows you to ask plenty of questions without raising too many suspicions. And the development world is suitably unthreatening. Neither Skarparov, nor his uncle Ibragimov, will take kindly to nosy parkers, so it's critical to appear innocuous.'

'Wouldn't I need to know something about development to pull that off?'

'I'm sure you can muddle through. Everyone else at DFID seems to. And as a new recruit you have a perfect excuse not to know anything. I love this view.'

Michael leans over a metal railing, gazing out across the lake at the centre of the park. On one side of the bridge, the water reflects the great facade of Buckingham Palace, its bulk rendered elegant by a framing of trees. On the other side, the spires and domes above Horse Guards Parade rise like an enchanted castle keeping watch over Whitehall.

'You start in Tbilisi,' Michael continues. 'That is where Skarparov has based his Foundation and seems to spend most of his time. Find out what you can about him, look into this Foundation of his and see if you can find a way to gain his trust.'

'Tbilisi, in Georgia?'

'It's a lovely place, have you ever been? The current government swept to power in a velvet revolution a couple of years ago and President Saakashvili and the bunch of teenagers he's put in charge seem to be doing quite a job at turning the place around. Despite its troubles, it has managed to hold on to some of its nineteenth century splendour—an ancient city on the up in an elegant state of dilapidation. You'll like it.' He pauses, staring at the lake. 'So, Sarah,' Michael drops his voice to a more serious tone for the first time in their conversation. He stops walking and looks her straight in the eye. 'Are you in or out?'

Sarah realises she's been following his lead again, her imagination already half-lost in a far-flung world, her mind already seeking the cracks and weaknesses in her opponent. She's forgotten she was supposed to be saying no.

'I'm in,' she says, taken aback with the confidence of her reply.

'And you are sure you are fully committed and that this is genuinely what you want? We won't have any more… wobbles?'

Sarah's breath sticks in her throat. She catches a scent of saffron in the air, a faint trace of the perfume Michael chose for her. Would he recognise it on her skin?

'It's okay to have a bit of a false start,' Michael says. 'I was nearly chucked out of the Service training programme myself, although the circumstances were rather different.' He trails off, obviously hoping she'll ask for details, but she's more curious about when she might be offered a training programme. Is this really all the preparation she gets?

'But once you are signed up, once we send you out there, we need to know that we are on to a solid thing.'

'Rock solid and wobble free.' Sarah holds his eye, widening

her stance to steady herself.

'Base yourself in the embassy but keep a low profile. Find out as much as possible about this foundation and use it as a way in to Skarparov. If it's for real—offer help. If it's a sham—work out what kind. Offer different help. Either way, you need to find a way to make yourself indispensable to him, to make him trust you. And then use him to get to his uncle.'

Sarah nods, making mental notes. Michael makes it sound easy.

'Our man in Tbilisi is there to help if you need it. I can have you on a plane in the morning.'

'Tomorrow?'

'That's not a problem, is it? You don't even need to pack.' Another half-wink.

'That's it? No tech? No training?' Sarah was expecting the great reveal, a formal welcome to the organisation, a full induction session, a chance to meet her fellow recruits and to swap stories of the mysterious interview process. She was looking forward to the legendary training sessions locked away in Portsmouth, learning to shoot and drive and blow things up, while badgering the locals in the nearby pub for personal details. Not being pushed onto a plane on her own.

'You've got a mobile phone,' Michael says, his jaw tight. 'That's more than I would want, but I understand everyone has them.'

Sarah blinks at the Cold War dinosaur.

'Don't take your own,' he adds. 'And only use it if needed. Stay off social media and never forget that all tech can be hacked or tracked. This is "humint"—human to human. We have the "sigint" chaps working on listening, but I doubt they'll come up with much. Ibragimov is even more of a dinosaur than me. Your job is to gain trust. You don't do that through a screen.'

Sarah nods, trying to mirror his confident tone but feeling none of it.

'Remember, you have a month at best to find out what

Ibragimov is up to and stop him.'

Sarah is reeling, playing through the different possible worlds. What if she fails? What if she is found out? What would Michael do if she turns him down?

'You are sure you're up for this?' Michael asks gently.

'I'm certain,' she lies.

CHAPTER 7

Bg5 c5

Arriving in Tbilisi in the early afternoon, Sarah pulls her anonymous black holdall off the luggage belt. She draws back the zip and peeks inside. Michael's selection of clothes lies crumpled but untouched.

She steadies her hand to pass her duplicate passport to an immigration officer in army uniform, his features rolling and bulging like a face drawn on a balloon. Thick lips pulled back in disdain, he studies the photo before thumbing slowly through the remaining pages. Sarah tugs at her collar, suddenly hot. She holds her breath as she watches him carry out his careful study of the fake entry stamps. Is the forgery obvious? Would he know what a British passport should look like?

He slams the stamp down on a clean page and offers it to her without a word.

Sarah accepts it in a sweaty hand, only releasing her breath when she's safely in the baggage hall.

She scans the arrivals area hopefully, unsure whether Michael has told anyone she was coming. Who would she call if no one was there? With relief, she sees her name written on a wilted piece of paper held by a driver beneath a cloud of cigarette smoke. He has round, careful eyes and a nose as long and thin as a falcon's beak.

'You are Miss Sarah? I am Vakho, Welcome to Georgia, Miss Sarah!' he approaches with quick bird-like movements, bubbling with an excess of energy, and whips the holdall out of her hand. 'You wait here, please.' She is left on the curb outside as he makes an elaborate show of reversing the embassy Land Rover. 'Please,' he flings open the door directly at her feet.

Sarah sits glued to the window as they drive at speed into town. She pictured grey crumbling concrete, faceless apartment buildings and faded revolutionary splendour. She is not prepared for such beauty. Crumpled green mountains run along both sides of the road with exaggerated craggy contours. Abandoned Soviet landmarks overgrown with splashes of pale almond blossom. Low buildings in pink brick line the streets, wooden balconies hanging off their sides like overripe fruit. The car sweeps past the old centre, allowing Sarah a brief glimpse of the rose-bricked domes of the bath square, before diving headlong into three lanes of traffic to cross the river.

Vakho stops the car in a courtyard, bright with white paint. He sweeps over to open Sarah's door. 'We are here.'

Beneath an imposing stone pediment, a wooden door slumps in its hinges. Inside the dark stairwell, two tiny kittens mewl at Sarah's feet as she waits for her eyes to adjust to the gloom. The air smells of ammonia and fried sausage.

She follows Vakho up the stairs, the ancient floorboards protesting under her cautious step, and through a tall door on the first floor. 'This is where you stay.' He swings her bag inside and breezes through the apartment, flinging open doors and removing dust sheets from chairs and sofas.

'It's nice here,' he opens the heavy curtains, 'and the balcony excellent.'

After the insalubrious entrance, Sarah is braced for something cramped and dark: a proletariat's functional flat. But inside she finds the elegant splendour of the intelligentsia. The front door opens straight into the main room of the apartment, flooded with light from double height windows. Two of the walls are entirely lined with bookcases, comfortably spilling over with yellowing paperbacks and leather-bound tomes. Two stern gentlemen in dress uniform and sculpted facial hair look down at her from drooping canvasses in wooden frames.

Vakho opens the door to the balcony and addresses the view. 'Ah, beautiful Tbilisi.'

The city spreads below her like a fairy-tale. The view dominated by churches, their conical domes like shiny gnome hats pointing towards the sky. A church rises from the rocky outcrop just beneath the balcony, balanced high above the river. Across the banks, another church lies wrapped inside the walls of a honey-stone fortress. The crumpled mountains frame the view and, above it all, an enormous silver woman looks down over her domain.

'Mother Georgia,' Vakho says. 'She has her sword in one hand to *shloop shloop* the enemy.' Vakho knocks off an imaginary head with his arm. 'And her bowl of wine to toast to our health. She's there to look after us.' Sarah was hoping for some more tangible protection than an aluminium woman, but will take what she can get.

'So, how you like Tbilisi?' Vakho asks, his eyes dancing.

'I hadn't realised it would be so beautiful.' Sarah feels the tightly wound muscles in her neck begin to loosen. 'It's magical.'

'Ah, you watch out, it's powerful magic, you never know what's going to happen. You'll love it, I can tell. Now I leave you to rest. I come to take you to the Embassy in the morning at ten. It's okay, not too early?'

'Thank you, Vakho.'

'Kho!'

'Kho?' Sarah mimics his guttural grunt.

'No, you say "Vako" like "Wacko"! You need to try the "kh" sound.' He rolls a soft purr in the back of his throat.

'Va*kho*,' Sarah tries again.

'Much better! You sound like a Georgian. You need me you call me, 55599955.'

'That's a good number.'

'Vakho has some useful friends.' He watches her, round eyes solicitous, hawk's beak tilted to one side. He waits, as if there is more he has to say. Is there a trace of warning in his eyes? Something he wants to tell her? Sarah can't read if his hesitation stems from shyness faced with a young female foreigner, or if it is something more. He gives a little nod, his fingers clasped together. 'Welcome to Georgia!' he says, disappearing out the front door.

Left alone on the balcony, contemplating the fairy-tale view and her sword-wielding protector, Sarah could be an intruder in somebody else's life. The events of the last few days accelerated her everyday existence into something she scarcely recognises as her own. She is not quite lonely—not with so much to take in— but she feels very much alone.

Propped up on the plump cushions of the swing seat, she unpacks a leather-bound notebook, the pages made of pressed paper. She bought it for capturing thoughts and ideas, but so far it contains nothing but lists. She opens to a clean page, hoping to capture some of Tbilisi's early magic in words, something she could fill out later in a letter. But the paper stays empty. It is too much to know where to start, and besides, she has no one to tell.

She spoke to her father that morning to let him know she accepted the job and was being sent immediately to Georgia, muttering something vague about a placement with DFID. She longed to tell him in person. His absent silences and careful pauses were difficult to read over the phone. Was that disappointment in his voice as he offered his congratulations, or was he simply watching the leaves dance outside the window? She drafted several emails to Jenny to explain her sudden absence from London, but sent none. Lying proved no easier in writing than it had been over the phone, and her excuses looked all the more unconvincing laid out on the screen. In her first real job as a journalist, Jenny often seems to feel it her professional duty to pick holes in Sarah's stories. Nothing Sarah can write would stand up to her fact-check. God, she wishes her mother was still here to offer vague reassurances and distract her with a story about Chopin in Paris.

But other than her father, no one but Michael knows she is there. Sarah looks up to Mother Georgia, shimmering like a zeppelin in the last of the evening's sunshine, her eye resting on the mighty sword arm. 'You'd better know how to use that.'

CHAPTER 8

d5 h6

The next morning, Sarah arrives at the British embassy's shiny new offices above one of the corporate hotels on Freedom Square. She hopes to be met by our man in Tbilisi but is told to wait for the Ambassador, who 'wants a look at her'. She sits in reception, gazing out the window over the central fountain and the blazingly bright statue of St George the dragon slayer, golden spear poised to deliver the fatal blow.

The building opposite is three stories of neoclassical splendour, newly restored and freshly sandblasted. Next door to the neat stacks of porticoes and balconies, another building is on the verge of collapse, the crumbled facade threatening to slide face-first into the square. Hoardings show an artist's impression of slick new buildings bathed in computer-generated purple light. The structures behind the boards slump against dusty scaffolding, sunlight catching their buckled floors through gaping holes in the roof. It's the public face of a city in transition, shaking off years of neglect to join its former glory with the modern and the new. And Michael is right: Sarah loves it.

A painfully tall man appears wearing a neatly tailored shirt with heavy cufflinks in the shape of rowing boats. His face has the flushed complexion of one almost permanently embarrassed. He lurches towards her, seeming surprised at the length of his stride, and offers a hand. 'You must be Sarah? I'm Ed, Third Sec Political. Pleased to meet you. HMA—sorry, Alistair—is ready for a quick word.'

Sarah follows Ed to the Ambassador's door where he stops and lingers awkwardly, clearing his throat. Over his shoulder, Sarah sees a pair of shiny mustard and brown brogues propped over the arm of a sofa.

'Um, Your Excellency, this is Sarah, the visitor from DFID.'

Sarah can now see the full figure of the Ambassador reclined on the sofa, his eyes focused intently on the middle distance. As she enters, he swings his legs down to the floor and stands up purposefully, straightening the crease of his pale linen trousers and brushing down his twill waistcoat.

'Jolly good. Do come in, please, have a seat.' From his name, Alistair MacLeod, Sarah had been expecting a Scottish accent. But the Ambassador's voice is pure Eton plum.

Ed scuttles towards the chair to remove a large pile of books. His Majesty's Ambassador paces the room.

'So what are you lot up to now then?' Alistair asks, staring absently out of the window.

Sarah hesitates, unsure which lot he is referring to and how far her cover is supposed to stretch. Michael had warned to keep a low profile.

'I didn't think you were interested in this part of the world now?' he continues. 'Too much money. As I understood it, the days of putting our aid money to some use as a political tool are out. It's all about helping poor people these days, regardless of what they're going to give you in return.'

DFID it is then.

'Frightful waste if you ask me. We could punch far above our weight here if we had a bit of your cash behind us to fund the pet projects of the new Ministers. I've scarcely got a budget to change the curtains in the residence, while the Americans are showering President Saakashvili's men with cash and calling all the shots. They've even got their president coming next month to fawn over everyone's favourite revolutionaries. So, are we about to buy a seat at the table?' He turns to her, eager-faced.

'Sorry to disappoint,' Sarah replies. 'I'm only here for some research. The Skarparov Foundation, have you come across them? They contacted our Secretary of State proposing cooperation in some of their activities in this region. I'm here to scope out areas for possible collaboration.' Sarah is pleased at how easily the story comes out.

The Ambassador looks put out. 'Skarparov,' he muses. 'Yes, I've seen the name plastered on a fleet of shiny new Land Cruisers around town, don't know much about it though. What are they doing? It's not another "governance" project, is it? Trying to launch another revolution? Skarparov sounds Russian; they're not terribly popular around here at the moment. Everyone's got the jitters about them pouring in to invade as soon as the snow melts.'

'He's an Azeri.'

'Ah, is he now? Anything to do with that pipeline? There have been far more of them over here since construction started on that beast. It's an extraordinary project, but it doesn't half make me nervous having it pass through under our feet.'

'Why nervous?'

'It's surely only a matter of time before someone tries to blow the thing up.'

How much of Michael's concern has been shared with the Ambassador? Surely the two must talk, although apparently not about her. 'Who would want to do that?' she asks.

'Anyone looking to put the brakes on Georgia's move into the light. It's all looking rather good here at the moment, and there is no denying Saakashvili has pulled off some minor miracles in cleaning the place up. But that stability hangs by a slender thread. It wouldn't take much to send it back to the dark days. Is your chap an oil man?'

'His father is,' Sarah fills her voice with confidence, 'among other things. It doesn't appear he has much of a business mind himself—owns a few failing casinos, that sort of thing—so we were all somewhat taken aback by his sudden jump into philanthropy.' She is particularly pleased with her casual use of the first-person plural.

'Interesting, and have you met him yet?' the Ambassador ceases pacing and settles himself into his chair behind his desk, level with Sarah. His very movements seem to come from a bygone era, he holds himself with an unwavering confidence, a dignified stiffness. Sarah can't tell how much of his posturing is for show and how much is real.

'Not yet, I've only just arrived. I'm hoping to start with Irakli Makmudov, his representative here, find out a bit more about the Foundation. Do you know him?'

'Yes, no,' the Ambassador trails off. 'Well good to have you here. We must have you over to the residence for supper one evening. I'll get Sopho, my secretary, to arrange it.'

'Thank you, Your Excellency, that would be lovely.'

'You needn't bother with all that Excellency stuff, only Ed here has to do that. You can call me Alistair, to my face anyway. There is a whole host of things I get called behind my back and you can take your pick.' He laughs and holds out his hand. 'Good luck with it all. If there's any money coming this way, I've got plenty of ideas of what we can do with it.'

Sarah turns to leave, relieved not to have been found out in her lie, but still unsure if she is supposed to have secrets within the embassy. Happily, his curiosity seemed untroubled. She feels as much of a fraud pretending to be a spy as pretending to work for DFID.

'By the way,' he stops her, examining his reflection in the window, pulling down the points of his waistcoat. 'Does it look like I slept in these clothes? The poker at the Frenchman's went on rather late last night and I didn't get the chance to change before my meeting with the President this morning. Do you think he noticed?'

Is he for real or just hoping to watch her squirm?

'No, Your Excellency—sorry, Alistair—you look quite, um, dashing.'

The Ambassador smiles appreciatively.

'Jolly good, jolly good. Now, Ed, can you do me one of your emails?'

Sarah understands that her audience is over.

CHAPTER 9

THE VAN

'This is for you.' The Castle slams the door of a white van and throws the Pawn the keys. 'Drive it on the day. Leave it parked nearby. And anything you need to do for us before then, use it. I've got a couple of guys who need some help bringing some stuff down from the mountains. I told them to call you; you can arrange logistics.'

The Pawn closes his fingers around the keys, weighing them in his hand. Ford Transit van, diesel, 1995 model at a guess. 'Who does it belong to?'

'No one you need to know. Paperwork is under the driver's sunshade if you ever need it. You won't. And put these on it.' He drops two battered license plates through the open passenger window. 'I'll leave you to it.'

The Pawn climbs into the driver's seat, sets the key in the lock and turns it a three-quarter turn, watching the yellow light of the glow plug. He counts silently until the light goes off, turns the key to start the engine, and gives the accelerator a tap to check the revs.

Where is he supposed to do it? He can't just get out a spanner in the street outside his mother's house and put on a set of fake licence plates. Anyone could be watching. They don't have a garage. And where else can you hide a van?

He wonders if this is some kind of test. Start with something small to check he is reliable. He'd like the chance to give them a test of his own—he knows almost nothing about them, and first impressions so far have been weak. The Castle hasn't been back to any of the group meetings since they started meeting privately. No one seems to know much about him. But if his plan is for real then at least they are after the same thing: freedom from the puppets stuck with their arses in the air as they kowtow to the west. And unlike all the others who just talk and talk, the Castle is a man of action. With deep pockets.

The Pawn drives out of town. Maybe he could find a quiet spot in a forest somewhere. The paperwork must be linked to the new registration. He flips down the sunshade and a creased stack of dusty papers fall into his lap. Shit. It is all in Azeri. He turns over the license plates sitting next to him on the passenger seat and laughs. At least no one would ever think it was his.

CHAPTER 10

Bh4 Qa5

His hand sits in hers like a wet fish. Sarah does her best to withdraw from the handshake without appearing rude, but Irakli Makmudov, the local head of the Skarparov Foundation in Tbilisi, is eager to linger.

'Welcome to the Skarparov Foundation.' His voice is deep and rough. His white shirt in thick starched cotton is cut a little too tight, his expensive-looking jeans accentuate his very long legs. His dark hair is swept in a side parting, a prominent cleft in his chin and a permanent dark shadow of stubble highlights his full red lips. Broad shouldered and undeniably handsome, Irakli carries himself with the quiet arrogance that suggests he knows it all too well.

'Please, sit down,' Irakli flashes another smile and takes a step too close, the fish hand now on the small of Sarah's back to guide her towards a heavy leather armchair. His eyelids curl with pleasure at himself.

Sarah tries to settle into the overly deep chair, designed for lounging. She can either perch primly at the front or mirror Irakli's indulgent sprawl. She goes for the perch, leaning into the armrest to look a little less uptight.

'I'm here to follow up on Mr Skarparov's letter to DFID requesting cooperation.' Sarah watches as Irakli ostentatiously runs his eyes down her neckline. She has left the top buttons of her blouse undone, not knowing what she might need to use, and now restrains the urge to button up. 'To explore how that cooperation could play, how we could complement each other, fit together,' she pauses, holding his eye, 'if you like.' His body rolls and purrs at her words. This is going to be easy. 'Tell me,' she leans forward deliberately, 'a bit about your work and the activities of the Foundation, and especially about your particular role.'

'Well,' Irakli rubs his palms down the front of his jeans, 'the Foundation was set up last year by Mr Skarparov. But it's early days, you know. Still finding our feet.' He opens his hands wide and flashes Sarah a grin.

'And what does the Foundation do?' she prompts, nodding encouragingly.

'Well, it's mostly livelihoods,' he adopts the slow, easy tone of one in the know, 'and capacity building and skills and stuff like that.'

'Of course.'

'We're tackling unemployment and jobs, especially in the mountains, you know?'

'Excellent. One of DFID's priority areas.' She's relieved that he's clearly no more expert than her. 'And can you tell me a bit about where you work?'

'Well,' Irakli glances over Sarah's shoulder out of the glass-fronted office, 'it's early days you know, we've still got the feasibility studies, stakeholder engagement and all that stuff to do first.' Irakli speaks as if he is pulling expressions off a shelf and trying them on for size.

'So nothing up and running yet?'

'No, no, the money's in place. Just working on the details now. No use rushing in, right?' He grins again, returning his gaze to her eyes, via the hem of her skirt. 'Our project manager in the mountains can tell you more if you really want to get down to the details. Most of our work is in the mountains, up in the border regions with Russia.'

'Can I go and visit the sites? I'd love to see the mountains.'

'The mountains are my home, where I'm from; I mean really from, you know? I grew up here in the city, but my roots, my whole family is up there. It's in my blood.' He thumps himself emphatically on the chest.

'So could you be my host?' Sarah tries to hide her distaste at the idea of putting herself into his hands. She needs him. And he seems easy enough to use so long as she gives him ample chance to talk about himself.

'Of course. Yeah, we could probably arrange something for you.' He's back to watching the window behind her.

Sarah expected the suggestion to be met with more enthusiasm. 'Sounds wonderful. And is Mr Skarparov currently in Tbilisi?'

'I think he's back this week. Hey, you know—'

'Do you think I could meet him?'

'We'd love to get you guys involved in our official launch. We're planning something big to announce our arrival on the scene, it would be great to add a bit of British classiness to the event.' He gives a very un-Michael type wink. 'You know, maybe get your ambassador involved, I hear he's quite a character, or a big shot from DFID. What do you think? Maybe you guys could even host it, make it your show?' He stretches his long legs towards Sarah. 'We'd cover all the costs. We throw the party, you get the kudos. What do you think?'

'I'm sure that is something we could consider. Once we've got to know each other a little better, of course.' She tries to look suggestive, but she's revolted returning his cheesy lines. She's done this before, she's batted an eyelid, she's smiled more broadly, she's held an eye a beat longer than needed. But this feels different. He's an easy piece to play. He'd flirt with his own reflection if there was no one else available. But it feels sordid, more consciously transactional. Is this really her job? Making eyes at creeps to get them to spill the beans?

Irakli is on his feet and staring out of the window. 'Hold on, Sarah. I just need to check on something.' He dashes out the door, leaving her hanging.

Sarah watches through the window as Irakli runs towards a van that has pulled up in front of the building. A small, cheerless figure, face partly hidden beneath curtains of greasy black hair, is struggling to unload something heavy from the back of the van, looking as if his legs will buckle under the weight. Irakli shouts at him, cuffs the youth around the ear and takes over his place, hauling the heavy load out onto the pavement. A solid, neckless hulk of a man emerges from inside the vehicle, pushing the cumbersome cargo onto Irakli, bracing himself to manoeuvre it from below. A third man, dark haired and bearded, sits at the wheel of the van, pointedly ignoring the others. Between them, Irakli and the bull-neck manage to unload the cargo, a bulging tube shape wrapped up in a garish bright cloth like a giant seal caught in a net. The greasy-haired youth looks on sullenly as they shuffle the tube down a passage at the side of the building.

Irakli is sweating under the effort, keeping up his stream of insults addressed at the other two men, at the hefty load, at the heavens. Sarah is struck by Irakli's transformation, by the speed with which he jumped in to help, his anger at them having arrived as they did and the resentment visible on the face of the surly youth. Being careful not to move too far from her chair, she fishes in her handbag for the camera from Michael's holdall. While pretending to be fiddling with the settings, she takes some surreptitious shots of the van with license plates, the driver, the three men with the wrapped dead weight. She edges closer to the window to get a better angle.

Irakli returns, wiping down his forehead with a handkerchief but leaving a glistening line of sweat on his upper lip. Sarah has just returned to her chair, her hand still inside her bag. 'Sorry, Sarah, I didn't mean to run out on you like that, just spotted a couple of our guys in need of a bit of help. That's the nature of a start-up, right? We all need to get our hands dirty.' His crisp white sleeves are rolled-up, revealing a collection of crudely drawn tattoos snaking up his forearms.

'What was that you were unloading?' Sarah asks. 'It looked like it weighed a tonne.'

'Carpets.' Irakli gives his palms another wipe before stuffing his handkerchief into his back pocket. 'It's one of the activities we've got going up in the mountains, traditional weaving techniques and all original dyes and materials. You know this region is famous for its carpets, right?'

'Of course.' The carpet wrapping looked garish and coarse compared to most of the Caucasian carpets Sarah has seen— with a shine straight out of a factory in China. And it would have to be woven in lead to require such effort to move. 'And what about in Azerbaijan? Is the Foundation also active there?' Sarah asks, hoping to lead Irakli towards talking about his link with Ibragimov without arousing suspicion. Michael mentioned they were close. Perhaps she could cut out Skarparov all together and reach Ibragimov through Irakli instead?

'Yeah, of course. That's Mr Skarparov's home. I think the work there is at a pretty similar stage to here—you know, early days.' He relaxes back into the leather couch. 'Did you hear about that train crash? Real mess, bet they're still scraping bits of body off the ground.'

'Yes,' Sarah says, her pulse quickening at the conversational swerve. 'I saw it on the news just before I came out. Have they worked out who's behind it yet?'

'Behind it?' he narrows his eyes. 'I heard it was points failure.' His voice is light and teasing. 'Or do you know something about it that I don't?'

Heart racing, Sarah tries to cover her slip. 'I heard a rumour that it was sabotage. But I've been told not to believe everything I hear in this part of the world. Everyone loves a good conspiracy theory, right?'

Irakli sits back into the chair watching Sarah as he recrosses his long legs.

She waits for him to respond, her breath uncomfortably loud in her ears.

'So, Sarah, why don't you tell me a bit about you? How did a good-looking woman like you end up working at a place like DFID?'

Her laugh sounds forced. 'I like helping those in need.'

'And they sent you all the way here just to talk to us? What else have they got you working on?' He is back to sprawling on the black leather, his top lip still beaded in sweat.

'I've got quite a portfolio to get to grips with, this just sounded like the most fun.' She wants to move the conversation away from her job. He is clearly no development professional, but it puts her on the back foot. She knows almost nothing about Georgia, about development, or about what DFID is supposed to be doing in the region. She would rather not put her ignorance up for inspection, even by Irakli. 'So what do you say about that mountain trip?' Sarah mimics Irakli's casual tone, folding one leg beneath her.

'Yeah. Sure.' Irakli wipes his palms again. 'I'm going up in a few days. You could come along. They'll probably organise a big *supra* for me, you know, a big Georgian feast? They normally do, even though I'm one of theirs. You'll see Georgian hospitality at its best.' He warms up at the chance to show off.

Saying goodbye, he takes her hand again in his big wet palm and pulls her in for a kiss on the cheek.

Queasy from the strength of his cologne, she hurries out to the fresh air, her eye struck by the security camera mounted above the pavement. She clocked it on arrival. But now she notices its strange angle, facing backwards towards the office rather than out to the street. Trepidation grips her stomach. Would it pick

61

up a clear picture of what was happening inside the building, or would the image be distorted by the reflection of the glass? She curses herself for not having noticed the angle before standing in the window.

Safely back in the embassy, she dives into the bathroom to wash her hands and face. It is not the first time she has endured the flirtations of a creep, but something about this encounter was different, more difficult to keep up the act. Or perhaps she was more conscious of the act as her professional duty? She actively objectified herself, rather than simply allowing the flirtation to happen. Sarah studies her reflection in the mirror, her wide eyes greener than usual in the harsh light of the bathroom, her pale skin a little sickly. A wave of nausea bends her double. She grips the cold edges of the sink for support. Flirting with scumbags like Irakli would probably be one of the easier compromises she would have to make in her new identity. She splashes more cold water on her face and scrubs her palms furiously with soap.

CHAPTER 11

Qd2 g5

'Sarah!'
She's stopped on the way out of the bathroom by a hand on her arm and an unfamiliar face.

'I found you!' He greets her as an old friend, but she's certain she's never seen him before. He has raw and ruddy cheeks as if he's spent years being whipped by a cold north wind and hair that hangs long over his ears. His shirt, in red stripes that clash both with his cheeks and with the flamingos on his tie, has been pressed down the front, but he's clearly not bothered with the sleeves or the back. He raises his eyebrows and pauses, waiting for her response.

'Sorry, you are…?'

He breaks an embarrassed smile, pushing his coarse hair back from his forehead. 'Of course, sorry. Steve. I work upstairs.' His eyebrows hang again in expectation.

'I… um…'

'Er, Michael told me you were coming?'

'Of course. Steve, our man in Tbilisi.'

He ducks his head as if to avoid an incoming blow. 'Look, would you mind coming up with me?' He squints around the room uncomfortably. 'It's better to talk up there.'

Sarah follows Steve upstairs and through two heavy sets of doors, each controlled by electronic passcode—presumably to trap unwanted visitors in the dead space in between. The airlock opens on a windowless corridor and another locked door. The walls are bare and painted the same light-sapping grey as the carpet. Steve opens the door with a key tied around his left wrist, tucked in under his watch strap. He guides her into a small office, empty and anonymous. Lowered ceilings make the air claustrophobic and the windowless room disconcertingly silent. Steve settles himself at the empty desk and gestures to Sarah to sit. A faint yeasty smell fills the air.

'Sorry about that. I'm never quite sure of who's listening down there. Local boys built that bit of the building, who knows what they slipped into the walls with the plaster work? Up here is secure. We had to bring in Brits to do the lot—plaster work, carpentry, carpeting, you name it, it was hand carried here by one of Her Majesty's subjects and banged in with a good British hammer. We don't have to worry about our Georgian friends earwigging. So, you're one of us then?'

'Us?'

'Yes, you know, the Friends from across the river? Softly, softly catch a monkey?' Again the hesitation, face frozen, an actor waiting for the prompt to be whispered from off stage. 'I'm Station Chief, Tbilisi,' he continues. 'Not that you'd call it much of a station, there's only a couple of us here.'

Sarah wonders where the rest of them are. There is no sign of anyone else in this strangely silent part of the building, no other desks, no other doors and no sound other than the gentle hum of an enormous computer and the ticking of a small alarm clock on the desk.

'You would have thought someone would have done me the

courtesy of letting me know you were coming.' His accent is hard to pin down. Civil Service received pronunciation, but with a trace of Estuary vowels. 'I had no idea until a message came through for you from Michael in London. I told them they were out of their mind. Then I had to go back rather red faced when Ed mentioned the new DFID girl. Does the Ambassador know you're one of us?'

'I'm not sure that he does. He seemed to think that I had been sent by DFID, so I played along with that.'

'Probably for the best, he's not known to be particularly discreet. If he did know he'd be humming the Bond theme every time you walked into the room. I had to have words to stop him introducing me at public functions as his resident spook.' Steve fiddles with his hair, pulling it forward over his ears. 'So you're the Skarparov bait?'

Sarah resents the image. Michael convinced her she was chosen for her skills, not as a pretty-coloured lure in a cocktail dress. Is Steve just lacking Michael's finesse or is he passing on Michael's description? 'Michael asked me to look into the Skarparov Foundation,' she says, heckles up. 'Do you know it?'

'I know Viktor Skarparov from the Tbilisi social scene. He's a regular at official functions, especially if the government are involved. And he's often hanging around the bar of the Sheraton late at night.'

'And it's work that takes you there?'

'You'd be surprised.' Steve gives her a sideways look. 'He always struck me as charming but essentially useless. What's he doing with a foundation?'

'No idea. I met the head of their Tbilisi office this morning but left none the wiser as to what they are working on.' Sarah breathes deeply to banish the memory of Irakli's clammy hands.

Steve fishes another key from inside the neck of his shirt, and leans in throat-first to open the top drawer of his desk, pulling out a plate of half-eaten toast and Marmite. He re-locks the empty drawer, leaving Sarah wondering if securing the Marmite is a conscious mitigation of an assessed threat, or simply force of habit.

'You don't mind if I finish up my breakfast, do you? Bit of a rush to get going this morning.' He takes a bite, the sound of spraying crumbs amplified by the bare space. 'Who have they got running it then?'

'Irakli Makmudov, do you know him?'

'That degenerate? I don't know him well; again mostly social circles.'

'The Sheraton nightclub?'

'Perhaps.' Steve laughs. 'Tbilisi is a pretty small town.' He wipes his mouth with the back of his tie, smearing a dark stain above one of the flamingos. 'I hope he didn't try anything inappropriate?'

'No, not really. Wandering eyes and some corny lines, but mostly harmless.'

'I wonder why they chose him. He's always struck me as a nasty piece of work—more at home with mafia street struggling than development projects.'

'He parroted some corporate-speak, but seemed more interested in looking up my skirt.'

'That's right.' Steve wipes his hands together and unlocks the drawer to return his empty plate. 'Wasn't he in Nakhchivan in the '90s? I seem to remember hearing he was part of a smuggling link to the Mkhedrioni.'

'The who?'

'Sorry, forgot you were new. The Mkhedrioni were a powerful paramilitary organisation during the civil war—mostly heavily armed thugs with Kalashnikovs and meat cleavers. I always thought that was more his crowd.'

'And Nakhchivan?' Sarah asks, struggling to mimic Steve's effortless pronunciation.

'A funny little enclave of Azerbaijan sandwiched between Armenia and Iran. Heydar Aliyev was governor after the fall of the Soviet Union before he became president of Azerbaijan.

Irakli's got links up in Chechnya as well, doesn't he? He had something of a network going during the last Chechen war.'

Sarah clocked the sleaze, but the arrogance she had written off as mostly harmless takes on a whole new life when paired with Kalashnikovs, meat cleavers and Chechens. 'Michael said he was connected to Skarparov's uncle, Ibragimov,' Sarah says. 'He told me to get close to Skarparov as a way in to Ibragimov. I wondered if Irakli might be a useful shortcut?'

Steve nods as if his mind is elsewhere. Sarah thinks he might be about to tell her more, but he dives under the desk to pull up his socks gathered round his ankles. 'We all thought Mikhail Ibragimov was yesterday's man,' he continues from under the desk. 'Very powerful under Heydar Aliyev, and as corrupt and nasty as you'd have to be to make a fortune out of the fall of the Union. But we thought he was out of the inner circle now that the son is in charge. It looks like he's gunning for another round, if that agent is to be believed. Poor bastard, it's stories like that make me wonder if some of these chaps know the risks they're running.'

'Ibragimov?'

'No, the agent that fingered him.'

'The one on the train?'

'Poor bastard. Of course, we don't know for sure. There is rather a lot we don't know about this one.'

'So you think the crash was planned, once Ibragimov realised the agent had turned him in?'

'That's what we have to assume. Too much of a coincidence that he was one of the few casualties otherwise. But something about it doesn't sit right for me. Surely there are easier, less public ways to bump someone off than an elaborate train derailment? Normally they just turn up in a ditch somewhere, minus fingertips and teeth.'

Sarah swallows hard; the tick of the clock grows more insistent.

'Sorry, I didn't mean to scare you.' Steve sits back in his swivel-chair and studies her, his eyes cautious. 'You're new, aren't you?'

'I arrived this week.' Sarah hopes her voice has more authority than she feels.

'No, I mean totally new. To all of this.' He gestures towards his empty desk and the windowless walls.

'Yes. Michael sent me.'

'Poor bastard,' Steve mutters at the computer screen. He sighs sharply through his nostrils, shaking his head. 'We have to assume,' he looks back at Sarah, 'that someone ratted the agent out to Ibragimov, so Ibragimov took his revenge. And of course all we have is this one dead guy's testimony linking Ibragimov to the weapons moving into Azerbaijan.' He pauses. 'Michael didn't discuss any of this with you?'

'He mentioned the weapons: 300 PKM machine guns, 6,000 AKM Kalashnikovs, tracer, RPG-7s...'

'Blimey, you were paying attention.'

'Force of habit.' Sarah smiles. It's something she's always been able to do, at least as long as she can remember. Lists, numbers, timetables, anything really—except names. She realised quite young that it made her unusual. At a children's birthday, a frazzled mother trying to make a room of sugar-high seven-year-olds do something quiet produced a tray filled with unusual objects. The aim of the game was to see how many you could remember once the tray had been taken away. A pair of binoculars... a hat... a spoon. Sarah couldn't understand why the other faces went blank when they were only halfway there. She reeled off the missing items. The birthday girl burst into tears and accused her of cheating. Since then, she preferred to keep her love of recall to herself. But the more complicated a list, the more her brain enjoyed fixing itself to the challenge, digging a hook into a Draganov Sniper, storing away the RPM in a specially labelled shelf where she could find it later.

'It's an odd list,' Steve muses. 'Sounds more like the armoury of a jungle warlord than what you normally find in the hands of the local insurgents.'

Sarah makes a mental note to work out how you would tell the difference.

'And did Michael discuss insertion tactics? If Ibragimov is willing to blow up a train just to punish an agent who ratted on him, God knows what he'd be willing to do with that amount of kit. The pipeline is the obvious target, but he's not a predictable type. We've got just over three weeks until the opening of that beast, when all eyes will be on the region and still no clue what he might be planning.'

'He told me to get close to Skarparov and use him to get to Ibragimov.'

Steve rolls his eyes. 'Seems a bit round about, doesn't it, given the urgency? But I suppose Mike in his wisdom has his reasons.'

It would have been nice if he'd shared them.

'There is an exhibition opening tonight at the Georgian National Museum, something to do with carpets. The President is due to make an appearance, so most of the Tbilisi elite should be there. I'm sure Skarparov would be keen to show his face.'

'Can I get tickets?'

'Sopho will get you on the guest list. I'll take you if you like, give you a quick run down on who's who.'

Sarah is hesitant. Is turning up with the embassy's resident spook really a good idea? At least it's a lead that doesn't involve another meeting with Irakli.

'I'll pick you up at eight. And wear your best dress; you'll want to make sure Skarparov spots you too.'

She's back to being a worm on a hook.

*

Sarah finds Sopho packing up her desk and preparing to leave. The Ambassador's secretary scoops up a large stack of files and shuts them in a precarious pile in the cabinet behind her.

'Sorry to stop you as you're on your way out,' Sarah says. 'Steve mentioned you could help get me on the guest list for the event tonight? Sorry, I don't think we've met. I'm—'

'You're Sarah. It's okay, I know.' Sopho gives a bashful smile. 'Sorry I did not come before to say hello before. You want to see the carpets?'

Sopho dials a number from memory, cradling the black plastic phone under her chin while decanting everything else on the desk—photo frames, three tubes of hand cream and a vase of artificial flowers—into a large leather shoulder bag with an elegant sweep of her arm. She speaks in rapid Georgian, nodding animatedly into the handset—'*ho, ho, britanetis saelchos, Sa-rah Black*'—she looks up at Sarah, covering the mouthpiece with her hand. 'No middle name, right?'

'No. How did you know that?' she asks as Sopho crashes the handset back into its cradle.

'It helps to know things.' Sopho gives another smile that lights up her broad features—wide cheekbones, large heart-shaped mouth, aquiline nose. Her wild chestnut hair has been wrestled into a large clip on top of her head. Her smile transforms her face from doe-eyed and watchful to radiant and mischievous.

'Will you be coming?' Sarah asks.

'Me?' Sopho shakes her head. 'It's not really my thing. I'm going to Mtskheta to light a candle and then straight to my parents.'

'Where's Mts…' Sarah falters trying to get her mouth around the five consonants.

'The Jvari monastery. One of the oldest churches in Georgia. I go as often as I can.'

There is something instantly endearing about Sopho—an openness mixed with a careful reserve, the way she looks down before meeting your eye but then smiles as if you shared a long-standing private joke. Sarah feels drawn to her warmth.

'Are you sure I can't convince you to come along?' She's confident Sopho would make a much better wing-woman than Steve, and probably knows just as much, if not more, about the Tbilisi elite.

'You'll be fine. You're meeting Skarparov, right?'

Sarah is thrown, how much does Sopho already know? She doesn't want to give away more than she should. If Steve could not talk freely downstairs in the embassy, how guarded should she be when talking with a Georgian secretary? She nods noncommittally.

'Can I give you some advice?' Sopho asks, her dark eyes suddenly serious.

'Of course.'

'Watch yourself around Irakli, he's trouble.'

Sarah laughs, she doesn't need the warning but appreciates the concern. 'Yes, he set my "creep radar" blaring.' She expects a knowing laugh but Sopho's round eyes still look worried.

'Please be careful. And if you ever need any help, you can always ask, you know? It's difficult here sometimes, especially when you're new and don't know your way around. I'm happy to help.'

'Are you sure you don't want to come tonight? You could help me fend off unwanted advances?'

Sopho looks torn and lowers her eyes beneath her thick lashes. Sarah realises she's asked the one thing Sopho can't offer. 'I'm sorry. You'll be fine with Steve. But if there's anything else, just ask.'

CHAPTER 12

Bg3 Nh5

An embassy Land Rover pulls up outside Sarah's apartment at five minutes to eight—Steve in the passenger seat and Vakho behind the wheel. Vakho dives out to open the door for Sarah.

'Wow, Miss Sarah, you look beautiful!'

Sarah laughs. Irakli's smarm had left her feeling licked by a lizard whereas Vakho's easy charm gives her a happy flush.

'Watch it, Vakho,' Steve admonishes playfully. 'You're on duty tonight. Sorry, Sarah, I take it you've met Vakho?'

'Yes, he picked me up from the airport.'

'He's the best guy we've got. Knows everyone and everywhere in Tbilisi, don't you Vakho?'

'Of course, Mr Steve! Anything you need.' Vakho grins at Sarah in the rear-view mirror.

'You do look lovely, Sarah. That's quite a dress!' Steve's cheeks flush from ruddy to magenta as he delivers the compliment.

Michael's red dress hangs beautifully and is surprisingly

comfortable for such a close cut. The movement of the cool cloth against her skin feels elegant and alluring, but not too obvious. It certainly looks better without the slippers.

The National Museum is housed in an imposing eighteenth century building on Rustaveli, central Tbilisi's elegant main thoroughfare. The museum is closed for renovation, but the large empty halls have been taken over for the evening by a display of hand-woven Caucasian carpets.

Security is visibly tight. All guests have to present identification and names are checked against a master list. Inside, the room is already crowded with groomed and glamorous guests decked out in their finest. Sarah is glad she's dressed for the occasion.

A girl sweeps past with a tray of drinks. The full skirts of her traditional dress skimming the ground, she seems to glide rather than walk. Spinning around, she offers a drink to Sarah and Steve, her pointed sleeves flicking out behind her. Sarah hesitates, unsure if she should be drinking while trying to make contact with a professional target. Steve presses a glass into her hand.

'You might be working tonight, but you certainly shouldn't look like you are.'

The serving girl tosses a long black plait over one shoulder and continues her round, showing off the crimson embroidery on the back of the dress that tapers to her slender waist. Sarah watches her float off, mesmerised by the impossibly smooth movements.

'It's like she doesn't have any feet.'

'Amazing, isn't it? God knows how long they have to practise before it looks that effortless.' Steve takes Sarah by the elbow and walks her around the edge of the room, pointing out the people of interest while making it look as if they are admiring the carpets on display. Sarah tries to add a little glide to her step.

'The chap with the bow tie over there is the head of USAID, the American equivalent of DFID. They've got plenty of cash to spread around, but even they are struggling to get the influence they think they deserve. He's still recovering from the ego bashing he received from the Minister in charge of donor cooperation. Told him to "get lost" in front of the President, but using more colourful language. Ah, yes, that's the Minister there, see the spherical chap with the little moustache?'

The Minister is in full rant, fingers jabbing at the chest of an older man with a wide shovel nose. 'That's Bendukidze. He's supposed to be the real brains behind the government's current reforms. Some of his views are pretty radical, but they seem to be working so far. He hates all donors. If he had his way he'd chuck them all out, but the President reckons the country needs the money.'

'That's one way to do donor cooperation. So I shouldn't introduce myself as DFID then?'

'Well it might be good for a laugh, he's a pretty colourful character, but let's warm you up a little first.'

'Who's he talking to?' Sarah is intrigued by Steve's description and the larger-than-life mannerisms of the Minister, still gesturing aggressively to keep up with his rhetoric.

'I think the other guy is the head of one of Tbilisi's biggest banks. Bendukidze doesn't seem too impressed with him either.'

'He would be a good person to ask about whether the Skarparov Foundation are actually doing any legitimate work. Shall I go and ask?'

'I would hold on a moment.' Steve looks nervous, if he had a tail it would be firmly curled between his legs. Has he had a run-in with Bendukidze in the past? He tries to manoeuvre Sarah away from the Minister and on to a less intimidating target, but she's not giving in. It's rare to meet people so unafraid to speak their mind. And if he has come across Steve before, she'd rather get to him before the Minister sees them together. Sarah channels her inner dragon slayer and, wriggling free from Steve's arm, makes her approach to the Minister.

'Minister Bendukidze?'

The spherical man drops off mid-rant, his clenched fist still raised. He turns to Sarah. 'And you are?'

'Looking for some of your advice.' Sarah offers her hand.

Bendukidze examines her like a caged lion surveying his lunch.

'Let me guess,' he throws a derisive glance over her outfit. 'You must be a donor. NGOs don't dress like that. Tell me, DFID or the World Bank?'

'Is it that obvious? I'm not even wearing sandals.'

Bendukidze's sneer softens. '*Vai me*,' he rolls his eyes theatrically. 'Another do-gooder. Why does no one want to come here just to make some honest money, instead of giving it all away with strings attached?'

'If it makes it any better, I don't actually have any money to give,' Sarah gives a tentative smile.

'Even better!' the Minster snorts. 'So you want my advice? My advice is get lost. All of you, let us get on with running our country.'

The banker that Bendukidze had been talking to visibly squirms at the Minister's raised voice. He looks glad to be out of the direct line of fire but concerned for Sarah's ability to hold up in his place. Sarah considers her response. Should she laugh? The Minister may be deliberately provoking her to get a rise, but his tone is deadly serious. Would her laughter disarm his attack or rile him further? She decides to try more flattery. 'Actually I'm after your advice on another Foundation working here— the Skarparov Foundation? I am told you have the best handle on everyone doing worthwhile work in Georgia and I would appreciate your honest opinion on them.'

'I've never heard of them. You?' he asks, turning to the shovel-nosed banker still standing beside him, fiddling awkwardly with the stem of his wine glass.

'Skarparov?' the banker purses his lips with a little wince. 'I believe, er, they are new.' He looks at Sarah, his eyes entreating her not to push for more.

She pushes on regardless. 'And do you know anything about

their work?'

'I... er...' the banker looks to the Minister for support.

'They haven't come to bother me yet,' the Minister says, 'so they can't be very serious. Or maybe I chucked them out before they told me their name.' Now he is laughing, delighting in his power. 'If I can give you some advice Ms DFID.'

'It's Sarah.'

'As you wish. If you really want to help Georgia, you send me more people like this man.' He slaps the banker on the back. 'You know who he is? He started off selling old computers and silk stockings off the back of a lorry in Moscow. Now he's one of the most prominent businessmen in Georgia, the head of one of the biggest banks. And a genuine philanthropist too, not like your... whatever his name was. This is the sort of person we need, someone who knows the value of hard work and is committed to the long-term future of this country. You donors with your offers of money—you're like an unfinished piece of knitting. It looks nice, but once you get caught up in all the strings the whole thing unravels, and you're left with nothing.'

Sarah couldn't help but smile at the image enhanced by the Minister's elaborate hand gestures.

'Foundations with flashy cars, talk shops, meetings to organise the next meeting. I don't need any of it. If you really want to help you can tell your colleagues to send me their bankers not their bureaucrats. Now please excuse me.' He gives Sarah a gracious nod and turns away.

Sarah has rarely met anyone quite so directly confrontational and yet there is something refreshing in his honesty.

The banker looks relieved that she's still smiling, if not a little impressed. He removes a business card and a silver pen from his top pocket and scribbles something on the back of the card. He hands it to Sarah, pressing it gently into her palm. He bows his head to acknowledge her thanks, before sliding off to follow Bendukidze.

'How did that go?' Steve reappears at Sarah's side.

'I think I got away with just a light mauling,' Sarah says, examining the business card. On the back, in spidery handwriting, the banker has written a name: Nikolay Kuznetsov. She slips the card into her evening bag.

'He must be in a good mood. Evening,' Steve nods a polite greeting to a heavy-set man in an ill-fitting jacket who nods in response. 'That's our main Georgian counterpart. I'll introduce you properly another time, it doesn't really do to hang around each other too closely at social events.' The Georgian pauses to take in Sarah as he walks past. 'And that's the Americans over there.' Steve points out a huddle of suits. 'And over there, one of the Russians.' A bearded character, drink in hand, stands with his back to the wall watching the crowd. Sarah is again conscious of what it might look like if she is seen too closely with Steve. Who else might be surreptitiously circling and noticing? She takes a step away and turns to face the crowd.

'Does the name Nikolay Kuznetsov mean anything to you?' she asks as they move towards another large display case.

'Not immediately, why?'

'The banker who was talking to Bendukidze wrote it on the back of his business card.'

'Intriguing. It's not anyone in Tbilisi, as far as I know. But it's a pretty common name. You might as well be asking about John Smith.'

Sarah's attention is captured by the exquisite carpet inside the display case—lit by spotlights from both sides, it seems to glow in the dark hall. She is drawn to the colours—neutral earth tones mixed with rich reds, eye-catching blues and highlights of golden saffron, unexpectedly bright despite its age. As she inspects the carpet, she begins to feel that someone is watching her. She flicks her head around, scanning the room, but spots no one looking her way.

'Great, aren't they?' Steve says, 'I'd love a few to brighten up my place, but the nice ones don't come cheap.'

'It's a real work of art,' Sarah says.

'Excuse me a moment.' Steve ducks away to intercept a man in full military uniform, braids and tassels gleaming. Sarah tries to catch their conversation, but Steve is master of the art of speaking in a crowded space without being overheard. She turns around to scan the crowd for Skarparov, hoping she will recognise him from Michael's photo. The collected guests are fascinating: a priest in a high black head-dress wearing an elaborately jewelled cross, military uniforms of every colour and rank, gazelle-limbed women in cocktail dresses, polished and pressed diplomats, a white haired couple who might be European royalty talking to a man in a scarlet waisted coat with a row of bullets tucked in pockets across the chest and a large dagger hanging from the belt at the front. But amongst the curious crowd milling among the carpets there is no one who fits Skarparov's description.

Steve reappears at her side and whispers in her ear. 'Have you noticed how the number of black suits with earpieces has just tripled? Saakashvili must be on his way, or they wouldn't be in such a flap.'

Sarah is impressed by how casually Steve seems to move around the room—taking in, noticing and observing while appearing to be doing nothing more than enjoying a cocktail party. As he showered her in Marmitey crumbs in the embassy, she took him for a bumbling low-level spook. "On duty", he is far more natural than she expected. Inwardly reeling from the newness of it all, she is glad for his support.

The crowd is parted by a line of drummers who spring into position, one foot pointed, one hand raised as if to grasp the sky. They form a column through the middle of the room for two male dancers, wearing the same scarlet coat and daggers Sarah spotted earlier. The dancers fling their bodies in the air like arrows, landing unflinchingly on their knees before leaping back up to full height. A deep male voice rises over the drumming, joined by others in polyphonic harmony. Sarah is spellbound by the display, scarcely noticing when the wall of security suits separates to flank the newly created dance floor. The room falls silent, as if a shock of electricity has passed through the hall. Everyone turns instinctively in the direction of President Saakashvili.

The beaming face she knows from posters plastered across the city, but she did not expect him to be so big. Toweringly tall and broad, he seems to expand in every direction, his presence further magnified by a springy lope. His eyes are ringed with heavy bags, but he's grinning broadly and shaking hands effusively and putting on a good show of being pleased to be there.

Sarah's heard so much about this bold new president with his ambitious reform plans; she's dying to find out what lies beneath the bluster and bravado. But her hopes of making an approach are quickly swamped in a crowd of people wanting to flatter and cajole. She watches him work the room, impressed by the elegance with which he moves through the crowd, finding a word for each without being waylaid by even the most persistent petitioner. A waiter hovers at his elbow with a bottle of wine, ready to replenish the glass after glass being gulped down the presidential throat.

'Sarah, what a surprise to see you again so soon. I almost didn't recognise you.' She feels an arm around her waist and a damp paw on the small of her back. Irakli is just as confident and slick in his manner, but there is less warmth in his voice. 'I see you are here with Steve.'

Does he labour on the name or is she imagining it?

'He offered to show me around.'

'How kind of him.' Irakli, watching the back of Steve's head, reaches out and grabs one of the serving girls around her tiny waist. The girl spins round and shoots Irakli a fiery look that he meets with a wink. Sarah is looking forward to the serving girl giving him a well-aimed slap but Irakli is shrinking, he looks almost apologetic.

'Irakli, I should have known I would find you here talking to a beautiful woman.'

Sarah braces herself for another brute come to try his hand at flirtation, expecting Irakli to join in the banter. But Irakli pulls himself to attention as if caught behind the bike sheds by the headmaster. The interloper is short and solid. His slicked hair gleams unnaturally dark on top with a band of grey at the temples and his skin has the hue of well-polished wood. His features bear the traces of a handsome man, or at least an appealing face, going swiftly to seed. Puffy eyes from too much drink, chin relaxing into jowls, soft lips. He flashes her a beguiling smile that seems to start at his ears and lift his whole face.

Sarah smiles back, her stomach writhing, her skin both hot and cold. He gazes at her with eyes an arresting shade of opal beneath heavy brows that seem to move independently from the rest of his face.

'And when are you going to introduce your friend?' Skarparov offers his hand to Sarah. 'Viktor Skarparov, a pleasure to meet you. I take it you've met Irakli, my right-hand man?'

'Yes.' Sarah is thrown. She had planned to approach Skarparov on her own terms, not for him to materialise at her side. She sets her shoulders and turns on her most charming smile, allowing him to hold onto her hand slightly longer than is comfortable. His skin is marble cool. 'Irakli was good enough to brief me about some of your work. I'm Sarah Black, I work for DFID. What a pleasure to meet the man himself.'

'The pleasure is all mine. Miss Black, could I take you for a tour of some of these delightful pieces? I wouldn't go so far as to say I am an expert, but certainly an admirer. Come. Let us admire together.' He links his arm through Sarah's, casting an appreciative eye over her dress before moving on towards the main display.

This is exactly the position she had hoped for, perhaps her only chance to press her advantage, but no words come when she tries to speak. She searches the room for Steve, looking for a nod, any sign of acknowledgement that he's seen her, that she's doing the right thing. She sifts through the list of questions she prepared, but now, arm-in-arm with her principal target,

Skarparov's blazer pressed up against her hip, the touch of his chilly palm still lingering on her own, none of them seem to fit.

'This is one of my favourites,' he says, releasing her arm to lay a reverential hand on the glowing glass case. 'Daghestan I think, wait,' he ducks round to the other side of the display. 'Yes, come and have a look at the underside. You see the deep ribbing? That is one of the key marks of a Daghestani carpet. Wonderful, no?' Sarah has never seen anything like it, delicate silk needlework on rough undyed yarn, colours that clash and complement woven into intricate geometric patterns.

'This part of the Caucasus I know very well; many of our suppliers come from here. It has been a centre of sericulture for centuries.'

'Sericulture?' Sarah gives him the chance to show off.

'Silk farms, the rearing of silkworms. Amazing to think that all this beauty is spun from those little grubs.'

Sarah is transfixed by the pattern, continuing perfectly without repetition. Each shape, star, spiral, triangle using a different combination of colours and backgrounds.

'I see we have another natural admirer.' Skarparov moves back to her side, watching her eyes read the codes spelled out in silk. 'So Irakli talked to you about our hopes for DFID's support with our launch? We would be deeply honoured if you would consider co-hosting an event with us. We are very new to this scene, and many people question whether we belong in your world. We could benefit from your wisdom, your reputation.'

Sarah stalls as he slips his arm through hers to continue their tour. 'Have you talked to any of the other donors?' Sarah asks.

'Of course. But we like the integrity of DFID. We like to know where we stand with our partners.' His eye lingers on Sarah, gently taking her in.

'Of course.' She lets him look. He is not subtle in his attentions, but nor is his gaze as sleazy as Irakli's. He studies her in the same way he looks at the carpets, something to admire rather than devour. 'We would need to understand a bit more about your Foundation first,' she tries stalling further, softening her voice, 'to be sure we find a natural fit.'

He does not respond, leaving her to fill the silence.

'And I would have to talk to the Ambassador about it. It might be a bit out of book for us to host a launch for an organisation that the UK is not directly supporting, at least not yet.'

Skarparov stops mid-stroll. 'You're a chess player!'

'What makes you say that?'

'Out of book? I've got you, haven't I? I can tell by that charming blush. A chess player! Tell me, what is your level?'

'Oh nothing too serious, I used to play at school.' Sarah is unprepared for the sudden feeling of intimacy that comes from revealing elements of her personal life. Her real life. She is supposed to be in character as Sarah the charming development worker. But the pretence feels weakened by Skarparov seeing through to Sarah the teenaged chess champion.

'Come on, you can tell me. Did you compete at national level? What was your Elo rating? Don't be shy.'

'No really, I played a bit as a hobby, an amateur,' Sarah lies.

Skarparov rubs his palms together. 'How intriguing. Well, no wonder you like all these geometric patterns. You noticed of course on that last piece how the pattern never repeats?'

'Really? How clever.' It feels safer playing the dumb blonde than allowing Skarparov any further into her head.

He gives her a sceptical look, one mobile eyebrow raised, unconvinced. He points to the next carpet in the display. 'What do you notice is special here?'

Automatically Sarah begins scanning the design to interpret the pattern, counting motifs and colour combinations. She doesn't have to tell him.

'You see these crosses?' Skarparov asks. 'These are typical of the orthodox church in this region. But this is a Muslim prayer mat, and look here—see how the crosses form a pattern with the crescents? It's like me. A true hybrid of the Caucasus.' His movements are gentle, elegant, the quiet, unhurried poise of one brought up amongst constant luxury. He gazes at the carpets, his eyes slightly closed, his fingers tapping out an unheard melody on the case.

'I thought you were fully Azeri?'

'Yes, by blood. I was born in Baku. My family is there. My father started the Skarparov Enterprises there and some of my relatives have been quite influential within the government for many years.'

Sarah is tempted to ask him about Ibragimov but waits; she doesn't want to give herself away too soon.

'But I have always felt equally at home here in Georgia, especially in the mountains. Baku is very unpredictable; it is starting to feel like a dangerous place.' He pauses for effect. 'Whereas Tbilisi is blossoming, changing for the better with new optimism. Tell me, have you been to the mountains yet?'

'No, not yet. Irakli offered to take me to show me some of your work.'

'Then you must go!'

Sarah lowers her eyes, trying to escape his gaze. She doesn't want to spoil the moment by telling him his right-hand man is a creep.

Skarparov gives a sigh of frustration. 'You must allow me to apologise for Irakli, he can be quite a blunt tool. I'm afraid he was foisted on me by an uncle who can be difficult to refuse. And I need someone with his connections if I am to operate in the mountains. They only trust their own. He knows all the right people, including some of the more unsavoury ones. But he is certainly well placed to show you around, even if he can be a bit, how should I put it, rough mannered at times.'

'No need to apologise.' Sarah is again unnerved by how accurately Skarparov penetrates her thoughts. 'He was perfectly gentlemanly.'

Skarparov raises an eyebrow. 'Really? That would be a first. But do join him on his next trip. I'll make sure he behaves. And when you come back, let's talk about this launch.' He takes

Sarah's hand in his and raises it to his lips. 'It's been a pleasure talking to you, Sarah, enjoy the evening.'

She watches as he floats off through the crowd.

Once he's out of sight, Steve appears back at her side. 'So how did your first contact go?'

'I'm not quite sure.'

'He certainly looked interested in the bait. Did you manage to set up another meeting?'

'Um, I think so.' Sarah is still watching the crowd. 'We agreed that we would follow up after I visit one of their project sites in the mountains.'

'Sounds like success to me. Congratulations on your first contact. Let's find you a refill, I think you've earned it.'

'Thanks.' Sarah tries to feel pleased, but she's daunted by the task. As a first contact it went as well as she could have hoped—he even mentioned Ibragimov, his pushy uncle, unprompted. Michael made it sound so easy: use the foundation, offer help, make yourself indispensable, win his trust. She memorised the steps. When the subject was just a smiling photo it sounded an easy recipe to follow. But now that he's a real human being, with an uncanny knack of seeing past her pretences, her confidence falters. She knows she could develop a good rapport with him, as herself, opening up and encouraging him to do the same. But could she encourage openness in him without giving too much of herself away?

She knocks back the glass of champagne that Steve presses into her hand. She doesn't have the time to over-think this. She has just over three weeks to get to Ibragimov and so far Skarparov seems her best bet. It's simple really. Just don't screw it up.

CHAPTER 13

Bd3 Nd7

Sarah reaches her father on the third attempt. The ancient telephone made of pale blue Bakelite has an old-fashioned rotary dial and a pleasing weightiness. But she's unsure if it can still reach the outside world. Having tried a combination of different codes to access an outside line and listened to a series of unfamiliar tones and beeps, she finally hears her father's voice. He sounds faint, half lost in the static, but the voice is reassuringly his.

'Sarah? Where are you? Are you underwater?'

'I'm in my apartment in Tbilisi.'

'Is it subterranean?'

'No: first floor, looking out over the most spectacular view of the old city.'

'No fish then?'

'No, Dad, no fish.'

'And what's Tbilisi like? Concrete and dreary?'

'Actually it's beautiful. Still emerging from the great social experiment, but happily with most of its ancient charm and churches intact.'

'Funny thing really. When I joined the Civil Service, I had to sign endless bits of paper to say I'd never go to these places. Wrong side of the curtain. And now there you are giving them our money.'

'You'll be pleased to hear I haven't got any money to give, not yet anyway. Just doing some due diligence.'

'Oh.' There is silence at the other end.

'Are you there?' Sarah asks.

'I went in again last week—Cabinet Office senior management called me in. Felt a bit strange on the train but much better once I had my toes back under a desk. Shouldn't be more than once a week, if that. It's good to feel useful.'

'And you're well? Is Angus there with you?'

'Who are you looking into then?'

'Me? Yeah. Um, it's a new philanthropic organisation—the Skarparov Foundation. They've just started working in the Caucasus.'

'And what does your instinct tell you? Are they a good lot?'

'It's a bit early to say.' Sarah listens to her voice repeated down the echoey line. 'Their local guy is definitely a sleazebag. I'm going up to the mountains later to have a look at some of their work.' She wants to move away from details of her assignment, but part of her wants someone who matters to know where she is going.

'If the sleazebag so much as—'

'Then I will knee him firmly in the groin. It's okay, Dad, I know the drill.'

'Actually a toe is generally better than a knee, unless of course you lose your balance.'

'Then any unwanted advances will be met with the point of my shoe in his crotch.'

'Are you allowed pointy shoes in DFID?'

'The buckle of my Birkenstock in his bollocks?'

'That'll do. And do watch out for Turco-Mongol invasions.'

'Whose invitation?' The creaking phone line does little to make her father more comprehensible.

'Tamerlane.'

'The chess set?'

'No. Didn't you read any history? The great conqueror and founder of the Timurid dynasty. He invaded Georgia eight times to try to get them to give up Christianity.'

'But, Dad, wasn't that in the fourteenth century?'

'Yes, but he didn't manage, did he?'

Sarah laughs. 'I'll look out for invading armies.'

'And Sarah? Trust your instincts, won't you? Don't put yourself in any situation that doesn't feel right.'

'Yes, Dad.'

'I mean it; there's no need for heroics. Not in that world.'

Sarah wonders which world he means. Even face to face it is impossible to keep up with her father's mental leaps of association.

'How's the game going?' she asks.

'I let him have that bishop. You should have seen him crowing. But he hasn't spotted my rook at h3.' Her father gives a little cackle of glee.

'Oh dear, I hope he doesn't take it too badly.'

'He's a lot of bluster, but tougher than he seems. Always know your opponent, Sarah. Play to his style if you want to have the edge. I should know how to work him by now, we've been playing almost a year.' His voice disappears into a high-pitch squeak that could be an impression of the neighbour or more interference on the line.

'Look after yourself, Sarah.'

'I will. You too. I'll call you when I get back.'

She replaces the heavy handset in its cradle, leaving her fingers still curled around the handle. Even across a broken line from many miles away, it is a comfort to hear his voice.

CHAPTER 14

WOOD PUSHERS

The Castle flings open the door of the office where Hasan and Seidov are waiting, letting it bounce on its hinges before slamming it tightly shut.

'What the hell were you thinking turning up like that with the equipment in the middle of the day?' he yells.

Seidov, the smaller of the two, beardy, looks pointedly at the ground. His frame is thin and wiry, and his tightly curled black hair grows so low on his forehead it seems to cover half of his face. 'I didn't touch the stuff. It was your new guy who nearly dropped it.'

'Well?' the Castle asks, turning to Hasan.

Hasan draws up his full, solid, neckless hulk. He is a good half a foot taller than the Castle but too solid, too slow. Forearms like breeze blocks and neck like a side of ham, he stares at the Castle with his big stupid face. He seems to wear an almost permanent shrug—an expression of disdain or just a shirking of responsibility. 'You never told us when to come,' he mumbles.

The Castle matches his stance, puffing out his chest. He's filled out a bit since his kick-boxing days, a bit softer round the middle than he'd like. But he could still take them. Even that big bastard. And they know it. 'You were supposed to call first. Have you any idea what mess you might have got us in?'

'Sorry,' Hasan looks at the floor. 'We didn't know.'

'Of course you didn't know, because you didn't think.'

'What did you want us to do? Drive around the city all day with that thing in the back of the van?' Seidov asks. He tilts his head towards the Castle, his eyes so closely set it is hard to tell whether he is looking him in the eye. 'Your guy couldn't wait to get rid of it,' Seidov says dismissively.

'But no one could see it in the van, could they?'

He is starting to worry whether it was a good idea trusting these two with the job. They all worked together in Nakhchivan in the 1990s. The Castle was just a skinny kid back then— messenger and courier for Ibragimov, proving his salt. These guys did the heavier lifting—helping the boss with smuggling routes through Turkey and Iran. Hasan was never the sharpest tool in the box and was more useful for his size than his brains. But Seidov is not as dumb as he looks. And his experience fighting in Nagorno Karabakh is going to be essential.

At that time, Ibragimov was the special one, anointed acolyte of Heydar Aliyev with an interest in all of his special projects. The Castle knew well enough that he was the guy to stick to, even then. And loyalty repays loyalty. Look at him now. Trusted by the boss to mastermind this full project with complete independence, while these two were simple foot-soldiers. Skarparov clearly doesn't like them around, probably worried they'll put a dent in his squeaky-clean image—but he can hardly refuse a favour to his uncle, can he? The Castle vouched for them, told him they were good guys. Now he hopes he was right.

'Just when you goons turned up with the van, I had a woman from the British Government, sitting in the front office, asking questions and watching your every move.'

'Did she see anything?' Hasan asks, his small reluctant eyes looking sideways at the Castle.

'I don't know how much she saw, but I know she was at the window trying to get a better look.'

'Shit,' Seidov mutters to the floor. 'So what do we do?'

'It's a headache I really didn't need. But don't worry, I'll take care of her.'

CHAPTER 15

Nge2 Ne5

Irakli appears at the embassy behind the wheel of a shiny black Mercedes G Class. 'Jump in,' he calls to Sarah through his open window.

Sarah's still fumbling for her seatbelt when Irakli launches the car into the traffic, engine roaring.

'We just need to pick up the other car and the driver, then we can set off,' he says.

'We're not taking your car?' Sarah is relieved at the mention of a potential chaperone. After Steve's briefing on Irakli and Sopho's word of warning, she's even more reluctant to put herself in his wandering hands.

'This one? To the mountains? Are you crazy? This car is just for looking good around the city and not getting stuck in Tbilisi potholes. We need a proper car for the mountains, and someone who knows what he's doing.' He laughs as he swerves across the lanes to avoid a flying minibus, brushing his hand against Sarah's leg with each gear change. She puts her handbag over her knee to bear the brunt of the brush.

At a petrol station just outside town, a sullen-faced driver with steeply sloping shoulders is waiting with an ancient Lada Niva, the original Soviet 4x4. The driver scans her suspiciously. His thick brows curl down around his eyes giving his face the cynical mark of one who has seen it all and declared it mostly shit.

'This is what you need in the mountains,' Irakli thumps his fist heavily on the bonnet. The car gives a worrying rattle. 'It's a terrible car, you'll feel like a coin in a slot machine by the time we get there, but it's the only one worth taking where we're going.'

'Which is where?' Sarah asks.

'You'll see.'

The road follows the river out of the city, and tunnels through steep rock-hewn cliffs and overhanging trees. Soon they are tearing up the main highway at a terrifying speed, weaving in and out of minibuses and trucks, overtaking and undertaking to avoid deep gashes in the tarmac. Sarah clings to the driver's headrest to stop herself from being thrown around the back seat. Irakli sprawls in the passenger seat. His body language is relaxed but his shirt is soaked in sweat and his fingers drum relentlessly on the dashboard.

Once off the main road, Sarah is able to loosen her grip on the headrest and enjoy the scenery, no longer needing to watch the road with dread and mumble a prayer on every blind bend. They pass a string of villages—single storey buildings with corrugated zinc roofs, houses with wide wooden balconies and overhanging gables, neatly tended gardens with climbing wildflowers next to abandoned plots of crumbling concrete and broken-down machinery. Fawn piglets with brown spots run squealing between the cars.

As the mountains loom larger, the road deteriorates and the asphalt gives way to a muddy track. The road ducks through thick forest and up into high-sided cliffs, growing narrower and narrower until it is scarcely more than a car's width across. The face of the mountain plummets beneath them into fast flowing streams lined with flint and shale.

The car stops. A vertical step of snow and mud blocks the road.

'What do we do now? Is there another way up?' Sarah asks.

Irakli snorts. 'We do nothing! The Niva will take care of it.'

Dato, the sour-faced driver, simply shifts the car into low gears and the little Niva, engine growling, picks its way over the obstacle. Clearly a car for the mountains.

They arrive at the village in the late afternoon. The road glows golden in the last of the light and shadows dance across the landscape in bright contrast. Loud blasts echo around the valley walls.

'Was that gunfire?' Sarah asks, hoping it might have been a rockslide or a car misfiring, its sound magnified by the natural amphitheatre of the mountains.

'Of course,' Irakli shrugs, scanning the bushes at the side of the road. 'They are celebrating the festival of Athena today, if we're lucky we might be able to catch the end of the celebrations and some home-made beer.'

'Athena? The Goddess of Wisdom?'

'It's her feast day,' he says still searching, not meeting Sarah's eye.

'So the people here aren't Christian?'

'They celebrate all the Christian festivals too, but many of the pagan holidays remain. They like to hedge their bets up here. Nature feels very powerful in the mountains, you need to pay respect. And it's a good excuse to drink more beer. Come on, this way to the sacrifice spot.' He points towards a narrow gap in a hedge where waist-high grass has been trampled down by the weight of passing revellers.

Sarah scrambles up the steep path after Irakli and Dato. At the top, a small wooden hut surrounded by a wire fence sits hidden in the trees.

'This is the place of sacrifice,' Irakli says, 'but it looks like we've missed the main event.'

A pile of red entrails lies on the ground outside the hut, sticky and glazed like a rheumy eye. An old man dressed in a black cassock with a beard of iron wool stands inside the fence. Irakli and Dato step inside, greeting him respectfully. Sarah makes to follow.

'No, you wait there.' Irakli's arm blocks the gate. 'He has invited us to join him in a toast to Athena.'

'And I can't join?' Sarah wasn't expecting Irakli to be a generous host, but this is ridiculous.

'You can toast,' Irakli looks confused by Sarah's questions. 'You just have to stay on the other side of the fence.'

'Are foreigners not allowed in?' Sarah asks, searching for the rule she is unwittingly breaking.

'No, of course,' Irakli says. 'Foreigners are our guests, a gift from God. But women can't come in the holy place.'

Furious, Sarah marches towards the entrance just to see if Athena would stand up for her. But she stops when she sees the look of horror on the old man's face and remains, quietly outraged, on the permitted side of the fence.

Eyeing her doubtfully, the keeper of the holy place enters the hut, emerging with a grimy jerry can of orange liquid and a bronze goblet. He hands a gobletful to Irakli.

'*Athenas gaumarjos!*' Irakli raises the toast towards the old man, who nods in acknowledgement. He raises the goblet again towards Sarah before lifting it to his lips and draining the cup in one mouthful. Sarah raises an empty hand in response.

'Wow, that's good,' he wipes his lips with the back of his hand and refills his cup. 'You'll be wanting this too, Sarah.'

'So pour me some.' Is he just an inconsiderate brute or is he taunting her?

'That's what you want, eh?' He squares up in front of the rusty chain-link fence, broad shoulders heaving, and stares at Sarah as he downs another goblet in a single draught. Sarah can't hold his eye. His flirtatious stare has turned heavy and lecherous and there is something savage in his bravado, freshly fuelled by alcohol.

He ducks inside the hut and returns with a small white mug. Patches of the enamel coating have chipped away, leaving a stain orange with rust. 'Here, try this: brewed right here for the sacrifice.' He leaves the enclosure to bring her the beer on her permitted side of the fence. Sarah preferred it when he was on the other side of the chain-link, like a penned-in animal. His cheeks are glowing and his body sways towards her as she takes the cup. Taking a step back, she raises her mug in a toast. The beer is warm and cloudy and tastes like ale pulled from pipes long overdue a clean.

'Delicious,' she says without enthusiasm.

'Like nectar from the gods,' he drawls into her ear, his breath hot and heavy down her neck. Sarah's eyes are drawn to the jellied pile of entrails on the ground and the liquid catches in her throat. What is she doing here? A solo trip with Irakli felt foolish enough when he was sober. Now that he's growing all the more unpredictable, she has no way to escape.

Dato the driver, on a low chair next to the old man, is working his way steadily through the jerry can of beer. His oversized nose no longer seems to match up with his cynical brows, as if his face has been twisted off its grid. Irakli interrupts them, swaying slightly, to refill both of their cups with a clear liquid that looks like kerosene.

'*Chacha!*' he declares. The three men down the spirit, shuddering as it hits the gullet. Irakli quickly refills their cups. The old man looks unaffected by the impromptu drinking session. He sits on his low stool, beard tipping up and back with each toast, staring steadily ahead, hands resting on his knees. Irakli, by contrast, is flushed with drink, his upper lip beaded in sweat. Sarah watches with alarm as Dato rises from his stool and stumbles, his legs moving a beat behind the rest of his body. He looks accusingly at his feet before rolling to Irakli for support. He gazes about him like a lost child, his cynic's face now the mask of a clown.

Sarah, her rusty mug now empty, wonders how long the forced celebrations will last. She pulls out her camera, through boredom more than professional duty, to take some tourist shots—a typical village drinking scene, a pagan festival in the mountains. But as she raises the camera, Irakli lurches towards her, knocking her sideways and grabbing it in his large wet-fish palm.

'There you go again, hey, taking pictures.' He fiddles with the buttons on the back of the camera. 'Let's see what else you've got on here, shall we?' His voice is lewd, as if looking for unedited bikini shots.

'Give that back.' Sarah's chest tightens. Luckily, she thought to empty the contents of the camera onto a thumb-stick that is safely stored in her apartment before they left. But she is thrown by Irakli's intrusion. And horrified by what it means.

'No great loss—there's nothing to see. Funny that.' Irakli throws the camera back at her. 'Come on, we're going.' He pushes Sarah towards the path down the hill with Dato reeling behind them. A man in a dark leather jacket is waiting at the bottom, crouched on the grass at the side of the road. A low-slung BMW in gunmetal grey hums next to him, engine running. Irakli greets him as a long-lost brother, gripping him round the neck in an affectionate head lock. Sarah watches horrified as Dato climbs clumsily into the driver's seat of the Niva. He looks scarcely able to control his breathing, much less handle a vehicle.

Irakli pushes Sarah roughly into the back of Dato's car. She flinches from the alcohol on his breath and the meaty pungency of his sweat. She tries to get out—this is crazy, she'd rather climb the mountain on foot than put her life in Dato's shaking hands. But Irakli has pushed up the passenger seat. She waits for him to climb in to the front but he straightens up, staring at her. His expression makes her stomach squirm. His eyelids, normally curled up in self-satisfaction, now slant down giving his face a vicious streak. 'I'm taking Luka's car.' He slaps his newly arrived companion on the back of the neck. 'We have some catching up to do. Dato will take you on. Drive safely.' He taps on the roof before climbing into the driver's seat of the BMW.

Dato stares at the steering wheel as if trying to remember what it is. He turns the key and looks startled when the car jumps forward, lurching across the road. Sarah wants to escape—everything feels wrong—but there are no back doors. She tries to scramble into the front seat but is thrown back as Dato lurches the car around a tight bend with Irakli following close behind. They race through the village, both cars swerving to avoid craters in the road and skidding on the loose gravel. Dato looks pale; his hands slip on the steering wheel as they pick up speed.

The road with its hairpin bends and stomach plummeting drops was bracing on the way up, but Dato's quiet competence had reassured her. Now that her driver has a gullet-full of home-brew, Sarah is terrified. Irakli's car is right behind them, forcing them to go faster, pushing them into each blind bend.

A scrawny chicken darts across the road in front of them and a small boy runs out after his pet. Dato does not notice them, staring ahead with glassy eyes. Sarah throws herself at the steering wheel to swerve the car away from the collision. She pulls hard towards her, sending the car skidding on two wheels and veering to the right. Dato gapes at her hanging over the passenger seat, his face uncomprehending. She waits for a thump or a scream. Time feels stretched as she waits for the inevitable, but nothing comes. In the rear-view mirror, she sees the boy cradling his chicken in a cloud of dust, watching the two cars scream by. She sees Irakli's face behind the wheel. He is laughing.

'Slow down you moron,' Sarah shouts at Dato. 'You could have killed him!'

Dato does not respond.

'Let me out!' She climbs over the front seat to reach the passenger door, but the inside handle is missing. Suddenly she is thrown into the dashboard by a sharp thump from behind. Irakli's grey car pushes right on their tail, so close now that his front bumper nudges the Niva onwards.

'Stop! What the hell are you doing?' Sarah screams at Irakli. He stares straight at her, his face set in a deranged grin. Is he mad? Or just blind drunk?

They approach another bend at lunatic speed. Dato steps heavily on the brake sending the car into a skid. Again Irakli rams them, catching the back of the car and pushing it sideways. Dato yanks at the steering wheel in panic as the back wheels lose traction and the car swerves into a giddy fishtail. He looks up, his face the colour of cold porridge. Then his head slumps forward and his body hangs limp over the wheel.

Sarah reaches for the pedals, but Dato's bulky form fills the footwell. The car is losing momentum, but the road ahead veers up to the right at an angle impossible to manoeuvre at this speed. Another shunt from behind as Irakli shoves past them sending the Niva off the side of the road. A narrow verge of weeds and gravel is all that separates the track from the vertiginous mountain drop. Sarah screams as the car approaches the edge until nothing is visible ahead. The car tips out into the void.

All is black.

CHAPTER 16

0-0 Ng6

Searing pain brings Sarah back to consciousness. She is crushed under the passenger seat, one arm pinned awkwardly beneath her. The car balances on its nose, tail end up, gravity pulling her down into the footwell. Dato is still slumped over the wheel, his body supported by the steering column, arms dangling at his sides. His face is hidden by a clump of black hair shot through with streaks of dirty white. She can see nothing through the windscreen, now a fractured spiderweb of shattered glass, and can't see what stopped their fall. She reaches with her free arm to Dato's throat, feeling for a pulse. He does not flinch as she pushes her fingers deeply into the creases of skin at his neck, but his back heaves slowly in the contented snore of a drunk. Amazingly, he looks unscathed.

No amount of pushing will open the passenger door, its frame warped by the impact. Setting her back against the dashboard and angling her feet towards the window, Sarah kicks against the glass but nothing moves. She tastes blood. A sticky trail seeps from her forehead down the side of her face. Summoning all the power she has in shaky legs, she tries again. Two kicks later her right foot smashes through the window. She leans back, legs in the air, delighting in the sound of the falling fragments of glass.

After a few more painful kicks to dislodge the last shards, she clambers out. Her knees buckle as she peers down the flint face of the cliff. The car is balanced on a lip of rock just below the road. Had it missed this small outcrop, they would be a mangle of metal and shattered body parts on the rocks below. Sarah is hooked over the car by the urge to vomit and braces herself against the crumpled side panel as the wave of shock passes. Blocking the chasm from her mind, she hauls herself back up to the road, grip faltering on the loose gravel.

At the top, a group of villagers gawk at her. Sarah looks for Irakli, but he is not among them. That bastard, why didn't he stop? An old woman approaches, shoulders bent into a hoop, hands outstretched. Her leathery skin is thick and strong but riven with deep splits and creases. Her eyes, sunk deep into their sockets, dance with an unexpected lightness. She gazes intently at Sarah, taking hold of her hands, muttering strange words. She examines Sarah's arm and unwinds her rough woollen head scarf to wrap the wound in a makeshift bandage.

'Someone's still in the car!' Sarah points over the edge. 'He needs help.' Two men, staring at her as if she is an apparition of the goddess herself, climb cautiously over the edge towards the concertinaed car.

The old woman, her arm locked carefully around Sarah's, leads her to a large house behind a fence overgrown with roses. Wide wooden balconies and carved balustrades encircle the house, protected from the sun by a deep overhanging roof. The amber wood is weathered, its varnish peeling, but the zinc roof shines with a brand-new lustre. A buffed and polished dark green Mercedes takes pride of place in the driveway.

A man wearing a leather jacket two sizes too large comes out to meet them. He takes one look at Sarah and wrestles the old woman away from her, muttering to her in Georgian, trying to lead her into the house. She prods him in the chest with a thick-knuckled finger and sends him shuffling back over to Sarah, tugging at his shirt collar. 'Come inside, please,' he says in accented English. 'My mother explained what happened. My name is Giorgi, we will look after you.' Giorgi's eyes have his mother's sparkle but where she is happy to gaze at Sarah in curiosity, he can't wait to get away. His eyes dart and shift and only fleetingly meet Sarah's before searching out the safety of his feet. He wears the uniform of the mountains—dark trousers and black leather jacket. But on him it looks wrong: his red t-shirt is too bright, the jacket so big it makes him look like a child. The gleaming car must belong to him.

Inside, the house is dark and cool. Giorgi leads Sarah upstairs to a spare bedroom, simply furnished with a sturdy looking bed frame piled high with blankets and pillows. At the sight of the bed, a sharp pain shoots through Sarah's arm and she wants nothing more than to burrow under the inviting looking pile.

'You stay here to clean up,' Giorgi instructs. 'My mother will see to your arm.'

She is glad to be alone. Her body is still reeling from the accident, flooded with adrenaline. She knows she's lucky to be so little hurt, but she can't shake the look on Irakli's face as he pushed her into the car, or the twisted sneer as the car lost control. Was he just drunk and failing to comprehend the gravity of what was happening? Or were his shunts intended to push them off the road? His disappearance after the accident suggests the worst.

Sarah is drawn to the window that looks out over the blue-tinged forest and the plummeting valley below. The golden afternoon light has faded to smoky grey, but even in the muted dusk, the sky is sweeping and vast. She watches the light fade, trying to dislodge the image of Irakli's lunatic grin. What would he do if he found out she had made it out alive?

Giorgi's mother enters with a bowl of water and a bundle of cloths. She sets to work cleaning the wound on Sarah's forehead, clucking sympathetically as Sarah winces with pain and fashioning a bandage for the injured arm, all the while talking in strange tones and singing a mournful lullaby. Sarah is overwhelmed by gratitude for her care, to be safe. She has to swallow hard to hold back the tears threatening her eyes.

Wounds well-dressed, the stack of pillows on the bed looks all the more inviting. But even Giorgi's mother's care is not enough to make her feel safe. Irakli can't be far away, and it wouldn't take much to track down a wounded foreigner in a tiny mountain village. She can hear voices downstairs, the sound of people she can't place, chairs being scraped across a concrete floor. She can't stay here.

'Is there a way to get back to Tbilisi tonight?' she asks Giorgi's mother but it's clear she doesn't understand. Sarah tries again in Russian and the woman embraces her, her shoulders shaking with laughter. 'Tonight? Of course not! Nobody drives that road in the dark. You must stay. Relax. You need to eat. Tomorrow you can go.'

Sarah is led downstairs. The house is dark but outside on the terrace a long table is set for dinner, small plates stacked on top of each other at each setting, oversized forks and spoons, low tumblers filled with chequered paper napkins. The same endless view from her window is just visible from the terrace, fading into black.

She counts the table settings with growing anxiety. There are dozens of plates. If she can't leave, she was hoping to be able to gulp down some chicken soup and go to bed, not to join a feast-day party.

Giorgi waves from the end of the terrace. It's more an acknowledgement than a welcome. He's talking to a European-looking man, unusually tall with red hair and grey-blue eyes. Sarah's insides shrink. The last thing she wants is a curious foreigner. At least amongst the Georgians she can hide behind the language barrier. What if he wants to talk? The stranger gives the impression of being curiously at home, his broad shoulders

102

radiate relaxation in his surroundings. They are talking in a strange mix of Russian and Georgian with the odd English word thrown in.

The redhead notices Sarah. In Giorgi's hurried explanation, mumbled into his ear between sucks on a cigarette, Sarah thinks she catches Irakli's name. Does Giorgi know him? Does he know what happened?

'Chechnya, with some of the locals,' the foreigner says matter-of-factly, swapping into perfect English. 'It's the best season for bear hunting.'

'So where's the big skin?' Giorgi asks.

'My companions were more interested in taking pot shots at beer cans. A mother bear walked right over my sleeping bag one night, but it did not feel right to shoot her. She had a cub with her. Not exactly fair sport.' The stranger turns to Sarah and offers his hand.

'Hello, I'm Elias. I don't think we've met?' His voice is a deep monotone, with an accent impossible to place. Sarah tries to offer her bandaged right hand, but Elias swiftly offers his left hand to help her out. Sarah shakes it, feeling small. He must be at least a foot taller than her.

'Hello, I'm Sarah. I'm from England.' Why did she say that? She feels awkward, nervous, unprepared for the stranger's intense gaze.

'A pleasure to meet you, Sarah from England. What happened to your arm? I hope that wasn't an Athena-related injury? It's amazing how many egos and senses of balance get offered up to the goddess along with the sacrifices.' His voice is deep and serious, but a suggestion of a smile crosses his eyes.

'It was nothing; some trouble on the road on the way up.'

'Nothing too serious, I hope. And what brings you up here?'

Sarah searches for an escape. She's in no mood to explain herself. She wants to ask Giorgi if there's a bus back to Tbilisi, or any other way to leave before morning, but Giorgi has moved away to welcome other guests. Elias waits for her answer, maintaining his careful study.

'I work for DFID,' Sarah speaks the awkward acronym phonetically, trying to sound like an old hand.

'Sounds like a breeder of Welsh daffodils. What does Diffid do?'

Sarah laughs, but is unsure if it's a joke. His voice doesn't waver from the deep monotone.

'The Department for International Development,' she says. 'It's the part of the British government that does overseas aid assistance.'

'Daffodils for the poor and needy then?' Another suggestion of a smile, his voice still deadpan.

'Wouldn't that be nice? Sadly it's a bit more prosaic. We're mostly focused on poverty reduction and achieving the MDGs.'

'Emdigies?'

'Sorry—it's a hopeless industry for acronyms. The Millennium Development Goals, a set of internationally agreed goals to reduce poverty, improve health, provide universal education…' Sarah is rambling. She was comfortable trotting out the development line in front of the Ambassador and Irakli, their casual disinterest made it easy. With Elias she feels more exposed.

'All sounds terribly worthy. And what part of world saving is taking place here tonight?'

'I've come to see the work of the Skarparov Foundation. Do you know it?'

'Skarparov Foundation? Of course. That's Giorgi's lot, isn't it?'

It's the last thing Sarah expects to hear. Giorgi works for the Skarparov foundation?

'Er, yes, I've come to look at some project sites, to see if there are any possible areas of collaboration.'

Elias glances across at Giorgi who is helping an elderly lady into a seat at the table. 'Collaboration?' he asks with a raised eyebrow. 'Good luck with that. And how long have you been in

Georgia?'

'Only a couple of days.' Sarah lunges at the chance to move the conversation away from her. 'What's your story? How did you end up here?'

'I've been coming here for years. I first drove through in an ancient rust bucket just after the fall of the Soviet Union and have been coming back ever since.'

'An adventure junkie then?'

He blinks, pale white lashes flashing over grey-blue eyes. 'It's changed almost beyond recognition. It was pretty wild back then, bandits and highwaymen and crooked policemen looking out for bribes. But already you could feel its magic. It all seems a little tame now by comparison.'

'I've heard Saakashvili has made some real progress in cleaning things up.' Sarah wishes she had something more insightful to say.

'Yes, Micha,' Elias smiles cautiously. 'He's certainly got his work cut out. I hope he's got the spine to see it through.'

She flounders a little longer, asking questions which he politely fails to answer in the same flat tone, a little brusque but with always a hint of humour just below the surface. His manner is intriguing, his unflinching gaze makes her nervous and her answers to his questions feel bland and prosaic next to his. What is it about him that renders her so awkward and ties her tongue? And why does she care? She is both disappointed and relieved when Giorgi comes over to guide them towards the table. The *supra* is beginning.

CHAPTER 17

f4 Nxg3

Her hopes for an early night evaporating, Sarah takes her seat in the centre of the long table. Giorgi to her right, an apple-cheeked uncle wearing an admiral's cap to her left, and Elias across the table. She feels a prick of envy as he falls deep into conversation with his neighbour in fluent Russian. But she is more relaxed out of his intense gaze.

Some of the newly arrived guests offer her a hand, their eyes swimming from the day's festivities. Athena has been well soaked in offerings. Giorgi gives each new arrival a hero's introduction: his uncle—the best singer in Georgia, a neighbour—the first person to kayak down the Pshavi Aragvi river in winter; a cousin—a world-class sculptor and poet. Each new guest is gently mythologised as they join the table. Giorgi seems to relax in the crowd, he has an easy warmth with his guests. All except Sarah. He still can't meet her eye.

Those who settle at the table are mostly men. Some of the cousins have brought their wives, but after greeting their host they busy themselves with the children or disappear into the kitchen. Sarah is pleased to see Giorgi's mother collapse in the seat next to her and continue her unintelligible patter, clasping Sarah's hands between her own and shaking them in rhythm with her words. Sarah tries to switch to Russian, to extract some meaning from the melody, but the matriarch of the table ignores her efforts and continues in musical Georgian, untroubled by Sarah's lack of response.

People begin picking at the plates of food as they arrive on the table, but the vast jugs of orange wine remain untouched. Finally Giorgi stands and raises his glass. The table falls silent as he makes the first toast, long lyrical cadences of syllables rising and falling around a mouthful of consonants. The sing-song metre of the language is starting to sound familiar to Sarah, but she understands nothing.

He finishes the toast, summarising for Sarah's benefit. 'For our meeting, for bringing you here as our guest together with our old friends,' he nods at Elias, 'and family, *gaumarjos*!' He raises his glass to the table who echo a response, some simply repeating the final words, others adding their own embellishment, continuing the story and making it grow as it spreads around the table. It feels wrong to be toasting their meeting, given the events that brought her here. And yet the warmth of the table, the embraces and smiles of the other guests who drink to their meeting as if a great prophecy has at last come true, leave Sarah feeling oddly happy to be among them. Her arm throbs and her head aches but in this unwanted feast, she finally feels safe. She raises her glass and returns the toast.

The food is simple but abundant: tomatoes and cucumbers dressed with walnuts and fragrant purple basil, salty cheeses that crumble under the knife, steaming bowls of lamb stew, surprisingly cold chicken soup and clay pots of soft, spiced beans. Invisible hands whisk away plates and replace them with clean ones, encouraging the guests to begin anew.

Giorgi is endlessly circling the table to greet a new arrival, or rearranging seats to accommodate the growing crowd. When finally he sits down next to Sarah, she grabs her chance.

'Elias tells me you work with the Skarparov Foundation?'

He looks strangely relieved. 'Yes,' he sneaks a sideways glance at her. 'I am the project supervisor for the work in the mountains.'

'Then you must be the one that Irakli told me really understood what was going on.'

Giorgi sinks deeper into his oversized leather jacket that sits around his narrow shoulders like a bookshelf. He takes a bite of chewy bread, his prominent Adam's apple jumping as he tackles the mouthful.

'Yes.' He looks down at his plate.

'And can you tell me a bit about what the Foundation is doing here?' Sarah tries to read what's guiding his reticence.

'We want to bring jobs back to some of the poorer parts of the mountains. Using their traditional skills and know-how, but with twenty-first-century technology to help make their craft more effective.' He raises his dark eyes as if testing her interest. Does she really want to know or is she just being polite? At Sarah's encouraging nod he continues, his eyes lit with earnest enthusiasm. He sits taller, filling out more of his stiff jacket. 'It's mostly carpets up here. They have centuries-old traditions, and we don't want to change any of that, but we've brought in some of the best kit from Germany to make their work quicker and more productive.'

'Has it been successful?'

His eyes flick up to hers again. 'It's been a struggle.' Giorgi pours a large glass of a bright green sparkling liquid and offers it to Sarah. 'Not everyone wants the same things…'

She sips the lurid green witches' brew—it is incredibly sweet with a vegetal flavour she can't place. 'What is this?'

'Tarragon lemonade—have some more.' Giorgi gives her his first real smile, eyes like two half moons and tiny lines crinkling across the brow of his nose. 'I can take you to the project site tomorrow if you like, show you our activities.'

Sarah hesitates. This is her chance to find out more about the Foundation, the key she needs to unlock Skarparov. And she's sure she has more chance of finding out what the Foundation is about with Giorgi than with Irakli. But what if he's there?

'Irakli was supposed to be—'

Giorgi's smile drops. 'Irakli knows nothing about development,' he says, his brows tightly pinched. 'He has no interest in the project. But he's respected here. Or maybe just feared. Excuse me.'

He stands to propose the next toast. This round is considerably more sombre, the smiles more muted as the table embellishes on Giorgi's words. The uncle at Sarah's side offers a rudimentary translation. 'We drink to those who have passed away, to the ancestors, to our friends who left us too soon.'

Giorgi drains his full glass of wine and sits down, the metal feet of his chair scraping against the flagstones. He looks at Sarah, his face bright with sudden courage. 'Do you know where Irakli went after…' his voice falters.

'After the accident?' Sarah prompts, amazed to hear him asking exactly the question that has troubled her all evening. 'No. I thought you might know. He just kept driving.'

'That animal,' Giorgi whispers between gritted teeth. 'Don't worry, you are in my house now.' He thumps himself loudly on the chest, puffed up with a swagger born in wine and simmering outrage. 'I'll make sure he's not coming back tonight.'

'Will he be at the project sites tomorrow?'

'Not if I can help it. He has no place in this work, I don't know what he even does. He only causes difficulties.'

Giorgi stands abruptly for another toast. Once again, the uncle in the admiral's hat—the "best singer in Georgia"—leans across to offer Sarah a translation in his rudimentary English. 'This one is for parents, Mama, Papa, yes?' he slurs. 'For their meeting and their love. We honour them. We respect them when they live, we respect them when they die. They look after us.' Giorgi acknowledges his mother standing in the doorway beaming with pride. 'And for everything they gave us that makes us who we are. *Gaumarjos*!'

The uncle refills Sarah's glass from the generous jug of tannin-rich golden wine. She has been trying to pace herself, sipping with each toast. The singer, who has greedily downed each round, teases her, 'What? You don't like our wine?'

'No, it's delicious.'

'Then why you no drink? You don't like the toasts? You don't like the parents?'

'No, yes, of course. I am just taking it slowly.'

'Slowly? What slowly? We are celebrating.' His words slide into each other. 'This is one hundred percent pure natural sun wine.' He holds up the glass to admire the colour. 'A gift from God, you can't get drunk on this wine and no hangover.' As he stands to tend to the other glasses around the table, Elias slips into his seat. Sarah is surprised. She thought her awkward attempts at conversation earlier had put him off but he's back, tipping a steaming dumpling onto her plate. 'Here, try this, they make excellent *khinkali* here.'

She prods the hot, heavy package with her fork.

'A *khinkali* virgin? Ah, I envy you. Here, let me show you how it's done.' He picks up the pleated knot of dough that seals the dumpling and carefully bites a hole in the top. Tipping the whole mushroom shaped cup towards his mouth, he slurps up the juices inside before biting into the meat filling. Sarah tries to copy his technique but is startled by the hot oily soup bursting into her mouth and manages to dribble some down her chin.

'Please, allow me,' Elias wipes her chin with a single sweep of a paper napkin. The gesture feels surprisingly intimate, but his eyes only linger on hers for the briefest of moments before he is back to chewing on his dumpling. Is she imagining his attentions or hoping for them? Her eyes fix on his long lashes, so pale as to be almost invisible in the light.

'It's a feast in a mouthful,' he says. 'Of course they are much better when you're really hungry after a long hike, or to mop up a hangover. I've never really understood their place at the end of a big meal. But they are delicious. So, how was it for you?'

'The dumpling?' Sarah raises an eyebrow. 'Delicious. Well, I'm not sure I'd have it every day, but it's tasty.'

'And the tarragon lemonade?' he nods towards Sarah's half-drunk glass.

'It's very… interesting.'

'You really are from England. In Dutch we say no.'

'So you're Dutch?'

'Yes.'

'That would be why you speak such perfect English.'

Elias shrugs off the compliment. 'I've never lived in Holland. My parents are Dutch.'

'So where did you grow up?'

'Here and there, we moved around.'

'But you are familiar with our British way of preferring not to say what we mean if we can shuffle awkwardly around a point instead?'

'Yes. I was thrown out of some of your best schools.' He grins at her, his gaze still just as intense but she's no longer intimidated by it. In fact, she's beginning to enjoy it.

Giorgi raises his glass in another toast.

'Ah, to love,' Elias says. 'This one is my favourite.' He translates Giorgi's words. 'To the magic that brings two people together, to the whisper of a hint when you first look into someone's eyes of a meeting of minds. The synapse snap that draws you closer, eager, hungry. To the heart that beats as though calling a thousand painted savages to battle where they will prance and cry only to elicit one of your beloved's smiles. To the unknown, the trepidation, the chance and chase of persisting happiness. To the love that binds us together and wraps us in its deep embrace, *sikvaruls gaumarjos*. To love, victory to you!'

The table circles through the rounds of additions and toasts to love. No one other than Sarah appears shaken by Giorgi's new-found eloquence.

'Did he really say all that?' she asks after a pause. 'I think I must have been missing something with his uncle's translation.'

'More or less. I might have helped him out a little. He's too earnest to be a really good Tamada. Not quite comfortable enough in breaking free, allowing the rhapsody to fly straight from the muse.' He mops up some of the juices on his plate with his bread.

'Can anyone be Tamada?' Sarah asks, wondering if she would get to try. It is starting to look like fun.

'He needs to be a poet, a wordsmith. Able to command respect, to tackle the more sombre themes with dignity and gravitas—'

'And he needs to be a "he", I suppose?'

'Sadly, yes. But I'm sure you could pass as a dashing man if that's what's stopping you.'

The pace of dishes finally slows, and uneaten remains lie untouched on plates. Down at the end of the table, three older men and the uncle, his admiral's cap now askew, begin to sing, their voices complementing each other in polyphonic harmonies that sound both familiar and new. Each voice picking out the different tones of a bagpipe, at once harmonious and discordant. The uncle calls over his young son, who joins in a striking descant over their deep bass notes. An old aunt moves in to join the singing, her dyed auburn hair swept elegantly to one side and her eyebrows squeezed into a tight triangle as she reaches for the high notes. The next generation up, an ancient lady with an embroidered shawl wrapped around her head, smiles over toothless gums and nods in time to the melody. A neighbour sits with a small girl on her lap, their dark hair intertwined as they listen, mesmerised by the song.

A gentle peace settles over the table. In the warmth of the enchanted evening, nothing seems quite real. Sarah's drive up with Irakli and brush with death begins to feel like a piece of the forgotten past. How could it be the same day? How could she be sitting here enjoying the wine, the singing, the celebration, when she had begun the evening wanting nothing more than to escape? She smiles, remembering Vakho's words, recognising the hand of Georgia's powerful magic at work.

The singers move off, leaving Sarah and Elias alone at the table. Their conversation flows playfully. Sarah's forgotten her awkwardness, her words come easily, her best self tickled to the fore. She has not noticed the others leave until Elias suggests they go to admire the view, illuminated by the nearly full moon.

They stand in silence, staring out over the valley.

'Extraordinary,' Sarah whispers, the word is woefully inadequate for the towering beauty of the mountains.

'It's lovely, but really nothing on Tusheti. That is where you must get to next.'

Sarah draws closer to the warmth of his body.

He continues as if he hasn't noticed. 'Nothing can prepare you for the moment you pass through the sky-scratching peaks to finally look down on the planes of heaven-high Tusheti. Can't you find an excuse for cooperation there? I'm sure they could grow some very fine daffodils.'

The call of a bird rises through the darkness. Its song swoops up in celebration—*Woo woo! Woo woo!*

'Was that real?' Sarah asks.

'A nightjar,' Elias smiles. 'Have you never heard one? There are dozens of different kinds. This one is rather fun with its whooping call, but my favourite is the one that trills.' He places his tongue on the roof of his mouth and starts making an extraordinary noise, like an elaborately rolled "r" rising and falling in a swooping parabola.

'It can't do that.' Sarah can't tell if he's teasing.

'Of course it does, have you really never heard them? You must have heard something similar walking in the forest at night.'

'And what do they look like—these extraordinary singers?'

'Small, mottled brown, with exceptional moustaches,' Elias

113

continues with the same deadpan tone and a flash of his invisible lashes. He draws an elaborate moustache through the air from his cheeks and twists and tickles the imaginary side feathers with his fingertips while continuing its churring call. 'Some of their moustaches are up to a metre long,' he waves his hands back behind him, 'and they are known for their mythic ability to steal the milk from goats.'

'You're making this up: a milk-stealing moustachioed bird that trills like an Italian? Sorry, I'm not buying it.'

'Why else would they have moustaches? They are there to tickle the underside of the mother goat and make her feel like she is being tickled by her kid. You find them everywhere. You must have heard one, even if you've never actually seen it stealing milk. I have to admit that is rather rare.'

Sarah can see her laughter reflected in Elias's eyes, despite his efforts at keeping a straight face. He draws her some elaborate moustaches, stroking gently against her cheeks with his fingertips before shooting them off in delicate arcs like a peacock's tail feather.

Suddenly he stops and looks straight into her eyes. 'Come with me to Tusheti tomorrow. I leave early in the morning with a local guide. We're planning to explore one of the lesser-known passes to see if there is an easier way of crossing the mountains than returning all the way back to the valley. I've crossed the other direction before but never going this way. It should be even more spectacular starting from here.'

'You're going by foot?' Sarah asks. Surely no one would be mad enough to take on these towering peaks without help.

'Yes, of course; it's the best way. It shouldn't be more than a few days' walking. You will love it, and I would appreciate the company. Mountain guides aren't strong on conversation and I'm sure your smiling eyes will make the walking much easier.'

'I would love to, but I can't.' Sarah says, her mind already playing with the idea of forgetting her mission and taking off through the wilderness with this dashing Dutchman. 'I have to report back to London after this trip and I'm not sure they are looking for new mountain passes.'

'Come on,' Elias urges. 'I can tell you now what to put in your report.' He adopts a mock-serious newsreader's voice, 'I do not recommend cooperation with the Skarparov Foundation, they are run by a bunch of drunkards and terrible Tamadas. British interests would be better served by exploring the possibility of breeding new daffodil in Tusheti. The mountain conditions are perfect for this important export of British culture and Welshness. I recommend continued study of the area with expert guide.' He smiles at her. 'There, how's that? They'll be funding your trekking holiday before you know it.'

Sarah laughs, trying to imagine the look on Michael's face on receipt of this report. It's almost worth trying, just to see what he makes of the code.

But the thought of Michael gives her pause. The headiness of the golden wine and the attentions of this mysterious stranger make her feel free and unrestrained. She feels a lightness with Elias that is all the more delicious after the shock of the crash and the after-effects of adrenaline. But she knows that allowing herself to be flirted with by an unknown foreigner, while doing her best to flirt back, is probably not approved behaviour of a secret servant of Her Majesty.

'So you're coming then?' Elias interrupts her thoughts. 'Or do you still need some persuading?'

'It sounds wonderful, but not this time. You do the difficult scouting, and I will come with you next time when you've found all the best places to picnic and perfect camping spots.'

'I've heard the highest mountains are excellent for spotting the long-moustachioed nightjars. You could compare your exquisite feathers.'

He touches his fingers once again to her cheek bones, standing right in front of her, his body so close she feels the heat radiating from his chest. As he draws his fingertips away, imitating the feathered arcs, he brushes lightly over the tops of her ears and suddenly his lips are on hers. The kiss is gentle, his lips soft like the ripe flesh of an apricot. Her whole body feels electrified. The touch of his skin, his strong hands exploring her back, his sculpted shoulders under her fingers—all seem to set her senses alight. She feels alert, invigorated and hungry, every skin cell celebrating his touch.

He draws away to look at her, his body still tightly pressed against hers and his arms cradling her protectively. 'I've wanted to do that all evening. In fact, since I first saw you standing right on this spot, I wanted to know if this elegant elfin creature tasted as delicious as she looked.'

Sarah is stunned. She had felt awkward and rambling under his inquisitive gaze. How could he have thought of kissing her? Her mind is clearer than it has been all evening, sharp and alert and reawakened, but her body feels punch drunk, reeling from an excess of pleasure and hungry for more.

She leans forward and touches her lips to his and the lightening shock floods her body once again.

'Now, what do you say about coming to the mountains with me?' he asks.

'So all that talk of heaven-high Tusheti was just an excuse to whisk me off to have your way with me? There was me thinking we were going to be true mountain explorers.'

'Oh we would be, but a real mountain explorer needs to keep a wide-open heart, to be alert and receptive to everything he sees around him. Come, I promise to keep you safe from bears and mountain lions and will bring you back to Tbilisi refreshed and ready to write your important report to London.'

Sarah allows herself to imagine exploring the inaccessible mountain scenery by day and this tantalising man by night. But then her common sense interrupts her reverie.

Gently, she withdraws from his arms, hoping her mental resolve is stronger away from the magical pull of his skin.

'Really, I can't.'

He studies her, as if weighing up whether to keep trying or to accept her refusal. 'Well, either way, if we have an early start we are going to have to get some sleep at some point.'

Sarah has not noticed the passing of time, but suddenly realises that the supra is well over, the guests departed, and the house is dark.

'You're right, I've got a head full of wine to sleep off before the morning.' She pauses. 'Where are you staying?'

'I was just planning on sleeping out here, I'm always happiest sleeping outside and I have a good plastic sheet to keep me warm.' He meets her eye, reading her cues. 'But perhaps you have a better idea?'

'I have a beautiful room at the top of the house, I think there should be space enough for two underneath the piles of cushions on the bed.' Sarah can scarcely believe her audacity. But somehow with Elias she feels different, not herself. Or perhaps only herself, without the need to follow convention. Her step impossibly light, she takes his hand and they walk silently back to the house.

Up in the room, she feels shy and unsure. But Elias seems entirely at ease and his confidence makes her bolder. He takes off his clothes as if it was the most natural thing to do, as if they have stood naked in front of each other countless times. He pauses for a moment in front of the window looking out at the tumbling valley. Sarah admires the line of his back, lean and taught, reaching up to his broad shoulders. He turns to face her and carefully, wordlessly, helps her remove her clothes before folding her into his arms and wrapping his limbs around her. Once again, she's shocked by his touch, but the electric pulse is no longer a cool shudder, more a warm and encompassing surge. They lie together, their limbs carefully entwined like jigsaw puzzle pieces, and mumble quietly into each other's ears until Sarah feels his body grow heavier and his breathing slow as they drift into sleep.

CHAPTER 18

Bhxg3 Bg4

When Sarah awakes the next morning, he is gone.
She wonders if she dreamed their unexpected encounter. But she still feels the shudder and tingle of his skin, and even sun wine could not create such exquisite dreams.

Sitting up, she is hit by the full force of her hangover. Her brain is too big for her skull and pushes painfully behind her eyes. Her injured arm throbs. So much for the pure natural wine. And with the nausea comes shock. What was she thinking, inviting a stranger into her bed? What if someone had seen Elias disappear this morning? How could she have acted so unthinkingly? She remembers every word they exchanged, the tender shock of their kiss. But it is like watching someone else, someone more daring and blissfully unencumbered by social scruples.

She lowers her feet to the cold floor and rests her spinning head on her knees. She is glad to be alone, to face this feeling of self-reprimand without being skin to skin with the very person who engendered her recklessness. She feels no regret, can no longer imagine never having tasted his delicious skin and would do it all again and more. But she wishes their meeting had been conducted with more privacy; that they really were as alone in the world as it felt at the time.

She makes her way downstairs, scarcely able to make eye contact with Giorgi's mother who is standing at the stove cooking an enormous pan of eggs, the air around her salty and steaming. She greets Sarah with the same welcoming smile and carefully inspects the injured arm and the dressing on the forehead before leading her outside to the terrace. Giorgi sits alone at the long supra table, swamped in his oversized jacket. His red t-shirt is streaked with sweat, and he sucks heavily on a cigarette while eyeing up a bottle of clear liquor on the table. Sarah is not the only one to have overdone it.

'Good morning,' she greets him tentatively, waiting for a reaction or a knowing smirk. Giorgi waves his cigarette in acknowledgement and remains crumpled in his seat.

'That was quite a feast last night.'

'Oh *vai me, vai me,*' Giorgi groans, 'I curse Athena, I curse Bacchus, I curse that delicious wine.' He stubs out his cigarette and pushes a small glassful of the clear liquid towards Sarah. 'Here, you need this. And breakfast. Deda?' he calls into the kitchen. His mother reappears, staggering under the weight of a cast iron pan filled with a vast fluffy omelette.

'What is it?' Sarah eyes the glass, suspecting she would rather not know.

'Chacha. Made from our grapes; you need it to balance out the wine.'

Sarah raises the glass to her lips, swooning at the smell of the alcohol. Her stomach churns in anticipation of another dose of poison as she throws it back. It's like swallowing a burning candle. Then a wave of comfort breaks over her body, wrapping her swollen brain in a warm towel and settling the pounding in her ears.

'You feel better now.' Giorgi raises a weary smile. 'Now eat.'

119

He pushes a plate towards her. 'You need food.'

The tower of eggs is surprisingly light, but Sarah has little appetite. She's thinking about Irakli. In her shock yesterday she did not fully believe that he could have deliberately pushed their car over the edge. Part of her was waiting for him to reappear, drunk and apologetic, having spent the evening enjoying the freedom of the mountain girls unleashed by the festival. But now the scene is more stark. She can't stop thinking about her amateur error at the Foundation offices and Irakli's drunken grab for her camera at the sacrifice spot. Had she really given herself away so easily?

'Do we still have time to visit the project sites this morning?' she asks Giorgi. 'What time is the bus?' She's eager to leave but she can't go back to Tbilisi with nothing more than a blown cover and an ill-advised romantic liaison.

Giorgi lights another cigarette, the lines across the bridge of his nose knotted into a deep frown. 'You're sure you want to go? You should rest from your accident.' He nods at her arm still wrapped in its makeshift bandage.

'It's fine; it doesn't hurt that much,' Sarah lies.

Giorgi taps his cigarette onto a glass ashtray and exhales deeply. Is it just his crashing hangover making him reluctant or is he also thinking about Irakli? 'Okay, we can go, but we have to be quick.' He looks at his watch. 'We'll go straight from there to the bus.'

*

With evident pride, Giorgi leads Sarah into the gleaming new project office. Photos of smiling women and dramatic mountain scenery encased in slick glass and metal frames cover the walls. A widescreen TV in the corner glows with a bouncing Skarparov Foundation logo. A hook-nosed youth swivels in a chair behind an oversized desk, its vast polished surface tellingly empty. He looks up as they enter, but quickly looks away when he sees it's a stranger. Something about his face strikes Sarah as familiar, but she can't place why.

Giorgi hurries her through into the next room, ignoring the boy completely.

'Who was that?' she asks.

'Him?' Giorgi asks. 'Oh him, that's just Levon, he's new. Great with computers, not too many social skills. An Armenian,' he says with a shrug, as if that explains all she needs to know.

Giorgi leads Sarah to the next room where a group of women, huddled round an old wooden loom, watch her with unguarded curiosity. Dwarfing the loom, but ignored by the women, an enormous machine in gleaming aluminium dominates the room, manufacturer's stickers in place and not a fingerprint to be seen on its polished surfaces.

'This is the machine I was telling you about from Germany,' Giorgi says. 'Top of the range and uses all the latest developments in weaving to allow the women to produce their carpets in a fraction of the time.'

A small radio playing tinny Tchaikovsky balances on the flat end of the machine and a frame of muslin cloths is strung from the top of the equipment, dripping liquid into buckets below.

'It's going to revolutionise the craftsmanship, but it still allows the women to use their traditional patterns and materials.' Giorgi pats the metal beast. It looks to Sarah like it is only being used to make cheese.

She kneels down to greet the women, picking her way over a stack of carpets woven in wine red, deep blue and beige. She is met with a flurry of giggles and embraces. Using a combination of sign language, smiles and basic Russian she tries to ask one of the older women, a proud grandmotherly figure who comes forward as the natural leader of the group, what she thinks of the new machine. The old woman smooths her skirts and re-tucks her headscarf around her ears. 'It's a little complicated,' she says softly. The other women giggle again and eye Giorgi cautiously.

He jumps in to answer. 'They are receiving all the necessary training. Eventually the machines have the capability to handle patterns digitally which will further ramp up the production numbers, but, well you know, these things take time.'

Sarah kneels to inspect some of the carpets on the floor. 'Where do you sell the work?' she asks a girl with bright intelligent eyes. The girl flashes a look at Giorgi and gives a silent smile.

'The main market is still Tbilisi,' Giorgi answers. 'But we are also looking at exporting to Turkey and Azerbaijan.'

Sarah tries a few more questions, but each time Giorgi interrupts the women to answer on their behalf. When she tries to use him as an interpreter to ask more complex questions, he answers himself without even going through the motions of translating her words. She is unsure if it is just his enthusiasm about the project and his desire for her to have a better understanding than she could gain from the unsophisticated answers of the women, or if he does not trust the women to say the right thing. Either way, she will get nothing useful out of the women in Giorgi's presence. There must be a way to get them on their own. She thinks as quickly as her hungover brain will allow.

'Is there a toilet here I could use?' she asks Giorgi, rubbing her stomach.

'No.' He gives the women a silencing glare. 'It's better to wait until we're finished. It's not good here.' He checks his watch, looking over her shoulder out of the window. 'Anyway, we have to go now to get you back to Tbilisi. The bus leaves soon. I can send you some more details about the project's aims and objectives. And maybe you could come back for another visit, when we have more time.' He tries to guide Sarah towards the door.

'Please, I'd rather go now.' Sarah puffs out her cheeks and bends slightly forward.

'Really, it's better to wait. We need to leave.'

The group leader is listening, her dark eyes watchful with concern. Sarah kneels down, hoping she will be more sympathetic than Giorgi. The woman throws a cautious glance at Giorgi, then arranges her skirts to struggle to her feet. Taking Sarah firmly by the arm she leads her out of the room. The younger girl follows behind them, her face alight with playful mischief, her long dark hair held in a plait that swings around her waist. She clearly does not want to miss the spectacle of this strange foreigner at the outhouse.

The leader of the women leads Sarah outside to the empty patch of ground behind the building. Giorgi follows closely, looking increasingly uncomfortable. Under a tree, surrounded by bright green ferns and nettles, a wooden outhouse is propped up on stones and precariously balanced wooden planks.

'Really, it's better if you wait. Let's leave now.' Giorgi moves to take Sarah's arm, but she bends over with a theatrical groan.

'Sorry, Giorgi, I won't be long.'

She pulls back the door—five wooden planks of mismatching length, held to a cross beam with rusty nails. The hinges squeal to a stop, leaving just enough space for Sarah to squeeze through. The old woman waits at the door, but Sarah pulls her through the narrow gap to join her inside. The girl with the plait slips in after them, flashing Sarah a bright smile. The air inside is thick and evil smelling. A cloud of flies, disturbed by their entrance, buzz around Sarah's head in protest. She swallows hard, her hungover stomach threatening to rebel against the stench. She casts a sideways look at the hole in the floor between two sagging floorboards—just in case. She might need to know which way to aim.

'So you make the carpets here?' Sarah tries her best school-girl Russian. The older woman looks at her in astonishment.

'The Foundation, do they help you make them? Provide training? Money?'

The younger girl giggles, looking at the floor. 'Some of them we make. Some of them they bring in,' she whispers, her bright eyes finding Sarah's in a nervous glance.

'Bring them in? So they're not all made here?'

'Some yes, we make as before. Some they bring them in, then

bring them out. They only send to Mr Irakli.' The girl looks at the older woman. 'We call them wrapping paper.'

'Wrapping paper?' Sarah acts out wrapping a large box to check she understood the term. 'What's in them?'

The older woman grabs the younger girl by the arm and yanks her into silence. 'We don't know what's in them,' she says, her eyes cautious. Sarah can see Giorgi through a hole in the door, pacing just outside and smoking a cigarette.

'Do you ever look?' she asks. 'Just a peek?' Sarah mimes peering into a carpet roll. The girl giggles. Sarah knows that Skarparov needs Irakli attached to the foundation to be able to operate in the mountains, to be accepted by the community. Even if he has nothing to do with Giorgi's well-meaning weaving endeavours. But then what is he up to receiving mystery deliveries? She remembers Steve's warning about Irakli's unsavoury connections.

'Have you ever seen...' Sarah's brain sticks when searching for the correct Russian word for guns or weapons. She resorts to more sign language, sticking her finger out, 'bang, bang?'

The girl giggles again, more nervous this time.

The older woman, ashen faced gives the girl another silencing jab. The whole hut shakes as Giorgi hammers on the outside. 'Everything okay?' he calls. 'We need to go, Sarah, if you want to get back to Tbilisi.'

'Yes, fine, I'm coming,' she calls out, before whispering to the women, 'what does Mr Irakli bring?'

The older woman grabs the girl's elbow and shoves her out of the door. Sarah feels she could probably get something out of the girl, but the older woman has seen it too and is not willing to risk it. Her heart sinks, she feels inches away from understanding but her best chance of information is being marched back to the workshop. Reluctantly she follows them outside, clutching her stomach and wiping her forehead for theatrical effect. The younger girl flashes Sarah an apologetic look as the older woman pushes her back inside.

Giorgi throws his cigarette butt to the ground and takes

Sarah's arm in a tight clasp, steering her towards the front of the house. She is searching for ways to escape, to be able to spend more time alone with the girl, but it's clear Giorgi and the older woman will never let it happen. 'If you want to reach Tbilisi before dark, you must leave now,' Giorgi says, not relaxing his grip on her arm.

Sarah admits defeat. She can't afford to hang around in the village any longer than necessary.

*

In the village square, the "public bus"—a battered looking minivan—is already waiting for passengers. Giorgi hands her a folded piece of paper. 'Elias left this for you.' At the sound of his name Sarah flushes with pleasure and a touch of embarrassment. She does her best to adopt a look of casual disinterest as she takes the note and stuffs it into her back pocket. Giorgi, looking shattered and exhausted, leaves her with a brief goodbye.

She climbs into one of the last remaining seats at the back of the bus, firmly wedged between two walnut-faced ladies. The air smells of hot metal and livestock. One of the women has taken a large basin of yoghurt on her lap to make space for Sarah and is struggling to keep it balanced alongside an unruly burlap sack. Sarah takes the basin on to her own lap with a smile. The old lady beams at her appreciatively, rubbing Sarah's shoulder in approval with a large-knuckled finger, before reapplying herself to the task of keeping the large bag from getting away from her.

With Giorgi safely out of sight, Sarah opens the short message written in an elegant hand:

I've gone to catch you a nightjar. I will be back in Tbilisi in three days, call me.'

Sarah reads and rereads the note, trying to hear the voice that wrote the words. She cannot help but smile at the thought of him—dancing eyes, tall stories of goat's milk stealing birds and promises of mountain adventures. Although she wishes for more, she is glad the note is cryptic enough to have passed through Giorgi's hands.

Her neighbour continues to struggle with the bag on her lap. It moves and squirms in her grip with a life of its own. Finally a small fluffy head emerges from the top and a bewildered looking chick cocks its head at Sarah. The old woman smothers it back in the bag.

Sarah is relieved to be in the company of strangers. The ancient bus rattles precariously along the mountain roads, but she feels safer in the crowd. Surely Irakli won't find her here? She finds herself glancing out of the window at each passing car, he must know by now that she had escaped from the wreckage. Was the accident an opportunistic attempt to get rid of her or would he try to finish the job?

She wishes she had more time with the girl in the project office to find out what he was really up to. It is clear he's using the office as a front for something, but what? She had assumed the weapons being transferred from Russia to Ibragimov were going directly to Azerbaijan, but what if Irakli was using the cover of the Foundation and the porous mountain border to take delivery for him? There is no reason why an attack on the pipeline would have to happen in Azerbaijan. The sections in Georgia are just as vulnerable.

Sarah wonders if Skarparov himself has any idea what Irakli is up to or if he's left his uncle's thug to his own devices. Skarparov struck her as more savvy than the bored playboy that Michael had described, but perhaps his interest in the prestige attached to having a Foundation persuades him to turn a blind eye.

Sarah can't wait to discuss her findings with Steve, but the thought that Irakli might hold the key to unlocking Ibragimov's plans makes her stomach turn more than the erratic turns in the mountain road. Could she really go back to him? She squeezes the basin tighter to her chest.

The bus stops at a makeshift truckers' stop—a small hut selling refreshment next to a rust-stained outhouse. Two large trucks stand side by side at the edge of a pit of gravel and grass. Sarah's pulse quickens. So long as the bus is moving, she feels safe. But each stop is another chance for Irakli to appear.

Most of the passengers in Sarah's bus are struggling to gather their belongings, stretching out cricked muscles and preparing to leave. A handful of other dilapidated buses have pulled up alongside, their destinations announced in hand-painted signs propped up inside the windscreen. She squeezes herself deeper into the back seat, willing the passengers to hurry.

'Tbilisi?' she calls nervously to the driver, hoping she is not about to be ejected from the safety of his back seat into who knows where they were.

'*Ho, ho,*' he nods, gesturing for her to stay put.

One by one the other passengers depart, leaving Sarah alone and exposed. Her neighbour staggers off last, squeezing Sarah's hand as she goes. The old woman has unloaded the yoghurt to another willing helper and Sarah watches her struggling to manoeuvre the burlap sack to her next bus. As she sets it down to adjust her grip, two yellow chicks run out across the stone-strewn ground.

Just as Sarah prepares to jump out to help, a car in gunmetal grey screeches into the parking area, sending up a cloud of dust and flying gravel. Her chest tightens. Surely it can't be? A tall figure climbs out of the car, shouting at the old woman with the chicks. Irakli. Does he know she is here? She swallows back the urge to scream. She still has the protection of a public space. Surely even a brute like Irakli won't try to take her out in a crowded bus station? She sinks into the seat and watches him, a cold sweat breaking at her temples and her stomach in spasms. His driver has popped open the bonnet and is leaning over it to examine the engine. Irakli paces furiously behind him, shouting insults and brandishing a lit cigarette like a weapon.

'Tbilisi? We go?' Sarah tries to instil some urgency into the driver, who only nods mildly.

Irakli's driver climbs back into the car and tries the engine, the bonnet still raised. The starter motor coughs and chokes, but the engine does not start. Irakli kicks the tyre before starting up another tirade. He flicks his lit cigarette towards one of the chicks still running startled around the dust.

Sarah doesn't dare move. Her only comfort is that he looks more concerned with haranguing his driver than looking for her. During a pause in his outburst, he looks straight at Sarah's bus and seems to move towards the open door. His slick grooming is gone, his shirt stained and his hair dishevelled. His skin looks sallow and shines like a waxwork. A tight pain throbs in Sarah's throat. *Please let us get out of here before he notices I'm here,* she thinks, relieved to finally see some new passengers board the bus and take up the row in front of her. What would she say? Would he try and bundle her into his car? She is preparing to scream blue murder if necessary. Anything to keep him away.

Finally, the bus driver climbs back into his seat and starts the engine. He swings the bus round, turning right in front of Irakli's car. Irakli throws them an aggressive stare but as the bus pulls onto the road he's back leaning over the engine of his car. Sarah sinks into the back seat, exhausted and fading, her hungover brain a wreck but finally able to breathe as the bus trundles on towards Tbilisi.

CHAPTER 19

e5 0-0-0

'There you are.' Steve is flustered and out of breath, his ruddy cheeks glowing with heat. 'I was about to give up on you. You're going to be late. You should have left ten minutes ago.'

Sarah arrived at the Embassy early the following morning, eager to discuss all that had happened with Steve, but when he saw her he almost knocked her over in his hurry to push her towards the basement carpark.

'Late?' she asks.

'For the meeting,' Steve says, as if she is being deliberately dim. 'Vakho's waiting for you downstairs. You'd better hurry.' He propels her out of the door.

'But where are we going?' What has she forgotten?

'Don't worry, Vakho knows the way. Sorry I can't join. But do say hello from me.' He gives her arm a reassuring squeeze before bounding back up to his office.

Vakho is waiting behind the wheel of an embassy car, engine

running. He jumps round to open the door for her, and they speed out of the garage as soon as her seat belt clicks into place.

'Where were you, Miss Sarah?' he asks. 'I thought you weren't coming. Steve told me you had to leave at eight.'

'Sorry, I got held up,' she says, still racking her brains for what she's forgotten.

'Don't worry, I'll get you there. I know all the shortcuts.' They tear through the streets of central Tbilisi, Vakho hunched forward, his eagle's beak darting over the steering wheel.

'Where are we going?' she asks, unsettled by the mystery.

'To the airstrip,' he glances at her, round eyes questioning, 'or that's not where you want to go?'

'No, no, Steve just didn't mention the location.'

'Mr Steve, he goes there a lot.' Vakho drums his fingers against the steering wheel.

'And did he mention who we would be meeting there?'

'Ha! Miss Sarah, now you're testing me!' he grins across at her. 'I know nothing about Mr Steve's work, just the driver. I take him places but I hear nothing. Only boring embassy work.' He taps his finger against his long nose as he pushes the car through a tight gap.

'Of course.' She watches out of the window as they race down the highway, past the main airport and into the industrial outskirts, flat fields littered with electricity pylons and unfinished concrete. Clumps of tall buildings rise in the distance, their facades cracked by the shadows of laundry and TV aerials.

As they turn off the highway, Sarah notices a silver sedan following them onto the smaller road. Her first thought is Irakli, but the colour is too pale to be the BMW he had tried to shunt her off the cliff with. It is too far away to make out the face of the driver.

They pull up in front of an abandoned station—a slab of cement overgrown with weeds; the faded blue roof held up by rusted columns. A railway carriage stands marooned on the grass—its former livery of purple and gold just visible beneath the dust, seats and wheels long gone. Sarah wants to warn Vakho about the silver car, but when she looks again it has disappeared.

'Are you sure this is the right place?' she asks, stepping out into the overgrown ruin.

'Yes, it's this way, follow me.' Vakho leads her past a Tsarist-era military barracks, now taken over by a family of pigs. A huge sow eyes her suspiciously as she tiptoes past in her office shoes. Beyond the pigs, a network of concrete paths winds between grass-covered bunkers and almond trees set to burst into blossom. They stop at a vast stretch of cement, fractured into a patchwork of grey.

'It's good, we're on time, he's not here yet. It's okay if I leave you now, Miss Sarah?' Vakho looks torn, his dark eyes apprehensive. 'I don't like to leave the car out here. We want to have our wheels and petrol when we get back.' He thrusts his hands into his pockets then pulls them out again. 'I'll wait for you at the car.'

Sarah pulls her cardigan tighter against the breeze. Alone in the military wasteland, she feels desperately underprepared. Her instincts tell her that neither Steve nor Vakho are the type to have deliberately set her up, but still, she is uneasy. And wishes she knew what had happened to the silver car.

The noise of an engine cuts through the wind and a tiny twin prop approaches the landing strip. Sarah shields her eyes as the wheels bounce down and the little plane slows to a stop only a few hundred metres after touchdown. The aircraft has an overextended nose like a pushy Afghan hound, glossy black and red stripes and swooped wheel covers that give it the curious look of a dog in high-heeled slippers. Two figures emerge from a door above the wing. The first is so tall that Sarah takes it for a man dressed head to toe in red leather, until the new arrival shakes out her glossy mane of dark hair. This extraordinary creature is followed by a silver-haired man in a well-cut suit—unmistakably Michael.

Even climbing out of a tiny plane on a windswept wasteland,

he looks immaculate. He greets Sarah with a kiss on both cheeks and introduces his companion. 'This is Dilara, a good friend and my taxi driver for the day.' Dilara flashes Sarah a painted smile and shakes her hand with a firm grip. Sarah can't help but gape, feeling very pale and plain next to this exotic creature, all eyelashes and lips and voluptuous curves poured into her red aviator's suit.

'You found the place then?' Michael asks.

'Vakho knew the way. Is anyone else supposed to be coming?'

'No. Why?' Michael looks alert.

'A car followed us off the highway.'

'All the way here?'

'I don't know. It disappeared before we arrived.'

'Did you tell Vakho?'

'No.'

'Why on earth not?'

'I wasn't sure, and then it was gone.'

Michael puts his hand on Dilara's arm and whispers in her ear, pointing over to the area behind the pig farm. It sounds as if they are talking Turkish. Sarah feels a stab of jealousy watching Michael cosy up to this scarlet apparition. She knows she's used to having his full attention, but she's annoyed that she even cares to see him so obviously enjoying the sight of the red leather vamp sauntering off towards the pigs.

'That was quite an arrival,' Sarah says, taking Michael's arm. She is not sure if it's the stab of the green-eyed monster that makes her want to be close to him or if she is just pleased to see a familiar face. She nods towards Dilara. 'Which film does she think she's in?'

Michael gives a vague smile. 'One I'd enjoy watching, I'm sure.

'Come on, really?'

'Dilara's an old friend of mine and owed me a favour.'

'Looks like a useful sort of friend.' Sarah watches Dilara bound through the fields with the unlikely gait of a cat on its hind legs. 'And what a charming spot you chose.' They walk arm in arm down the cracked cement of the landing strip.

'I always prefer a face-to-face meeting where possible, and this is the best place to get in and out quickly. There are no border formalities, and air traffic control is light.' He nods towards the ancient tower with its blown-out windows. 'We'll be off again soon, but I have something I wanted to tell you. You look cold, take my jacket.' He slips off his suit jacket and has it around Sarah's shoulders before she had the chance to protest, wrapping her in a warm cloud of sandalwood.

'So, what was it?' she asks.

'Where have you got to on Skarparov?'

'I met him earlier in the week at a reception.'

'First contact made, excellent. How did it go?'

'He was better than I was expecting: more charming, less sleazy.'

'I knew he'd be your type.'

'I meant as a potential source.'

Michael nods, acknowledging her point.

'Skarparov was keen for UK support for a launch event for his Foundation, to give it an official seal of approval.'

'That could be useful. Is it something we could ask the Ambassador to go along with?'

'I don't think the UK Government should have anything to do with it. Irakli, the local head, knows nothing about development.'

'And you should know,' Michael says with a wry smile.

'I might know nothing about development, but I can smell a braggart.' Sarah is eager for Michael's approval, to prove that she's got a brain, even if she doesn't have six foot of voluptuous curves to pour into a flying suit. 'The project offices in the mountains look like a sham. There is obviously money up there, new buildings and shiny machines. The local coordinator seems genuine enough, but I think even he is in the dark about what they are really up to.'

'A front then?'

'Possibly. Or the noble carpet weaving is just part of the story. One of the women I spoke to mentioned "special deliveries" being brought in and out disguised as carpets. Do you think Ibragimov might be receiving the weapons through Irakli in the mountains? They are definitely close.'

'Look at that, that's an old Mil Mi-6.' Their stroll has taken them to the end of the runway where an ancient helicopter, riveted metal patches starting to curl at the edges, has been left to rust. Michael admires its drooping rotors. 'You know this was the world's largest helicopter when it was designed? The cutting edge of Soviet technology. We were moved about in one of these when I was doing my training, like the school bus. I think someone was tickled by the name.' Michael hops up under the wing to peer through the windows. 'I haven't seen one for years. And what was in these special deliveries?' he continues seamlessly.

'Weapons, possibly; I'm not sure. The girl I talked to obviously didn't want to say. And there's only so much you can cover while perched over a drop in an outhouse.'

'An outhouse?'

'Needs must,' Sarah grins.

'That border is particularly porous. I wonder what they are bringing in.'

Sarah walks on in silence, wondering how to broach what is weighing on her mind. She is reluctant to tell him, to show weakness. But if she can't tell him, who can she tell? Her shoes, not chosen for a stroll through a muddy field, are starting to rub and her laptop bag weighs heavily on her shoulder. 'Something happened in the mountains,' she pulls Michael's jacket tighter against the cold chill catching her neck, 'and I'm not sure what to make of it. It left me rather shaken.'

'Oh?'

Sarah tells him about the car accident and her suspicions that Irakli deliberately shunted them off the road. Michael walks on, his gaze focused, before responding.

'Well, that was sooner than I had expected. But I'm glad you are mostly unhurt.'

'You were expecting this?' Sarah asks, riled by his coolness.

'They were never going to welcome someone openly snooping into their business, but I didn't think they would be on to you that quickly.'

'You could have warned me.'

'It's always a possibility.'

'Do you think they know who I work for?' Sarah wants Michael's reassurance that it isn't as bad as it looks. That these things always happen in the first weeks of a mission.

'I'm sure they have their suspicions, but I doubt they have anything concrete. They would probably try to warn off anyone who comes asking too many questions.'

'So that was just trying to warn me off? It certainly felt like more than that. If it hadn't been for that ledge of rock, I would have been killed.'

'They are rattling you, Sarah, to see if you will run away.' Michael bends down to pick something up from the concrete in front of them. A small tortoise pokes its head cautiously from its shell. 'You'd be much better off on the grass old chap,' Michael whispers gently to the creature before setting it down under one of the almond trees. 'Your shell won't do you much good beneath the wheels of Dilara's Beechcraft.'

Sarah wishes Michael would show her the same degree of concern. 'How can you be sure it was just a warning?'

'Because if they had really wanted to kill you, you wouldn't be here.'

A light drizzle brings a cutting edge to the air. Sarah swallows hard, smoothing wisps of hair away from her eyes. This time, she is certain, Michael is wrong. Irakli is not that subtle. Her survival was pure luck.

They walk back towards the runway.

'So, what is your next move?' Michael's blue eyes look dark

and far away.

'I've been trying to work that out. If the foundation is suspect then the DFID cover may be more of a threat than a help, they're hardly going to want someone poking too closely into what they're doing. But what else can I offer Skarparov that would win his trust?'

Michael says nothing.

'If Irakli is helping Ibragimov with the weapons, then perhaps he should be our target,' Sarah says, trying to focus on the logic of the suggestion over the horror of the idea.

'You'd go back to him after he tried to have you killed?' Michael asks. Sarah can't tell if his brow is raised in surprise or admiration.

'If it meant getting to the bottom of what Ibragimov is planning sooner.'

'That's certainly bold.'

Is he offering his approval?

'Or perhaps foolish,' he adds, snatching it away. 'Luckily for you, I might have a way to speed things up.' He gives her one of his half-winks. 'Ibragimov has requested a meeting in Baku. The request came in through an untested source, so we need to do a little digging before we can agree to anything. But it could give us another way into Ibragimov, without having to use the Skarparov route. Or indeed Irakli.'

'Who does he want to meet?'

'That's what's interesting. He hasn't even tried to dress it up as a meeting with the Ambassador; he's cut straight to the point and asked for a meeting with MI6.'

'Ibragimov wants to talk to us?'

'If this source is to be believed. You're not off the hook just yet. Gifts like this don't fall into our lap without strings attached somewhere. But it is worth following up. BOG are hosting the Baku Energy Forum next week; Ibragimov and Skarparov should be there. You could approach both if necessary. Meanwhile, we can do some digging on this source. You're booked on a train leaving tonight.'

'Doesn't that sound a bit off? If Ibragimov is planning to blow up the pipeline, why would he be asking to meet MI6 around a major oil and gas event?'

'Don't forget he's an old hand in this game. It's the best kind of cover, hiding in plain sight. Or it's research, to see who turns up.'

'Leaving tonight?' she asks.

'An overnight sleeper gets into Baku tomorrow morning. Much finer way to travel than by plane I find. The embassy can fill you in on the rest. Be ready to leave at five o'clock, the tickets will be waiting for you at the station. Not a problem, is it?'

'No. I'll be there.' Sarah's head is spinning but she's glad for the chance to put some distance between herself and Irakli.

Dilara returns, her hair tumbling in bouncy waves over her shoulders, her cheeks flushed from exertion. 'It's done,' she says to Michael who replies in Turkish. Dilara takes Sarah's hand and leads her back towards the pigs' barracks. There is a familiar scent to her glorious mane of hair, something heady and exotic that Sarah struggles to place. Just over the crest of the hill they stop and Dilara points to a figure, trussed and bound, face down in the mud of the pigsty.

'That your guy?' she asks, her accented voice rich as double cream.

'I only saw the car. Are you sure it's him?' Sarah's stomach is gripped by a wave of nausea at the sight of the body.

'You don't need to worry now. Pigs make short work of corpses.' Her pumped-up lips curl into a grin.

Michael approaches. 'You are going to need to tread more carefully, Sarah. They know we're interested now. The cover is still fine to use, but it no longer gives you any protection.'

'Who was he?' Sarah asks, shocked at Michael's sangfroid. 'Why did she have to kill him?'

Michael shrugs. 'I don't know. But he certainly isn't listening anymore.'

Dilara returns to her plane.

'And who the hell is she?'

'She's a friend. A daughter of the Saban clan. Like I said, she owed me a favour and agreed to get me across the border.' What did Michael do for Dilara to earn this kind of service?

'Who are the Saban clan?'

'Wealthy Turkish entrepreneurs. Very wealthy. Manufacturing, steel, mines, real estate, supermarkets—not much they don't dabble in. Her brother has been set up as the crown prince to inherit when their father dies, but Dilara is by far the better suited to the task.'

'So the family business is manufacturing and murder?'

'Dilara just happens to have some unique skills. And when she decides she likes someone, she is extremely loyal. I have helped her out in the past, now she's helping me. It's always useful in this business to have people you can call on for help.'

'So she's a spy?'

'No. Just a useful friend.'

'I'd better hope she likes me too.'

'I expect she will. If only because you come from me.' He faces her. 'But I need you to be very careful from now on. Don't forget who you are dealing with, and please don't take unnecessary risks. In general, you should trust nobody.'

'Of course.' Does Dilara count as part of this warning?

'Nobody. Not even those who sound, or feel, like God's own good guys. In fact, those are the ones you should be especially careful of. Sorry,' he reaches around her shoulders and delicately removes his jacket. The wind whips her damp skin. 'I'm afraid I'll be needing this back.'

Sarah feels a little chastened—could Michael's warning have something to do with Elias? The thought of him sends a thrill soaring through her body, warming her blood. She knows their encounter was impulsive, but she still can't bring herself to regret it. Her thoughts keep slipping back to the way he made her feel, alive and inspired, like her insides were being tickled. Even so,

Michael is right. Delicious or not, Elias is an unnecessary risk.

'Good luck, Sarah. Keep me posted about Baku.'

The noise of propellers rises to deafening. Dilara gives a thumbs-up from the cockpit and blows Sarah a kiss. Michael turns back to wave before climbing the ladder. Moments later they are thundering back down the runway towards take-off.

Dilara's perfume still hangs in the air. Sweet but earthy and slightly bitter. It was saffron—Safran Troublant, the same perfume that came in the mysterious holdall. Honestly, Michael? Is that your pick for all the women in your life, or did Dilara help you choose it? Sarah is not sure whether to feel cheapened or flattered. But there is definitely something sweet in catching him out.

CHAPTER 20

LINES OF SIGHT

Irakli strides back and forth in front of the red brick building, checking and re-checking the lines of sight. He isn't exactly sure what 2.5km looks like, but this is definitely less. Definitely. It is the fifth building he has looked at and the real estate agent is going to start getting suspicious. He is already asking difficult questions that don't have answers. But it was worth the effort. This is the one.

He looks up at the windows facing the street—a fancy plate of metal work is bolted in front of each window, but there lies the beauty of this plan. It doesn't matter. The glass in the window is cracked in places but intact, its frosted finish covered with centuries of grime. No way anyone will be nosing in through here—they might even be boarded up from the inside, they look so murky.

He paces around the back of the building, checking the other entrances and exits. A tree grows right out of the side of the building, its roots causing the pink brick to bulge and buckle but the wall still looks sound. The nearest buildings are far enough away. An old man shuffles past, stooped over his cart piled high with pomegranates and a rusty metal press. Otherwise, the street is deserted. Yes. This is going to work.

The agent unlocks the door with an enormous iron key and takes him inside. Plenty of space. One room at ground level and a trap door leading down to the cellar below. Most of the light comes from a skylight in the roof. Irakli can see a patch of grey sky through the glass. Should mean they can see what they're doing without the hassle of connecting up to the power. And no one is going to be looking in from up there.

He smiles at the agent. 'Yes, this is the one.'

CHAPTER 21

a3 h5

Tbilisi train station hangs with dilapidated grandeur. Its high ceilings are fallen in through decades of neglect, its windows blackened with grime. Designed in an age when the railway was the pinnacle of luxury travel, the echoing cavern now serves only a handful of freight and passenger trains that rattle asthmatically across Georgia to the Black Sea. The roads are much faster, and the comforts that once made train travel a more elegant option have long since been battered out of the creaking coaches and threadbare upholstery.

Sarah is lost. There are no signs, the departures board is blank, and the ticket offices deserted. She wanders through an open door at the back of the building to find a dozen empty platforms. At the far end of one, a solitary train is dwarfed by the expanse of concrete. *"The American Express,"* it announces in bold letters down the side. An improbable name for a trans-Caucasian railway.

As Sarah approaches the first carriage, a man in blue bell-boy's uniform hops towards her. 'Ms Black? Ms Black? We are here for you, I have your tickets, wishing you a wonderful journey today, Ms Black.' He breaks into a high-pitched giggle, making his moustache bounce, and thrusts an envelope into her hands while wrestling her bag from her grip. 'Come, come please, I show you your cabin, very nice train, the American Express,' he says proudly.

Sarah surrenders her holdall and follows him into the carriage. The train has the spruced-up feel of a refurbished museum piece. The wooden walls of the compartments gleam deep amber under fresh varnish but the doors clatter in their hinges and the windows, dressed with bright blue curtains, are stained with soot. The effect is rather charming. Sarah has been on sleeper trains before but only the faceless smooth and efficient kind, packed with backpackers and businessmen. This is far more fun.

The guard leads her to her cabin, one of six sleepers in the first-class carriage, and shows her how to pull down the bed. The cabin is small but cosy, with furnishings that might have been taken from a guest room at her grandmother's house—an orange and pink crocheted blanket on the bed, a lace cloth on the table and orange lampshades on the wall.

'I'll show you how to lock the door,' the bellboy closes the door behind him, locking them in. 'When you are asleep, be sure to lock both bolts, the top and bottom, you must make sure it's fully locked.' He slams the bottom bolt in place as if to demonstrate its strength. 'And take this,' he pulls a small rubber door stopper from the pocket of his jacket. 'It's good to use too, just in case.' Another high-pitched giggle. 'It's good to feel safe.'

His manner is unthreatening, his giggles endearing, but his heavy-handed warnings are making Sarah nervous. Why is it necessary to take such precautions? The guard smiles, his neatly trimmed moustache bobbing reassuringly. This extra cautiousness must be a remnant of Soviet paranoia. Or perhaps they are unused to young women travelling alone. Sarah takes the small rubber stopper. 'Thank you, I'll be sure to use it.'

He stands in the doorway, hands behind his back as if waiting for something.

'Thank you for your help with the bag.' She rummages in her wallet and offers him a handful of Laris, but he waves her money away.

'I am here to help, Ms Black. I am in the cabin at the end of the carriage. Anything you need, please ask me, and Jim's your uncle, I am here for you!' He pauses again, then bows out of the cabin, shutting the door behind him.

Sarah unpacks some of her belongings, checking her phone optimistically for signal but there's nothing. She opens up Michael's laptop and tries to draft an email to Jenny to send later from a safe connection. She wants to share some of her recent adventures, to laugh about the ridiculousness of her situation and caricature some of the stranger characters she has met. But it's impossible to find the right tone. She is not ready to share her encounter with Elias, still unsure what to make of what happened. And Jenny would only want more details than she is prepared to give. A description of her visit to the mountains could be made to sound like a convincing first-week tale of a new DFID recruit. But the story is soured by the spectre of Irakli. His deranged grin, the sweaty sheen to his face, his cruel laughter creep into every phrase. Sarah tries to write a few light-hearted sentences to make Jenny giggle, to reassure that all is well, but her mind keeps returning to the bound and trussed figure in the pigsty. Her cheery words sound hollow. She deletes everything and starts again:

'Tbilisi is weird and wonderful. On my way to Baku. I miss you.'

That will have to do.

Sarah shoves the laptop back in her bag, then thinks better of it. She used it to write up some of her findings on the Skarparov Foundation—nothing too different from what a real DFID officer would have remarked, but still drawing attention to her interest. She removes it and the notebook from her bag and slips them under the mattress. No, too obvious. She finds a stack of towels in the tiny ensuite bathroom and wedges the laptop inside so that they look undisturbed. She locks the door of the cabin carefully behind her and goes to explore the train.

The first-class carriage is a narrow corridor with six identical doorways. Two of the cabins are empty. Raised voices in musical Georgian rise from behind the third door and the last two cabins are occupied by a young family, the father trying valiantly to comfort a crying infant as the mother swats at two older children bouncing on the bed. To pass to the next carriage, Sarah has to step from a small ledge behind a wooden door to the equally small space on the other side. She grabs the large handles on either side of the door to steady herself but still she can't look down at the tracks rushing by beneath her feet.

The cabins in the second-class compartment are larger, with four beds to a room. Inside one, a group of rosy-cheeked men in black leather jackets are playing cards across the lower bunks. Luggage piles up in the corridor. The end cabin is packed from floor to ceiling with branches of sweet almond blossoms, filling the air with their rich scent.

Sarah fords another gap to enter the restaurant car, high backed benches squeezed between wooden tables. She is not yet hungry, but curious to discover her fellow passengers on this bizarre journey.

The television above her head plays an American high school movie dubbed into Russian. A girl in a blue and white striped tunic stands at the bar in the corner, her chin resting on her hands, staring absently at the screen. Only half of the tables are occupied—a couple reading magazines while their teenaged son stares wilfully out of the window; a pair of Georgian women talking animatedly, hands flying with each sweep of the conversation, their feet resting on plastic bags filled with their worldly goods; a soldier wearing pristine desert army fatigues chews his way through a pile of sunflower seeds. Sarah watches an older man in a brown suit, shiny and worn at the elbows, slowly make his way through the carriage, greeting several of the other passengers.

Outside the window, the crumbling rows of apartment blocks that border the city give way to verdant green. The girl in the tunic shuffles down the carriage with a trolley. The choice is stew, grey and greasy and straight from a cast-iron cauldron, or sweaty sandwiches wrapped in cling film. Sarah is glad she is not hungry, but takes a sandwich filled with a slice of something pink in case of desperation.

The restaurant car begins to fill as those who joined the train at the last minute come to take their places. The man in the brown suit sits down at Sarah's table.

'Do you mind if I join you? It seems we have picked the busiest moment.' He speaks in immaculate English, words carefully chosen. His hair is combed long over his head, perhaps to disguise a balding scalp, or just the way he has worn it for forty years. His cheeks are dotted with brown marks of age, but his eyes are keen and alert.

'Of course, please—' Sarah is about to add 'sit down' but he already has.

'May I ask what brings you here? Your colouring suggests you were not born in the Caucasus.' He studies her. 'England, I would guess. But you are neither tourist nor traveller.'

Sarah is taken aback by the directness of his question, but tickled by his elegant way of asking. 'You would guess right; I am from England. I'm on my way to Baku for the Energy Forum,' she says, happy to have a solid cover story.

'Ah, yes, the black gold, and how it will turn around the fortunes of the region. That is the story, is it not?' He touches his fingers together on the table in front of him.

'Yes, there is a lot of optimism about how the opening of the pipeline will bring prosperity to the region, especially to Azerbaijan.' Sarah feigns the confidence of a seasoned professional.

'More optimism, just what we need.' His voice is melancholy but his eyes still smile.

'Optimism can never hurt, can it?'

'What good has optimism done for Georgia?' he asks. 'They came with their revolution and roses and optimism, always lots of optimism, but now I see only disappointment.'

'Disappointment? I thought things were changing for the better?'

'The truth is really very simple, I can explain it to you very easily,' he watches her. 'There is always someone who benefits from change, but what about the rest? Our optimistic friends came by revolution. How can they talk of democracy when the lesson they have taught is that if you want something, you just take it?'

Sarah lets him talk, intrigued as to where he is going.

'The government say they want change, but they are the ones that need to change, and they will never change because they have what they want.' He speaks slowly, the cadence of his voice rising and falling as if reciting poetry.

'You are the first person I have heard who wasn't in favour of the revolution,' Sarah says. 'Most people seem to think it was a good thing, bringing well-needed changes for the country.'

'That is because you sit in your bubble, and you talk to people who tell you the things you want to hear. Come and visit me on my farm, talk to my neighbours, my labourers. You will see how much this optimism has brought them.'

Sarah feels chided, but only gently. 'You have a farm?'

'Of course, any society is built up from its agricultural base. If we want to make real changes, we have to go back to the beginning.'

Sarah realises that she is talking to an unreformed Marxist. Not the youthful idealistic type she came across at university, but one who lived through the painful Soviet experiment and yet emerged at the other end, ideals intact.

'You speak excellent English for a peasant farmer,' she says, her turn to provoke a reaction.

He places his hands in his lap. 'I studied international relations

147

in the United States and public administration in Belgium and Poland and social sciences in Moscow, and I delivered lectures in mathematics in England, when they let me. I was a lecturer at the Tbilisi State University before the revolution, but now I do not see the point. Why do we need more young people with heads so stuffed full of facts that they think they know all there is to know? So I went back to my farm, which I had left to pursue my dream of academia.'

The train grinds to a halt and Sarah hears the sound of doors slamming. She looks out the window but there's nothing to tell her where they are. His face suddenly breaks into a wide grin. 'I am sorry, I did not mean to burden you with my story. There is great joy in suffering, if you know where to look.'

'And how can you turn suffering into joy without being an optimist?' Sarah is enjoying their curious debate.

'Through knowing how to use your despair. "The whole art of living is to use the people who make us suffer simply as steps enabling us to obtain access to their divine form and thus joyfully to people our lives with divinities".' He gently closes his eyes as he recites the lines, his voice returning to its lyrical cadence. 'Do you know the quote?'

'I've never heard it.'

'Then you have a real treat in store. It's Proust. If you haven't read it, your life can only become lighter. Find a copy to take with you to your Energy Forum, it will bring sparkle to your mind and help keep their optimism from turning to despair.'

The train slowly chugs back into motion. 'I will try and find a copy in Baku,' she replies. 'Thank you for the recommendation.'

'It is not a recommendation. Just a reminder of what you already knew.' He studies her, his face broad and open. 'I must apologise, you came here for your dinner, instead I have burdened you with my sorry story, so now I leave you with Proust to make your soul blossom.' He stands, touches his hand to his chest and gives a little bow.

'No need to apologise, it has been a pleasure. Thank you for

148

the reminder.' She is charmed and bemused by her philosophising train companion, by his strange mix of melancholy and joy. She can't tell if he's teasing her or playing up a caricature, but nonetheless he has provided entertainment for her journey. And a welcome distraction from thinking about Dilara and the pigs.

The guard in the blue uniform appears at their table. 'Ms White, is this man bothering you?' He shoots a hostile glance at the older gentleman.

'No, thank you. We were only talking. I'm quite happy.'

'I wish you a pleasant journey,' the older man nods at Sarah and again at the guard before making his way down the corridor. The guard watches him suspiciously.

'Anything you need, Ms White, you ask me. You be careful please, Ms White.' He smiles at her with a look of concern, no giggling now. Sarah does not bother to correct him on her name—he got it right before but it's an unimportant mistake. 'Of course,' she nods.

She picks her way back to her cabin through groups of people sitting on towers of luggage in the corridor. The card players now look merrily doused in wine and the carriage is ripe with the smell of tightly packed bodies and almond blossom. As she enters the first-class carriage, a door ahead slams shut. Sarah turns her key in the top lock of her cabin and is startled when the door springs open. She closed both locks on leaving, but now the bottom one is fully open.

Instantly she switches to high alert. The room looks much as she left it. Her bag in place, the clothes folded as she remembers packing them. But somehow it looks too neat. She would have left behind more of a mess when she unpacked her things. The items she removed from the bag are still lying on the bed.

She checks the bathroom for the laptop and notebook.

They are gone.

She collapses on the bed, heart thumping, sifting through everything that was on the laptop, what an outside eye might be able to decipher from the pages of handwritten notes and reminders in her notebook. Luckily most of it was written in a private shorthand, notes to jog her memory rather than fully worked out sentences. But the laptop—the careful folders of people she was planning to approach, the angles on the train crash she was considering. How was she so careless as to leave a physical trace of her thoughts, and so naive to think that hiding them in her cabin would keep them safe?

Her cheeks burn with humiliation; what a complete fool she is. What was she doing sitting in the restaurant car talking philosophy while her cabin was being searched? Was her intellectual Marxist sent to provide a distraction, an accomplice to whoever took her notes? It could have been coincidence, an opportune theft while her cabin was empty. But who would be able to access this compartment without drawing the attention of the guard? Sarah trusted the guard, took his over-the-top warnings at face value, but it could also have been a bluff. What if he tipped someone off that she was out of the cabin?

She double checks that both locks are now securely shut, wedges the door stopper firmly in place and yanks at the curtains to seal herself off from the darkness outside. The thin strips of fabric don't cover the glass. She throws herself on the bed fuming, wishing for a rewind button, something to repair the damage. How could she tell Michael what had happened?

She's been so keen to prove herself to him, to show that she's worthy of his trust, that she's lost sight of the mission, her mission, the reason she's here at all. She's spent the last week waiting for instructions, she's been bumped from pillar to post at other people's request. Get this plane, take this train. Where was she in all of this? Is she just a piece being shuffled around the board? This is her mission, or supposed to be. And she is the one who is going to end up dead if she doesn't start taking charge of her own game. Enough of waiting for instructions, enough of trusting people to be there to help her. She's on her own.

She listens to her heart hammering blood around her body, firing up her instincts for self-protection. This is no time to cower in her cabin.

She can't be scared. No one is going to help her.

She needs to stand up for herself and fight back.

She wrenches out the door stopper and storms out, letting the door clatter behind her. What is the point in locking it? And where is that bastard? She thunders through the first-class carriage, throwing open the doors of the empty cabins in the hope of surprising the Marxist or whoever took her belongings. How can you hide in a moving train?

She steps across the gap into the second-class carriage, drawing curious glances as she scans every face for signs of guilt or collusion, trying to place who she has seen before, who could have moved since she first passed through. Beyond the piles of luggage at the end of the carriage, she sees the brown suit of the Marxist philosopher trying to slip unnoticed into the restaurant car.

'Wait! Stop!' she shouts, almost tripping over a pair of outstretched legs in her hurry to catch up with him. She grabs him by the sleeve. 'Who are you?'

'I'm sorry,' he looks like a wounded animal. 'You seem disturbed, is everything okay?'

'No it's not okay. My cabin has been searched and my notebook stolen.'

A dark blue vein throbs on the side of his forehead and his eyes dart behind her. 'I'm so sorry to hear that,' he says, trying to prise his arm out of Sarah's grip.

'I bet you are. It seems like too much of a coincidence, don't you think?'

'I don't follow—'

'Don't give me that bullshit. Are you working with the guard?'

'Sarah, I'm sorry, I really don't know—'

'How the hell do you know my name?'

He turns to run into the next carriage, trying to pull the door shut on her. She sticks her foot in the door and pulls back with all her force, throwing him off balance. His foot misses the step across the gap and seems to drop in slow motion. He lets out a whimper as he falls, landing on the small ledge with one foot trailing helplessly towards the tracks.

'Please help me.' He's staring at Sarah with wide, terrified eyes, trying to reach for one of the door handles.

'Tell me who you are.' Sarah stands over him, her feet straddling the gap, blocking both handrails with her body.

'I've told you. Everything I told you was true.' His voice breaks over the words.

'How do you know who I am?'

'They told me your name.'

'Who are they?' She keeps a tight grip on the doors, edging her foot away in case he should grab her down with him.

'I don't know, I have never seen them before. They asked me to keep you in the restaurant car until we had passed the customs stop.'

'They were Georgians? How many?'

'Two. Azeris.'

'And why did you agree?'

He peers down at the ground rattling past beneath him. 'I am not in the privileged position to turn down that sort of money.'

'Pathetic. So much for the gentleman Marxist.'

'Sarah, please. Help me.' He holds out a trembling hand. She yanks it up, making space for him to climb back up. 'Thank you,' he stammers. The door to the restaurant car opens and the soldier in the shiny new fatigues stares at them both open-mouthed. The man takes his chance to disappear into the safety of the crowd.

Sarah returns to her cabin feeling restive and finds the guard backing out of her door. 'What are you doing in my room?'

'Ms Black, thank God you are okay.' His relief seems genuine, and he's got her name right this time. 'Your door was open, I was worried.' He holds out her laptop and notebook. 'I found these in the bin at the end of the carriage.'

'The *bin*?' Sarah takes back her belongings. The pages of the

152

notebook are soggy with cold coffee.

'I came to bring them to you, but you were gone.'

'Thank you for your concern.' Sarah slams the door in his bewildered face and jams the rubber wedge in place.

'Please be careful, Ms Black,' he calls through the door. 'Anything you need, you tell me. Okay?'

And risk more of my possessions going walkabout? Sarah doesn't trust him. Why did he call her Ms White in the restaurant car if he knew her real name? She does not trust anyone. Who were the two men who paid off her philosophising Marxist? And why go to the effort of stealing the laptop only to dump it in a bin? She thinks through who might want to give her a scare. Perhaps this is Irakli's next attempt to put her off. Or maybe Ibragimov? But how would either of them know where she was or have time to arrange the hit?

She kicks off her shoes and lies down on the bed. The story of the two men could be a ruse. The guard is sure to have keys to her cabin. Did she interrupt him as he was trying to slip them back unnoticed? He is the only one who knows her full name, she has no idea what else about her he might know.

The landscape outside the window is swallowed up in blackness. She closes her eyes and hopes for sleep. Rocked by the motion of the train, she manages to drift in and out of consciousness, startled awake by every sudden sound—a door slamming or window banging—transformed by her unsettled mind into intruders entering her cabin.

The windows slowly streak with dawn. The green leafiness of Georgia has given way to a desert moonscape, flat and featureless and stretching for miles with little sign of life. Only the occasional nodding donkey, backlit by the orange burst of a gas flare, reveal that they are now in oil country. Sarah watches the desert roll by, grey hills appearing and vanishing in the distance, until a city begins to take shape. The train pulls into Baku with the early morning sun.

CHAPTER 22

Rfb1 e6

The embassy in Baku buzzes with the promotion of British industry. After the quiet cosiness of its Tbilisi counterpart, it feels more busy showroom than diplomatic centre. Sarah accepts a cup of strong coffee and waits in reception, her fingers wrapped around the mug, her body still rocking with the jerk and sway of the train. After her sleepless night, she is grateful for the caffeine and takes comfort to be somewhere safe, surrounded by noise and movement.

A man offers Sarah his hand. He's wearing a dark blue suit with a hint of pinstripe, but it looks like the suit is wearing him. He is so slender his shoulders and elbows protrude from the fabric at odd angles, as if his muscles were attached inside out. His hand in Sarah's feels like a pile of pencils, grinding together in a thin crepe-paper case. The skin of his face stretches tight across his skull, his sandy hair thinly combed against his scalp. He casts Sarah a sceptical look, like a customer buying a second-hand car, unwilling to show interest that might raise the price.

Sarah dislikes him immediately.

'You made it; I am pleased. I'm Jim. Mike told me to expect you. I hope you had a smooth journey?'

'Yes, thank you,' Sarah says automatically. 'Very smooth.' She sinks deeper into her chair and tightly crosses her legs.

'And did Gela take good care of you?'

'Gela?'

'The guard on the train, he's one of ours. Well not really ours, but sympathetic, and very helpful when he needs to be. I asked him to keep an eye out for you. Just in case of any… well, just in case.' Jim tries to smile but it looks more like a grimace, skin pulled tight over triangular cheek bones.

Sarah now understands the guard's expectant pauses and knowing looks. Why he only ever used her real name when no one else was in earshot. 'Yes, he was very attentive.' So someone else must have taken the laptop. She wishes she could talk to Michael; she doesn't trust Jim, isn't ready to open up to him, to admit to her naive errors that allowed someone access to her things. She'd rather not tell Michael either, but at least he was a known entity, and he had more reason to be on her side. Nothing in Jim's crisp manner, in his red-rimmed eyes or sceptical gaze makes her want to take him into her confidence, to admit to her mistakes. But she hasn't been able to reach Michael on the number he gave her. He appears when he wants her, but she can't summon him when she needs him.

'And you weren't bothered at all?'

'No,' she says, hoping her sleepless night is not too evident in her drooping eyes.

'Very good.' From the pointed politeness of his tone it's clear he knows she's lying. He must already know about the laptop; Gela must have already reported the incident. But it's too late to backtrack now.

'Now, for that meeting. I understand you're the bait?'

That term again. Sarah's heckles are up. 'I am not the bait; I've been asked to follow up on a request for a meeting.'

'Calm down.' Jim looks affronted by her assertiveness. 'It's just a bit of shorthand, no need to take it personally.' He speaks slowly as if to a child. 'You will be the stand-in for our mysterious source requesting a meeting with Ibragimov. Better?'

Sarah grits her teeth and nods.

'It's a new source, they insist on communicating solely by dead letter box, as if it's still the cold war. Most people these days prefer an anonymous Gmail account. We keep the drop spot open for those who don't trust technology, but it makes negotiation a touch tricky. So you're the bai— Sorry, the "decoy deep cover agent" to flush him out.' He made inverted commas in the air with his pencil fingers. 'We've told him an agent will be at three locations this week for him to make contact. You have tickets for the ballet tonight, you're to do some tourism in the old city tomorrow and you'll attend the Energy Forum the following day.'

There is something in Jim's attitude that makes her uncomfortable, something unpleasant in his fleshless face— is he just cavalier or covertly hostile? He certainly seems to be enjoying himself firing instructions at her.

'And why me?' she asks. 'Why can't one of you meet him?'

Jim shakes his head, removing an invisible speck of lint from his trousers. 'The staff in the station here are all known faces, they could hardly pose as tourists in the bazaar. And if the plan goes wrong, it would be easier to get you out without too much explaining.'

'And how will I recognise him when he makes his approach?'

'You will carry a copy of *The Economist*. And the recognition word is pomegranate.'

'Pomegranate?' Sarah laughs. 'I'm supposed to slip that casually into conversation?'

'It's the national fruit,' Jim says dismissively. It must have been his personal choice.

'You can use this one.' He hands her a copy of the magazine. The headline is "The Sex Business" and shows a curvy silhouette of a woman clad in red satin, a large red-handled pair of barbecue tongs propped on her ample posterior.

'You're kidding, right? It's not even this week's.' Sarah throws the magazine down on the table. 'Which sniggering twit found that funny?'

Jim neither laughs nor apologises. 'I'm afraid the current edition seemed even less appropriate.' He tosses her another copy with two houseflies shown in grimly close up detail. The headline is "The Spy Game".

Sarah has to laugh. Reluctantly she shoves the shiny scarlet rump into her bag.

'And when I've made contact?'

'You've not done one of these before?'

'I was sent out straight from recruitment.'

'One of Michael's recruits?'

'Yes.'

He sits back and studies her. His gaze suddenly less hostile, less posturing almost sympathetic. She's no longer a second-hand car, she's a lab rat in a cage. 'I did wonder…'

'Wonder what?'

'What Michael's involvement was here. I know he and Ibragimov have… history, shall we say.'

'History?' Sarah asks. Why has Michael never mentioned this? 'What kind of history?'

'Oh, rumours, that's all. I don't know any of the details.' He gives her an understanding smile, his crepe paper skin folding into fine points at his eyes. 'I'm afraid there's not much you can do to prepare for a job like this. Just go along with it and eventually it will start to seem normal. You'll have plenty of time to polish your craft.' What is behind this sudden change from arrogance to sympathy? Why does coming from Michael make her suddenly less of a threat?

'Just see what you can pick up. See if you can ascertain why they want to meet. The go-between is unlikely to give much away, but do what you can to establish trust.'

157

'Do you think Ibragimov knew I was coming?' Sarah's mind is still on the train.

'I don't see any reason why he would. Why?'

'Just want to know how to play an approach.'

'You'll be fine.' He looks at his watch. 'I'm afraid I have to dash. There's a demonstration planned by the opposition for tomorrow. London are getting excited and want me to look into my crystal ball to tell them how it's going to play out.' He pauses at the door, speaking over his shoulder.

'Love and Death, tonight at eight.'

'I'm sorry?' Is this more code?

'The ballet. It's the new Bulbuloglu piece. One of Azerbaijan's most popular composers and the former Minister of Culture. I'm sure you'll enjoy it. Let me know how you get on.'

CHAPTER 23

b4 Qb6

The Azerbaijan State Academic Opera and Ballet Theatre is a blue and yellow confection, the twin towers of the faded facade capped with elegant onion domes. Its grand neo-classical style still leaves a striking impression, even if long in need of renovation. It's holding on to its former glory as a glamorous older lady gone slightly to seed.

Sarah collects her tickets from the dimly lit booth. She holds her copy of *The Economist* prominently under her arm, red top clearly visible but scarlet tail covered up. It is strangely difficult to remember how she would normally hold a magazine without feeling so self-conscious. The wizened lady behind the window takes some time locating the envelope with Sarah's ticket. 'Miss Black, Miss Black, Miss Black,' she mutters as she flicks through a yellowing pile of index cards.

Sarah holds her magazine a little higher in case this long show was part of the approach. The ticket lady gives no flicker of recognition.

Before the performance begins, she wanders through the crowds, taking in the collection of shabby soviet intellectuals and eager-eyed students smelling of beet soup. An elegantly dressed woman bumps into her, grabbing at the magazine as they collide. Sarah smiles at her expectantly, wondering how to throw out a casual 'pomegranate'. But the woman mutters apologies and drifts off.

Sarah takes her seat, still watchful for a signal as the lights dim and the grand proscenium arch is bathed in raspberry pink. She is soon lost in the performance. In place of leotards and tutus, the dancers wear traditional costumes of the Caucasus. The female dancers float across the stage in long skirts and head-dresses while the men, wrapped in sashes and daggers, perform mesmerising leaps in front of the backdrop of mist-covered mountains. The programme is entirely in Azeri, and she struggles to follow the storyline, but the spectacle is pure pleasure. She finds herself disappointed when the lights come up and she is back on duty.

During the interval she reads her magazine, propped up on a cocktail table in the bar, careful to raise her eye often enough for anyone trying to catch it.

'Are you following me?' Sarah feels a cool hand on her shoulder and looks up to see Skarparov's curious opal eyes. 'I didn't think I'd find you here. What brings you to Baku?'

He is the last person she expects to see. She gathers her composure, trying to work out the quickest way to get rid of him without seeming rude. Talking to him could put off Ibragimov's go-between from making an approach.

'I'm here for the Energy Forum later in the week. Just taking the opportunity to soak up a little of the local colour.'

'A happy coincidence.' Skarparov rocks back on his heels, his thick black eyebrows dancing. 'So am I. What interest do DFID have in big bad oil? I thought that was covered by commercial teams?'

'There is World Bank money going into the pipeline, so our

Minister is responsible for ensuring environmental promises are met and the social and developmental impact of the project are not forgotten.' Sarah sticks closely to the background briefing, hoping he won't probe any further. She glances over his shoulder, trying to keep her eye open for anyone else who might be trying to catch it.

'If I were the British government,' he spins a small wooden cocktail stick casually in his fingers, 'I would be more concerned about the security risk posed by the pipeline than the token development projects promised alongside.'

'You think someone might want to attack it?' Sarah asks.

'I don't know why anyone would. But you never know these days.'

It's impossible to tell from Skarparov's breezy manner if he's trying to warn her about something or just making conversation.

'And tell me, Ms Black,' Skarparov offers his hand and guides her towards the bar, 'how was your visit to the mountains? Did Irakli look after you?' His smile is warm, genuine, there is nothing in his manner that suggests he's trying to rile her.

'Irakli?' She snatches away her hand. 'He left me high and dry. Didn't he tell you?'

'No.' Skarparov stops twiddling the cocktail stick and holds it stiffly between pinched finger and thumb. 'What happened?'

'We had a car accident on the way up. Irakli disappeared. Luckily, I came across Giorgi who took me around the sites.'

Skarparov's face darkens, his fleshy earlobes seem to drop, pulling down the rest of his features. 'He left you?' His words are stilted, as if stuck in his throat.

'I haven't seen him since. I thought you'd know.'

'I must apologise on his behalf.' He snaps the cocktail stick violently in two. 'I know he can be crude, but this is an unforgivable way to treat a guest. Please do not hold it against us. I will ensure that he is reprimanded. I hope Giorgi was at least able to show you all you wanted to see?'

'He was very helpful.' Sarah is reassured by his concern. After

Michael's warning, it had been troubling her that Irakli might be acting under instruction from his boss. Skarparov is certainly putting on a good show of having known nothing about it.

'Do you always bring something to read at the ballet?' he points to Sarah's magazine.

Her heart quickens, her hands suddenly clammy against the edge of the table. 'I like to keep myself well informed.' Could this be the signal? Could Skarparov be the one who asked for the meeting with Ibragimov? It seems ridiculous.

'I hope it's not distracting you from the story. Love and death, friendship and betrayal… It's a powerful piece.' He calls the waitress's attention. 'Can I offer you a drink?'

'I'd like a pomegranate juice please,' Sarah lingers lightly on the trigger word.

'I'd recommend sour cherry, if I can't convince you to join me in champagne.' No flicker of recognition.

'Are you visiting family in Baku?' Sarah asks, offering him a chance to steer the conversation towards Ibragimov.

'Yes, I promised my daughters I would take them to the Energy Forum. They tell me they are interested in joining the family business, but I think they are hoping to bag themselves a rich husband.'

'Would that be Ibragimov's business?'

'You know Mikhail?' He looks as if she has just said something unexpectedly crude. 'No. I would not trust my beautiful girls with a man like him.'

'I thought he was your uncle?'

'Sadly so, but we are no longer close.' Skarparov watches her, his opal eyes turning through a kaleidoscope of ideas. 'How well informed you are, Sarah. Have you been briefed on all the well-to-do of Baku or am I attracting special attention?'

'I like to do my homework.' She feels the conversation slipping out of her control. Skarparov is attentive and charming, he has the easy graces of the over-privileged, people for whom life has always turned out right. But she knows he is smarter than he seems. And she has the feeling he is trying to tell her something, to hint at something he is too well-mannered to mention. Are his words about Ibragimov to be taken as a warning? She wishes she knew how to break through the pleasantries and dig for more information without giving herself away. 'Your uncle is an intriguing character,' she begins but she's interrupted by the bell ringing to announce the second half.

'Let's talk some more.' Skarparov leans in to kiss Sarah on the cheek. 'I hope that clod Irakli hasn't put you off our little project. We are still hoping for your support.'

'Of course.' Sarah maintains her smile as Skarparov breezes off through the crowd, but drops it as soon as he's out of sight. She's lost him just at the moment he might have been willing to open up and she's no closer to having made contact with the anonymous source. It can't have been Skarparov, he showed no response to the recognition word and made no effort to arrange a meeting. Has she allowed herself, again, to be distracted just at the wrong moment?

She stays on high alert throughout the second half and hangs around in the linoleum-lined corridors after the performance, her eyes roaming the crowd hoping to spot someone doing the same. No further approach is made.

CHAPTER 24

Na4 Qa6

As instructed, Sarah spends the next morning wandering through the old city, where traces of Arabic, Persian and Ottoman history mingle with the shabbier underside of a modern city. Newly sand-blasted buildings gleam golden in the sunshine. Those yet to be restored have eroded into black and calloused ripples.

Baku is a world away from Tbilisi. Oil wealth has brought more investment, the buildings are higher and shinier, an influx of foreign workers has given it a more cosmopolitan feel with Turkish kebab shops, international high street chains and Irish pubs. But despite the western influences, there are many signs that the country still faces firmly to the East. Heydar Aliyev, the former president and current president's father, looms down from billboards on every street corner looking austere and authoritarian. The public buildings are monuments to Soviet aesthetics. Even those built in the nineteenth century as copies of the world's great cities are grand and imposing—watchtowers rising over the city. The streets are choked with an army of Ladas and an air of faded glory hangs over the sea front.

Sarah takes to her task with little enthusiasm. She feels self-conscious trying to blend in with the groups of tourists in the medieval city centre while keeping her eyes peeled for a mole. She wishes she had a better idea of who she was looking out for and where they were likely to try to find her. Jim's instruction to just 'do some tourism' feels frustratingly vague and the longer she is left without any sign of approach, the greater her restlessness. It doesn't help that she has the distinct feeling she is being watched.

With her copy of *The Economist* sticking out of her shoulder bag, she climbs the Maiden Tower and listens to a guide explaining how a young girl had thrown herself from the tower to her death in the sea below. Sarah studies the faces in the rest of the group listening to the guide. Is anyone trying to catch her eye? Or is anyone paying her undue attention? She finds herself uncharacteristically affected by the tragic foundation myth—gazing out onto the oil-slick surface of the water, she imagines herself hurtling headlong into its rainbow sheen. What persecution could bring on such desperate resolve? And why has this particular misadventure come to symbolise a monument with eight centuries of history to tell? She feels unsteady in her legs and steps back from the edge.

She moves on to the Old Caravanserai, studying the familiar faces among the other tourists who seem to be following the same route. Are they just ticking off the obvious sites or following her lead? She decides to try out some counter-surveillance techniques to shake off a trail. It is something she had been looking forward to learning in her training—she's read about "dry cleaning" in spy books, using unpredictable movements to lose anyone following her. But it was one of the many things missing from Michael's briefing. Without really knowing what she is doing she swerves away from the standard tourist circuit and weaves unlikely routes through the maze of medieval streets—doubling back on herself unexpectedly, walking in circles, looking over her shoulder, watching reflections in windows, trying to spot anyone else following her unlikely patterns. All without drawing too much attention to herself. After one double-back she thinks she spots a tall figure in a pale shirt duck into a side alley. But when she follows in pursuit, there is no one to be seen.

She stands in front of a carpet shop, pretending to admire the stacks of woven silk kilims and dusty woollen rugs piled around the door while actually studying the street behind her in a small display mirror. Was that the same figure in the pale shirt?

'Ah, you like the soumaks?' the owner of the carpet shop has spotted her. 'Then you have very fine taste. They are very special to this region. Inspired by the climate of the Caucasus— smooth and flat on the top to protect against the dust and heat of the summer in the desert, but thick and uneven underneath to provide warmth in the winter in the mountains.' He turns the carpet over to show Sarah where the weaver has left threads hanging long and loose, an impressionist image of the pattern on top. 'Each one is unique, hand-woven over many weeks in the villages. Each pattern tells its own story. Come inside please, I have many more beautiful things to show you.'

'Thank you.' Sarah tries to move away as the carpet seller's hand reaches for her elbow to guide her into the shop. 'Really, I'm just looking.'

'Yes of course, please look. My carpets need to be looked at every day. Come, you don't need to buy. Just come to look, make them happy, come and hear their stories. You are Samir's guest.'

Sarah lets herself be taken into the shop, carefully removing her arm from Samir's clutch. At least no one can follow her in without giving themselves away

'Please, sit down. Some tea?'

'Thank you, I'm fine.'

'You cannot appreciate beauty if you are thirsty. Black, with a little bit of sugar, yes? Ali! *Çay!*

Moments later, a young boy appears with three small glasses of tea. Sarah takes one and settles herself into the chair as Samir begins rolling out his wares. She has no intention of buying anything, but surely there is no harm in looking. Carpet after carpet is pulled out of neatly ordered stacks and spread on the floor in front of her. Samir barks instructions to Ali, what to find and where, but still manages to keep up his constant patter, telling Sarah the provenance of each carpet, its age and history, imbuing each story with romance.

'This one was made during the war, in a small village by women whose men had gone to fight. They had been gone for many years and the women did not know if they would ever see their loved ones again. To keep themselves from despair, the women would tell themselves stories and they would weave the stories into the carpets. You see this one, this is a shield, this lady thought her lover was strong and protected. This one has lots of white for peace, and here with the red for blood. I don't think this lady thought the war would end well. But a beautiful carpet, no?'

Sarah nods.

'And here you see the pomegranate motif, typical of Azerbaijan with its golden crown and blood red pearls symbolising fertility and health.'

Sarah jumps to attention, ears open, mind alert. 'Did you say pomegranate?' she asks, watching carefully for a reaction.

'Yes, the fruit of paradise. And these birds are also typical of the region,' Samir continues describing the pattern of the carpet without looking up. Is it too absurd to think that Ibragimov might be trying to set up a confidential meeting through a carpet seller? Sarah wonders how to linger on the signal without appearing ridiculous.

'I was told to look out for the pomegranate motif,' she tries, 'to recognise a carpet from the region.'

'Of course, many motifs are important to Azerbaijan.' Samir gives no indication that he wants anything from her beyond a potential buyer for his carpets. During a pause in his story, Sarah hears voices from the back room.

'I'll give you four hundred dollars for the lot but not a penny more. You know as well as I do that it is a fair price; in fact, I think it is pretty generous for this factory produced stuff.'

'No, sir, all of these are hand-made, nothing here is from a factory. Please, sir, I think you can try a little more, these are very beautiful carpets, you have very fine taste.'

'Hand made of course, in a factory in Pakistan and probably laid down on the highway for the traffic to achieve this charming weathering. But yes, they are beautiful, so I'll give you four hundred dollars for them. And if you argue any more the price will drop to three fifty.'

Sarah can't help but be drawn to the voice. Deep, with a trace of an accent she can't place. It reminds her of Elias's deep monotone. She reprimands herself for being so foolish, blushing over her cup of sweet tea at the sound of a deep voice.

'No, sir, of course, sir, four hundred is a good price, for you, sir, you are a good customer, sir, we make you special price.'

'And you can wrap them for me? I leave tonight and I'd like to take them with me.'

'Yes, sir, we will make a strong wrapping for you.'

The voices are coming closer. Sarah tries to interest herself again in the stack of carpets on the floor.

'Well, well, and what brings a nice girl like you to a seedy place like this?'

Elias is striding towards her carrying a stack of carpets over one shoulder. She recognises the pale shirt that has been shadowing her morning.

'You've been following me!'

'Well yes, okay, I'll admit I did notice you listening earnestly to the Maiden's tower story and didn't want to interrupt. But when I saw you come in here, I thought I'd better come and help you haggle.'

'But why not come in with me?'

'You came in the tourist door. I always go through the back. Force of habit, and that's where they keep all the best stock.'

Sarah's body jumps to attention as he squeezes onto the chair next to her the smell of his skin, the warmth of his shoulders, all remind her of their ill-judged but delicious evening of pleasure.

He gestures to the large pile of carpets spread out in front of her. 'I hope you haven't allowed yourself to be taken in by all of Samir's stories. Ladies in the villages pining after their loved ones in the war, has he given you that one yet? Of course it's a more romantic image than Iranian refugees darning away in a dingy room upstairs, but don't let yourself be taken in by it all. Our friend Samir here is a master storyteller, but he has never been one to let the truth interfere with the beauty of his tales.'

Samir looks sheepish and sets to work refolding the carpets. Sarah's attention is drawn to a stack of rugs near the door. They have a long pile and catch the light with a garish gleam. The patterns are less delicate than the others, the colours busier. They remind her of something, but she can not immediately place what. They are nothing like any of the pieces she saw at the exhibition. Is it the carpet in her cabin on the train? The bright magenta hue of the red dye sticks in her mind.

'Mr Elias you are unkind to my beautiful things. If you did not think they were wonderful, then you would not buy so many of them. My dear,' he says turning to Sarah, 'if I had known you were a friend of Mr Elias I would not have started with these ones. These are beautiful, but not the most special. I apologise, I should have known as soon as I saw you outside you were most special. Please, allow me to show you what we have in the next room.'

'Where are those from?' Sarah asks, pointing at the shiny pile.

'No please, those are not for you. We keep these for some of our clients who want to pay bottom dollar for top silk.' He picks one up and runs his finger through the long pile.

'You mean cheap viscose,' Elias says.

Samir responds with a pained nod. 'These, I will admit, are not made by hand. You see the coarseness of the pattern,' he points to a flower that had a chunky pixelated finish, 'they are

169

mass-produced. Made in Russia. We have to cater for all tastes.' Carelessly, he rolls it up and flings it to the floor.

Seeing it lying on the floor, a hastily rolled tube, Sarah realises where she has seen it before. Irakli's delivery at the foundation office had precisely that shade of artificial red, the same sheen of fake silk. It must have been from a similar batch. How could he claim he was bringing it straight from the weavers in the mountains if it was cheap crap made in Russia?

Elias jumps in. 'I think my most special friend has probably seen enough of your carpets for today and she looks like she is in need of some fresh air. Anyway, we have an important lunch date, and we must not be late. Shall we?' He stands up and offers Sarah his hand. 'I promise I'll bring her back next time we're in town. I'll come by later for the carpets. Thank you, Samir, it has been a pleasure, as always.' With that, he leads Sarah out of the shop, still casually holding her hand as they walk down the street.

Elias leads her through the back streets of the old city, around corners and down alleyways until Sarah has lost her sense of direction and is surprised when they arrive back at the sea front. She keeps her eyes open, making sure the battered magazine is visible to everyone they pass, remembering reluctantly she is still on duty. But surely even bait worms need their lunch? They enter an unmarked doorway and Elias leads her up to a terrace with a few metal tables and a panoramic view of the Maiden's Tower and the sea.

'You sit here with the view; I'm happy just looking at the most beautiful woman in Baku. What are you doing here anyway?'

'I wanted to ask you the same thing—I thought you were up in the mountains?'

'I was, but the weather changed suddenly and we had to turn back. There are no prizes for bravery in the mountains when the conditions aren't right, only body bags. I tried to look you up in Tbilisi, but they told me you had left. I was rather hoping you would have called.'

'How did you look me up?'

'I walked the streets with a billboard asking for the address of the girl with the emerald eyes until I found your house.'

Sarah is caught between laughter and incredulity. 'You did what?'

'Well, what was I supposed to do? You didn't leave me your number and you didn't call mine.'

'But, how…?'

'Don't worry, I went to the embassy and asked where they had snaffled away their foxy blonde. They didn't want to tell me at first, I'm sure this must happen all the time.'

'You did not!'

'No need to look so worried, I'm teasing. I was very professional, entirely in keeping with talking to a servant of Her Majesty. Anyway, they told me you had gone away so, somewhat crestfallen, I decided to come here. I had some business to take care of and always enjoy the chance to spend a few days here. And what brings you here, other than looking at overpriced carpets?'

'The Baku Energy Forum tomorrow.'

'I thought you were looking at hopeless Foundations? What has that got to do with big bad oil?'

'That's what I'm here to find out.'

'You're trailing Skarparov across the Caucasus?' Elias asks, his face twisted in mock-disapproval.

'No,' Sarah says a little too forcefully, uncomfortable by how close Elias's teasing is to the truth. 'I'm on the look out for more hopeless foundations to add to my collection.'

Elias calls over the waiter.

'What would you like?' he asks Sarah. 'I can recommend everything.'

Sarah studies the endless list of unfamiliar names. 'Surprise me.'

*

171

The food arrives, a wide spread of small dishes with salads and cold dips, rice wrapped in vine leaves and a bottle of white wine dripping with condensation. Sarah is not used to drinking this early in the day and intends to go back to research what she was supposed to know about the oil pipeline. Lunchtime boozing is unlikely to make the Energy Forum any more enticing. But Elias diligently keeps her glass filled and somehow the bottle quickly disappears.

'What first brought you to Baku?' she asks.

'Oil. I was twenty-two, straight out of university and wanting to get my hands dirty.' Sarah finds herself surprised that Elias has done something so prosaic as attend a university.

'A friend of a friend of the family chartered state-owned oil tankers out there,' he gestures towards the sea, 'so I went to work for them. Dirty business, but what a cast of characters. Half of the crew were Russians: hard working committed alcoholics with fantastically filthy language. That's where I learnt all of my best Russian swearing. It's a real art form, the levels of obscenity you can layer into a single insult. But they worked hard, and I learned a lot about the business, and it gave me a taste for the Caucasus. I hadn't even discovered Georgia at that point, but I was already falling in love.'

Sat in the sunshine above the harbour, the wine going straight to her head, Sarah listens to Elias tell his unlikely stories and slips once more into the happy insouciance that took her in the mountains. She knows that allowing herself to get drunk with a mysterious foreigner twice within the first week of a mission is an elementary mistake. But she cannot bring herself to do the sensible thing—thank him for lunch and go back to her hotel to sober up. He makes her feel bold. He tickles her imagination with his stories and teasing and he seems to bring the best out of her with his disarming questioning and curiosity. They linger over their lunch until all the plates have been picked clean and the waiter brings them the bill, keen to be rid of them to prepare for the evening setting.

They leave the restaurant and wander through the streets of the old city, washed with the lazy glow of lunchtime drinking, grinning widely and giggling at nothing in particular. Elias yawns. 'I think I'm due an afternoon nap, what about you?'

'My hotel is not far, I came by foot,' Sarah says, outraged by her own boldness.

'Lead the way.'

*

As soon as the lift doors close, Elias sweeps his arm around her waist and pulls her in.

'Wait,' she wriggles out of the embrace. 'What if they have cameras in here?'

'What if they do? That poor boy on reception looked like he could do with a bit of excitement. I'm sure he's seen worse things than a girl being kissed in a lift.'

They hurry from the lift into her small bedroom and after a quick check that she has not left anything out that he should not see, she pulls him down on top of her. He undresses her, taking his time with each button and clasp, his touch careful and confident. The curtains are open, and the afternoon sunlight pools across the bed.

Tenderly, they explore—he traces the curve of her back with a fingertip, following up with his lips. Her skin calls out under his touch. They make love softly, urgently, pausing at moments to smile at each other in disbelief until sated and slaked, they fall deeply asleep.

When Sarah awakes, it is already dark outside. She looks at Elias's long and lean body, amazed that he is real, amazed that he is here. He is sleeping with one leg thrown proprietorially over hers, his face at peace with a trace of a smile around the mouth as if enjoying a good dream. As she reaches out to stroke his apricot skin, his eyes open and he grins, folding her into arms.

'Did you sleep well, beautiful nightjar?' he whispers in her ear.

'Blissfully. It was a good idea of yours to come back for a sleep.'

'I'm pretty sure it was your idea.'

'Mine? Couldn't have been. I'd never have been so presumptuous,' Sarah says, trying to disentangle herself from his arms as he pulls her in more tightly.

This man is unlike anyone she has come across before—the confidence, the brashness, the gentleness of his touch. The playful joking and poetic declaration of feeling, all delivered with the same deep and unwavering voice. She is drawn to him, intrigued by him. When he is not there the world seems dull and characterless by comparison. But as much as her heart seeks him out, is hungry for more, her head is ringing the alarm. Do people like him actually exist? Is there a place in the world for philosophising, story-spinning, carpet-buying mountain men who appear in the least likely of locations?

He releases her from the embrace and pulls his shirt across his shoulders.

'Where are you going?' she asks.

'I have to leave tonight, back to Tbilisi, and if we are lucky with the weather, on to the mountains for another shot at that pass. My plane leaves in just over an hour so I won't have time to pick up those carpets. Will you bring them for me? It would make me very happy to know you are looking after something that is mine.'

'Of course, I'll pick them up tomorrow. I'll even try and wangle another hundred off the price if you like—I think I had Samir sussed.'

'I don't suppose I can persuade you to come with me now? I've got stacks of carpets in my house in Tbilisi, you could take your pick which you want to take with you to turn our tent into the abode of a Bedouin sheikh?'

'I'd love to, but I have to be here. The Energy Forum—'

'Of course, your seedy little Azeri. I am getting rather fed up with playing second fiddle to a man in a shiny suit. I'll have to work on my powers of persuasion. I'll be back in Tbilisi sometime next week. Call me when you get back or I'll have to come and make another scene at the embassy.'

'It might be worth it just to see you attempting your charm on that strait-laced receptionist. Good luck in the mountains.'

'When the mountains decide to take you, there is not much you can do to prevent it. But it's not a bad way to go if you have to die young.'

'Well please try not to, not just yet.'

'Don't worry, Sarah, everything is bliss and happiness. You must laugh throughout. And if you die, you die well. See you in beautiful 'blisi.'

He bends down to kiss her, his hand stroking the nape of her neck. She pulls the sheet up, suddenly conscious of her nakedness.

'No, don't,' gently he pulls the sheet away. 'I want the image that stays in my head to be of you in a glorious state of undress.' He kisses her again and leaves.

CHAPTER 25

THE MOBILE PHONE

'Here, take this,' The Castle hands over a small blue handset. The rubbery buttons are grimy around the edges and the numbers beginning to fade.

The Pawn takes it and instinctively pulls off the battery cover, lifts up the battery and checks the SIM card. No visible evidence of tampering. It would need a thorough clean.

'Use it,' The Castle instructs.

'When?'

'Just use it as you would any phone, make calls. They may be listening so act normal.'

'What if I don't want to be listened to?'

'Call your mother, complain about the dinner. I don't care. Make it up. It's more about making a record. Even if they aren't listening, they'll look through the call logs.'

'And if I want to talk to you?'

'There's a number in there you can use to talk to me. Never use my other one again—clear? Delete it from your other phone.

You never had it. From now on, this is how you reach me. But remember, watch what you say.'

The Pawn opens the contacts—he scrolls down to find the Castle, listed along with a string of other names he doesn't know. 'Who are all the others?'

'Probably people we made up. Don't worry too much about them. Remember to use it, make it look like it's your normal phone. And make sure it's the only one you're carrying on the day.'

CHAPTER 26

Nec3 dxe5

The British Oil and Gas (BOG) Pumping Station stands out along the desolate coastline south of Baku, the head of the pipeline that snakes a thousand miles through the Caucasus to Turkey's Mediterranean coast. Sarah watches from the car window as the city vanishes into a faceless grey desert, rimmed by the Caspian with its rainbow sheen. The terminal lurks in a crater, flattened out of the dusty moonscape as if by nuclear explosion. Workers in fluorescent yellow overalls swarm the site, planting trees, laying turf and putting in place the finishing touches for the opening celebrations. Sarah is impressed by the size and scale of the installation—vats, cylinders, tanks and miles and miles of piping, arranged in brightly coloured loops and curves. Would Ibragimov really be bold enough to target such a massive installation? And if so, where? Here at the terminal would make the biggest bang, but anywhere along its length would have the same effect. A thousand miles gives plenty of options.

'You're with the embassy team?' a girl with a glossy blow-dry asks in an American accent, flicking her pen down her clipboard. 'Please wear your badge at all times. The program will start in the main hall in ten minutes.' She speaks with business-like efficiency, polite but disinterested. She is the only other female in sight.

Sarah has opted for the well-cut, conservative black suit from the holdall. Having never worn a proper suit, she feels like a child in her mother's clothes, but she is glad to blend in with the army of dark jackets and blazers. She rearranges her dog-eared copy of *The Economist*, trying to cinch it casually under her arm as she wanders the crowds.

The hall is decorated with a dazzling array of safety posters— bright-eyed workers celebrating their full complements of fingers and toes and young children successfully crossing roads. Hard hats in every colour. Thick honey-coloured oil, pouring out of a large Perspex pipe, foams into a fountain like the centrepiece of Willy Wonka's Oil Refinery.

She spots a table in the reception area bearing ranks of name tags and scans the names and titles, trying to form a picture of who is here and who is representing who. As she reaches across to straighten one of the rows, a pale hand grasps her arm. She looks up, *Economist* at the ready, to see a distinctly English-looking man—large nose, small pinched mouth and troubled eyes that look like he's been haunted for years by the feeling that he's forgotten something. Gripping her wrist, he is shaking her arm in an awkward greeting. 'You must be Sarah; I'm told we have a mutual friend called Michael.'

Sarah's pulse quickens, is this the approach? 'Yes.' She casts around for how she could possibly mention a pomegranate.

'Didn't mean to startle you, I'm Hayden Blaine, the British Ambassador to Azerbaijan.' Sarah releases her breath. 'Sorry I wasn't able to meet you personally when you arrived, Jim told me I might find you here.'

'Your Excellency,' Sarah removes her hand from his odd

grasp, 'Michael told me to track you down.'

Hayden nods, smoothing his perfectly parted hair with his hand. 'I spoke to Michael last night and was filled in on some essentials. I'm happy to help in whichever way we can.'

Sarah is relieved that the British Ambassador in Baku seems a little more clued-up than his counterpart in Tbilisi.

'Have you made contact yet?' he asks.

'Not yet. I ran into Skarparov at the ballet, but I don't think he can have been Ibragimov's source.'

'Skarparov? Working with Ibragimov? Surely not. They seem to go out of their way to avoid each other. I don't see why Ibragimov would be using him.'

Sarah nods, disappointed with another confirmation of what her conversation with Skarparov had suggested. She's still reluctant to accept that Irakli could be the only useful link to Ibragimov but it's starting to look inevitable. 'Michael asked me to get close to Skarparov as a way into Ibragimov.'

'You were told to approach Skarparov?' Hayden looks sceptical. 'I don't see what help he'll be, given the urgency. But I'm sure Mike must have his reasons.' Hayden cranes his neck around the busy venue. 'Anyway, Ibragimov is here so you can make a direct approach. Always easier to cut out the middleman.'

'Can you point him out?' Surrounded by the fanfare for the opening of this geopolitical asset, the gravity of the threat feels more real than it had over a restaurant table in London. The pipeline is the fruit of a new era of cooperation and stability, an opening to the West that would not have been possible ten years ago. But such a valuable asset is by its nature vulnerable: an explosively high-profile target to anyone wanting to threaten that change.

Hayden looks at his watch. 'I've not got long; I left the Grand Old Duke of York's team with the President's protocol people hammering out what he will and won't do at the big pipeline opening shindig in a couple of weeks.'

'The Grand Old who?'

'Prince Andrew. He's our secret weapon. They love him out here. His team are doing an advance visit to agree on photo ops and make sure he avoids having to wear any silly hats. I'm supposed to be looking after them. Let's go through to the coffee area outside the VIP section. That's where most of the real business happens. Here, cover up your badge a moment.'

Sarah slips her name tag into her jacket as the Ambassador guides her elegantly through the security cordon to the VIP area where the hot shots come to see and be seen. The room is walled with heavy, blue velvet curtains which, in the dim lighting, cast a ghoulish glow across the faces of the delegates. The status of each attendee can be gauged by the numbers of hangers-on in their orbit, assistants scanning the room for potential contacts, wide-necked security agents ponderously circling.

Sarah spots Skarparov with two very glamorous young girls on his arm, presumably his daughters. Their glossy manes and cocktail dresses look ludicrously out of place in a room of dark suits. One is dark and a little horsey, her eyes blank in a perfectly made-up face as she scans the room for potential money-matches. The other is blonde and looks as if she has far more going on behind her eyes—a copy of her father's unlikely pale green. Scuttling around Skarparov, whispering occasional cues into his ear, is a small man Sarah assumes must be his chief flunky. The man's sharp, pointed features and creeping, obsequious posture make Sarah think of a rat, sniffing around for tasty snippets of information and delivering them into his master's ear, hoping for praise. His dark eyes look distrusting and harried and Sarah can't imagine why you would want such a person hanging around you. Perhaps having a "bad cop" on hand allows Skarparov to more easily keep up his well-mannered act.

Skarparov catches Sarah's eye and raises his glass of tea in greeting. She nods in return, wondering whether to approach him to pick up where they left off at the opera, or wait for the real target.

A white-haired man with a gnomish grin and round glasses

expounds the virtues of the pipeline, his top-level status signalled by his face, conspicuously powdered for the stage. 'It's a genuine marvel of engineering, crossing mountain ranges, fourteen active earthquake faults, extremes of temperature and altitude…' His audience nod enthusiastically, their moustaches stretching as they smile.

'That's Ibragimov over there.'

Sarah follows the direction of Hayden's nod. Ibragimov is holding court at a glass table, surrounded by acolytes, huddled in deep leather armchairs. He has an unnatural gap between his nose and his top lip as if something is missing, but the stretch gives his face a certain grandeur. There is a yellowing tinge to his skin, taken from the same colour palette as his brown suit, carefully styled for another era. His thinning hair is dyed auburn and held in place with a thick layer of lacquer. His benevolent smile expresses both his dissatisfaction with all around him and the comfortable knowledge that he has the power to change it.

'He looks like a dinosaur,' Sarah whispers.

'Yes, and a nasty piece of work by all accounts. All those who flourished at the time of his peak had to have a mindset of hierarchy and suspicion and be familiar with the dirtier ways of making money. But he was known to be especially ruthless. He once controlled the lamb import licences from the US and China, then spread rumours of a "fake" foot and mouth outbreak to boost his business. When that didn't work, he unleashed the real disease into several herds throughout the Caucasus.'

Keeping her eye on Ibragimov, Sarah moved the Ambassador towards the edge of the crowd where they could talk without being overheard.

'Bit odd him being here, isn't it, if he's planning on blowing the whole thing up?' she asks.

'Well,' Hayden seems flustered, 'we don't really know what he's planning. Men from the old regime are notoriously difficult to approach through official channels. Then out of the blue we get this strange message, purporting to be from him. And of course the train derailment.'

'Was he definitely behind it?'

'We're almost certain. They've released some more details on the passenger lists. According to local police, two people who bought tickets were unaccounted for after the accident. Their names are probably fake, but we've traced the purchase of their tickets to a small company in Nakhchivan.' Hayden's eyes light up as he reveals his nugget. 'Turns out the company is a subsidiary of one of Ibragimov's businesses.' He studies his coffee, stirring as he speaks, slipping the words out under cover of innocuous conversation. 'I assume Michael told you about the "Russian deliveries"?'

'The weapons?'

Hayden coughs loudly.

'Also for Ibragimov?' Sarah asks.

'So it would seem.'

'Do we have anyone's word for it, other than the agent on the train?'

A waiter in red velvet waistcoat carrying a tower of tulip-shaped tea glasses pushes up uncomfortably close to Sarah, smelling of hair oil and turmeric, proffering a glass of tea with a lecherous smile. The stack of glasses hover over her at an impossible angle yet somehow maintain their precarious balance. She backs away from his greasy grin and waits as he swings his improbable turret on to the next group.

Sarah draws Hayden back towards the edge of the room where the velvet drapes help muffle their conversation. The room feels uncomfortably full of eyes and ears. 'What if it's not the pipeline? What if he has something else entirely planned for his newly acquired arsenal?'

'It could be a straightforward power grab. Ibragimov was a powerful ally of Aliyev Senior, the current president's father. But these days he has fallen out of the inner circle. For the last few years, he has been steadily stripped of his official roles and thus of his clout and influence. It would be hardly surprising if he sought ways to reverse that trend.'

Sarah's mind turns through the possibilities, but it's too much to take in. How has she been thrown into this? Two weeks ago her biggest concern was where to find the obscure book Jenny wanted for her birthday. How did she go from rifling through second-hand shelves to weighing up the likelihood of a coup in just a fortnight? 'So you think he might be planning to use the weapons to attack the President?' she manages to ask.

'Perhaps.' Hayden's words are clipped, his narrow mouth barely moves but his troubled eyes express a growing urgency. 'But either way we need to find out now. There are just over two weeks left until the big shindig. The great and the good will all be here, including HRH, and we have to rule out any chance that it could be the target. I understood that this was your mission?'

The question is designed to sting, but Sarah disarms it with a smile. 'It is, and I appreciate all the help you can give.' Surely this can't all fall to her? They must have someone better placed, better connected or just more familiar with the region. Sarah wonders if this is just a growing sense of imposter syndrome or if there is a reason no one else wants to touch it.

Hayden stiffens, fixing in place a professionally courteous smile. A man in a tight navy blazer, gold buttons straining, is elbowing his way in their direction. Their spot at the edge of the room offers no escape.

'Ah, Sergei, I thought I would run into you here,' Hayden says, smoothing his brow with a fingertip.

Sergei squeezes the Ambassador's hand while holding his elbow in a tight grip. His face is pink and shiny like a boiled ham, his clove-black eyes lit by a mischievous smile.

'And I bet you were hoping you would get away first.' Sergei gives a fat laugh, still clutching the Ambassador's arm.

'No, no, of course not.' Hayden's chin seems to retreat into his neck. 'It's always a pleasure,' he looks to Sarah for help.

'May I introduce Sarah; she's visiting from Tbilisi. Sarah, this is Sergei Babikov, the country Chairman of Lukoil in Azerbaijan.'

Sarah holds out her hand. 'Pleased to meet you.'

'Tbilisi? You don't look like a Georgian, luckily for you!' He kisses her hand before turning back to the Ambassador. 'Now tell me, dear Hayden, is there truth in what I have been hearing about your lobbying efforts? Because none of us would be very happy to know that you were trying to get your hands on a bigger piece of the pie without us all being allowed a taste.' He oozes with delight at sticking the needle in.

'Dear Sergei, I trust you understand how this all works.' Hayden fiddles furiously with the spoon on the edge of his coffee cup. 'You know as well as I do that these are nothing more than rumours. I don't know where they came from, but I assure you they have nothing to do with us.'

'Ah, but you are British, so I can't expect you to tell me the truth anyway, could I?' He slaps Hayden on the back. 'You're so reserved. Who knows what you are up to under that stiff upper lip, eh?' he says, jabbing the Ambassador in the chest.

Hayden blinks twice, summoning his composure. 'I assure you; we always like to be frank with our friends.'

'Ha! That's good,' Sergei turns to Sarah, still laughing. 'His Excellency has a silver tongue. Well, Hayden, I do hope you count us among your *friends* and don't do anything,' he pauses, moistening his lips, 'that would jeopardise that friendship.'

'Of course.' Hayden gives a gentle nod. 'Good to see you, Sergei. Enjoy the forum. Do excuse us, we have an appointment.' He leads Sarah into the crowd.

'What was that about?' Sarah asks when they were out of earshot.

'Nothing really, at least I hope it's nothing. There is a rather persistent rumour doing the rounds that we've been lobbying the government to reopen our production sharing agreement— BOG's, I mean—to give them a greater share of the resources, at the expense of some of the other producers. There's no truth in it, but I keep being questioned about it. And our Russian friends delight in teasing us whenever there is a suggestion of reputational risk. Nothing they like better than a good scandal.'

'Any idea who is spreading the rumour?' Sarah stands well back out of the path of another waiter brandishing a large teapot.

'Any of the other oil companies could benefit by putting us on the back foot. Especially now—with the opening of this pipeline, BOG are in the spotlight. The press here are not the most professional bunch, they're happy to pass on rumours without troubling to check facts. It could even have started within government itself. There is a strong pro-nationalisation lobby who want to see all the deals ripped up and control given back to the state oil company. In short, any number of people have good reason to try and weaken our position.'

Hayden makes a grab for her arm. Alarmed by his sudden force, Sarah spots a small man with statement red-framed glasses making a beeline for them. Hayden acknowledges him with an apologetic wave, gesturing to his watch, before pulling Sarah behind a massive metal installation in the middle of the room and out of sight. The man with the glasses looks bemused by the manoeuvre but allows the Ambassador to escape.

'Who was that?' Sarah asks, inching through the middle of a giant replica of a cross-section of the pipeline, buffed to a gleaming shine.

'Oh dear, was it really that obvious?'

'It wasn't the most subtle of retreats, you nearly pulled my arm off.'

'I'm sure he's used to it, especially in this crowd. He's one of the new government advisers. Quite junior but loud and, for the time being, very influential. He's the leading voice calling for renegotiation of oil agreements. We'd never be able to put those rumours to bed if I were seen talking to him, here of all places.'

Sarah stares at her reflection in the gleaming metal, grossly distorted by the curvature of the giant wall and reflected into twisted infinity by the back wall of the tube. The dwarfing effect makes her dizzy and she reaches to the wall for support, edging her way along the slippery, cold pipe to the opening. But just as she's about to return to the comfort of flat ground, she catches sight of Ibragimov's stooped figure, silhouetted against the light. She freezes, unsure whether to approach him or shrink back into the tunnel. Hayden has disappeared out of the other end of the pipe. Leaning back into the rounded wall she watches Ibragimov, her eye falling on his shiny teeth and unusually long, sharp canines. His face is composed, but his eyes roam the room as he delivers an irritable series of instructions to his assistant, backing up his words with a series of short stabs to the assistant's kidneys with a silver pen.

'There you are.' A skull-like face appears at the far end of the tunnel. Sarah is thrown by the ghostly apparition who appears to be talking to her, until she recognises the sharply-angled suit—Jim, the intelligence officer from the embassy. He makes a grab for Sarah's arm, but she's had it with being manhandled and bats him away.

He looks shocked at her insubordination. 'This way,' he hisses, leading her to a meeting room at the edge of the VIP area where the Ambassador is waiting. He slams the door behind them, leaning his insubstantial weight against it. 'Ibragimov is here, have you approached him?' His breath is short and laboured.

'I was just—'

'We really don't have time to lose,' Jim continues in an urgent whisper. 'We know the weapons have left Russia. An attack could be imminent and you're wasting time waiting for him to come to you. Sir?'

'I was—' Sarah tries again.

'I have to say I agree with you, Jim.' Hayden fixes Sarah with his troubled eyes. 'We don't have time to wait.'

'Look, you've got to go straight to Ibragimov,' Jim continues, 'Get close to him—'

Sarah is fit to explode. 'If you would just let me get on with it instead of holding me here fretting.' Sarah pushes the two men out of the way and storms out of the door to find Ibragimov.

CHAPTER 27

bxc5 exf4

Sarah races back to where she last saw Ibragimov, but he's vanished. She returns to the lounge area where she had first seen him holding court, but the space is deserted. All the delegates have moved on. Waiters shuffle between the high tables, removing empty cups and discarded napkins. She roams the conference venue, trying not to look as harried as she feels, until finally she sees him. Amongst the crowds of people gathering by the exit, his distinctive brown suit is unmistakable. She pushes her way through his hangers-on and walks straight up to him, grabbing hold of the first excuse she can think of for making such a bold approach. 'Mr Ibragimov? Do excuse my intrusion, I know you are a busy man. I wonder if I might have a few minutes of your time.'

Ibragimov glances at his gatekeeper, clearly surprised that she has not been intercepted. The assistant, small sharp teeth bared, shoots her a vicious stare. He moves in as if to barrel her away from the boss, but Ibragimov calls him off. He's intrigued.

Sarah offers her hand. Her pulse soars at the touch of his large liver-spotted hand in hers. She turns up her smile, hoping to cover the rush of responses provoked by finally finding herself in front of him. The epicentre of the threat—the man ruthless enough to introduce a disease for his own financial gain; brutal enough to stage a train crash to kill the agent who reported on him; and the recipient of a major arsenal of weapons for use in another imminent attack. What she would give to peer inside his head, to see the world as he sees it, to understand what makes him tick. Is he the only one who knows the extent of what he has planned? Sarah wonders how many others he can trust to carry out his dirty work. The tools available to her to communicate as a stranger feel woefully inadequate. How can she hope to understand this man, standing before her with the refined poise of a *grand seigneur*, clicking the sharp tip of his silver pen? It would take weeks to win his trust. She only has minutes.

'How may I be of service?' his words are muffled by heavy lips and a lazy tongue.

Sarah's cheeks quiver with the effort to hold up the smile while choosing the appropriate attack. 'My name is Lisa Spalding; I am a freelance journalist and I'm working on a story about family business empires in Azerbaijan. I was wondering if you might consider giving me a little of your time to share your thoughts?'

Ibragimov considers her, a curious smile creeps over his elongated face, his eyes inscrutable.

'You would like to interview me?'

'Well, it need not be as structured as an interview; just an informal chat to hear your views.' Sarah channels Lisa's imaginary boldness.

'I do not speak to the press,' he replies flatly, the half-smile still in place.

'I know you are not a fan of journalists, but I was hoping you might consider making an exception.' She slips in one of Michael's half-winks. 'This will be a positive piece. I want to illustrate the success of some of the leading family-run businesses in Azerbaijan, and explore how the culture lends itself to this model.' She congratulates herself on this moment of improvisation while thinking ahead for what to do if he refuses. 'It would be a chance to showcase the elements of your company of which you are most proud.'

'And if I say no?' Ibragimov asks. 'Will it still be a positive piece?'

'If you say no, it would be my professional duty to ask again.' Sarah steps a little closer, bringing her fingertips to the ends of her hair.

Ibragimov laughs, looking across to his right-hand man who watches them impatiently.

'What do you think? Should I talk to this lady?'

The assistant mumbles something about another appointment.

'It really shouldn't take too long,' Sarah insists.

Ibragimov studies Sarah as if weighing up his options. Finally he raises his thick lips into his satisfied smile that reveals his prominent canines. 'Do you need a lift back into town Miss…' He looks down at her chest for her name badge.

Sarah dives for her bag, ensuring the fall of her jacket conceals her DFID identification. 'Please call me Lisa.' She straightens up, clutching a notebook to her chest.

'Lisa, of course.' He pauses. 'Well, Lisa, I have to be back in Baku this afternoon and, as my colleague will no doubt remind me, I have a full schedule for the rest of the day. But perhaps you could join us in the car? Then you could ask me your questions and I could, what was it again, put forward my best side?'

Sarah feels a warm rush to her stomach. She could not have wished for a better opening than to spend time alone with Ibragimov and his close advisors. He's unlikely to give anything away during their journey, but it's a perfect start to get a handle on what sort of creature she is dealing with.

'Thank you, that would be perfect. I promise I won't let you down.'

'No,' he smiles his warm, calculated smile again. 'I'm sure

you will be most kind. Please allow me a moment, I need to say goodbye to a few people before we leave. Perhaps if you wouldn't mind waiting for us outside?'

'Of course, take your time; I'll be ready when you are.'

Sarah stands outside the front exit, scarcely able to believe the success of her last-minute cover story. She had expected a journalist to be brushed off immediately, but it was the best she could think of with no time to plan. Under her DFID cover she had no reason to connect herself to him, or to ask him the kind of questions that a journalist could get away with. She waits at the door watching the dark-suited VIPs ducking into limousines, lower-level flunkeys looking for transport back into town and journalists dismantling their equipment before hurrying back to file their stories.

As the crowds continue to thin, she can't help but wonder if she has been brushed off. Did he prefer to let her down discreetly, saving the embarrassment of a direct refusal by quietly slipping away through another door? Just as she is losing hope, Ibragimov appears, carrying a briefcase.

'Sorry, Ms Lisa. I hope I didn't keep you too long.'

'Not at all.' His assistant is no longer with him.

'Follow me, I have a car waiting.' He leads Sarah across the car park to a black SUV and opens the back door for her. She scoots across the seat, expecting him to climb in after her, but he stands outside, looking down at her, smiling benevolently.

'Well, Sarah, my driver will make sure you get safely back.' She is rocked by a wave of nausea. Had she misheard him, or had he just called her Sarah?

'You're not coming?'

She wants to disappear into the seat.

'Don't look so sad; you tried your best.' He places the briefcase on her lap. She stares at it, unable to move.

'You can give this to Michael.' He taps the briefcase, drawing out the name with his heavy tongue and deep nicotine-stained voice, then closes the door.

Sarah stares at the case, half expecting it to explode in her lap. The door opens again, and another man climbs in beside her. She recognises the red-rimmed glasses immediately—the government adviser that the Ambassador went to such pains to avoid.

He gawps at Sarah. 'I thought this was Mr Ibragimov's car? Who are you?'

'I'm sorry,' Sarah tries to open the door. 'I think there's been a misunderstanding.'

She is fumbling for the handle when the door whips open and a camera lens pushes in, shutter snapping. The government adviser looks as panicked and confused as she is. The photographer outside lines up another shot, crouching level with them and blocking their exit. Sarah instinctively hugs the briefcase to her chest, hiding her ID pass, while searching for an escape. Another journalist at the opposite window is now angling his lens into the car. She ducks her head into the footwell, pulls off her ID badge and tries to scramble into the front seat without having a camera pointed up her skirt. Suddenly a strong hand pulls her arm and a deep voice orders her out of the car.

CHAPTER 28

c6 bxc6

Sarah recognises the voice with astonished relief. 'Elias? What are you doing here?'

He pulls her up, shielding her from the journalists with his broad shoulders. 'I'm going to try and get you out of this. Come on, we're going to have to hurry.'

Elias half-drags, half-carries her across the car park, keeping her head closely tucked into his chest and pushing away the camera lenses that follow. He pushes her into the back of a battered yellow taxi and jumps in the front passenger seat. 'Tural! Go!' he shouts. The driver, a shock of long white hair falling into his eyes, throws the car into gear, brimming with excitement.

Through the back window, half-obscured by a thick carpet and a large box of tissues, Sarah watches the photographers still gathered around Ibragimov's car taking pictures of the government adviser cowering in the back seat. Ibragimov himself is nowhere to be seen. Elias gives instructions to the driver in rapid Russian, pointing out the quickest exit while Sarah checks for a tail. She realises she is still clinging onto Ibragimov's briefcase. What did he mean by saying she should give it to Michael?

They hurtle over a speed bump towards the exit, windows rattling and suspension screaming as they land with a thump in front of a pair of shocked security guards. Before the pair have time to react, they are speeding down the main highway along the coastal road back to Baku.

'What the hell just happened?' Sarah asks, still shaking. 'What are you even doing here?'

'I was about to ask you the same thing. How did you manage to get yourself into the centre of a media circus? And who was that creep in the car?'

'A government adviser, one of the lobbyists for reopening the oil and gas deals. The Ambassador went out of his way to avoid him.'

'Which is presumably why the press were so interested in you getting into a car with him. What were you thinking?' Elias watches the road, urging the driver to overtake whenever possible.

'I didn't know he was going to be there. I was supposed to be getting in the car with Ibragimov. And you were supposed to be leaving yesterday?'

'Ibragimov? Why the hell would you do that?'

'I wanted to…' Sarah stops herself. She is deeply relieved to see Elias, but can't let that throw her off guard. 'The Ambassador suggested I should take the opportunity to talk to Ibragimov as part of my research.'

Elias looks unimpressed. 'The Ambassador sent you into that car?'

'No, he sent me to talk to Ibragimov. I fell for the car trick; I should have known it was too good to be true.' As she speaks, she feels the tug of doubt. Could there be truth behind Elias's suspicions? Hayden and Jim had pushed her to follow Ibragimov immediately. Could they have known what he was planning?

'And what's in the briefcase?' Elias asks.

'I have no idea; Ibragimov gave it to me.'

'Hadn't you better open it up?'

She examines it cautiously, afraid it might be booby-trapped or set to implicate her further in the scandal.

'Go on, I'm curious.' Elias watches her inspect the fastenings. 'Here, I'll do it.' He reaches across and grabs the case.

'No wait—'

He flips open the lid. 'Wow! That's a lot of cash. Hardly very subtle, is he? What are you supposed to be doing with this?'

She peers over Elias's shoulder at the carefully bound stacks of hundred-dollar bills.

'Hardly enough to fund a revolution, but you could have a lot of fun with it.' Elias is laughing. 'What is it for?'

'No idea.' Sarah does not see the funny side. 'Presumably part of the set up. A British official getting into a car with a government adviser might make a good picture but it's a better story with a suitcase full of cash.'

Sarah hopes to dampen Elias's curiosity, but her mind teems with questions. Was it really just a prop for the sting or was it part of a wider deal? Could Michael be expecting it? She recalls Jim's revelation that Michael and Ibragimov had a history and curses herself for not having taken the chance to quiz him further on what he meant.

Elias thumbs through the notes, holding a couple up to the light to inspect the watermarks.

'Is it real?' she asks.

'I don't know. Dollar bills always look like Mickey Mouse money to me, but I think it's real.' He checks the rear-view mirror. 'Damn. That didn't take long. Sit back, we're being followed. We're going to have to try a different route.'

Elias gives rapid instructions to the driver, who pulls the car down a gear while stamping on the accelerator. The ancient vehicle lurches into the outside lane, then dives back across the traffic towards the exit through a shower of car horns and skidding tyres.

They are still in the desert no man's land between the pipeline filling station and the city, the landscape littered with nodding donkeys and oil pumps. The side exit leads to a dusty village of sand-coloured houses and a low-rise mosque. Tural leans out the window to look behind at the chasing cars, then back just in time to swerve out of the path of a wandering goat. The confused-looking animal is left in a cloud of dust as the battered taxi fishtails back on course, sending Sarah skating around the back seat.

The single track tarred-road stops at the last house in the strip—they have reached the end of a cul-de-sac and will have to double back on themselves to find another way out of the village. Sarah can see a dark vehicle pull off the highway, a motorbike following closely behind. But Tural doesn't drop speed, swerving at the final moment before the car crashes into an abandoned garage and bashing through an open wooden gate at the back of the garden onto a gravel track. As the taxi barrels on, Sarah watches the other car slow down at the end of the asphalt. She hopes her pursuers will be forced to turn back, but they're soon on the move again.

The track becomes steadily less clear. Sarah grips the back of the driver's seat, hoping the tyres can take the thrashing across rocks and gravel. Elias points Tural towards a rocky escarpment ahead.

'Do you have any idea where we are?' she asks.

'More or less.' Elias sounds confident, but that might be for her benefit. 'There must have been a coastal road to link these villages before the highway was built, the trick is to find it and hopefully lose some of our hangers-on in the process.'

Sarah leans her head out the window for a better look. Her ears are whipped by the wind, her face stung by the lash of her hair. How can Tural anticipate the bumps in the road at this speed? 'They seem to be multiplying.' A second car has joined, along with at least three motorbikes flinging up a growing cloud dust. 'Who are they?'

'How should I know?' Elias replies. 'It's you they're chasing. Who have you pissed off?'

'Until just now, I thought I was pretty innocuous. I haven't been here long enough to make many enemies.'

Sarah is flung forward as Tural brakes suddenly to soften the blow from a deep rivet in the gravel, almost invisible from a distance. The car slams into the ditch and flies out the other side, the back suspension rearing like a bucking bronco.

'Well, it's fair to assume at least one of them has been sent by Ibragimov. Having set you up, he's also given himself away and will certainly want to keep an eye on you.' Elias takes tighter hold of the briefcase that's sliding off his lap as he braces himself against the thrusting of the car. 'And presumably the contents of this. One of them will be from the Interior Ministry. It might seem like a sleepy little oil town, but it's also a pretty tightly run police state. So whether they are working on behalf of Ibragimov or keeping their eye on him, they'll be watching us now. The bikes must be journalists. Sorry, but we didn't make the most subtle getaway. I wanted to get you out as quickly as possible.'

'I'm glad you did,' Sarah says. 'But if they thought there was a story to chase before, they certainly won't give up now.'

'We're in good hands. Tural has been driving taxis in Baku for thirty years, he'll be able to lose them once we're back in the city.'

'It's a rally driver we need out here.'

The car flies from bump to stomach-churning bump, like a fairground ride stuck at top speed. With each landing, Sarah can feel the chassis twist and torque. She has one hand pushed into the ceiling to protect her head, the other locked against the door panel to anchor herself on the backseat. The fatigued metal beneath her hands feels flimsy and strained. The ancient car was built for city driving, not for flight. But Tural seems oblivious; in fact, he seems to be enjoying it.

'Here.' Elias grabs the wheel, and the car rolls off the track and through an abandoned field, ploughed ridges just visible between rocks and gravel. With an arresting clunk, the whole ceiling panel comes away from the chassis. Sarah's hand is now all that is preventing it from collapsing on their heads. Tural laughs as he bats the flapping edge away from his eyes. Sarah manages to fold the detached piece away from the front seats, clearing the driver's view. The newly exposed metal of the roof amplifies the sound of the doors clattering in their frames and the loose change dancing on the dashboard.

The chasing cars have caught them up. The taxi ducks into a narrow lane between two farm buildings with the cars in close pursuit. The lane ends at a low stone wall. The only way out is back the way they came, but the cars and motorbikes hem them in, blocking their routes for escape. This is it; they're going to have to admit defeat.

'Through there, through there,' Elias shouts, pointing at the wall.

'Are you mad? That's a solid stone wall.' Sarah cranes over the passenger seat to see if there is a hidden gap she's missed. The wall isn't high but it's definitely there and they are heading straight at it. Sarah slams her foot into the floor, pummelling the brake pedal that isn't there, her hands grasp at the door handles. Tural adjusts his grip on the wheel and throws the car on.

The wall hurtles closer, ready to smash into the front bumper. Is Elias mad for suggesting it? Or Tural for following his instructions? Either way they're going to get them all killed. Sarah folds her head between her arms and braces for impact against the back of Elias's seat.

The impact doesn't come. The taxi launches off the final bump and somehow sails straight through the obstacle, the tyres passing over two lower sections where the stones are missing, miraculously avoiding scraping out the car's innards on the bricks between. Tural gives a whoop as they fly on. Sarah's stunned that they are still alive. The two cars behind them draw to a halt.

'That should buy us some time.' Elias appears entirely unruffled by their near-death collision. 'It looks like this track joins up to another road ahead so we should be able to make some speed again soon while they work out how to get round that farm.'

The road, when it comes, is not much wider than the track. The patchy asphalt forces the car to spring and start over the potholes. At least there is less dust. Elias pushes Tural to go faster as Sarah scans the landscape behind them. For the moment, at least, the hangers-on have disappeared. But the relief is short-lived. As they approach the next village, their pursuers are once more closing in.

When the road peters out, Sarah, with growing confidence in Tural's abilities, is quietly looking forward to seeing what unlikely route he will find to escape this time. But Elias motions for him to rejoin the highway. Amongst the traffic entering the city, it becomes more difficult to spot the tail cars, but the little taxi is able to make more speed. They weave through the traffic, Tural accelerating towards stationary cars before pulling into gaps that don't exist, cutting up cars that narrowly miss ploughing into the back of them. With each push of speed, Sarah ducks her head, expecting the car to fly into a spin as it catches a bumper in the closely packed traffic.

They speed through the outskirts of the city, where the maze of oil derricks gives way to low-rise buildings along the Corniche road towards downtown. As they approach the centre, the traffic becomes heavier and, despite Tural's best efforts and masterful shortcuts, he is eventually brought to a halt by a bank of cars stopped at a red light. Sarah can see the tail cars not far behind and the motorcycles threading up towards them. As the lights change, Elias points Tural to the maze of small streets and alleyways of the Old City.

'This isn't going to get any easier.' He gives Sarah a reassuring smile, but his eyes suggest his confidence is beginning to waver. 'Don't worry. Tural knows every shortcut there is.'

They sail through pedestrian zones and barrel the wrong way down one-way streets. Tural handles the car with the grace of an acrobat, oblivious to the screeching of the wheel rims, and the straining of the chassis. The taxi performs like a work mule being forced into a dressage routine. Somehow, even with their unlikely and accomplished manoeuvres, the dark cars still manage to keep pace. Sarah is amazed by Tural's feel for the size of his car; he squeezes it through gaps that look scarcely wide enough for a bike without hesitation. Up ahead, a pavement cafe sprawls across the shared space. Tural leans on the horn, sending pedestrians and bystanders flying, and scattering the patrons of the cafe just in time before the taxi ploughs through, catching one of the cafe tables in front of them like a cattle guard. They push on, sparks flying from the metal table scraping against stone. The road bends round to the right at a sharp angle, but it's too tight to make at the speed they are going, especially with the added length of the table in front. The only option is to carry on straight, thumping down a narrow flight of stairs, tyres slapping against the stone steps, Sarah's teeth chatter together in with her tightly clenched jaw. She can't believe they are still moving. 'Where are we going?' she asks.

'That rather depends on how long it takes to shake them,' Elias says, watching the cars in the wing mirror. 'I was hoping they'd have given up by now but they're a stubborn bunch. Let's try to cut through to the north.' Back on home territory, Tural is no longer taking instructions. He will decide how to drive through the warren of streets and alleyways designed long before the car, diving deeper into the maze.

Elias searches ahead for escape routes. He tries again to direct them, but Tural brushes him off, still grinning as he flies round a corner, two wheels lifting clear off the ground. Suddenly the car pounds to a stop throwing Sarah against the bare-metal roof. A solid concrete barrier blocks the road from edge to edge.

Tural looks dismayed. This barrier is evidently not yet part of his near-perfect mental map of the city. He tries to turn the car but needs several attempts just to edge the nose round. With a shriek of tyres, the other vehicles appear and slam to a halt in front of them. Tural sinks his head into the steering wheel.

Men in dark suits emerge from the cars. Journalists with cameras at the ready push past them to get closer to Sarah, swarming the vehicle. Elias flings open a door, flattening the first to approach the car but there are more. Sarah's door is wrenched open and a hand grabs her, trying to pull her out of the car. Unfamiliar faces fire questions at her that she does not understand. The crowd push closer, shouting and shoving cameras and microphones towards her. Tural sits with his head in his hands. Elias has disappeared.

'Can you confirm you are with the British Embassy?' one of the journalists shouts.

'No.' Sarah thinks quickly. 'I'm just visiting.'

'And who is with you in the car?' The pack thrust forward to get a closer look at the vehicle.

'No one, just the taxi driver, he's taking me back to my hotel.' She does not have to lie this time. There is no sign of Elias anywhere. One of the journalists peers around the passenger door, as if expecting to find a government adviser cowering in the footwell.

'What was in the briefcase?' Another pushes forward, joining the crowd around her like ants on a jam spot.

'What briefcase?' She does her best to look nonplussed.

'The briefcase you were holding.'

'Was it a bribe?' shouts another.

'How much will it cost the British government to get the best deal for BOG?' another jabs his microphone towards Sarah.

'I don't know what you are talking about; I never had a briefcase.' Thankfully the briefcase has disappeared along with Elias. Two of the journalists clamber into the back seat, pulling up the crochet rug that covers the splits in the ancient leather and grabbing for Sarah's handbag. Tural, finally revived, remonstrates with them in Azeri as Sarah tugs her bag out of the journalist's grip.

'That's private property. I don't know who or what you are looking for, but you've made a mistake. I'm just visiting. I never had a briefcase; I'm just trying to get back to my hotel.'

Tural sets on the journalists, chasing them out of the car with a folded newspaper.

Two men appear through the crowd. At their approach, the journalists back off as one, taking some final snaps of Sarah and the taxi before disappearing. One of the new arrivals succeeds in pulling Sarah out of the car.

'You must come with us,' he says in heavily accented English. He is not in uniform and displays no identification. 'You must come,' he repeats, squeezing her arm more tightly.

'Who are you?' Sarah asks.

'We are the police; we take you to the station. Get into the car.'

'Where are your uniforms? Where are your badges?'

'It is better for you to come easily. We do not want to make it difficult.'

With no other option, Sarah allows herself to be pushed into the back of their dark car.

CHAPTER 29

c5 Qa5

Sarah has been staring at the police station wall for three hours. She has studied every crack in the yellowing paint, clocked every cobweb casting soft shadows in the corner and has named the dying fly that buzzes discordantly against the clouded windowpane. The black suits who brought her in have disappeared, leaving her in the care of some more conventional-looking policemen. Having taken down her details, the officers sat her in this airless holding room, soaked in the smell of over-boiled cabbage. And here she stays, mostly ignored, but unable to leave, until the Ambassador arrives.

Hayden's face is pale with concern, or perhaps embarrassment. He is wearing the same blue pinstripe suit from the forum, but his collar is now askew and he has loosened his tie. Sarah can't imagine he ever looks more informal than this. He looks like the type whose dressing gown has a collar and fine creases ironed down the sleeves.

'My goodness, what happened? How did you end up in here?'

Sarah doesn't stand to greet him. She's in no mood for ceremony. Instead she huddles deeper into her bench of curved metal and cracked orange leather, leaving him nowhere to sit. Hayden hovers over her awkwardly, clasping and unclasping his hands.

'How do you think?' she asks. 'Ibragimov set me up.'

'Ibragimov? What did he do?'

'You sent me right into a trap.'

Hayden looks aghast. 'You don't think I set you up for this, do you? Sarah, please, I had no clue he would be out to compromise us. Quite frankly I didn't think we even hit his radar.'

'So it was just bad luck, was it, that you hurry me over to talk to him just as he is planning a sting?' Sarah feels a hot ball of fury rising up her throat.

'I assure you I had no idea. Look, of course you are shaken up and have been through a lot, but please don't place the blame on us. We are on the same side, you and I. You need to trust us, otherwise you are out here entirely on your own.' Sarah does not feel much benefit from his support. 'Can you at least tell me what happened?' he asks, still leaning over her, his tie dangling towards her face.

Sarah shuffles across the bench to make space for him to sit.

'I was with the prince's people when I was told you had been arrested following a car chase in the Meydan. I came at once.'

Sarah watches him with suspicion. The face of a career diplomat, and a British one at that, is not an easy face to read. She is not sure she trusts him, but she does need his help. Begrudgingly, she explains.

'I went to talk to Ibragimov,' she begins, picking at the yellow foam spilling out of the seat cushion.

'Yes, as we had discussed.'

'As *you* had suggested,' she says sharply. 'He offered me a lift back to Baku which, of course, I accepted. But when I got in, the government adviser you dodged at the reception got in next to me.'

'Oh God, not him.' Hayden raises his eyes to the ceiling. 'What on earth did he want?'

'He looked as surprised as me. But the journalists knew who he was, and someone must have tipped them off that I was from the embassy—before I knew it they were swarming the car.'

'The slippery bastard, pardon my language. So it must have been Ibragimov behind those rumours. I wonder what he wanted out of it.' Hayden stretches his legs out in front of him and examines his shoelaces. 'Wouldn't put it past him to use this opportunity to put forward his own oil company. Never one to miss the chance to benefit from others misfortune, or create it. Just need to discredit BOG and swoop in to the ensuing chaos.'

'BOG? It was me he pushed under a bus. I have nothing to do with British Oil and Gas.'

'He doesn't know that. It would look even worse for them if BOG have got the government doing their dirty work.'

'And then there was the briefcase full of cash.' Sarah watches for Hayden's reaction.

'The what?' He appears genuinely surprised. 'Whose briefcase?'

'The briefcase full of cash Ibragimov handed me as I got into the car,' Sarah says, unblinking. The fly gives another death rattle as it flings itself against the window.

'Oh good lord, I had genuinely no idea that Ibragimov was behind these rumours or had any reason to suspect who you were.'

'So how do you explain it, then?'

Hayden is too restless to sit. He paces the small room with evenly measured strides, his heels squeaking on the tired linoleum. 'There are plenty of ways he could have found out. Nothing can be taken for granted, Sarah, everything here is watched, noted and recorded. Especially foreigners. From the moment you entered Azerbaijan, you will have been observed and monitored by a number of agencies, official or otherwise, any of whom could have had links to Ibragimov.'

Sarah considers mentioning the incident on the train but doesn't want to let Hayden off the hook.

His pacing comes to a stop in front of her. 'Don't tell me the journalists got hold of the briefcase?'

'No. I left it in the taxi that helped me get away.' It seems best not to mention Elias's involvement. She is in no mood to face questions on who he is and how she knows him.

'You took a taxi?' Hayden looks horrified.

'Yes, and he will have had a hefty tip if he finds that briefcase. But from the way he drove he probably deserves it.'

'A taxi?' Hayden repeats incredulously.

'I needed to get away as quickly as possible, and I wasn't exactly going to jump in the embassy flag car, was I?'

'No, I see your point.' He resumes his pacing.

'But we attracted a fair bit of attention, and a crowd of journalists and whoever it was that brought me in here followed us. The driver tried to shake them off in the old town and that's how I ended up here.'

'What a mess.' He rubs his brow with a forefinger with such force he might be trying to etch in another frown line. 'I'm going to have to get on to the press team for some handling lines straight away. Do you think they knew who you are?'

'They knew I was from the embassy.'

'God, we're going to have some work to do picking our way out of this one. I feel like I've landed in the middle of an exam for the senior civil service.' Hayden shakes his head. 'But of course the main thing is that you're all right and unhurt. I'll see what I can do to get you out of here. It should be relatively straightforward to pass this off as a case of mistaken identity—you are simply a tourist who got shaken up. But then you will need to leave Azerbaijan immediately and you won't be able to come near the embassy before you go.'

'Can't say I'll be sorry to leave. But what about Ibragimov? And the weapons? How are we going to find out what he is planning?'

'We'll have to leave that to Jim.'

'But Jim has done nothing. He said himself he wasn't well placed to get close. I just need to—'

'Sorry to break it to you, Sarah, but after today, pretty much anyone is better placed to get close to Ibragimov than you are.' His tone is gentler than his words, but Sarah still wants to punch him. The thought of abandoning her mission to Jim and his dry incompetence leaves her devastated. She slumps into the bench and pummels the leather with her fist.

CHAPTER 30

Qb2 Bd4

On her return, Tbilisi is in full swing preparing for the upcoming visit of the US president, coming to cement Georgia's standing as friend and ally of the West and to give his bright, brash seal of approval to Saakashvili's new government. His visit will send a clear message to the Russians that their days of influence in the South Caucasus are over. Saakashvili, known for his micromanaging perfectionism, is clearly keen to make an impression. The road from the airport is being repaved and renamed to honour the visiting president, with tarmac thick enough to withstand the hefty cavalcade of dignitaries and entourage. The buildings along the route are being repainted in bright and gaudy chalkboard colours. Those whose structural faults cannot be hidden by a lick of pink or blue have been covered in vast swathes of fabric like unused pieces of stage set.

The colourful gaiety jars with Sarah's mood. She is mortified by how badly her efforts unravelled in Baku and plagued by not knowing whether her own naivety and inexperience are to blame or whether she was deliberately set up to fail. She feels knocked off balance, cut loose, batted from one spot to the next like a pinball in a machine by Michael or Jim or Hayden or any of the other men who seem to feel responsible for her mission, but are willing to let her take all the risks.

She tries to wrestle back control of the furious force of her mind, to decide for herself what and how to follow up next. But she knows it's too late. The last smash of the flipper sent her sailing down the gutter back to the beginning. In fact it's worse than that—now that Ibragimov knows she is connected to the British Government, she won't be able to get close to him again, let alone get him to spill his secrets. Michael gave her a month. Now almost half-way through her time, what has she got to show for her efforts? A broken cover, a media circus and a humiliation at the hands of her target. It's worse than if she'd done nothing at all.

How will she face Michael and tell him what happened? How will she face her father with his idealised expectations of her brilliance? Sorry Dad, I lost, and lots of people died because I screwed it up. If Ibragimov succeeds in launching another attack, how will she face herself?

She starts walking with no destination in mind, hoping the repetitive thud of sole against pavement will settle the questions churning in her mind and reveal a solution she hasn't yet considered. But today, even the city is against her. The chaos of its hurried renovation amplifies her own disorder and frustration.

The pavements have been ripped up to make way for the relaying of the road, replaced by clouds of dust and the smell of bitumen. Sarah picks her way through the rubble. The meeting request from Ibragimov makes no sense. Did she miss something at the ballet or in the old town while distracted by Skarparov and Elias? Or was the whole request just part of Ibragimov's sting to flush her out? Sarah replays Ibragimov's words as he handed over the briefcase—*You can give this to Michael.* Was this personal? Had he been hoping Michael would come himself? Michael has never mentioned a personal connection to Ibragimov, but there is a great deal that Michael has never mentioned.

She crosses the river, under the great bronze statue of King Gorgasalis on his horse. Mother Georgia stands high on the opposite hilltop, looking down, one outstretched arm offering wine and the other her shlooping sword. 'I thought you were supposed to be looking out for me?' Sarah asks the giant aluminium protector. 'Or does your sword not stretch to Baku?'

She forces herself to re-examine the options, to bat away the enticing despair and search for what can be salvaged. Ibragimov would never trust her now, that much is clear. Irakli is also too suspicious, and too dangerous. Which leaves only Skarparov. She could perhaps convince him to rat on his uncle. But if they were as estranged as Hayden suggested, then there is no reason why Skarparov would know anything worth telling. She could try the other members of Ibragimov's circle. But after the fiasco in Baku they would all know her. She considers the disgruntled assistant—might he be driven to disloyalty by one too many stabs in the kidneys? It's a hell of a long shot.

The air is gritty and dry from the hasty demolition, stinging her eyes and sticking in her throat. She crosses the road, chancing a break in the traffic at a run to avoid a speeding *marshrutka*. Why did Michael ask her to follow Skarparov if Skarparov's antipathy to Ibragimov was well known? She wants to trust Michael, she's royally stuffed if he's not on her side, but what reason does she have to be sure that he did not set the whole thing up to take delivery of Ibragimov's money? And why does he never answer his bloody phone? She stumbles over a loose shard of tarmac, swearing like a Russian sailor as she catches her balance.

And then Elias. It seemed almost too good to be true when he turned up unexpectedly in Baku, with carpets and wine and tall stories. But she had been willing to write that off as a happy coincidence. It is not so easy to explain how he magically appeared to rescue her from Ibragimov's sting. What was he even doing there? He'd said he was off to catch a plane. She wonders how much else had been a lie.

A banner waves above the road, emblazoned with the US president's towering grin. 'You can get lost, too,' Sarah snaps at his shiny teeth and flared nostrils. She needs a drink, something strong and sweet. The bar in the building next to her flat has tables up on the roof where at least she would have the fairy-tale view for company.

She orders a glass of Mtsvane—a straw-coloured wine that tastes of summer fruit and honey—and a plate of white sulguni cheese. As she sips the wine, her frustrations slowly melt into the glow of evening. A round slab of stone catches her eye, crossed with the light and dark markings of a chess board, ready set with roughly hewn pieces. Sarah sits down to play white. The feel and weight of the pieces in her hand brings a familiar comfort, a strange mix of relaxation and anticipation. Perhaps the concentrated discipline will loosen whatever is lurking in her mind.

She weighs a pawn in her hand, examining its possible avenues. But her concentration is snapped by a gentle cough behind her shoulder. She looks up into the pale green eyes of Viktor Skarparov.

'Ah, my dear Sarah, what good fortune to find you here. Would you mind if I joined you?' He is already pulling out a chair.

'Yes, in fact, I would.' He really has a knack of turning up at the worst possible moments.

'Of course, chess! I'd almost forgotten our shared pleasure. May I play black?'

'I was quite happy playing alone.'

'Surely you can do an old man a favour. I know it's vain, but I like to feel, for just a moment, that I could still manage to convince a girl like you to have a drink with me. Humour me, just for one game. Be kind. I promise I won't bite.' Skarparov smiles entreatingly, a twinkle of playfulness behind the mock-modesty.

They play through the opening moves, Skarparov moving his knight to set up a King's Indian defence, giving Sarah control of the centre. Sarah is pleasantly surprised. The King's Indian is her preferred opening for exploring unusual attacks and unexpected combinations. She feels reasonably confident to play against it.

He signals to the waiter who reappears with a new bottle of wine and another glass.

'I owe you an apology.' Skarparov moves a knight to bring both black knights to the left flank.

'For ruining my quiet drink?' Sarah edges forward a pawn and loses her bishop to his advancing knight.

'No no, I'm sure you have forgiven that already.' He tops up her glass. 'An apology for that situation in Baku. It was me who gave you away to Ibragimov.'

His words work through Sarah like a punch to the gut. She scrabbles to maintain a composed expression, steadying herself against the cold marble of the table as she takes his knight with a pawn.

'Of course I wasn't certain you were a spy, but we did have our suspicions. It seemed rather unlikely that the Brits would take such a keen interest in me for my philanthropy alone. And I rather hoped that you were—you're far more intriguing as a honeypot than as an earnest development worker. But I'm rather hurt if you were just using me to get to my uncle.' He castles on the queen side.

Burning bile rises up Sarah's throat and she takes a gulp of wine to avoid retching. This is everything blown. Both of her targets, Skarparov and Ibragimov, know that she's a spy. The pinball machine has spat her out and she's rolling across a grimy floor. She bites down hard on her lip to steady herself. She should deny his accusations, convince him he's got it all wrong, but what would be the point? She covers her knight that is threatened by his queen, hoping to disguise her defence as an attack.

'I mentioned my suspicions to my uncle when I saw you approach him at the forum. Very unkind, but how was I to know what he had up his sleeve? Had I known, I would have kept it to myself.'

'That's not much help to me now.' Sarah studies her opponent. The pouches of skin underneath his protruding eyes exaggerate their roundness, giving him a disarmingly open expression. But can she trust it? He is confessing to having set her up in a dangerous sting and yet he seems to be asking her to humour him, to laugh it off as a little misunderstanding. With Skarparov's unusual attacking style, the board is looking oddly lopsided. All of Sarah's pieces are aimed at the black king.

'But really, you need to be more careful with someone like my uncle. He is a dangerous man. What did you want with him?'

Sarah fixes her eyes on the board to avoid giving an answer.

'Maybe I can help? Perhaps I could offer you a favour by way of apology?' He runs his finger around the lip of his glass.

Sarah's hands again seek out the cool stability of the stone table. Her gut clenches, warning her to share nothing—she does not want to feel in his debt and does not trust his intentions. But her cover is already blown—what does she have to lose by confessing the little she knows? Placing herself in Skarparov's hands might give him enough of an ego-stroke to make him a useful informant on Ibragimov. She moves her queen forward, putting his king into check.

'The embassy think Ibragimov is planning something in Baku,' she says.

Skarparov gives a wry smile, withdrawing his king to safety but leaving his queen open. 'Ibragimov is always scheming over something. What is it now?'

'They think he may be planning an attack.' Sarah watches as Skarparov continues to run his finger around the top of his glass.

'And they may be right.' His eyebrows pitch up in the centre to a point.

Is that it? Has she really given herself away for this cryptic response? Sarah cradles Skarparov's captured knight in her palm, waiting to see if he would elaborate.

'They suspect he is assembling quite an arsenal of weapons for use in this attack,' she prompts.

'Yes.' Skarparov looks directly at her, the playfulness replaced by something colder. 'From Russia, large quantities.' His face unmoving, his pale green eyes alert. Sarah holds his stare, waiting for more.

'Is he planning a power grab in Baku?' she asks.

'It is probably nothing that simple. My uncle is a complex man. He has enjoyed a position of privilege in the shadows for many years. I see no reason why he would suddenly seek a seat at the head table.' Skarparov sits back, lowering his eyes and adjusting the thick strap of his watch. Sarah studies his body language attentively.

'So what is he after?'

'Instability? Chaos? A difficult environment for friendly relations and secure investments,' he says casually, moving his bishop.

'Why?'

'Azerbaijan is about to become a very wealthy country. When that tap is turned on and the black gold starts to flow, unknown wealth will pour into Baku. If that prosperity is handled well, there is a chance for growth and real development, for our country to shake off its Soviet past.'

'Surely a good thing?'

'For some, yes. But for someone like my uncle, the status quo of all being hidden beneath a cloak of corruption works very well. Nothing is permitted, everything is possible, if you know which wheels to grease.' He keeps his eyes fixed on Sarah, nudging forward a pawn. 'The current government has been flirting with the path to righteousness - but opening up means transparency and regulatory authorities and audits and all things that strike terror into the heart of a man like my uncle. He is a creature of the shadows; he has grown rich from holding the strings that control the flow of money and influence in his country. The last thing he wants is to open that system up to public scrutiny.'

'Hasn't he already lost some of that influence, since Aliyev Junior took over?'

'Yes. And that will have made it all the more urgent for him to regain that power. You are too young, Sarah, to understand the sort of power that was wielded by those who ran the republics in the late Soviet Union.'

She sits forward and adjusts the hang of her blouse around the neckline.

Skarparov watches appreciatively. 'You could not know what it does to a man to have it, how it shapes him and colours him, and how difficult it is to give it up. People say it is like an addiction, but it is more than that. Power becomes part of your identity. To lose it, is to lose yourself.'

'So he wants to destabilise Baku to regain his position of power?' Sarah asks, trying to bring Skarparov back to the concrete threat. She moves her queen back into check.

'It may not stop there.' He sidesteps his king to safety, delighted to have Sarah hanging on his every word. He has removed his watch and is toying deliberately with the strap. 'The Russians have a clear interest in destabilising this region,' he says, 'in keeping their former satellite states down at heel and out of the rich world's club, to hold onto their sphere of influence. If Russia is involved in the supply of these weapons that your cloak and dagger friends have picked up on, then his target may stretch well beyond the government in Baku.'

'So the pipeline?' She moves her rook forward to threaten Skarparov's queen.

'He's too clever to let me into his plans, his trusted circle is very small and I do not qualify. He probably knows I have too much of a soft spot for pretty girls asking questions,' he smiles his unctuous smile. 'But yes, possible. I would have thought that was too obvious for him. Too low-level terrorist. But it does look tempting. In any case, something big enough to bring instability across the region. Dragging our progress backwards to where an old-fashioned operator can flourish.'

Sarah waits for him to continue, working through what his motives might be for taking her so far into his confidence. But he is strapping his watch back on to his wrist as if to indicate that the lecture is over.

'Well, how was that for an apology? Am I forgiven?'

'Not quite.' Sarah swoops in to take Skarparov's queen with her rook, tilting the board back in her favour. Her chest tightens as she absorbs her quiet moment of triumph, but Skarparov's face is frustratingly calm. How could he not be more rattled by the loss?

'What about Irakli? Why would you take on a guy like that who's so closely linked to your uncle to run your foundation?'

'I told you before: my uncle can make it very difficult to say no.' Skarparov pinches at his fleshy right ear lobe.

'Do you even know what he's actually doing for you?'

'I know he has a lot of dodgy friends, but I also know he's lazy, too pleased with himself to get into real trouble.'

'The first time I visited Irakli,' Sarah says, with growing confidence in her position, 'he had to run out to help some guys unload something from a van. He claimed it was carpets coming in from the mountains, but it clearly weighed a tonne and was wrapped up in some crappy made-in-Russia factory rug. I don't know what was in it, but it looked dodgy.'

Skarparov opens his mouth as if to speak, but stops. His cheeks, which always bear a ruddy shine, flush a deeper shade of red. He studies the board in silence, calculating his next move. 'I wouldn't be surprised if Irakli is engaged in some underhand dealings for my uncle,' he says, addressing the board. 'Perhaps I had better keep a closer eye on him.'

Has she overstepped the mark? Now was not the moment to risk losing his trust. She tries again in a gentler tone. 'Given that you just got me locked up by the Azeri police, how am I to believe that you are telling the truth?' She takes a bite of salty cheese, holding it near her lips. 'Can you give me a real reason to trust you?'

'To you, it might look as if we have nothing in common. You probably see me as an ageing playboy to be humoured and milked for what he's worth.'

She laughs. 'And you probably see me as a naive young spook to be taken advantage of and fed whatever information suits you.'

His eyes regain their levity. 'However we choose to see each other, and whether or not we are right, I am certain that there are some things we share. Neither of us wants to see my uncle succeed. He is a relic, a Soviet man through and through. I am not. I may look like a craggy old dinosaur to you, but I am a different generation from my uncle, and I want a different future for this region. I don't want to see the tentative progress that has been made since independence destroyed.' He moves his rook all the way across the board to Sarah's home rank.

She holds his eye.

'I have some loyalty to him through our blood. But that is where our connection ends. I also have loyalty to my country and my home. If he is determined to sabotage the chances for progress in the region, then I don't see it as too strong a betrayal to help derail those plans. And if all I have to do is share a glass of wine and a few musings with you, then it is a very easy kind of betrayal.'

'The best kind,' Sarah smiles. His efforts at flirtation are faintly ludicrous, but unthreatening. With the warmth of the wine softening her earlier mood, she might even be starting to enjoy the exchange. It would be easy enough to keep up this play-flirtation so long as he keeps talking.

'Okay.' Sarah sits forward, feeling bold. 'So the motive stacks up. But can you give me any proof of Ibragimov's plans?' She sees Skarparov's pawn edging forward but chooses to play the attack.

'Proof?'

'A token of trust.'

'I presume you know about the train crash?'

217

'Of course.'

'And so you know that it was no accident. I would advise you to follow up the passenger lists if you want to find out who was behind it. I'm fairly certain you'll find links back to Ibragimov.'

'Anything you can offer that we don't already know?'

Skarparov raises a smile that begins at his large ears. 'Okay, a tip just for you, to earn your forgiveness.'

'This better be good.'

'The Kentucky Derby is coming up next week—the tenth of May.'

'That's the following week.'

'Pay attention to the board, Sarah, not in trying to trip me up.' He moves his pawn to the end of the board, regaining his lost queen. Sarah's control begins to slip.

'So what does that have to do with Ibragimov?'

'He is sure to be there.'

'And?'

'If I were in your position, I would make sure I was there too.' His fingers creep back to the rim of his glass.

Sarah moves her rook forward one square to protect her king. 'What has horse racing in the US got to do with his plans for the Caucasus?'

'Very little. But these are exactly the kind of events he likes to attend when he has, shall we call it—*business*—to arrange. Big international events, flooded with money and foreigners, are the perfect place to be anonymous. Against that backdrop, who would raise an eyebrow at an Azeri public figure meeting with Russian arms suppliers and mercenaries, so long as they both have money to spend and can feign an interest in the horses? If you want to know what he's up to, watch who he meets. And there, at least, you can blend in. Your chances of getting back into Baku unnoticed are pretty remote, but you could easily be lost in the crowd in Kentucky.'

'I'll be sure to look into it.' No point appearing overly grateful for the tip.

'I really am sorry for what happened in Baku.' He takes her bishop with his rook. 'I hope you did not suffer too much. As soon as I realised what was happening, I sent Elias over to help. I hope he managed to make it better than it could have been.' Skarparov places both hands on the table. 'I understand you had already met?'

Sarah feels like a bucket of cold water has been dumped over her head. 'You sent Elias?' she manages, regaining her composure.

'Well he didn't just appear miraculously at your side, your knight in shining armour, did he?'

'Of course not,' Sarah ignores the insinuation that Elias might be anything more to her than a convenient accessory to escape. 'I just didn't realise you knew each other.' She retreats her king to the safety of her home corner.

Skarparov moves his rook. 'Check mate.' His rook and reclaimed queen line up to seal his win. Sarah stares at the pieces. Beaten and broken, she squeezes a stone pawn in her hand so hard it hurts.

'Of course I know Elias, he works for me. What else do you think he was doing up in remote parts of Khevsureti? And why else would he be in Baku?'

Bear hunting and carpet buying do not feel like convincing answers, although she had happily believed them at the time. She is crushed. Everything she thought or felt about Elias is now soiled by this revelation. Every moment of pleasure is soured by Skarparov's words. Her eyes prick with fury—fury at Elias for playing her, at Skarparov for his part in it and at herself for allowing it to happen.

She drains the remainder of her wine and says with a steady voice, 'I hadn't given it much thought, but I'm glad he was there. He certainly got me out of the worst. Thank you for the game, it has been most informative.' She rises quickly and offers her hand.

He draws it to his lips, placing a kiss just below the knuckles. 'I'm sorry if I touched on something that isn't my business. You

219

look hurt; I hope I didn't cause any offence?'

'Of course not. I never like to hang around after a loss.' She pulls her hand away.

'Thank you for our little game, Sarah, I did enjoy myself. I hope we can do it again soon.'

She nods in response and leaves, nearly stumbling over a chair in her hurry to get away.

CHAPTER 31

SERGEI

'You got it?' The Castle calls down the trapdoor into the darkness below.

His question is met with a string of colourful swearing, accented by a few throaty grunts. It is worryingly quiet until Hasan's huge head appears through the gap in the floor.

'You're really telling me we have to get the whole thing down there and then we bring the whole thing back up again when it's time?' Hasan asks, wiping a coating of sweat from his forehead with the hair on the back of his colossal forearm.

'Yes,' The Castle says. 'That was the heaviest single part, but there's loads more up here so keep at it.' He takes a drag on his cigarette and grinds the ash into the cement floor. Seidov is lounging on a chair in the corner watching the two bickering from his narrowly set eyes.

'Why can't we just put it together now?' Hasan asks. 'There's no one here. There's no one anywhere near here most of the time, other than that great piece of metal.' He jerks his head in the direction of the hulking structure outside.

'Because I don't trust you two not to screw this up again. The carpet cock-up was enough. I don't want to take any more risks. I want it and you out of sight as much as possible. Then, if anyone comes asking questions, we've got nothing to hide.'

'Are you going to tell me what we're doing out here with this thing? Or am I just your removal guy now?' Hasan asks.

'In good time, yes. But for now, the less you know the better. Trust me.'

'Why would I do that?'

'Because it's all in Ibragimov's plan.' He knows that mention of the boss will settle the mutinous mood.

'So why are we all here? What are we all doing in Georgia?'

'Boss's orders, Hasan.'

'But I thought—'

'New orders.'

'When did you see him? Where do you get the orders? Last I checked he doesn't trust the phone.'

'He sends me messages disguised in jam and tea. His idiot nephew brings them over, but he has no idea.' The Castle gives a snort through his long nostrils.

'I know what that is,' Seidov says, examining the pile of boxes they brought from the car that Hasan is donkeying downstairs. A rough smile creeps across his face.

'You've used one before, I hope?' The Castle asks. 'I'm counting on you to know how to operate it.'

'We had them in Karabakh, used to call them Sergei. Do you have replacement barrels? They're a real splinter in the ass when they overheat.'

The Castle shrugs. 'And you think it will have any problems getting through those metal plates on the windows?'

Seidov twists his finger at his temple. 'Are you crazy? These things pop out bullets as long as your fist packed with explosive. That whole wall would be gone in the first couple of rounds. Even without replacement barrels you could squeeze out two hundred to two hundred-and-fifty rounds - that's enough to destroy anything within a 2.5km range. But what the hell have you got planned for it here?'

'Next set of instructions are coming tonight. Skarparov's been in Baku and should have taken delivery of my next package of "tea".' The Castle snorts again, still tickled by how brazenly Ibragimov takes advantage of Skarparov's good nature.

Hasan shoulders the next box. 'Are you two going to help?' he asks with a contemptuous look at The Castle's pristine white shirt. 'This would go a lot quicker with three you know?'

'Sorry,' the Castle replies with the smile of one only too happy to see the tables turned. 'I've got the wrong shoes on today,' his eyelids curl in taunting delight. 'Anyway, one of us has to stay up here as lookout.'

'Lookout? Where are you looking? The windows are boarded up?'

'Seidov can keep watch up here. I'll stay outside with the van. I don't want to leave it there too long. Once you've got all the boxes in, I'll be back.'

Hasan adds another layer of obscenity to his previous stream of insults and balances the box back down the ladder to the cellar.

CHAPTER 32

Kf1 Kd7

The moment Sarah puts her key in the lock, her front door swings open; but she remembers locking it when she left. She tiptoes silently from room to room, searching for signs of intrusion. The living room looks untouched, her work bag still sitting on the table, cardigan flung over the arm of the sofa. The balcony door stands open, heavy curtains sighing in the evening breeze. Sarah grabs a poker from the fireplace, edges around the curtain and out through the balcony door.

Elias is on the swing-seat reading, wearing nothing but a loose-fitting pair of pale blue trousers. Sarah is furious.

He looks up and smiles. 'You're a sight for sore eyes. I had almost given up waiting for you. What on earth are you doing with that poker?'

'What are you doing here?' she asks, laying down the poker. 'How did you get in?'

'I thought you'd be pleased. Your doorman let me in; he's an old friend of my favourite taxi driver and owed me a favour.

Now come here and stop looking so alarmed.'

He takes a step towards her. His trousers hang low around his waist, low enough to make it clear that he is not wearing anything underneath. Sarah stands speechless, her eyes drawn to the contours of his abdomen. She left the restaurant wanting to confront Elias with what Skarparov had revealed. But not yet. She needs time to cool off from the double humiliation that Skarparov managed to pull on her. She is certainly not ready for Elias here in her apartment, or his naked skin.

'We need to talk,' she manages to say, addressing his feet.

'Of course we do, but first I need a taste of your lovely lips. I've been dreaming of eating peaches since Baku.'

'No, I'm serious. Can you please put your clothes back on?' She throws him his shirt.

'Oh, we need a fully clothed talk? How disappointing.' He pulls the shirt across his shoulders and fastens the buttons. Sarah squeezes in next to him on the swing-seat, trying to find the words, but thrown by the arresting presence of him in her space.

'Not out here.'

'As you wish.' Elias follows her inside.

She sits cross-legged in an oversized armchair, upholstered in a stripy fabric salvaged from an old carpet, pulling her knees in tightly. Elias throws his arm over the back of the sofa opposite. They stare at each other in silence, his lips curled into an amused smile, her eyes blazing.

'Well spit it out, you look fit to burst,' Elias says.

'You work for Skarparov?' she holds his eye, ignoring the weight of her question hanging between them.

His shoulders deflate as he lets out a slow sigh. 'Oh…'

'Oh? That's it? Well do you or don't you?'

He studies the backs of his hands. 'It would seem that I do.'

'What does that mean?'

He jumps to his feet and disappears into the kitchen, returning with a bottle of wine and two mismatched glasses. He pours the wine, setting the larger of the two in front of Sarah, before draining his glass in one and heading back to the balcony. 'I need a smoke.'

'Wait, you can smoke in here, as long as I can have one.'

'You don't smoke.'

'I will now.'

Her hand brushed against his as he offered the light. The slightest of touches, the momentary press of his skin against hers, was enough to set her synapses ablaze. She feels the hot rush of desire, she's hungry for his touch, she wants to drag him into bed, not to fight. But first she needs answers.

She pulls her hand away, watching the smoke spiral towards the ceiling. She wishes they could step out of the physical—bodies with appetites, desires and memories of shared pleasure. She would be just a voice asking a question and him the giver of an answer. Without the layers of physical desire, hurt and confusion intruding on the simplicity of what she needs to know. The cigarette turns her stomach.

'It started as just a few favours for Giorgi,' he addresses the table between them. 'Make a few connections, arrange a few meetings, that sort of thing.'

'And you did?'

'Of course I did; why not? I thought it was a favour to a friend. But then they insisted on paying me and stupidly I took it. I was running short and there's not much to be made in mountain guiding. And then, they had me.' He rubs stiffly at the side of his neck. 'We were in a business relationship. It's harder to distance yourself on principle when you've taken someone's money. Like it or not, you're connected.'

'You've been playing me since the moment we met?' Sarah can't believe how candidly he could admit his deception.

'No! Look, I know how this must seem, but everything you have seen concerning you is purely me. This has nothing to do with Skarparov and his dirty money.'

He reaches for her hand, but she snatches it away.

'But he sent you to rescue me in Baku?' The wine tastes sour and warm.

'I would have come anyway if I knew you were in danger.'

'You lied to me repeatedly. You made out that you'd never even met him.'

'I never said that. You never asked.'

'You told me you were leaving Baku that day?'

'I *was* leaving Baku.' He tips the ash from his cigarette into an ashtray. 'I picked up a message at the airport telling me to come to the Energy Forum, so I changed my plans.' He looks up at Sarah, chin raised, all warmth drained out of his eyes. 'I was rather pleased at the idea of seeing you again.'

The moustachioed portraits hanging on either side of the mantelpiece stare down at Sarah disapprovingly. *Don't tell me you two are taking his side.*

'And what did you do with that briefcase of cash?' she asks.

'What do you think I did? I kept it. I did you a favour, didn't I?'

'Did you give it to Skarparov?'

'No. I spent it. What, you wanted to give it back?'

Sarah bites down too hard on the inside of her lip. 'Why should I believe you?'

A change comes over his face. Tension pinches his cheeks and jaw; a trace of bitterness narrows his eyes. 'It's not as if you have been entirely honest with me,' he says.

Nausea laps at Sarah's throat, the rough wool of the upholstery scratches her bare skins. 'What do you mean?'

'Oh come on, you can drop the act. Yes, it's a lovely line you spin about wanting to save the world, but you don't honestly expect me to believe that the British government is so interested in some tinpot oligarch's Foundation they would send someone like you out here to look into it? There is clearly more to this than holding hands and selling cheeses. If you want to trust me, then we both need to come clean. I can stop pretending to be just a mountain man without the need for a salary, and you can stop pretending to be an earnest development worker.'

Sarah feels ripped open—as if everything private and personal now lies strewn across the living room. Her inner life laid out before the censorious gaze of the stern gentlemen on the wall. He watches her with an unsettling reserve, standing at the doorway in expectant silence, waiting for her to respond.

She wants to come clean, to match his apparent honesty with her own. But to do so seems naive. Her instincts are telling her to confess. But her instincts had also told her to jump into bed with him at their first meeting.

'I told you, I've been asked to look into Skarparov,' she says, sticking with as much of her flimsy cover story as remains. She stubs out her cigarette and reaches for his crumpled packet to take another.

'Yes, Sarah.' His use of her name seems to discard the intimacy between them. 'You've told me that. But by who?'

'The British Government. For DFID,' she perseveres.

'And why Skarparov? This country is awash with foundations and NGOs. Why on earth would DFID be pouring resources into this bunch of jokers when there are so many other do-gooders?'

'I don't know, no one really explained.' Sarah hears the insincerity in her voice. The portraits seem to shake their head in stern reproach.

'And it didn't strike you as strange?' Elias asks sharply.

'Didn't it strike you as strange that they are suddenly pretending to care about carpet weaving?' Sarah shoots back.

'It's not my business where a rich man wants to put his money.'

'But it *was* your business because he was also giving it to you. You didn't want to know what they were doing? You haven't tried to find out what the Foundation is covering up there? You can't honestly expect me to believe you were just an innocent bystander who happened to be on the payroll.'

'Don't make it into something it's not. Yes, I've taken Skarparov's money. And I've enjoyed his hospitality and I've drunk litres of his wine. But no, that does not mean I'm on the inside. If his Foundation is up to things they shouldn't be, then I'd rather not know.'

'But how can you not care?'

'Because that isn't *my* job.' A muscle twitches below his eye but his voice has softened. He takes a step towards her. 'Sarah, you can put yourself out of your misery. I know.'

'You know what?'

'I know why you're here. At least, I've got a good idea. And I know you can't talk about it, not with me, and not here,' he raises his eyes towards the corners of the ceiling. 'I won't push you. But don't think that I'm an idiot.'

Sarah climbs unsteadily to her feet, overcome by an urge to escape. She was supposed to be confronting him, but now she is under interrogation. She needs time to think, but where to go? Where to hide in a one-bedroom apartment? She retreats to the tiny Soviet bathroom—seeking comfort in its pale blue light, its exposed pipes and blue plastic mirror covering a colossal crack in the plaster. She opens the taps on the bath and undresses, balancing on the narrow edge, the ceramic cold against her bare skin. Her thoughts swirl among the whistles and shrieks of the water rushing through ancient pipes into the tub.

What grounds does she have to trust him? However much he might have played it down, he is working for Skarparov. For all she knows he could be a loyal employee sent to sabotage her. Could he also be a plant by a foreign service? There is no reason why the UK would be the only country interested in Ibragimov. The risks of admitting who she was are surely too high. She climbs slowly in, dropping her head beneath the steaming water as it pounds in around her feet.

The risks of admitting who she is are surely too high. But what choice does she have? He already knows. Skarparov already knows. Even Ibragimov already knows. Why persist in hiding from the one person who might be able to help her? She longs for greater faith in her own judgement.

He appears in the doorway. Gone the cheerful swagger he greeted her with on the balcony, but gone too the hostility of their fight. His eyes are red, but their hard edge is softened with solicitude. Wordlessly, he walks towards the bath. His approach is hesitant but tender. Sarah feels vulnerable lying naked beneath him, unprotected. Slowly, he climbs in next to her, without even removing his clothes—oblivious to all but her. He folds her in his arms, her head coming to rest against his chest, her cheek pressing the wet fabric of his shirt. She feels safe, for the first time in a long time.

'It's okay.' He kisses her head gently. 'I'm on your side.'

She raises her chin to look him in the eye. 'I don't know what to believe anymore.'

'Don't worry, Nightjar. We're in this together.'

CHAPTER 33

Qb7 Ke8

'Sag—ham—o—' Unusual sounds boom from the office of the British Ambassador to Georgia.

'No, Alistair, sa*gh*amo, the "g" and the "h" go together, like a French "r".' Sopho, Alistair MacLeod's ever-patient secretary, holds up a large sheet of paper covered with letters written in black marker. Sarah watches from the doorway, bemused.

'Sarrrrrrrrramo,' Alistair tries again, hamming up the trills.

'Not quite. You're speaking Georgian, Your Excellency, not Italian. Think of the sound at the end of *bonjour*.' Sopho makes a sound that seems to come from the back of her throat and the tip of her tongue at the same time.

'*Saghamo, saghamo, saghamo*,' Alistair intones, practising the elusive consonants.

'Good morning, Ambassador,' Sarah says, sorry to interrupt the performance.

'No, it's good evening, *saghamo mshv*... Sopho are you sure you've written that right? How on earth am I supposed to say four consonants together before I get a vowel to help me out?'

Sopho laughs and amends the giant flash cards with her marker pen.

'Ambassador, you asked to see me?' Sarah says.

'Ah yes, of course I did. Sorry. Sopho and I were starting our practice for the speech at the Queen's Birthday Party next month. I might have led some people to believe that I can speak Georgian, so now I don't want to leave them disappointed. Sopho has kindly agreed to help me learn the speech phonetically, but it's a beast of a language to get your tongue around.'

'You are doing very well, Ambassador,' Sopho says smiling. 'Try once more, *mshvidobisa*,' she holds up the card again. The letters are so large the single word fills the side of A3.

Alistair imitates her pronunciation as she nods encouragingly.

'And now together.' She holds up both pieces of paper.

'*Saghamo mshvidobisa, saghamo mshvidobisa*,' he begins pacing the room in time to the intonations. '*Saghamo, mish*— what was it again?'

'It's sounding pretty good,' Sarah says.

'Well, there are the first two words anyway. I think we're going to need quite a lot of practice.'

'And quite a lot of paper.' Sopho gathers the piles of discarded cards on the desk. 'Shall I get some more?'

'No, no, you stay there, I won't be long distracted from my work.' He raises both eyebrows towards Sarah. 'I have something for you on your Skarparov.'

'About the Foundation?'

'No of course not, you're not really interested in that, are you? I had a rather embarrassing conversation with Hayden about you yesterday.'

Sarah should have anticipated that Hayden would communicate with his Tbilisi counterpart.

'He called to apologise for the mess in Baku and I had to pretend I knew what he was on about. I had to get Steve upstairs to fill me in. You know you didn't have to play the DFID line with me.'

Sarah squirms at being caught out in her lie; but mostly she does not want to admit to working for MI6 in front of Sopho, a Georgian secretary.

'Sorry, Your Excellency, for the misunderstanding.' Sarah's eyes widen in warning.

'Please call me Alistair. Look, I know the Michael lot don't trust me to be able to keep my mouth shut, but it's a lot easier if we don't have secrets within the embassy.'

Sarah glares at him, willing him to stop. She glances at Sopho, discreetly rearranging her flash cards, pretending not to listen.

'Oh, you don't need to worry about Sopho, she's the soul of discretion. Knows all the secrets we have, don't you, Sopho?'

Sopho looks at Sarah through her thick lashes. She smiles apologetically, a blush creeping into her wide cheeks.

'And anyway, Steve uses her for all his back-office paperwork, so I'm sure she knew all of this before I did.' Alistair pulls down the points of his waistcoat. '*Saghamo mshvidobisa!*' he says with a flourish, watching his reflection in the glass of the portrait of the Queen. 'How was that?'

'Brilliant, Ambassador,' Sopho says. 'Are you ready to try the aspirated T?'

'Only if it comes in a pot with a splash of milk—you couldn't get me a cup, could you? I don't think I can wrap my mouth around any more of your crunched consonants without a bit of lubrication.'

'Okay, but we still have a lot to do.' Sopho tidies her sheets and goes to fetch the Ambassador a cup of tea.

'You said you had something for me on Skarparov?' Sarah says.

'Ah yes. Sopho picked it up actually. He's off to Dubai next week for the World Cup.'

'The World Cup? What has that got to do with Dubai?'

'Not the football, the horses. It's been an annual event for the last ten years, ludicrous amounts of money for the winner and a good day at the races for everyone else.' Alistair settles at his desk and begins doodling with Sopho's black marker.

'And Skarparov will be there?'

'Apparently so. I'm going. Not really one for the horses, but it's supposed to be good networking. I always ask Sopho to do a bit of homework on these invitations—who is going to be there, who I should try to meet, who better to avoid. She flagged that Skarparov was one of the confirmed attendees.'

'And Ibragimov?' Sarah is not confident that Skarparov has much more to divulge. He clearly thinks the suspicions around his uncle are well founded, but she doubts he knows the details. She can't afford to wait another ten days to follow Ibragimov to Kentucky. And something about the way Skarparov offered her the tip has been bothering her.

'Why do you want to go back into that lion's den? I don't remember his name being mentioned. Hold on, Sopho!' he calls through the open door. 'Was Ibragimov going to Dubai?'

Sarah cringes at hearing her mission boomed through the embassy. Sopho reappears, carrying a tray of tea in white crockery with gold rims. She closes the door behind her. 'Ibragimov? No, he wasn't on the confirmed list.'

'So then, how about you tag along? You can follow your funny little Azeri character and we can have a jolly time at the races,' Alistair says.

'I'd love to, but I think I have too much to be getting on with here.' Sarah would rather use the time she has left to dig into Ibragimov's contacts in the Caucasus rather than swanning around in Dubai.

'Oh come on, it will be fun. You don't have to decide now, I don't leave until Wednesday. Sopho can look after the travel arrangements.'

Sopho pics up the next card in the pile, *britanet'is saelch'os*. 'We need to practice the aspirated "t",' she coaxes. 'Try saying the "t" with a little puff of air.'

Alistair holds his head in his hands. 'How the blazes are you supposed to puff a "t"? I'm not sure I can take much more of this. I'd rather save my puff for the pipes.' He rummages in his top drawer, pulls out a practice chanter and starts playing with the fingering.

'Have you heard the Ambassador play the bagpipes?' Sopho asks Sarah with a glint in her eye. 'He's very good. He pipes himself in to all his receptions.'

Sarah stifles a giggle. 'I can't wait.'

'Why do I feel you two are making fun of me? Anyway, I need to give my poor old glottal a rest for now or I won't be able to make it in.' He marches slowly out of the room puffing on his chanter.

'Is he always like this?' Sarah asks.

'A lot of the time, yes,' Sopho nods, 'but it's mostly for show. He can also be serious, if he has to. It's quite a good trick. No one knows how to deal with him when he suddenly stops acting the fool. It can be an effective way to get things done.'

Sarah is impressed at Sopho's level of insight. No wonder the Ambassador trusts her so completely.

'Don't worry about him giving away your cover, I'm sorry if it was awkward, but I already knew you were working for the service. Steve asked me to take care of the paperwork and Mike wanted help with local arrangements. I didn't want to say anything until I was sure Alistair knew. He's not always that discreet.'

Sarah laughs. 'No, Steve did warn me.'

'If there's anything else I can help you with, please remember you can always ask.' Her conspiratorial smile is hard to resist.

'In fact, there is something.' Sarah moves her chair closer. 'Could you do some research for me?'

Sopho's face lights up. 'Where would you like me to start?'

'I'm trying to find out about all the business connections that Ibragimov has throughout the Caucasus, especially anything that links him to Georgia. I'm curious who his partners are here, what networks he's involved in, that sort of thing. I can't find anything useful online, at least not in English.'

'Okay, I'll see what I can do.'

Sarah pauses, remembering Skarparov's mannerisms as he offered his apology. 'And, Sopho? Let's look into Skarparov too.'

CHAPTER 34

THE EXPLOSIVE

'We want you fully mobile; that way you can pick the best position close to the target. Movements on the day could be quite unpredictable, and we don't know exactly where you will be. This way you can stick close and choose your moment. First up, this baby.' The Castle hands over a pale green hand grenade.

The Pawn takes it confidently, examining the metal ring at the end of the safety pin, flicking it back and forth in his fingers.

'Watch what you do with that.' The Castle takes a step back. 'You used one of these before?'

'No. Seen plenty though. I like these ones. Classic pineapple shape for better grip and maximum fragmentation.' He examines the serial number on the bottom of the device. 'Is it Israeli?' he asks.

'How the hell should I know? Yeah, I guess. So you know how to throw one, right?'

'I—'

'You've got to keep your thumb over the lever, like this.' The Castle takes back the grenade, places his thick thumb over the catch, tweaks the pin and pulls his fist back over his shoulder. He grunts as he launches it with all his weight into the air.

The Pawn watches its flight. They are standing in a rock-strewn field, half an hour out of town. A bony cow is tethered under a tree by an old rope tied around its horns. The Pawn ducks as the grenade strikes the ground at the animal's feet. The cow sniffs at it suspiciously.

'No need to jump,' The Castle laughs, 'I kept the pin in. Your go,' he nods towards the grenade.

The Pawn runs off to retrieve the device and comes back to where The Castle is standing. He lifts it to his shoulder.

'No, no, no. Not like that. Use your right hand.'

'But I'm left-handed?'

'Shit. Never mind, you'll have to throw it upside down.' He watches as the Pawn takes up the position, hardly bothering to conceal his contempt. 'Aim for the cow.'

The Pawn throws, trying to copy The Castle's stance and following through with all his body weight. But his slight frame does not carry the same force. The grenade lands five metres short of the bewildered animal.

'Okay, you're going to have to get in some practice. You should be able to throw the thing about thirty-five metres, but, well, you're going to need to work on that. The kill zone is five metres, and you'll have about a fifteen-metre damage radius. So you need to get it as close as possible while staying far enough away yourself.'

The Pawn goes to pick up the grenade. He still has time.

CHAPTER 35

Qxc6 Kf8

Elias is waiting outside the embassy. Tall and redheaded, he is unmistakable amid the afternoon rush hour on Freedom Square. He greets Sarah with a respectful kiss on the cheek before helping her into an old Lada taxi, the paintwork so weathered and rusted it is impossible to tell what the original colour had been, doors so warped they need to be shut with a sharp bang.

The car rattles off through the streets of the old city, dodging potholes and skidding round corners on bald tyres. This part of town is Sarah's favourite—buildings of elegant brickwork with wrought-iron balconies, facades of crumbling stucco in pastel hues with wide wooden balconies hanging out over the street. It has a down-at-heel elegance. The real and shabby underside to her rooftop fairy-tale view.

After a steep climb, engine protesting, they stop at a gate half-hidden by a rocky outcrop bathed in green.

Sarah peers through the gates. 'Where are we?'

'You haven't been here before?' Elias asks. 'Then you're in for a treat. The Botanic Gardens, Tbilisi's most beautiful, forgotten spot. You said you wanted somewhere quiet we could talk. This is it.'

The gardens are like the forgotten great park of a country estate—once part of someone's grand design, now wild and given back to nature. A river flows beneath them with surprising energy along the valley floor. Sarah is intrigued to see an aluminium structure towering above them on the ridge of the cliff. At first it looks like a lighthouse or watchtower, wide panels of silvery metal riveted together in zeppelin curves. But then she sees it.

'Mother Georgia?' she asks in amazement.

'She looks rather different from up here, doesn't she?'

'She's huge. She looks so elegant and dainty from my balcony. From here she's enormous. And look at that sword! I thought it was some kind of ceremonial sceptre, but it's more like a Viking broadsword, ready to swipe off the head of anyone who displeases the mighty Mother Georgia.' Sarah gives her imaginary sword a head-rolling thwack.

The path narrows, paving stones giving way to beaten earth. As Sarah steps over a large root, Elias takes her hand to steady her step. Back on the flat, she does not let go.

They reach a small pavilion, where a white wooden bridge crosses the river. Behind the bridge, a waterfall emerges from the cliff-face, thundering down to a pool below. 'Is that perfect or is that perfect?' Elias asks.

'What?'

'This spot? One of the world's best views, hidden nature in the heart of the city. Completely secluded, overlooked by nothing and if anyone were trying to listen in, they wouldn't hear a thing over the noise of that.' He nods towards the waterfall pounding relentlessly behind them.

Sarah peers down over the drop. 'Were you serious about wanting to help?'

'Of course. Look, I don't know who or what you are after. But if you are digging into Skarparov and Ibragimov, you are in dangerous territory. I want to help, if only to keep you safe.' He pauses expectantly. 'So are you going to tell me? One minute you are looking at Skarparov's Foundation, and the next you are diving into a car with Ibragimov?'

Sarah hesitates, listening to the unstoppable roar of the water. To take Elias into her confidence is a step that cannot be undone. But she needs all the help she can get.

'We think Ibragimov is planning something that will disrupt the whole Caucasus. But our network on the ground in frustratingly thin.' Sarah sits on her hands.

'And I suppose I don't have to ask who we is?'

Sarah cages up, she can't spit it out. Surely it's obvious.

'It's okay,' Elias takes her hand. 'I know this must be difficult. You don't have to say anything more. What information do you have?'

'Very little.' She faces the waterfall rather than look at him directly. It makes it easier to say what she is unsure if she should be saying. 'A substantial arsenal of weapons has been moved out of Russia and we have reason to believe it was sent to Ibragimov. The embassy in Baku think he is planning some sort of power grab and they are nervous that he will target one of the oil installations, possibly the pipeline. But Skarparov thinks the target could be the stability of the entire region.'

'He told you that?' Elias asks, his face hardening.

'Yes, he was apologising for having tipped Ibragimov off about me in Baku.'

'Ha! That's a bit rich. So it was him who set you up? I can't say that I am surprised, but what made you want to go and talk to him after that?'

'It's my job.' Sarah manages a wry smile.

'So he ratted you out to Ibragimov, and then he ratted Ibragimov off to you?'

'Yes, that was pretty much it.'

'And you believe him?' Elias asks.

'I'm not sure. There is obviously no love lost between

Skarparov and his uncle, and if Ibragimov is planning an attack on the region, then it's reasonable that Skarparov would want to stop him. But I'm not sure I trust him.'

'Why?'

'There were signals. Don't laugh, but when I was younger I played a lot of chess.'

His face breaks into a smile.

'I said don't laugh. It was something I enjoyed, I liked the game, I still like the game. And I learnt a lot about reading people, especially when they're nervous.'

'Go on,' Elias says. 'I'm intrigued.'

'Well, it's not infallible, but there are certain things that people tend to do, especially when about to make a move they're not sure about, or that they know is flawed but are hoping you won't notice.'

'What sort of things?'

'It depends on the person, but Skarparov had a couple of mannerisms when he was telling me about Ibragimov that reminded me of players under pressure.'

'Such as?' Elias folds and unfolds his hands. 'You're making me feel self-conscious now.'

'It was the way he fidgeted more than any particular movement. He kept playing with his watch, adjusting it, taking it off, putting it on again, a classic sign of discomfort. He fiddled endlessly with his wineglass. There was something in the way he did it, the pacing of his movements, that brought to mind someone attempting a bluff.'

'So you don't believe him?'

'I don't know what to think. He had plenty of reasons to be nervous—he was, after all, turning his uncle in to a foreign intelligence agency. And beating me at chess. Real life is sadly never as straightforward as a game.'

'Did you question him at the time?'

'I didn't have the chance. He went straight into talking about you and that threw me completely. I know I can be spectacularly naive, but it didn't occur to me that you were working for him.'

'I told you. I'm not working for him.'

'Okay, taking his money in return for work done, then.'

'Look, it's not like that.' His voice is hard, refusing to match Sarah's playful tone. 'Skarparov could be right about Ibragimov, but that doesn't mean you should trust him. He may come across as a harmless playboy, but he definitely has a ruthless side.'

'And you should know.'

A shadow obscures Elias's face and Sarah immediately regrets the dig. 'Sarah, I don't know what you take me for, but I do hope you don't put me in the same category as that creep. He is violent and very dangerous. Given that he now knows you were sent out to spy on him, I think you would be wise to treat him with extreme caution.'

The sound of the freezing meltwater powering out of the cliff face is suddenly magnified.

'How much have you seen of his organisation?' Sarah asks.

'Not much. Not enough to know what they are up to.'

'The Foundation's set up in the mountains seemed pretty unconvincing. At least, it looked like the women and the carpets were not much more than a cover for what was actually going on.'

'That's probably true. I've never noticed much interest in development work. Poor Giorgi is trying his best, but I don't think he knows the half of it. And that section of the Russian border is almost impossible to control.'

'Do you think they are bringing in weapons?'

'I've seen bits and pieces. But mostly small fry, untraceable stuff. Nothing particularly out of the ordinary. Everyone in the mountains has a gun. I've met all sorts up there—Meskheti Turks, Armenians, Yezidis, occasionally even lost-looking West Africans. But all weird kids, misfits. You know the type? They're either going to be into computer games or fundamentalism.' Sarah remembers the edgy teenager in the project office with Giorgi.

'And you've never asked them what's going on? Never wondered?'

'Are you trying to catch me in a lie? Sometimes I can't tell if you even want to trust me.'

'Of course I do. I do. I just still can't understand how you can have been so casual in your relationships with a group who you think are crooks.'

'Life was a lot easier when I didn't have to care.'

'Why do you care now?'

'I care about you.' He brushes his finger down the nape of her neck. The small hairs on her neck rise to attention and a shock of energy shoots down her spine. 'If you're going to keep running in after them, then I'm coming with you.'

Sarah loops her fingers around his knuckles. 'So how does Irakli fit in? He showed zero interest in the work of the Foundation, but he's a regular up in the mountains. Do you think he's using the cover of the Foundation to do Ibragimov's bidding?'

Elias withdraws his hand. 'Irakli using Skarparov? I always thought it was the other way round.'

'Do you think Skarparov trusts him? He told me he was forced on him by Ibragimov.'

Elias nods, taking on board this suggestion then shakes his head. 'Sadly for Irakli, I think he's probably the fall guy.'

'Ibragimov's?'

'Possibly. But certainly Skarparov's. Other than the name of the Foundation, nothing links Skarparov himself with any of the activities in the mountains. I don't think he has even been up there. Everything goes through Irakli. I'm sure it makes Irakli feel very important, but it would also allow Skarparov to cut him off, if necessary, and deny all knowledge. I'm not sure Irakli is bright enough to realise how dangerous his position is. But it would be pretty easy for Skarparov to hang him out to dry.'

'Couldn't happen to a nicer person,' Sarah mutters.

Elias spins towards her. 'Did he try anything with you? If he so much as touched you—'

'No. He didn't do anything like that. But…' She hesitates.

'What?' Elias faces her directly, eyes cold and sharp.

Sarah picks a flake of green paint from the bench. 'You know the accident we had on our way up to the mountains? It could have been a genuine accident; the driver had definitely had too much to drink. But I am pretty sure Irakli deliberately pushed us off the road.'

'He tried to kill you?'

'I don't know. I suppose so.' The sudden ferocity of Elias's tone makes her shiver. 'It was so quick; I don't really know what happened.'

'Why didn't you tell me? I'd have hunted him down and chucked him off a cliff myself.' His face is thunderous.

'I hadn't even met you,' Sarah forces a laugh. 'It's not much of an introductory line, is it? Hi, I'm Sarah, could you take care of a failed assassin for me?'

Elias does not reply. His eyes are fixed on something in the water below, his shoulders hunched and tight. He rubs his thumb against the pad of his fingers.

'I need you to try and find out more.' Sarah tries to bring him back from wherever he's gone.

'Hmmm?'

'There's only two weeks left before the big pipeline launch, and we need a way into whatever Ibragimov is planning. I don't think Skarparov knows any more than he has already shared. But you can do what I can't. He trusts you. You can make yourself indispensable to him. Then he can introduce you to Ibragimov.'

Elias nods.

'Or Irakli? If we find out what he's up to in the mountains we might have some ammo to use to convince him to help us?' Reading Elias's cautious reaction to her enthusiastic urging, Sarah feels a twinge of conscience. Is this what Michael meant by using all available means—using your lover to get dirt to blackmail the guy who tried to kill you? Maybe she did have it in her after all. 'Do you think you can try?' She slips her arm around his waist and nuzzles a kiss into his neck. 'I will make sure you are duly rewarded.'

Finally he nods, his face white and far away. 'Don't thank me yet.' He stands up, brushing off her embrace. 'I'll be back in a week. Don't get yourself into trouble while I'm gone.'

'You're leaving now?' Sarah was looking forward to picking up their romantic walk.

'If I'm to get to the mountains today, I had better set off. There's not much I can do here. But you have no reason to hurry. This place is full of hidden beauty. See if you can get yourself lost.'

CHAPTER 36

Rb5 Ne5

Steve's call came early the next morning.

Wearing flat shoes with no grip, Sarah has to be careful not to slide down the riverbank in the mud. She spots Steve at the bottom near the water's edge, just in front of the police cordon. His ruddy windswept cheeks match the unsettled weather. He hurries to offer his hand, passing her a neatly pressed handkerchief.

'Here, take this. The smell can be a bit overwhelming.' He pulls a second hanky from his pocket and holds it to his face.

'What's going on?' Sarah asks, taking in the scene. Policemen in thick black raincoats and waders have cordoned off most of the riverbank. A man with heavy jowls is shouting instructions to a winch operator pulling a vehicle out of the river.

'Sorry to bring you here unprepared. But I thought you should see this.' Steve's face is pale and he has marked circles under his eyes. 'Recognise the car?'

The black vehicle is now almost fully out of the water. The

windows are smashed, and water pours from the open front door. But the boxy shape of the Mercedes G Class is unmistakable.

'Irakli's?' She covers her mouth and nose with Steve's handkerchief.

'I'm afraid so. The body was found early this morning. I hope you haven't had your breakfast yet.' Steve mumbles some words of Georgian to the officer at the cordon who looks around reluctantly before letting them duck under the rope.

Two more officers in dark coats are examining a body laid out on the muddy riverbank. They are a little outside town, where the river runs through a steep gorge, the pounding water masking the noise of the busy road above. Sarah braces herself as she moves closer. The body lies prone, arms and legs spread like a starfish. The face is the colour of pounded aubergine. Sarah shudders, taking in Irakli's swollen and distorted features, the shiny and bulbous protrusions where the eyes should be, lumpen and uneven fleshy mounds for cheeks. The mouth is grotesquely inflated, bloodied and black. His top lip glistens with beads of muddy river water. Sarah turns away, inhaling deeply through the handkerchief.

'Not such a pretty boy anymore, is he?' Steve looks as if he wants to put an arm around her for comfort but settles on a quick pat on the shoulder. Sarah focuses on Steve's face to avoid looking at Irakli's bruised and battered corpse.

'What happened?'

'The police are treating it as a drink-driving accident. Young guy has too much to drink, gets into a fight and tries to drive home. But I wouldn't be surprised if there was more to it than that. It's hard to tell after he's spent a night at the bottom of the Mtkvari, but those injuries look to me like he wouldn't have been breathing before he got in that car.'

'Won't the autopsy show whether or not he drowned?' Sarah forces herself to look. The clothes are deeply stained and one of the legs falls at an unnatural angle. But she has no idea what a body should look like after being pulled from a car wreck.

'Only if they bother to do one,' Steve says.

'Why wouldn't they?'

'A drink-driving accident is an easier explanation all round. If they discover he's been killed, they'll have to launch a murder investigation. It's easier to write it off as an accident. It's a plausible story to anyone who's seen Irakli tearing around Tbilisi in that car.'

Sarah watches as they cover the body with a plastic sheet. There is a sense of relief that she will no longer have to worry that he might try again to give her a similar end. But more than that, there's frustration that one of her only remaining links to Ibragimov is gone. She wonders who he had angered enough to end up wrapped in plastic in the mud? Had he betrayed Ibragimov's trust? Or could Elias have been right about Skarparov using him as a fall guy? She remembers the look of fury on Elias's face when she had told him about Irakli and shivers.

'Come on, we should get back to the office.' Steve offers his hand to help her back up the steep bank.

CHAPTER 37

Qb7 h4

The sight of Irakli's body hangs heavily on Sarah's soul for the rest of the day.

With the approach of summer, the sun rises stronger in the sky, turning the soaring windows in Sarah's apartment into a greenhouse. Even the moustachioed gentlemen look uncomfortable, sweating in their stiff collars and woollen coats. She closes the heavy curtains against the blaze outside, but in the daytime darkness, the flat feels stale and close. The musty smell of ancient damp and old books that she had loved at first, now reminds her of the organic stench at the riverbed.

The telephone startles her.

'Sarah!'

She breathes a sigh at her father's voice.

'I'm glad I caught you. You never seem to be in.'

'I've been away—Baku. I tried you when I got back, but you were out. Do you ever turn on your mobile?'

'Ah, Baku—the city of God. How was it?'

'I rather liked it. But I don't think I'll be back anytime soon.'

'Oh dear. Why not?'

Sarah longs to come clean, to unload the whole sorry tale of how she had winded up in a police station. But it is impossible. 'A case of mistaken identity. I had to leave in rather a hurry.'

'Reminds me of Yesenin. How does it go again?'

She can hear her father trying out whispered words of Russian as he rifles through his prodigious mental library. He is renowned for having a quote or snippet of literature to apply to almost any circumstance.

'Ah yes, *Прощай, Баку!* Farewell Baku! I'll see you no more. Sorrow and fright are now in my soul.' He recites triumphantly.

'Sounds about right.'

'Everything okay, Sarah? You sound as if your soul has had its own touch of fright?'

She swallows hard, clasping the receiver tightly against her cheek with both hands. 'I think I may have bitten off more than I can chew.'

'Well spit it out then! No point in choking out of politeness.'

'No… I mean… I'm not sure I realised…'

'It's okay, Sarah. I've been in Whitehall long enough to know how these things work. I think I know what you're trying to say.'

She closes her eyes in relief. There is nothing she can say over an open line, but she takes comfort in knowing that her father has quietly understood. She need not speak with words.

'I'd have advised against it, had you asked, but that would only have made you more keen.'

'It's just… I feel outplayed. Always struggling to keep up.'

'I find that hard to believe. Tell me about this chap—the Foundation fellow. What's he like?'

'He beat me with the King's Indian.' She carries the phone to the high-backed armchair and pulls her legs up beneath her.

'How did he manage that?'

'I let him promote a pawn.'

'I see.' He manages not to sound too disappointed. 'So he

plays the King's Indian. He's a player who likes to give you the illusion of control, while duping you with distractions. An aggressive style?'

'Not really. He was so relaxed that I thought I had him until the end.'

'The worst.' Sarah's father draws the word out in distaste. 'Don't let him beat you again, will you?'

'I'm not sure I'll get a rematch.'

'All the same. With a player like that, never forget to watch the pawns.' He lays heavy emphasis on his words as if imparting an important life-lesson. His best advice often came cloaked in chess strategy. Sarah wishes she knew what he meant.

'I won't. Thank you, Dad.'

'And call me from time to time. I worry you know.'

Sarah laughs. 'It's okay, I do too.'

CHAPTER 38

Rxa5 hxg3

'I can't get over the amount of booze they have.' Alistair MacLeod's eyes widen as he inspects the bar in the VIP suite of Dubai's Nad Al Sheba racecourse. 'I thought they didn't drink here? Ever since we got here, these lovely ladies have been trying to ply me with fizz.' He casts an eye over a young girl in Arabic dress circling the room laden with glasses of champagne. 'You're going to have to watch me, later on. Make sure I don't overdo it. But allow me to indulge a little first. They even have a passable selection of whiskeys. Can I make some recommendations?'

'I'm not much of a whiskey drinker,' Sarah says. 'I like the idea of it, but I tend to feel wretched the next day.'

'You don't have to go for a full sledgehammer of a whiskey, there are ladies' whiskeys too. What about this one, that's even milder than a ladies' whiskey. I'd call this a sort of… ladies-before-breakfast whiskey.'

'Thank you, I'm happy with champagne.' She takes a glass from a passing tray, held aloft by yet another beautiful girl:

Russian-looking, bleached blonde. Sarah surveys the crowd from behind an antique pair of binoculars she had picked up in the hotel shop—the perfect racegoer's accessory with the added benefit that they kept her face mostly hidden while scanning the room.

Women of all shapes and sizes are decked out in creations of organza and silk in the vibrant colours of tropical birds. Hoisted cleavages pop over the top of low-cut dresses, and bare shoulders rub alongside those well-covered in flowing and modest traditional Arab dress. Women adorned with the flowers and quills of Lady's Day at Ascot, chat to men in baseball caps and jeans, Savile Row suits mingle with designer T-shirts and the immaculate white robes of the Emiratis.

'Shall we go and find your man?' Alistair asks after knocking back a second whiskey.

'I'd rather he didn't know I was here. I don't want to put him off his stride.' Sarah had decided to follow Skarparov to Dubai after all, while Elias was in the mountains. With Irakli gone, he is her only remaining link to Ibragimov. But his readiness to rat out his uncle, his odd display of bluffer's behaviour during their chess game and Elias's warnings had planted too many questions that didn't add up. If he is going to be a useful informant, she needs to know if she can trust him.

'Everyone looks reasonably shifty in here; I'm not surprised it's tricky to track down your particular dodgy character.' Alistair gestures with his whiskey glass towards a group of dark-haired men. 'That's not him over there is it—Asiatic bunch by the over-the-top flower display, shiny suits and pointy shoes?' Sarah peers through her glasses and recognises the rodent features and creeping posture she had seen in Baku: Skarparov's right-hand man.

'Well spotted, Your Excellency. That's definitely his guy. No sign of the boss though.'

Skarparov's assistant finishes his whispered conversation and heads towards the exit with the hurried scamp of the eternal underdog.

'I'd like to see where he's off to,' she says. 'You don't mind if I leave you here a while, do you? I'm afraid you might be rather recognisable.' The Ambassador is wearing a tailcoat and is the only man in the room sporting a gleaming black top hat.

'Not at all, I suspect I'll find a way of keeping myself busy.' He wanders back in the direction of the bar.

Sarah follows Skarparov's man out of the VIP area and down the corridor towards the executive suites. In the towering heels from Michael's holdall, she struggles to keep up with the pace of her target without tripping. He turns into a corridor of meeting rooms, and disappears into the door marked "4".

Sarah totters past, shaking her hair down to cover the side of her face closest to the door. She sneaks a look through the gold, porthole-shaped window. Seated at the head of a table in a black leather armchair, tapping the ash from his cigar into a gold ashtray, is Skarparov. The other people in the room have their backs to the door. She keeps walking, aware that she is being watched by the stern-faced concierge at the end of the corridor. She approaches the desk with her best 'please help me' smile.

The concierge's stony grimace does not respond to Sarah's warmth. 'Can I be of assistance, madam?' He speaks in a South Asian accent, one of the city's army of migrant workers.

Her smile makes no impression, so she tries to bulldoze him with fast-talking assertiveness. 'I'm meeting my boss down here somewhere, but he forgot to give me the room number. Can you tell me where I'm supposed to be? It's a Mr Skarparov.'

A slightest flicker of the eyelids confirmed Sarah's suspicion. 'I'm sorry, madam, I cannot help you. All our clients' details are strictly confidential.' Sarah spots a list on the desk in front of him. He draws it away from her prying eyes.

'I'm not asking you to give me the number. I could just take a quick look at your list to work out where I need to be. I don't want them to wonder where I am.' Sarah tries to force her way forward.

'Names of our clients and guests cannot be shared.' The concierge leans in, bodily blocking Sarah's view of the list.

'Can't you at least tell me if he's down here?'

'Sorry, madam, but I cannot help you.' His face remains inscrutable, immune to her charms. She goes in search of back-up.

Alistair is still over by the whiskey bar. His cheeks and nose have taken on a rosy sheen.

'Alistair, I need your help.'

'Gosh, I've been hoping you were going to say that. I've always wanted to have a go at this spy game.' He rubs his hands together.

'Please,' Sarah shoots him what she hopes is a sobering look. 'I need you to create a diversion. Skarparov is downstairs in a meeting room. I'd like you to try and get the humourless watchman off his post, so I can have a look at who is with him.'

Alistair follows behind Sarah like a pleased puppy. Sarah waits at the end of the corridor as he makes his approach.

'Excuse me, young man, there's a lady outside making rather a scene.' The Ambassador takes the concierge by the arm and tries to manhandle him down the corridor.

'I'm sorry, sir, can I help you?'

'Yes. I'm afraid there's a lady who looks like she might need a bit of help. I fear she might have had rather too much to drink. She's gabbling and swaying all over the place.'

The concierge looks annoyed. 'I'm sorry, sir, you will have to talk to security.'

'No time for that. She looked like she was going to be sick. Gone a bit green around the gills, you had better hurry.'

The concierge lets out a sharp sigh, then shoots a look up and down the corridor. Alistair takes him firmly by the arm and marches him up the stairs.

With the concierge gone, Sarah slides the list from its hiding place. Room four is indeed in the name of Viktor Skarparov and, to her delight, the list includes the names of all guests cleared for access. Sarah whips out her phone and photographs the page before returning the paper to its spot. She hurries unsteadily back to the VIP area.

Pushing through a crowd of cigar-smoking teenagers, Sarah spots Alistair, supporting a nun in full black and white habit on his arm.

'Sarah,' Alistair looks suitably entertained by his predicament. 'Can I introduce you to Sister Margaret Conaghan? Dear lady is working in a mission in the tropics and is feeling rather giddy with local hospitality.'

'Is this your first time at the races, my pet?' Sister Mary speaks slowly with a strong Irish lilt, bringing her thread-veined face uncomfortably close.

'Yes, my first time in Dubai.'

Alistair could always be relied upon to boost the absurdity of any moment.

'We like to come every year,' Sister Mary says. 'It's fantastic fundraising; amazing what you can get people to promise in a place like this.' Her tongue struggles to keep pace with her words. 'I ran into this fine gentleman on my way downstairs. I want to try and corner a Mr Skarparov, you don't know him at all do you?' she asks in her broad Irish twang.

'No, I'm afraid I don't.' Sarah glances at the Ambassador, trying to contain her surprise.

'He's a difficult man to get hold of. I've been wanting to talk to him for months about whether his company could support our mission's work in Kenema. I've heard they've got stacks of money and to think what the sisters could do with just a bit of it. They are really doing some fantastic work, and the good Lord knows how much it is needed.'

'I don't doubt it.' The Ambassador raises his eyebrows in bemusement.

'Well, I'm going to have another try downstairs,' Sister Margaret slurs, 'I hope that Indian gentleman doesn't get in my way again. I thought he was quite rude.' She marches off, legs widely spaced to steady her step.

Sarah admires her perseverance. 'Who on earth was that?'

'A rather charming Irish nun who might perhaps be a little worse for wear. I'm afraid I set your po-faced concierge on her and then had to step in when it looked like she was going to hit him with her handbag. But what are the chances of that, eh? She's also after Skarparov. I wonder if she's one of yours.'

Sarah wonders which of Skarparov's companies the nun could be referring to. She can't see how a carpet-making foundation or a few failing casinos could be of much help to the nuns.

A resonant voice floats out of the tannoy, 'Ladies and Gentlemen, I invite you to take your positions by the viewing window. The evening's main event is about to begin.'

'Ah yes, the horses! I'd almost forgotten why we were here in all the excitement. Shall we watch?' Alistair offers Sarah his arm, and together they walk over to the glass wall of the VIP suite where the race can be watched from the comfort of icy conditioned air. Sarah pulls out her antique binoculars.

'Shame we can't have a bit of a flutter,' Sarah says. 'It always makes it a bit more exciting, don't you think? It seems a bit odd that at the most expensive race in the world, gambling is banned.'

'Oh, I almost forgot. Now where has Hamid got to?' Alistair looks around the crowd of spectators.

'Hamid?'

'I spotted him earlier, has a link to some bookies in London. A "placement facilitator", I think he called himself.'

They spot a man in the corner wearing an impeccably white and pressed dishdasha, juggling two mobile phones while scribbling notes on scraps of paper. He is flanked by two assistants, one Arab and one South Asian, who are trying to follow his gabbled instructions while catching the papers as he tears them off the notepad. Sarah watches as Alistair strolls over, cutting through the crowd of would-be gamblers. He seems to engage one of the assistants in a jovial chat as they point out the window, then moves off, slipping a handful of notes into the assistant's hand.

'I put a few dirham on the British horse, got to keep the side up. Although I think he might be owned by the Sheikh. Still, drinks on me if he places.'

'Brilliant. Who are we cheering for?'

Alistair consults his race notes. 'Elmustanser, apparently.'

'Fine British name,' Sarah grins.

Down on the track the horses are warming up, circling nervously as jockeys whisper in their ears. They cast four-way shadows under the floodlights, like jacks in the sand beneath a blackened sky. Sarah finds it odd to look down to the edge of the track and not see the standard row of bookies with chalkboards, endlessly adjusting their odds as the final bets come in. In their place, the standing pens are segregated into the different layers of Dubai society. At the end closest to the grandstand are the elite in flowing robes and red and white keffiyehs. Further away, packed tightly in the pen, are the migrant workers—Indians and Pakistanis in lungis, West Africans in crocheted skull caps and pristine voluminous silk robes.

Death of a Rose breaks slowly, allowing a pack of four to draw ahead and sniff the possibility of stealing his much-anticipated victory. But the early leaders are not able to keep the pace across the two thousand metres. The favourite whips around the outside of the field to take the lead as they come into the straight, the red and white silks of the jockey mirroring the ubiquitous branding of Emirates Airlines. Hamid, the surreptitious bookie, grows ever more animated as the race progresses, shouting into his battery of mobile phones in a confused mix of English and Arabic. A skinny assistant hastily retrieves one of the phones that had been flung to the floor, punching at the keypad to regain the connection before the end of the race.

As the horses thunder past an oasis of towering fake palm trees and into the final stretch, the skyline of Dubai comes into view—glass boxes and blades reaching incongruously out of the desert. The leading jockey glances over his shoulder, before charging ahead for the final five hundred metres to win by three lengths. The crowd erupts into applause.

'Well, that was that then.' Alistair looks a little let-down. 'All that build-up and fanfare for just over two minutes of excitement and then everyone is back to their evening. But six million dollars for the winner. Can you imagine! I'm afraid our British horse seems to have come in last.'

Hamid, by now breaking a sweat in his immaculate robes, is quickly surrounded by a crowd of punters eager to collect their winnings. Sarah spots Sister Margaret, face flushed and beaming, staggering towards one of his assistants, waving a slip of paper.

Down at the podium, the owners and trainers are gathering for the prize presentation. A three-foot-high cup, suitably gold and gaudy, is handed to the winning owner by Sheikh Mohammed, flanked by a line of uniformly smiling Emirates Air Hostesses. As the owner, red-faced and sweaty but grinning ecstatically, staggers down from the podium clutching his monster cup, Sarah sees a silver suit approach. She double-checks with her binoculars—definitely Skarparov. She can make out the shovel-shaped nose and a flash of his pale opal eyes. He accosts the winning owner and whispers something in his ear. A group of men hang back behind him. Sarah slips out her phone and takes a few more shots, hoping the resolution would be high enough to capture the faces. Moments later, Skarparov and his entourage have disappeared, leaving the crimson-cheeked winner to his next round of congratulations. Sarah wishes she knew what he was doing there and what had been said. It surprises her to see him so comfortable in wheeler-dealer mode. Up until now he has always been more fin-de-race playboy—too well mannered to ever dream of getting his hands dirty with work. Now, watching him flanked by his shifty-looking crew, he looks like the man in charge.

The Ambassador sways gently at her side. 'What do you say to a nightcap to round off all that excitement?'

'Why not?' she replies. 'I think we can celebrate a job well done.' Sarah takes the Ambassador's arm as he leads her towards the exit.

After a tour of several soulless hotel bars, the evening ends in the small hours with Alistair, still in his shiny top hat, holding court in the Filipino guest-workers' disco near the creek. Sarah, who is struggling to hold her head up after a string of lurid cocktails, is glad to have sent the photos and names back to Steve in Tbilisi before heading out for the evening. She can't relax into Alistair's carefree mood, she's too impatient to find out whether Steve can identify anything useful. Is it too much to hope that someone he met here might have some connection to Ibragimov or the Russian weapons? The number of questions she has is stacking up but she's still woefully short of answers.

CHAPTER 39

TARGET PRACTICE

Inside a disused barn, at the back of a friend's farm, the Pawn sets up a target range. At one end, a bucket placed on a bale of hay. They said it didn't need to be too high. He carefully paces out the five-metre radius and marks it with two brown plastic chairs, one on either side of the bucket. Then he paces back towards the centre of the barn, fifteen full strides, plus a little extra for good measure. He scuffs out the arc on the floor with his toe, drawing a line in the dust and loose pieces of hay. He stands back, taking in the set-up. Inside the chairs, everyone dead. Inside the line, maimed or injured. It looks bigger than he expected. Even if his aim is off, he should have no trouble at least wounding the target.

He has prepared a variety of objects to throw. He doesn't like to use the real thing. It feels too risky: repeated impact might damage the device, or shake loose the pin. Besides, he doesn't like having it around, even in their van. It is safely stashed for now in his basement, his mother's basement, but his workshop, where he knows it will be safe.

A naval orange—not heavy enough, but a good size, and satisfying to throw—lands with a juicy pop just inside the chairs. A bag of flour—weighed out to measure precisely four hundred-and-fifty-four grams, the weight of the device, clunky and difficult to handle, poor aerodynamics, but the weight was exact. He fluffs the throw and it lands five metres from his feet. He is dead. But the aerodynamics are shit. That doesn't count. A pair of rusty metal balls—good size, but not heavy enough, good practice for the arm action. He sets up the stance, shoulder blades together, chest pushed out, imitating the confidence of The Castle. The first ball hits a chair—good enough, the second lands at the foot of the bale of hay—better. Finally, the head of a hammer, handle removed - half a kilo so fifty grams over, but solid, and feels good in his palm. He draws back once again and throws. The solid metal head rebounds off the bucket with a gratifying clang. He pictures the puppets' strings snapped, their crumpled figures falling to the floor. Mission accomplished.

CHAPTER 40

Ke1 Be3

Sarah punches in the code to access Steve's "upstairs" section of the embassy. He had told her to come in early as he had something to show her. She had scarcely slept the night before in anticipation. But just as the first door in the airlock clicks open, Sopho catches her arm.

'Sarah, I have something for you. Have you got a moment?' Sopho's face is alight, struggling to contain her excitement.

Sarah is torn. She's tempted to leave Steve hanging to see what Sopho has uncovered, but she's just as curious to follow up on Skarparov's hangers-on in Dubai. Her heart beats solidly in her chest—after weeks of getting nowhere she might just have two leads at once. 'I've just got to pop in to see Steve, I'll come straight down to you afterwards.'

'Don't be long,' Sopho cautions. 'The Ambassador will be in soon.'

Sarah slams through the airlock doors and takes the stairs two at a time. The door at the top opens onto a wall of heat. She finds

Steve sweating at his desk, his thick hair plastered to his head.

'Have you got something for me on those names? God it's hot in here.'

'AC seems to have packed up so now we're sitting in a hermetically sealed box with no windows.' He wipes his forehead with his sleeve. 'I'm wondering if this is training for advanced interrogation techniques.'

'The names?' Sarah prompts.

'Yes.' Steve passes her an annotated list, the limp paper feels damp to the touch. 'The good news is we've got positive IDs on most of them. Odd bunch, don't know what to make of it.'

Sarah runs her eye down the list of unfamiliar names.

'This guy,' Steve points to top name, 'Yiorgos Komodromos, is the head of a Cypriot shipping company. We've done a bit of digging into the company and haven't found anything too untoward—reasonable sized operation, handles goods going from everywhere to anywhere. Mostly European and African routes. They were investigated for shipping agricultural goods to Rwanda just before the genocide, so may have a few dodgy clients. But that doesn't make them arms dealers, does it? Any idea what you're looking for?'

'Not really, just anything that might unlock what Skarparov is up to other than heading a phoney foundation.'

'The next guy is more interesting. Osa Adebayo, Nigerian, works for the African Union in the Security and Defence Team. He blotted his copybook a few years ago trying to bribe officials in Eritrea but was let off. Seems to travel to some pretty unsavoury places, but then that's not surprising in his job. No clue what he was doing in Dubai. God, I'm sweltering.'

Steve loosens his tie and goes to punch optimistically at the thermostat on the wall. His shirt looks like an archipelago of sweat islands. Sarah feels a damp patch growing in the small of her back, she can't wait to get back to the relative comfort of downstairs.

'And the last name?'

'UN Logistics, Omar Said, a Libyan. A career UN staffer—pops up all over the place, keeps his nose mostly clean but there's always dirt if you dig enough. Mr Said was investigated for fudging expense claims in Darfur, but it was pretty low-level stuff. We ran all the names through the Service and Interpol lists, but nothing came up. No smoking gun, I'm afraid.'

Sarah was hoping for more—a link to Ibragimov or some more concrete clues. She reads the names again, committing the details to memory and trying to piece together what could link this odd cast of characters to Skarparov.

Steve fans himself with his notebook. 'I thought you were supposed to be getting closer to Skarparov as a way to Ibragimov?'

'I was, but I'm starting to realise there is much more to him than meets the eye.' Sarah checks her watch. 'And the photos?'

'Now, those are interesting.' Steve spreads the enlarged prints Sarah had taken at the racecourse across the desk. 'I recognised a couple of the faces myself and had the rest verified by our North Caucasus team in London. Chechens, a nasty bunch. Two of them used to be bodyguards for Dudayev, known for gun running, drug smuggling, relatively minor stuff around the border, but they're on our watch list. God only knows what they are doing hanging around Skarparov at the races.'

'Any links to the Foundation?' She peers more closely at the grainy images.

'None as far as we know, but we don't really know much about the Foundation. That,' Steve gives her a teasing look, 'was supposed to be your job.'

'From what I've seen of it, I wouldn't be surprised if this bunch were its main beneficiaries. A convenient cover for smuggling things across the border. Thanks, Steve, this is great. I've got to run.' She gathers up the papers and photos.

He places a sweaty hand on the papers. 'Better leave them there. I'd rather they didn't leave this section.'

She nods and turns to leave but Steve has beaten her to the door. He stands in front of the heavy handle, blocking her exit.

'You know you can always call on me, I'm here to help you, Sarah. I'm on your side.' He gives her a meaningful look.

Sarah nods. 'Of course, thanks.'

'Really, there's no glory in striking out on your own with characters like this, and you could be putting yourself in considerable danger. Please don't be afraid to ask if you need back-up.'

Is he trying to reassure her or make her feel in danger? If it's the former, then he definitely needs to work on his technique. She nods her thanks for his awkward warning and hurries downstairs to find Sopho.

'So what did you find?' Sarah asks as soon as Sopho has pressed closed the door to the Ambassador's office.

'Not much on Ibragimov, at least not outside Azerbaijan. His business doesn't seem to extend far beyond Baku. He's got a few interesting connections in government, but surprisingly little outside the country. I tried to put it together here for you.' She hands Sarah a meticulously drawn map with Ibragimov at the centre and lines leading to different sectors of the political, business and government circles in Baku. Each name written in a careful hand with a line of background. The type of relationship was colour-coded, creating a precise web of connections, alliances and influences.

'This is brilliant, Sopho.'

'But here's the interesting thing—he's got a Service pay code.'

'You mean he's being paid by SIS?'

'I can't tell whether it is currently in use. But it means either he has been paid in the past or someone was preparing to pay him.'

'Ibragimov has received payment from British Intelligence?' Sarah is stunned.

'Like I said, I can't tell when. But someone was certainly thinking about it.'

'How did you find all this?'

'Steve lets me use his access codes when I need them.' She

gives a shy smile, lowering her thick doe-like lashes.

'Can we see when the last payment was made?'

'Unfortunately not. I can't see record of any payment or even when it was opened. But I'll keep digging.'

Sarah's mind is racing through the possibilities that this information might unlock. Why would the Service have been paying Ibragimov? She wonders if this is yet another thing Michael hasn't told her or whether he himself doesn't know.

'And there's more.' Sopho hands over another stack of papers, unable to hide her excitement. 'When I looked wider in the region, I couldn't find much on Ibragimov, but Skarparov started to show up.' Skarparov's web extends across two sheets of A3 with the same colour-coded lines of connection. The map stretches into Georgia, Russia and Turkey, with two fresh pages dedicated to Europe and Africa.

'And that's just the start. He seems to have connections in Africa, particularly West Africa. But nothing is publicly listed, at least not under his name. For someone with an international profile, he has very little registered officially in his name.'

Sarah's eyes fall to a photo on Sopho's desk. A young girl of perhaps twelve in a navy school uniform smiles at the camera. She has Sopho's bright intelligent eyes.

'Is that your sister?' Sarah asks.

'My daughter,' Sopho blushes. 'Tamuna.'

'She looks just like you. I didn't know you had a daughter. I didn't think you could be old enough,' Sarah smiles, meaning to give a compliment but reading in Sopho's reaction that she has been indelicate.

'She lives with my parents.' Sopho's eyes linger on the photo. 'The hours Alistair likes to keep are not that easy for childcare. But I see her at the weekends.' Sopho stops herself and glances at Sarah apologetically. 'I hope you don't mind—'

'No, of course not,' Sarah cuts her off, trying to put her at her ease. She remembers Sopho's reluctance to join her at the carpet exhibition on a Friday evening. She's eager to find out more, to open up the human connection, but is worried her questioning will send Sopho back into her shy shell. 'I'd love to meet her.'

Sopho brushes away Sarah's awkwardness with a broad grin. 'Of course. She'd love you. But I meant I hope you don't mind that I started following up on his casinos.'

'Of course I don't mind. Michael mentioned something about casinos. But weren't they mostly sold off?'

'Most of them, yes, or changed formal ownership. But there's one remaining in Amsterdam.'

'Amsterdam?'

'It's not the only business he owns there. He's also on the board of a diamond polishing business.'

'Diamond polishing? What has that got to do with casinos and oil companies?'

'Just what I thought! But that's as far as I've got. It's hard to track down concrete information. I think he likes to hide.'

'I bet he does. Thank you, Sopho, this is excellent. How were you able to find all this? I spent hours online looking for information on him, but he has almost no digital footprint at all.'

'Like I said, Steve lets me use his access codes for admin work.' Another sheepish smile, this time with a definite hint of mischief.

'Can I give you one more name?' Sarah is kicking herself for not realising sooner what a useful asset Sopho would prove to be. Did the Ambassador have any idea of her value or was she just used for making tea? 'Nikolay Kuznetsov. I've tried to find him, but it's such a common name I can't find anyone who makes sense. There's a Soviet naval officer, a rocket engine designer and a painter, but they are all dead. And a footballer and a rower but I can't see a link with Skarparov. Can you have a look?'

'I'd be happy to. By the way, Sarah,' Sopho seems suddenly uncomfortable, her easy grace faltering. 'I was filing your expenses for the Dubai trip. I expected your contract to be the same as the others upstairs, but it all looked quite different. You are an employee of the Service, aren't you?'

'Yes, of course. I mean, yes, they are my employers.' Sopho's question unpicks a seam of doubt. The recruitment process and interviews with Michael had been so carefully intriguing and obtuse that Sarah had never thought to ask about terms and conditions. Their discussions on moral dilemmas had never touched on pension plans and leave days. Then everything had moved so fast that she had no time to ask about a contract. She had assumed that the offer she had accepted was to join the Secret Intelligence Service, as a full employee. It had not occurred to her that Michael may have made different arrangements.

'Oh, well perhaps it was my mistake.' Sopho's lowered eyelashes tremble.

Alistair marches into the office. 'Sarah, what brings you here?'

'I was just helping Sarah with her expense claims, Your Excellency,' Sopho cuts in. 'Have you got any contacts in the HR department?' she asks Sarah. 'I asked my usual contact how I should process it, but she didn't seem to know who you are.'

Sarah cheeks begin to burn. 'I've only ever met Michael.' She looks to Sopho for reassurance, but her deep brown eyes are fixed firmly on the desk.

'There's not an actual person called Michael, is there?' the Ambassador interrupts looking amused. 'How very confusing that must be!'

The seam of doubt rips open, but she doesn't understand. Alistair's still laughing, 'Oh come on, Sarah, you get it? Michael? Mike for short? MI6? It doesn't actually refer to a real person. It's just the accepted way of referring to the Service, a little joke I suppose, but handy when you're in public. Surely you knew?'

Sarah swallows back the lump in her throat. 'Yes of course, I just... well, my contact is also called Michael.'

'That's what he told you eh? The slippery fish. Did he give you a fanciful surname as well? I worked with a spook once who called himself Cumberbatch. He was a military chap and some bright spark had elevated him to the rank of Quartermaster

Sergeant so that he could be known as Q Cumberbatch. Didn't believe it for a minute, but you certainly remembered who he was when he picked up the phone.'

Sarah is no longer listening. Her mind is in flux, reeling from what Alistair had just let slip. Her relationship with Michael had always felt one-sided—he fed her information on a need-to-know basis, and she followed his lead. But she never doubted that Michael was who he claims to be.

'What's your Michael's fanciful surname?' Alistair asks.

Sarah is too mortified to admit that she doesn't know.

'I knew a Michael in the service once,' he continues, seemingly unaware that his every word is sending Sarah into free-fall. 'Came across him in Moscow years ago, a bit of an odd fruit, always looked immaculate, three-piece suits and perfect hair. Impressive chap, but somehow a bit too slick, a bit too condescending to be charming.'

'And where is he now?' Sarah manages to ask, suspecting she already knows the answer.

'God only knows. He was put out to pasture years ago after getting caught out in some bribery case.'

Rising unsteadily to her feet, Sarah mutters words of apology and runs upstairs to Steve's office.

'Steve,' she says, supporting herself against the door frame, 'I need to talk to Michael.'

'Do you want to sit down? You look terrible. Has something happened?'

'Michael, who was here, at the airfield.' Sarah tries to control the rising pitch of her voice. 'I need to talk to him.'

Steve does not meet her eye.

'He gave me a mobile number, but it doesn't work anymore. I need to speak to him.'

'Is it something I can help with?' Steve fishes out a handkerchief to wipe his forehead.

'Alistair has just mentioned an SIS man who sounds remarkably like my Michael, except that he was chucked out years ago.'

Steve's cheeks glow fire-engine red as he pulls off his drooping tie and ensures the door is firmly shut. He offers Sarah a chair which she reluctantly accepts as an alternative to her jelly-like legs. 'He was never actually chucked out, just side-tracked off his stellar rise.'

'For doing what?'

'For accepting a briefcase of cash from someone he shouldn't have done, so I heard. He always claimed he was set up, and well, they didn't fire him…'

'So what is he doing offering me a job?' Sarah explodes.

Steve squirms deeper into his chair. 'I think you should be asking him that, not me.'

'How can I, if I can't even speak to him?'

'Look, I don't know the details, but from what I understand, in recent years he's had a bit of a reprieve. Everyone realised we'd taken our eyes off the ball. We'd lost our edge in good old-fashioned human intelligence. We had too many spooks getting comfy in embassies and not enough putting themselves in the front line chasing the intel. I don't know much about Michael's outfit other than that it's mostly off the books.'

'So I'm a deniable pawn?' Sarah asked.

'Again, you'll have to ask him. Do you want me to try the switchboard?'

'Don't bother. I think I know how to get him to pick up the phone. I need to get in touch with a wealthy Turk—any ideas?'

'Ed had his last posting in Ankara, he might—'

Sarah is already flying down the stairs.

Ed, the gangly Third Secretary who had first introduced Sarah to the Ambassador, is sitting behind his desk poring over a car magazine. Hearing Sarah's knock he springs up, catching his kneecaps on the underside of the desk.

'Sarah?' he smooths his foppish fringe back, drenched in embarrassment. 'Good to see you, come in.' He tries to perch casually on his desk but is let down by the awkward fold of his arms and an uncertainty about what to do with his legs.

'Dilara Saban. Do you know her?'

'Dilara? Of course, everyone knows her. Her family's pool parties are legendary. I've never been fed so much tequila before midday. What on earth do you want with her?'

'Helping out a friend. Do you have her number?'

'I used to. Not sure if it will still be the same. Girls like her have a habit of changing their phones pretty regularly. Let me have a look.' He pulls out his phone and begins scrolling through the contacts. 'Here it is.' He hands Sarah the phone.

'You've saved her under DD?'

'That's what we used to call her.'

Sarah raises an eyebrow.

'Honestly, *I* didn't make it up. Do you need—'

'I'll bring it back.' Sarah runs back up to Steve's office, still clutching Ed's mobile.

'Steve, I need a secure line.'

Steve looks unsure whether to help her or to sit her down with a nice cup of tea.

'Now.'

He leads her into a small cubicle—the floor, walls and ceiling are lined with padded grey felt. Sarah's ears swell in the silence as if a dense blanket has been drawn close over her head. The air in the room feels thick in her lungs.

'Weird, isn't it?' Steve says. 'Always gives me the creeps being in here, I feel like I'm in a morgue. You can't even hear yourself breathe. But you can be pretty sure no one is earwigging. The phone's over there. Know how it works?'

'I'll manage.'

He slips out, closing the padded door behind him.

*

'Helloooo?' Dilara's voice sounds rich and warm in the silence.

'Dilara, it's Sarah.'

273

'Sarah? Do I know a Sarah?'

'Michael's friend. We met in Georgia, at the airstrip.'

'Oh yes! I helped you out with your little problem,' she purrs.

'I need your help.'

'More pigs to feed?'

'Not this time. I need to talk to Michael.'

'So call Michael.'

'I can't. His number isn't working.'

Dilara stays silent for a moment. 'Why would I give you his new number if he didn't give it to you himself?'

'Because he gave me your name.'

'One moment.' Dilara shouts something in Turkish. 'I'm at my aunt's Botox party. Never been more bored in my life.' Another peal of honeyed laughter.

'So can you give me Michael's number?' Sarah is fit to explode.

'No. I can't.' She sounds as if she is about to laugh again.

'Please, it's important.'

'Of course it is, or you wouldn't have called me. I'll get him to call you.'

'Thanks.' Sarah's voice echoes back through the receiver. Dilara has already hung up.

Moments later the phone rings.

'Michael?' she feels self-conscious using this name in case it was also a half-truth, but has no other way to address him.

'No darling, it's me again,' Dilara says. 'He's in Vienna the day after tomorrow. He says to meet him there, Cafe Mozart on the Ringstrasse at eleven.'

'Thank you. I'll be there.'

'No need to thank me. Next time you help me. *Güle güle, ciao!*

CHAPTER 41

Bf1 Rh1

Sarah boards the flight to Vienna feeling sick. Fury writhes in her stomach like a wounded snake. What the hell has Michael led her into and how could she have been so naive not to question him more when she had the chance?

Her seat is sandwiched between two heavy-set Caucasian men, shiny suit jackets spilling over the armrests. She waves away the offer of chicken-or-beef, staring at the film playing in silence above her head while her turbulent thoughts epicentre around Michael.

Why didn't he tell her she was part of his pet project? And why was he using her for this mission? She has only ever met *him*, never seen a colleague, never signed a contract. What was she thinking? She shifts in her seat, sending static sparks flying from the grey polyester headrest. Jim in Baku had alluded to some personal history between Michael and Ibragimov. Had Michael recruited her just to settle a personal vendetta? A conveniently deniable pawn to be sacrificed if the risk becomes too high.

It would explain why he had made it so difficult to contact him. Having to beg Dilara for help only added to Sarah's humiliation. Did he expect her to just carry on with no help or support? For all the people who have told her they were "on her side", she has never felt more alone.

The man to her right tosses in his sleep, crushing her under his hefty shoulder. 'Fuck Michael,' Sarah shouts, the shock of the impact giving voice to her thoughts. The owner of the offending shoulder, woken by Sarah's sudden outburst, pulls off his eyeshade and looks at her in bleary bewilderment. Sarah snaps shut her eyes and pretends furiously to be asleep.

*

Vienna droops in the heat of an early May morning. Oversized youths sweat in Mozart costumes, shiny velour clinging to thick thighs, their faces red beneath curly white wigs. Pyjama-clad pensioners fill the parks with the slow coordinated movements of tai chi, and yoga mats lie rolled out over concrete courtyards. Sarah watches from her taxi as men in business suits speed by on futuristic modes of transport, sporting extraordinary hairdos and over-the-top eyewear. After the homogeneity of the Caucasus, where men wear uniform black leather jackets and women are modestly dressed, the array of colour and sheer diversity of the Viennese make the city look dressed for carnival. Sarah is wearing a bright blue hooded sweatshirt bearing the logo of the Italian football team. She bought it on impulse at the airport, attracted by something that would never have been chosen by Michael. It is uncomfortably hot, but at least she blends in.

She plans to arrive a little after the appointed time, to be sure that Michael would be there first, asking the taxi to drop her several blocks away so that she can approach on foot. She feels weary to her core, her head unusually heavy, but as she turns on to the Ringstrasse she becomes instantly alert. Something catches her attention and snaps her awake, like a mental twang of elastic. The world feels closer, the volume cranked up. She scans her surroundings, but nothing in the scene registers as unusual. She sees the cafe ahead of her, shiny silver-topped tables crowded on the pavement. Tourists, students and businesspeople enjoying a morning cup of coffee sit elbow to elbow. A horse and carriage veer into the centre of the road to avoid the path of a bright yellow tram. She scans the austere facades of the buildings opposite, stacked rows of pedimented windows, broken by wires and the branches of trees. One window is propped half open, but it is a hot day. Nothing looks obviously out of place.

From some distance away she sees him, crisp blue shirt at the centre of the crowded tables on the pavement. Sarah is surprised he is so visible, almost on display. Normally he prefers the edges of a room, where he can see but not be seen.

'Sarah?' He rises to greet her with a kiss on the cheek and guides her into her chair, his grip surprisingly firm on her arm. 'I thought it might be you.'

'Dilara didn't tell you I was coming?'

'She didn't, but she made it all sound so deliberately mysterious, I had my suspicions. Why didn't you call me directly? Why go through all this charade?'

'How could I call you? The number you gave me either doesn't work or you don't answer.'

'Oh? I do apologise.' He speaks as if it was entirely inconsequential whether or not he had left her stranded. 'So, what is it?' He straightens a small cup of coffee on its saucer and shakes out a sachet of sugar.

She has rehearsed in her head how to confront him without sounding naive. But, as always with Michael, his presence throws her. The impenetrable stare of his blue eyes, the careful charm that is both beguiling and deliberately distancing. She never knows how to play him.

'Who are you?' is the best she can manage.

'I'm sorry. I think I might need another coffee if we're going to get existential.'

277

'Drop the act. I need some straight answers. Starting with who you really are. Who do you work for?'

He glances over his shoulder, 'Perhaps we could discuss this elsewhere?'

'No, here is fine,' Sarah says. 'Answer the question.'

'I work for Her Majesty's Government, as you well know.'

'And who do I work for?'

'You work for me.' He gives her a lop-sided smile, revealing his scarred top lip. It is the only part of his face that shows any trace of softness.

'Why didn't you tell me this wasn't a normal recruitment?'

'What do you think constitutes normal in this business?' A slight raise of his groomed brow. 'When I first take people on, particularly if they are very fresh, I find it helps to have a little distance to begin with. I've learned from experience that people work best when they've earned your trust.'

'So we're sent out like cannon fodder and you can deny all knowledge if it goes wrong?'

'You're given the chance to prove yourself.' Michael leans back to allow a waiter to squeeze past with a tray heavily laden with glistening cake.

'And do I officially exist?' Sarah lowers her voice. 'Does anyone in headquarters know who I am or am I your pet project?'

'I have a small team; we are responsible for you.'

'And is Dilara part of that team?'

'No. As I told you before, Dilara is a friend. We have no official relationship.'

'So I'm part of some off-the-books disposable group that you can do with what you will?'

'Now, Sarah, you're being hysterical. Our embassy friends have taken good care of you, have they not? You've hardly been chucked out on your own?'

'I'm not being hysterical, but I think I deserve to know where I stand.'

'Of course you do. What else would you like to know?'

He has a way of making everything seem so simple, of making all of her concerns sound trivial, her questions unnecessary. But she knows she deserves more.

'Ibragimov. Why didn't you tell me you knew him?' she asks.

'What makes you think I know him?' he adopts a quizzical look, but it doesn't fly. Sarah can smell his discomfort beneath the bored nonchalance.

'When he set me up, he gave me a briefcase and told me to give it to Michael.'

'So where is it?'

'I lost it.' Sarah enjoys Michael's flash of impatience. If he's going to be impossible, she's happy to join him.

'And what was in it?'

'I don't know, I didn't look. Why would he want to give it to you? Why would he know your name?'

'How do you know he meant me? Lots of people use Michael as a euphemism, a way of—'

'Yes, I know.' Sarah snaps. 'He has an SIS pay code; he is known to the service. Why did we need this elaborate approach? What am I doing chasing after him if someone already knows him well enough to pay him?'

'Does he? How do you know?' Michael's disinterested act finally slips. This is obviously news to him.

Sarah pauses, not wanting to give away Sopho's secrets.

'It's okay,' Michael nods. 'You can protect your source—for now. But I'll look into it. That might change everything.'

He watches a horse and carriage pass by the busy street, his eyes suddenly far away. Sarah can almost see the cogs churning in his mind, but in which direction? She often feels he is playing more than one game at once. From time to time he would disappear, dip out of conversations mid-flow to make a silent move on another board. What possibilities has she unlocked with that information?

'You didn't answer my question—why send me if there was already a relationship established?'

'I assure you, I had no idea.'

'But you knew him? Why not go yourself?'

'He is hardly going to spill his secrets to me just because I ask. I thought you might have more luck with a fresh approach. And besides, our last encounter didn't end all that well.'

'Was he the one who set you up?'

'Who told you about that?' Michael's face hardens.

'Just a hunch. Am I right?'

He shifts in his chair. 'That's really a story for another day.'

Sarah feels again that same ripple of acute awareness. She scans the faces at the next-door tables, searching for something she might have recognised. Her ears filter the different noises of the street, the chatter of the cafe and clink of cutlery, a blackbird calling overhead.

'Is everything okay?' Michael asks. 'You look distracted?'

'Something doesn't feel right.'

'What? What doesn't feel right?' There is a quiet urgency in his voice, another crack in his polished shell but this time Sarah catches a glimpse of a human being inside, and he's scared.

In truth, nothing feels right—her being here at his bidding but without his support. His knowing so much about her while she knows so little about him. His unwillingness to discuss anything with her without turning her concerns into trivialities. Her inability to voice any of these concerns out loud.

'So you know Ibragimov, but you don't trust him?' she asks.

'Of course not, would you?'

'But still you sent me in to meet him?'

'That is how this works. Would you rather I sent you to Disneyworld?'

'No, Michael, I'd rather you explained what you want me to do. I'd rather you gave me a proper background to the mess you've thrown me into. I'd rather I could get hold of you without having to go through your Turkish vamp.'

'I really am sorry about that. It wasn't my intention to be so remote. I told you I don't like mobiles. But you seem to have managed perfectly well without me. Are you any closer to working out what Ibragimov's up to?'

'Do we have any concrete proof that the pipeline is the target?' she asks. 'Skarparov seemed to think he'd want something more damaging to the region.'

'And blowing up a newly opened, internationally-funded asset isn't that?'

'Skarparov thought it was too obvious.'

Michael taps his fingers on the shiny chrome tabletop. 'He's probably right. So what else then?'

'Ibragimov's networks outside Azerbaijan seem very thin. Could it be just a power grab in Baku, an attempt to regain some of his lost influence?'

'What was Hayden's view?'

'He was very careful not to give one.'

'And Skarparov?' Michael tips his head to one side, his subtle eyes give nothing away.

'He's definitely involved in all sorts of dodgy activities; I just haven't worked out what yet. But the more I learn about him, the less I trust him.'

'Follow your instincts, Sarah. Don't be blinkered by the obvious answers. Sometimes we just have to re-examine the question.'

Sarah starts to share the details she gathered in Dubai, hoping Michael might be able to uncover the link between Skarparov's odd collection of business associates, but Michael stops her.

'I'm sorry to be so short, but I'm afraid I can't stay. Talk to Steve—he'll be better placed than me to know who's who.' He sounds as if he is making excuses to leave a tedious cocktail party.

Sarah is flabbergasted; she's travelled all the way here to see him and that's it? 'But—'

'It's normal to have these moments of questioning; it's something that we all have to endure.'

'But can't you—'

'We all feel lonely, Sarah. It's part of the territory.' He stands to leave, bending to give her a swift kiss on the cheek. 'I have full confidence in you, but there is still work to be done. Keep to your brief and finish the job.'

'Michael, wait! Can't you at least tell me your full name?'

But he is already walking away across the crowded pavement.

Sarah watches him disappear through the crowds. The bastard. She came all the way here for that? We all get lonely. How many times has he used that line? Well, this time she is not going to stand for it. She hurries to chase after him, elbowing a passing waiter's tray. A thimble of espresso splashes across the next table and onto a businessman's morning newspaper. He jumps to his feet. A sharp sucking crack pierces the air, the sound of a wet rag being slapped against a wall. The businessman lurches forward with a low cry, his paper flies up and flutters in a dozen sheets in the gusty breeze.

Another shot rings out and Sarah dives to the floor, pulling the table down on top of her, exposing a long tear of splintered wood where the first bullet smashed through. She searches for Michael but there is no sign of him amongst the crowds of panicked people running from the scene. Would he come back for her?

She curls herself into a tight ball, rocking back and forth, sweat clinging to her plasticky sweatshirt and knees pressed against her teeth. Something in the rugged grain of denim against enamel brings comfort, a root to the physical world that is swooning around her. Everything is loud—movement everywhere, people scattering, people rushing in, teeth chattering under tables. Will there be another shot? Is it safer to stay or to run?

Sarah glances back at the figure slumped across the table, a dark stain blossoming across the back of his shirt, blood pooling to the aluminium edges of the cafe table. Who was he? At least it was a clean shot—he must have died before even hearing the crack. She searches her memory for anything she might have noticed about him before he took the bullet. He was sat so close to her, his elbow must have almost touched her own. Her mind replays the scene, lodging in the moment she jumped to her feet. What if she hadn't elbowed that waiter? What if she had stayed in her seat? Would she still be here to be having these thoughts? Her tongue feels covered in clumps of concrete and dust.

The blare of sirens helps scatter the crowds as two ambulances mount the pavement. Where the hell does she go from here? Paramedics rush towards the slumped form, scanning the terrace for casualties. A hand lifts her up, tries to coax her towards the ambulance, but all she wants to do is run.

The police string up black-and-yellow tape to cordon off the area, encouraging gawping tourists to move away. Staying with the bustle of other people feels safe, but she knows it's a false security. A gunman who opened fire on one of the busiest streets in Vienna would hardly be put off by a crowd. The noises around her are deafening, her legs feel too shaky to keep her moving forward. Who would want to shoot her? Ibragimov? Skarparov? She doesn't want to consider the possibility that Michael had a reason to leave when he did. Was his hurried departure part of a pre-arranged plan?

The city air feels thick and restrictive. She had booked a hotel not far from the city centre and flights to Kentucky the next morning. But if she is being tailed, that is the last place she should go. The historical centre with its grand squares and monumental buildings is too public, too exposed. She follows her instincts away from the cobbled, polished *Plätze* towards the dingier back streets, where the white stone palaces are streaked with grey. She ducks into an alcove to watch the street behind her. No one is following.

She slips inside a busy cafe, down a spiral staircase at the back and seeks out the toilets. Locking herself in the small single cubicle, she leans her forehead against the mirror above the tiny sink and heaves in a lungful of stale air. Graffiti-covered wallpaper makes the space feel oppressively close, her face reflected in the tarnished mirror looks bloodless and clammy. 'Fuck Michael,' she shouts for the second time that day. Why did she follow him

283

into this bloody mess?

Outside, a dim corridor leads to the service kitchens under the main cafe. Checking first to make sure no one is around, she bolts through the kitchens and straight out a back door, propped open for relief from the sweltering heat. She needs somewhere more permanent to hide than a toilet cubicle. Around the next corner, she finds what she is looking for. A dingy hotel, two grubby stars illuminated above the name *Pension Verner*, windows to the street blocked with heavy net curtains.

A lady with tortoiseshell glasses greets her, peering over the dark rims. Sarah checks in under the name of her school Geography teacher—Ms Perkins, sorry no reservation, no ID required. She is shown to a simple room on the second floor—the bed is tiny and a rusty orange stain blooms around the sink but for now, at least, she is safe. She tries to wash her hands and face in the basin, struggling to open the flimsy plastic that clings around the complimentary bar of soap. The un-graspable greasy strip is marked "Sealed for your Protection". Brilliant. She's being shot at, but the soap is watching out for her protection. She tugs the brown curtains closed and throws herself down on the sagging mattress.

If only she knew what Dilara had told Michael. If he was expecting Dilara to be there, then at least she could feel confident that he had not set up the shooting. But he had not seemed that surprised to see her. Did he hurry away from the cafe to avoid any more of her questions or had he known what was about to happen? Nothing is clear. Ibragimov has been on to her since Baku—if he was on the cusp of an attack, this would be the moment to get her out of the way. And if Skarparov had found out she'd been tailing him in Dubai, he might try to stop her digging any further. She pulls a lumpy pillow over her head.

*

Her mobile rings for some time before she dares to answer it.

'Hello?'

'Sarah, where are you?' Elias's voice is tense and hurried.

'I'm in Vienna.' She tries to adopt a lightness that hides her fragile state.

'What are you doing there?'

'I— I came to meet a friend.'

'Who? Who are you with?'

She almost laughs at the edge of jealousy in his voice. She wishes he could see her, pale and sweating on her dingy single bed. 'It doesn't matter. I'm alone.'

'You need to get back here. I think Skarparov is planning something, in fact I'm sure of it.'

'Skarparov?' Sarah pulls herself upright. 'Planning what?'

'I don't know, Giorgi won't talk to me, Irakli is no longer around to pump for information. But something is up. The women have been moved out of the project offices, there is a bluster of activity and a lot of nervousness, but no one is talking. Sarah? Can you hear me?'

'Yes, I'm here,' she answers weakly.

'You need to come back.'

'Yes, all right.'

'Are you okay? You sound distracted? Are you sure no one's there?'

'Sorry, I've had a bit of a rough day.'

'So you're coming?' there is an urgency in his voice she has never heard before.

'I was planning to go from here to Kentucky to follow the uncle.'

'Ibragimov?' he bulldozes over her attempts to be subtle on an open phone line. 'How do you know he is going to be there?'

'Skarparov told me. It starts in four days time—the tenth of May—apparently Ibragimov goes every year for the Kentucky Derby.' Something tugs at her memory and makes her pause 'Hold on.' She rummages through her bag for her notebook, but does not need to see it written down—she has it. 'Elias, that is the date of the US president's state visit to Georgia.'

'The same date Skarparov told you to be on the other side of the world? You should be here. Sarah?'

'I'm coming.'

CHAPTER 42

THE STRAWBERRY

Giorgi is closing up the project office when they burst in. This is the second bunch of goons this week. The last lot chased away the women and disconnected all the machines. No explanation given, they didn't even seem to notice Giorgi as he stood at the doorway trying to block their entry. This time Giorgi stays at his desk and lets them come.

But this pair are different. Giorgi has seen them before: Irakli's guys from Nakhchivan. He knows they have something to do with Irakli's logistics work, but he has no idea what. He always thought the less he knew about what Irakli was up to the better. Until they burst into his office and slam him against the wall, a thick meaty fist wrapped around his neck.

'I'm sorry,' he splutters, his tongue caught up in his mouth from the upward pressure of fist against larynx. 'I've got no idea what job you were doing and definitely don't know about your money.'

'Don't play dumb with us,' the bigger of the two and owner

of the meaty fist says, crushing Giorgi's full strength of resistance with a single arm. 'We know Irakli was getting his orders from the Boss via here. Then Irakli gets himself killed and some new guy turns up, tells us our target and disappears. You guys are crazy! You're going to need to pay us a hell of a lot more to pull this off.'

'I told you already, I don't know a thing about your money. This is a carpet-making Foundation.'

'Oh pull the other one,' the owner of the meaty fist laugh, not loosening his grip on the choke hold. 'So where are all the carpet makers, eh?'

'They're gone.'

'Uh huh.'

'They were cleared out by more of your lot,' Giorgi says. 'I promise that's all I know. I'm as much in the dark as you are.'

'Bullshit.'

The skinnier, beardier of the pair starts rummaging through the filing cabinets of Giorgi's office, pulling out the drawers of the desk, flinging carefully ordered papers and receipts onto the floor. 'The Castle must have told you something?' he says as he upturns another drawer onto the carpet.

'The Castle?'

'Yes, your boss. The one who they just pulled out of the river.'

'Irakli? I have no idea what Irakli was working on.'

'But he ran this place?'

'He used the job title, but he never had any interest in the Foundation's work.'

'So what are we supposed to do with the kit then?'

'What kit?' Giorgi asks, growing afraid of the shadow of panic in the aggression of his attackers. They are clearly out of options, and Giorgi doesn't like the thought of sharing a confined space with a pair of cornered beasts.

'The Sergei?! The big fucking strawberry under the giant iron lady you moron!' the neckless-hulk thunders, shaking with rage.

Giorgi sees the fear beneath the anger. Who are these goons?

Are they totally unhinged? What the hell had Irakli got them into? 'I'm sorry, I still have no idea what you are talking about.'

The smaller man heaves the solid wooden desk up on its side and tips it crashing to the floor, its glass top shattering as it strikes the ground.

The neckless hulk releases Giorgi from his vice against the wall to jump out the way of the flying glass. 'What the hell did you do that for?' He stares at his partner in disbelief.

'Fuck this shit,' the beardy goon shouts as he storms out of the office.

The hulk points a meaty finger at the point between Giorgi's eyebrows. 'You watch it. You hear anything, you tell us. You see anyone who knows about the plan, you tell him we want our money.'

Giorgi manages a small nod as he sinks to the floor.

CHAPTER 43

Qb5 f3

Elias meets her at the airport. Having not slept properly for days, Sarah almost falls into his arms.

'Are you okay?' He shoulders her bag, casting a sceptical glance at her incongruous sweatshirt. 'Do you want to go home and freshen up?'

'No time for that. I know I look like shit, but we've got work to do. Besides, I feel like if I lie down now I might never get up. What have I missed? How much do you know?'

He takes her hand and leads her out into the tarmac-rich heat of the airport car park. She blinks against the bright sun clawing her weary eyes.

'Skarparov has disappeared,' Elias says as he slings Sarah's bag into the back of a purple Lada Niva. 'There's no sign of him anywhere, no one's heard from him in days.'

'Any more news from the Project Offices in the mountains?' she asks as she climbs into the passenger seat.

'Poor Giorgi got a nasty roughing up yesterday from some

of Irakli's brutes. Came in ranting and raving about money and instructions and then trashed the place. He said they seemed half-mad.'

'Irakli's guys? Where are they now? Did Giorgi know who they were?'

'A pair of Azeris, from Nakhchivan. Apparently they know Irakli from way back. But God knows where they are now.'

The car gives an unpromising choke as the key turns in the ignition before the engine finally ticks over.

'Great.' Sarah taps her thumb against the open window. 'So all we know about them is that they were connected to a dead guy. Anything else? What about the offices here in Tbilisi—have you checked there?'

'The Skarparov Foundation offices? They've been shut up for weeks. I don't think anyone's been there since Irakli was… removed.'

'He was using it for his deliveries. I saw some guys there bringing something dodgy-looking during our first meeting. He must have been storing stuff somewhere round the back.'

'But surely he wouldn't have been stupid enough to keep anything there?'

'You never know. Any better ideas?'

'Let's go.'

*

The glass front of the Foundation Offices in Vake is covered by a metal shutter, marked with freshly-sprayed graffiti. The security cameras Sarah spotted on her first visit are still strangely angled back towards the window. They bring back the same hot flood of foolishness and regret. Such an amateur mistake for the sake of a few photos.

She leads Elias down the side passage where Irakli took the carpet-wrapped delivery. It ends at a garage with a pull-down door, locked fast. Elias kicks the fence at the side of the passage and see-saws and pulls loose a piece of wood. He shoves it under the garage door and jumps on it with all his weight to crowbar the lock. After a couple of jumps, it clatters open. 'After you,' he says, handing Sarah through the gap under the door. She has learned to love the advantages of being small, but there are times when she envies Elias the simple power of pure brawn.

Inside, it looks like a bomb has gone off in Ali Baba's carpet shop. Brightly coloured carpets stacked, piled, unrolled, flung down where they fell. Flashes of crimson and navy, webs of cream coloured warp and twine. Stacks of cardboard boxes and wooden crates with Cyrillic script down the sides line the walls. Sarah pulls down a pile—the boxes are empty, save for a few discarded cigarette butts and a sticky coke can.

She recognises the bright magenta hue of the carpet she saw on her first visit, but it lies empty on the floor. She pored over those photos after her trip to the mountains, hoping for a clue as to what had been in that heavy package. But they gave her nothing. She did not recognise the wide-necked thug who emerged from the van, or the driver, but on re-examining the pictures, she had realised why the greasy-haired "IT guy" in the mountains had looked so familiar. Levon had been on the receiving end of a sharp cuff from Irakli when he nearly let the cargo fall.

'Shit, look at this!' Elias holds up a large metal tin in dark green khaki. The lid curled off in jagged, sharp edges as if it had been prised open with a knife.

'What is it?' Sarah asks. 'It looks like a military-grade Popeye spinach can.' She takes the box from Elias to inspect the Cyrillic stamp on the lid.

'It's an ammo box,' he says. 'You see lots of these hunting in the mountains. But they're not normally that big.'

Sarah pushes back the lid—inside is a rough wooden box lined with white papers like an empty cigar box.

'Only thing that would take cartridges that size is an anti-aircraft gun.' His voice is quiet, the blood drains from his face. 'You don't think Irakli could have got his hands on one of those do you?'

'He was certainly well-connected with all kinds of dodgy types in Chechnya during the war. I don't see why not.' The pieces fall together in Sarah's mind. 'So that's what Skarparov is going to use to attack the US president?'

'That's what we're going to have to assume until we find anything else. But where the hell is it now? All these boxes are empty.' Elias kicks over a stack of wooden crates.

'The main event for the visit is in Freedom Square, isn't it? Security teams have been staking out the area outside the Embassy for weeks. What's the range for one of these things?'

'I don't know—a couple of kilometres maybe?'

'Well it can't be that easy to hide a massive gun like that.'

'Well, yes and no. It's big, sure, but with something that powerful you don't even need a window or line of sight. You could be sat behind a brick wall and would eventually punch through to your target. We can't possibly check every building within two kilometres of the square.'

'Are you sure there were no other clues from Giorgi? Who else in Tbilisi they're connected to? Where they stay when they're here? What's their favourite restaurant? Where their mother-in-law lives? There must be something we can go on.'

'He just said they were in full panic mode—ranting and raving and clearly out of options. Apparently they wanted Giorgi's help with a giant strawberry under an iron lady—clearly cuckoo.'

'An iron lady?'

'I think that's what he said, they must have lost the plot.'

'Can you see Freedom Square from Mother Georgia?' Sarah asks, trying to place the giant aluminium statue on the mountainside above the old town.

Elias drops the box he was holding. 'Get in the car.'

He chucks Sarah the keys and climbs into the passenger seat. 'Can you drive? I want to make some calls. If what we suspect is happening, is happening, there's not a lot we can do about it, going in alone.'

Sarah takes the wheel and follows Elias's pointed directions as he makes call after call, speaking a rapid mix of Russian and Georgian that she can't follow. They barrel down Rustaveli, past the shiny rotunda of the Philharmonic building, the hulking mass of a high-rise hotel now used to house refugees, the Rococo splendour of the Rustaveli theatre and out onto Freedom Square. As Sarah stops in the traffic snarled up around the great golden statue of the dragon-slayer, she finds herself picturing the carnage that would be wrecked by heavy artillery fire on a packed square.

Mother Georgia looks down on them from her hillside—staring munificently ahead, brandishing her sword and her bowl of wine. From down here, she lacks the intimidating size that had surprised Sarah up close in the Botanic gardens, but in terms of range, she is terrifyingly close. This is not a targeted assassination of two presidents; this is a spectacular show of overwhelming violence. Each of those shells is designed to explode an aeroplane out of the sky. What carnage would they create pointed at such close range on human targets? They would smash through bullet-proof glass as if it were cellophane, maim and kill anyone in their path—a massive exploding blanket of death laid down across the square.

Sarah pushes on, up through the narrow and winding streets of the old town, climbing steadily through the criss-cross of dangling electricity wire, crumbling pink brickwork, exposed rusty poles and red metal roofs. When she turns onto Sololaki Street, the aluminium statue rises like a beacon above their heads. Elias motions for her to park the car and carry on by foot. She looks up at her sword-wielding protector, willing her to spill her secrets. What has she seen? What has she hidden behind that enigmatic smile? Viewed from below, her curves seem more womanly—the swell of her abdomen more prominent, the roundness of her hips more ample. Her breasts look like an armoured plate - perfectly solid and round, and her arm muscles bulge under the weight of her offerings. The idealised female protector—welcoming and warrior-like, soft and feminine but unbendingly strong. Would she stand by while Skarparov's goons unleash blind slaughter on the square below?

'That one. That's where I'd choose.' Elias points out a red brick building near the foot of the statue. 'It looks deserted, and it's got the perfect angle down to the square.'

They circle the building. The windows are boarded up and the only entrance is locked.

'Maybe we should wait for back-up—what are we going to do if it's there?' Elias asks.

'But we don't even know if it is. We can hardly send in the riot police based on the ravings of one nutcase,' Sarah says. 'I think I can get up onto the roof—will you give me a foot up onto that tree?'

Elias helps her climb out across the narrow boughs of the tree that grows out of the building. The slender branches bend under her weight but prove just strong enough for her to catch onto the gutter and haul herself up. Maybe it isn't so bad to be a lightweight after all. She steps cautiously onto the flat felt roof covering and lies down, commando crawling towards the skylight in the centre. Inching forward as silently as possible, she pokes her head forward just far enough to see down through the window.

She clamps a hand over her mouth to silence her gasp, blood sloshing in her ears. Inside the building, directly under where she is lying, are the twin cannons of the biggest gun Sarah has ever seen. The whole apparatus takes up most of the room, the cannons pointing straight at the boarded-up windows. It is mounted on a kind of trailer that has been clawed to the ground on spiked metal plates. Two car tyres flick up from the sides like a massive military Transformer. One man sits in the seat, swivelling the barrels gently back and forth. Another sits on the floor next to the gun eating a pale *khatchapuri* cheese bread from a greasy square of paper. Sarah feels sick to her stomach. She tries to edge her way back, but she can't move; her muscles are locked in place, unable to look away.

'Are you all right up there?' Elias calls from below, rocking Sarah out of her paralysis.

'Shhh,' she hisses urgently. 'They're there.'

'Then come down, we can't let them leave.'

Sarah crawls back to the tree and shimmies into Elias's waiting arms. He's on his phone already as they run back past Mother Georgia to the car. They watch the building, scarcely able to breathe—what would they do if the guys came out? What if they'd seen her or heard her moving on the roof? What if they'd heard Elias? It was mad to turn up here without protection.

Her heart rate soars again as the first of the vans tears up the narrow street and screams to a halt outside the red brick building. She watches, speechless, as dozens of Georgian soldiers, kitted out in the finest new American-bought uniforms, heavily armed in full riot gear, pour out into the quiet street. The door to the building flies off its hinges with one swing of their battering ram and half of the soldiers pile in behind it. Loud shouts and the thunder of heavy boots follow, but not a shot is fired. Moments later, the two men Sarah saw inside the building are dragged outside, their hands secured behind their backs in cuffs, and pushed into the back of one of the windowless vans.

Was that it? It had happened so quickly Sarah could scarcely compute all that she had just seen. Less than twenty-four hours has passed since they worked out Skarparov's target, less than one hour since they realised the full devastation of his plan, and now the horror of the threat has fizzled out. These two men must be the pair who had turned on Giorgi. The weapon they were in charge of was unmistakably intended for an attack on the square. And now that attack would never happen. Sarah is reeling from the speed of all that had happened, but somehow her brain refuses to process any feeling of relief. It seems all too easy, too quick.

She turns to Elias—to share her uncertainty, her disbelief—but he is plainly jubilant.

'My god I love the way your brain works!' he declares,

sweeping her into his arms. 'It had never occurred to me that the rantings of those goons could possibly mean anything. But you brought us here. You pulled this off. Sarah? This is amazing, why do you look so crestfallen?'

Sarah shakes her head. 'Sorry, I don't know, it just seems a bit unreal.'

'Of course it does, it is unreal. But you did it.'

'Yeah,' Sarah looks up at Mother Georgia. Is there a suggestion of a smile on her massive forbidding lips?

'What do you say we get out of here now?' Elias takes her hand and strokes the back of her knuckles. 'Tbilisi's going to be chaos the next few days preparing for that visit. I for one would like to be as far away as possible when the Americans do finally turn up. Now that we know no one's going to try and blow the President to pieces with an anti-aircraft gun, I'd say we can leave the rest to the secret service. It is their job after all.'

'Yeah,' Sarah says again, wishing she could share in Elias's certainty.

'I've got a friend with a vineyard in Kakheti, nestled in the foothills of the Greater Caucasus with sweeping views down over Alaverdi. It's only a couple of hours drive from here but feels like another world. Would you allow me to invite you for a wine tasting tour?'

Sarah forces a smile. They did, after all, have reason to celebrate. 'And I don't even need to pack,' she says, nodding at her bag still on the back seat of the Niva.

CHAPTER 44

gxf3 g2

They drive the main highway out of Tbilisi to the East, Elias in buoyant mood. His spirit seems to swell, fed on the exhilaration of the day's events, the adrenaline kick from watching Skarparov's plan come unravelled and the thought of a romantic escape. He talks at length about the vineyard, the *qvevri* wine made in huge ceramic amphoras, the Ikalto Academy—a centre of learning in the Georgian enlightenment whose ruins they would pass on the way—pausing only to point out things along the road to make Sarah smile. She is glad he can lead the conversation and the mood. She still feels inexplicably flat. It could just be exhaustion, her brain too tired to take in the speed of the events. But she can't shake the feeling that she missed something. That there are more pieces on the board than she has taken into account. The gun must have been the Queen's move—a devastating attack with a weapon powerful enough to wipe out half the square along with the deck of VIPs.

'Are you all right?' he asks after another of his stories is met with little more than an 'mmmm'.

'Sorry, I think I'm just tired.'

'Don't worry, a good glass of *qvevri* wine will revive your spirit. And then you'll sleep like a baby.'

Just after they turn off the main road, heading steeply up towards the Gombori pass, a red light flashes on the Niva's dashboard.

'Exquisite timing,' Elias sighs. 'Sorry, but we're going to have to find some engine oil before we attempt that pass. This car is a temperamental beast. The friend I borrowed it from warned me this might happen.' Elias turns the car around and pulls in at the next tyre repair shop. A harsh-faced man with sloping shoulders and a grimy blue shirt appears out of a darkened shack and Elias speaks to him out of the window in Georgian.

'He thinks he has a friend who can help,' he explains, climbing out of the car. 'Stay here, I won't be long.' He follows the man in the direction of the next building, a hundred metres further down the road. Sarah watches them go, admiring Elias's broad-shouldered confidence, his ability to jump into anything without ever seeming to be bothered by the change of plans. They disappear into the next building.

Sarah sits alone, listening to the birds call back and forth in the forest beyond the road. A double call, met with a repetitive trill, both repeated. Until all noises stop.

A firm arm is on her arm, she is dragged backwards out of the car by an unseen figure with unyielding strength. A dirty cloth slithers over her face, covering her eyes, its slimy fibres jammed into her mouth by a bind that bites into the back of her scalp. She tries to scream, to call for Elias, for help from anyone, but the filthy rag muffles all sound. Her lungs suck at the noxious air, struggling to take enough oxygen through the hot mask. She tries to kick, to flail her arms, to scratch or strike but every movement is shut down by invisible hands and arms. She is thrown to the ground; but it is not the ground - the smell of wet carpet caked in mud, an uncomfortable metal bump raised into her hip. Her chest feels crushed, something sharp presses into her arm. And then black.

CHAPTER 45

fxg4 g1=Q

Her head hurts. Her tongue is swollen and her mouth rancid. Her flesh is cold as morgue-slab marble. She is lying on her side, knees tucked close in to her chin, but her arms are somehow stuck. How long has she been here? The numbness against the stone floor suggests several hours. Could it have been days? She does not know if she slept, she scarcely knows she is awake. Something hard and sharp digs into her wrists, clamping them behind her back.

Sarah pieces together all she can remember, hoping the effort of recall might bring clarity. The road to Kakheti, the tyre repair shop, Elias gone, the harsh-faced man. Was anyone else there? She tries to remember another face, another car, any clue she had not registered at the time. She can still taste the fabric of the foul-smelling cloth used to muzzle her.

It had happened so suddenly, the movement of one breath. Did Elias hear her struggle? Had he turned around in time to see her attackers? She tries searching through the fog, replaying the scene again to reset the flow of memory, but nothing comes.

Now here. How had she got here? Had they carried her or had she walked? Who were they? It is all claustrophobically close, like a night terror just before sleep. Everything viewed from inches above her nose—a hand, the cloth, the damp carpet in the foot well of a car.

Here is a windowless room, the bare stone floor chilled by damp. The walls are lined by ranks of metal cabinets and a bucket and chair stand alone next to the door. The light of a single neon strip, bright enough to hurt her eyes, makes the space feel tight and blank. Her hands are bound behind her back to a solid pole in the centre of the room. She tries to work out what she can reach. The metal cabinets are too far away, and how could she hope to open a drawer with her feet? But the chair, perhaps she could use the chair, a metal leg somehow slipped inside the binding might help her to yank herself free.

She tries sitting up, then working her arms up behind her back, to slide into a fully stretched position on the floor and hook the chair with her toes. But she does not get far before her shoulders jam. She tries another way, sliding sideways, first with hips angled towards the side of the room, then hips angled towards the pole. She must be able do it, it isn't even that far, she just needs to find the right position. But each attempt ends in an awkward sitting position. She must be missing something. There must be a movement to her body she has forgotten, a way of twisting or turning that would unlock the space she needs. But her joints do not cooperate. She remembers a Chinese acrobat she had seen at a circus, how she had seemed to pop her bones out of place to perform her bends and contortions. But no amount of mental effort will persuade Sarah's shoulders to simply pop themselves out. She slumps back against the pole. Okay, so not the chair. What else does she have?

Her watch is gone, her phone, her handbag. She has nothing to place herself in a day or a time. They have even taken her shoes. There is a vulnerability about being barefoot, the touch of the stone floor against her bare soles triggers something childlike, a sensation reserved for somewhere you feel safe and at home. Here it makes her feel more exposed.

But her socks. She had been wearing socks when she left for Kakheti. The thought of someone removing them from her unconscious body fills her with revulsion, the curious intimacy of the act, the needless and uninvited physical closeness from an unknown hand. What else had they touched?

Come on, Sarah. Optimism. You need it. Lots of it. It usually comes to her unbid, a steady natural flow assuring her that so long as you keep on fighting at something, things will come good in the end. But what does she have to fight in here? How can she keep up that clear determination that she is going to get herself out, when time continues to pass but nothing changes? She runs through her options again; there must be something she missed—the chair, the bucket, the door. She pulls at her binds until the skin around her wrists is chafed and raw. The simplicity of it is maddening. The chair, the bucket, the door and her trussed in the middle unable to move.

She finds herself longing for someone to come. A sign of life, a noise, any indication that she has not been abandoned. It is a curious thing to want. Here, alone, she is safe. Mostly unhurt, and mostly unharmed. But it is not enough, she needs someone or something to fight. Her mind frets over what she might already have missed. Has the state visit happened? Is this Skarparov's punishment for having foiled his attack or is it to stop her from uncovering Plan B—surely it could only be Skarparov's order that brought her here. What possible worlds have unfolded beyond her control? The thought makes her paralysis harder to bear.

*

After a timeless wait, the door opens. A man enters, his gaze fixed on the floor as he places a plastic tray at her feet.

'Who are you? What do you want with me? Why am I here?' Sarah resists the urge to rail, forcing herself to speak calmly. She can't talk herself out of here by screaming.

The man is short, portly. Dark hair flecked with grey and cropped close. A perfectly white scar cuts across the dark stubble of his cheek. He kicks the tray towards her. 'No talk. Food.' His monosyllables offer little comfort.

'Can you tell me where I am? Who do you work for? Is it Skarparov?'

He makes no response. She tries again in Russian but this is also ignored. Finally he responds in broken English. 'You, no talk.' He sits heavily on the metal chair by the door. 'Eat.'

On the tray is a plate of salty Georgian bread and a slice of cheese. She kneels towards the food but gets stuck in a painful crouch, hands lodged behind her.

The guard maintains his steady gaze at the floor.

'Can you release my hands while I eat?'

Sarah tries to read his expression, his brows set in a sharp crease, a small tremor to his lips. She tries to see the human being hiding behind his averted eyes.

'Please,' Sarah tries again, keeping her voice unthreatening.

He stands up, scraping the chair along the floor, and leaves the room.

Even desperately hungry, she can not bring herself to eat like an animal from a trough. She waits until the guard returns, a massive pair of wire cutters swinging from his right hand. He approaches Sarah, brandishing the metal tool. The reek of sweat and stale alcohol is overwhelming as he lunges behind her. The cold metal digs at her skin, and with a snap, her hands fall free. She shakes the blood back into her wrists and tries to thank her captor, but he is back to staring at the floor.

Should she run? She is free, nothing holds her here but the guard. But she does not rate her chances if she has to overpower him. Suddenly ravenous she picks up the bread and, too hungry to pace herself, bites off a large hunk. It is chewy and springy and unexpectedly delicious, but her throat and tongue are dry. The cheese is a sheep's cheese soaked in brine. Each mouthful of the salty food soaks up more of her remaining saliva, the bread forming tacky balls that stick to her tongue and grate in her throat. She takes another bite of cheese but the effort to swallow makes her gag.

'Please could I have some water,' she asks the guard.

He does not look up.

'Water,' she says again, more insistently this time. Is he deliberately ignoring her, or does he really not understand? 'I need to drink.'

He shakes his head. '*Ara*, no,' he mumbles.

She could smash the plate over his head. She could attack him with the tray. He is considerably bigger than her and probably twice her weight. Or she could just run. She pulls herself up, moving slowly, as if sharing a cage with a wild animal.

He snatches another industrial cable tie from on top of the metal cabinet next to the door. 'You, here,' he pushes Sarah back towards the pole with the wire cutters. He is behind her; if she runs now, she would have a head start. But she has no idea who or what is behind the door, even if she did manage to make it out of the room. She allows him to replace the binds securing her to the central pole.

'Finish?' he nods towards her half-eaten plate of food. Without a drink, it would be easier to swallow a wad of cotton wool. Sarah looks away in response. He picks up the tray and turns to leave.

'Can I have some water,' she calls after him, her voice rising, but he slams the door without looking back.

Sarah slides back to the floor. It's a game. A childish game to make her uncomfortable, they want to see her panic, but she must not give in. She tries to swallow down the last crumbs of dry bread still sticking to her tongue and the roof of her mouth. Think of something else. Her mind starts filtering through every decision she had made that had brought her here. What could she have done differently? Is there a move she missed that would have given her more protection? She imagines having rejected Michael straight out, following her first instincts and walking away when she had the chance. But her fantasy brings little comfort. She is too far gone. There is too much that she now knows, there is too much riding on her. She has to find a way out.

CHAPTER 46

Ra2 Qg3+

'Hello, Sarah.' A small man enters, followed by the guard. Sarah recognises him immediately as Skarparov's assistant from Dubai, twitchy rat features and underdog shuffle. He had given her a nasty feeling when she'd first seen him in Baku—his whole demeanour seeps ill-humour, an absence of feeling. She suspects he enjoys doing Skarparov's dirty work, allowing the boss to remain everybody's friend. At least it's clear why she's here.

He holds a glass of water, a tall glass, filled almost to the brim. Sarah's eyes fixate on the curve of the surface tension, the drops of condensation beading the sides of the glass.

'You're awake.' His sharp voice punctures the silence. He paces the brightly lit cell with small furtive footsteps, the heels of his shoes ringing on the stone with each step.

'What do you want with me?' she asks.

'It is funny you should ask this.' He stops his shuffling and stares at her, eyelids shot through with heavy purple veins. 'We have been asking the same question about you. What is it you want with us?' He brings his face so close to Sarah's chin she smells his hair oil like bitter almonds. 'It seems as if everywhere we go, there you are, sniffing around.'

'I'm doing my job.'

'Your job?'

'You know what I do, I work for the Department for International Development. I was looking into cooperation with the Skarparov Foundation. But my project is clearly over. The British Government does not work with criminals.'

'And what would your government think about your research practices?' He pauses, wetting his lips with a darting movement of the tongue. 'Is it common practice for development workers to seduce a member of staff to get access to information?'

'I don't know what you're talking about.'

'Don't worry, Elias told me everything. How sweet.' He pauses to take a long deliberate sip from the water.

'Told you what?' Her blood rises at the mention of Elias's name.

'He told me how you tried to seduce him while pressing him with questions about Skarparov Enterprises.' His quivering lips are inches from her face. 'I don't think that was very subtle, was it?'

'My dealings with Elias have nothing to do with you.'

'On the contrary, it has everything to do with us. Elias is a loyal employee. Are you in the habit of taking all your contacts to bed, or did we receive special treatment?'

Sarah holds on to her silence.

'Ah, I see I have hit a little close to the bone. I did not mean to embarrass you. Or did he seduce you? Which one of you was being played do you think?'

She tries to swallow, but her tongue sticks in her throat.

'Were you hoping he might come and rescue you? I'm afraid that is unlikely, given that he was the one who told us how to find you.'

Sarah's chest feels caught, a metal hoop tightening around the slats of her rib cage. The tyre-repair stall—Elias had brought her there and then disappeared. Surely he can't have planned this? She stifles any reaction. He's playing her. She won't give him the satisfaction of a response. She holds his eye, a vein erupting at her temple. 'Can I have some water?'

'I'm sorry. Are you thirsty?' He takes another ostentatious slurp from his glass. 'Did no one give you anything to drink?'

'No.'

'Here, perhaps you'd like to share mine.' He gulps water into his mouth then presses himself into her, locking one arm around the back of her head and forcing his thin lips against hers, ejecting a stream of water into her mouth. The water is shockingly cool against his hot flesh. Her whole body convulses as she feels a jab of his tongue. She wretches, hawks and spits, aiming the vile fluids from her mouth straight at him.

'You fucking animal, get away from me.' She coughs up another mouthful of bile and phlegm.

He retreats, dabbing the trail of fluids left hanging on his cheek with a handkerchief. 'They told me you are feistier than you look.' The leer on his face is more arousal than disgust. 'You said you were thirsty? And I only have this one glass.' He dangles it in front of her.

With a well-aimed kick, Sarah smashes her naked foot into the glass that flies from his grip, shattering on the floor. He stands motionless, hand still raised in front of her, features frozen. Sarah is expecting violence, retaliation, escalation of threats. But his sudden stillness holds far greater terror. Not knowing what level of depravity he is capable of, the quieter and calmer he becomes, the more threatened she feels under his gaze.

'I don't think that was a good idea.' Slowly he reaches to the floor and selects one of the shards of glass.

Sarah clenches her fists behind her back.

'I was told not to touch you. Viktor must be going soft in his old age. He didn't want you hurt.' He makes a noise somewhere between a grunt and a snort. 'But if you are going to be like that,' he moves towards her, pivoting the shard in his yellowed nicotine-stained fingers. 'I might have to defend myself.'

She leans into the pole with all her strength, crouching to shield as much as she can. He draws the sharp edge of the glass against her cheek, tracing it across her forehead, the pressure just enough for her to feel the bite without breaking the skin. She dares not move. The shard passes down over her eyelid, sweeps a circle down her cheek then draws sharply across her mouth. She holds her breath, eyes squeezed shut, hiding in her head, retreating into her body away from his touch. One hand holds her skull in a lock while the other slowly drags the glass across her skin. She is so numb she does not even know if he hurt her. She feels the trace of where he led the glass, but no pain.

'No. Not your face. That would never do.' The hand on her head jerks back. He takes a thick handful of hair and yanks her neck until the base of her skull cracks against her shoulders.

The glass is now at her throat, pressing down at the tender flesh to the right of her windpipe. Her chest heaves, her breath comes in deep and heavy gulps through her exposed and constricted throat.

'Oh, it would be so easy from here. A slip of the hand, a tweak of your carotid artery, and you would be out of the way.'

Sarah's whole body shakes, her muscles gripped by uncontrollable spasms.

'Who would cry for you, Sarah?'

She thinks of her father. How would he cope if he lost her too? Would he ever recover if he knew the way she had been disposed of, batted around like a cat's toy before the kill. She thinks of Elias and remembers his parting words from Baku: 'Don't worry, everything is bliss and happiness. You must laugh throughout. And if you die, you die well.' The absurdity of the advice in this moment makes her shake, a sigh heaves out of her chest and her stomach contracts. She jerks her head up, staring into the purple-rimmed eyes of her attacker, and laughs.

He steps back, thrown by her reaction. 'You're laughing, Sarah. Do you like that?' He lifts up the blue sweatshirt and drives the glass into the skin of her naked stomach, a look of excitement crossing his face.

'No,' Sarah holds his eye. 'I'm laughing at you.'

He slashes the shard across her abdomen, lashing out with none of his earlier control. She hears ripping. As he withdraws his hand, his fingers drip with blood. Still riven with fear, Sarah has to look down to confirm that it is hers. At the sight of the broken flesh she doubles over in pain.

He staggers backwards, looking from her to the glass in disbelief. 'What did you do that for?'

Sarah can't tell if he is talking to her or addressing his blood-stained hand.

'I think that will do.' He pulls a fresh handkerchief from his pocket to wipe off the blood, flinging the shard of glass at the guard who is cowering close to the door. 'Make sure to clean that up.' He nods at the remainder of the smashed glass. 'Wouldn't want her to hurt herself.' He forces a laugh. The guard's face remains impassive. A sign of humanity or fear?

'We'll talk again tomorrow.' He leaves the room, a new urgency in his scurrying steps. The guard hurries out behind him carrying the hastily gathered fragments of glass.

Sarah huddles into a ball and feels herself shiver, a tremble growing into an uncontrollable shake. Her lips are taut, they begin to squirm and twist as if filled with too much blood. She realises she is crying silent sobs, her mouth contorted with uncontainable rage.

CHAPTER 47

PREPARATION

The Castle still isn't picking up. He's gone quiet, ever since he revealed the target, and the Pawn has no one else to call. He tried calling his mother one day, to make it look natural for the record, but she didn't understand. Just come upstairs if you want to talk.

He has to escape her. She sucks him dry. He feels like a child around her, powerless to act. But is this really his only way out? He would have the money, but would he really then be free to go?

He wants to talk to The Castle. This seems crazy. He must have misunderstood. And who else is involved? How big is the plan? Who else is there with him? Surely something this big isn't down to him alone? This is nuts.

He goes to inspect the device, again. It is covered, a loose wrapping they said. Something you can hold in your hand discreetly. He's chosen a piece of brown felt, sufficient size, light weight, he can hold the wrapped device comfortably in his hand with only the pin exposed through a fold in the cloth. He paces up and down the workshop floor but catches his reflection in the window, standing awkwardly, clutching on to a weird bit of brown felt, looking red-handed. It's no good. He needs something less obvious.

He goes up to his mother's bedroom. Luckily, she's out, but she would know he has been here. He'll need a good excuse. The smell is unmistakable—cloying, heavy sweet air. Pointless shit everywhere—he picks up a statue of a shepherdess with a broken neck that has been clumsily fixed with superglue. Why does she keep this crap? He rifles through the drawers, grabbing an armful before hurrying back down to his workshop. He tips the fabrics onto the countertop—scarves, shawls, a white blouse—trying each, how it felt in the hand, size and texture, trying to catch his reflection.

Would he really go through with this? He tries to imagine what would happen to him if he didn't. The Castle was clear. They are long past the moment to back out. They would find him, he has nowhere to hide. But would it be worse if he does go through with the plan? At least the puppets would get what they deserve. If he dies, it is as a martyr, freeing the country, the world, from those who understand nothing. He refolds the pieces of fabric, nothing seems natural. He picks up the device, wraps it in a tartan handkerchief, tries tucking it up the sleeve of his shirt, then pulls back his fist taking aim at his reflection in the glass.

CHAPTER 48

Kd1 Qf3+

Sarah is back on the train to Baku, but this time it is her hanging hopelessly between the carriages, feet dangling towards the hurtling tracks. A stranger stands above her, offering help, but the further she reaches for his hand, the further she feels herself slip. The stranger's hand, like a mark at the bottom of a glass, looks solid and graspable until her hand slashes through the refracted image. In her desperation, she reaches up with both hands at once and feels herself plummeting towards the ground.

The ripple of fear knocks her awake, doubled up, hands still locked behind her, shoulders painfully compressed and cheek lying on the cold stone floor. For a moment she is lost, her brain stubbornly refusing to acknowledge the reality of her captivity.

Then the pain in her stomach brings it back. She cannot see the wound, but the blue of her sweatshirt has turned a muddy shade of brown and sticks to her skin. Her flesh feels hot and tender. It can't have gone that deep, the shard of glass was too short, the movement too brief, an impetuous slash more than a targeted stab. The blood stain is not wet, so at least the wound must have clotted. She wishes she could see it. Her toes throb where she made contact with the glass—at least that is a pain she can be proud of. It might not have brought her any closer to escape, but it was worth it for the look on his face. Bliss and happiness.

Elias's words had brought her courage, but she cannot forget what Skarparov's brute had said about Elias telling them where to find her. Surely it was just another ploy to unnerve her? Elias worked for Skarparov, or was at least connected to them—of course they would use this. But Sarah is troubled by the anti-aircraft gun—he seemed to know all the details in such a short time. And a surprising amount about anti-aircraft guns. He was so confident that their hunch was right—too confident? It all felt too easy, too smooth, the SWAT team arriving just as they were needed. But surely a scene like that couldn't be faked, could it?

The suggestion that he might be playing her strikes at something deep. A fear that she had tried to keep within the darker corners of her mind. She wants to believe he is on her side; his actions so far suggest that he is. But he also called her back to Tbilisi and led her into their trap.

She tries to think of the Elias she knows: the Elias who gives her goosebumps, who makes her laugh and swoon, the poetry-spouting mountain-man who makes her heart sing. The Elias who rescued her in Baku, the Elias who took her into his arms and made her feel safe. He swept her off her feet, but how much about him does she really know? She knows what makes him laugh, she knows the sound of his voice and the smell of his skin, but she does not even know his full name.

*

She is back on the train; this time no one offers help, just the blur of tracks below and endless space above with nothing to hold, no handles to reach, no doors, only the stillness of the open sky. She wakes before she falls, a white-hot pain on her stomach and the smell of stale sweat and fresh alcohol. Someone is touching her.

'Get off me!' She writhes away, slamming her spine against the column. The guard lifts her shirt and presses a wad of soaking wet cotton wool into her stomach. She breathes in the stringent fumes. The pain is scalding hot, and his clumsy administrations feel like another violation. 'Stop!' she screams, trying to kick him away with her legs. Is he shushing her? He does not meet her eye, but continues to apply himself stubbornly to the task of cleaning her wound, shushing softly as a tired parent might try to calm an overwrought baby.

'I'm fine, please stop.'

He backs away, looking unsure, then hurries from the room. A few minutes later he is back, carrying a tall glass of water and a beaker filled with orange liquid.

'Drink.' He places both glasses at Sarah's feet.

'My hands,' she says.

Keeping his uncertain eyes fixed on her, he backs out the door, returning moments later with the wire cutters. Sarah studies him, taking in as much as she can. The deep bald scar down his heavy stubble that looks so vicious on his resting face but disappears into his cheek when he speaks. The slight twist to the lips that suggests his sombre expression needs effort to maintain. His eyes dart furtively, rarely looking up or meeting hers, but they tremble more from fear than from threat. She tries to read his movements, the way he looks at her, the pauses of hesitation and doubt. He shows none of the sadistic pleasure of his co-conspirator.

As he releases her hands, she falls on the water, draining the glass in one delicious gulp. Never has anything tasted so good. She could drink ten more. She raises the second cup and gives it a tentative sniff. It has the heady tannin-rich smell of homemade wine and a deep amber colour that comes from months fermenting beneath the ground. Are they really serving her wine? Only in Georgia, she thinks and knocks it back in one. God that was good.

The guard's face breaks a smile. 'More?'

'Yes, please,' Sarah says. Why not? What harm could it do? If it is drugged, at least she would have rest. Hurriedly, he secures her in place with another cable tie and leaves the room. When he returns, he is swinging a large five-litre jerry can half-filled with the golden liquid. He releases her hands and tops up her glass—the serving considerably more generous this time. She drinks half of it in two large mouthfuls, her eyes on the guard who watches her with a mixture of curiosity and admiration. Yes, she could drink, and right now she can think of nothing better than to get herself blind drunk. She feels the alcohol getting to work, seeping in through her mouth, her tongue, her stomach, gently washing through her nervous system, leaving the taste of summer fruit on her tongue and dulling the pain in her abdomen. She is about to finish the glass when she pauses. It isn't done to drink alone, especially in Georgia. She pours the remainder of her wine into her water glass and offers it to the guard.

At her unexpected movement, he jumps to his feet, waving the wire cutters at her to hold her back. 'You sit,' he orders, jabbing the cutters towards her place on the floor.

She curses herself for being too bold, too quick. 'Yes, of course, I sit.' She crouches lower to show she intends to obey. 'Would you like some?' she asks, offering him the glass of wine.

'No.' He brushes her away.

She places the glass next to his chair and slowly sits back in her place, raising her own glass in a toast. '*Gaumarjos!*' He nods in acknowledgement without touching his glass.

'What's your name?' she asks. He looks at her blankly. 'Your name?' she tries again. 'My name is Sarah,' she gestures towards her chest slowly, deliberately, as if speaking to a small child. 'What is your name?' His face lights up with sudden comprehension, before remembering himself and replacing his frown. 'Niko,' he touches his chest. Sarah raises her glass again, '*Nikos Gaumarjos!*' She drains her wine. He has not touched her offering.

'Could I have some more?' Sarah waves her empty glass. He pushes his wine towards her with his toe.

'No,' Sarah presses her hand to her heart, 'that is Niko's wine, for you.'

He refills her glass from the jerry can.

'*Madlobt,*' Sarah accepts the glass with exaggerated thanks, trying to unearth any words of Georgian. '*Kartuli ghvino?*' she tries to ask whether the wine was from Georgia, unsure whether her pairing together of words would be comprehensible to her captor.

'Ho, *kartuli,*' he nods, eying his glass still sitting on the floor.

'*Sakartvelos Gaumarjos!*' Sarah raises the toast to Georgia with all the enthusiasm she can muster. By now the alcohol is firing through her blood, making her ears feel hot and her cheeks flushed, but she's watching Niko closely. Seeking signs of humanity. Signs of weakness. As she hoped, her toast works to prise out another half-smile. Finally, he takes a small sip. Thank God for the dual appeal of wine and nationalistic pride.

She presses ahead, trying to recall as many of the traditional toasts from the supra as she can, searching her wine-fuddled memory for the explanations she had heard from Giorgi's uncle and Elias's more poetic interpretations. She can remember most of the themes, but none of the Georgian words or details of the toasts. 'To our meeting,' she tries. He looks blank. 'You,' she points at the guard, 'and me,' she thumps herself on the chest, 'coming here together, to share this meal,' she gestures to the tray on the floor. '*Gaumarjos!*' The guard laughs coarsely through his nose and drinks, muttering his response.

Sarah pauses, leaning back into the pole. She does not want to lose his goodwill by seeming too eager.

'To family!' she says, picking up her glass once more.

'Femily?' He repeats her word without understanding.

'Mother, father, sister, brother, children?'

'*Deda, mama?*' he answers, joining in the game.

'*Ho! Deda! Mama! Gaumarjos!*' They drink again. Their glasses are soon empty, and the guard tops them both up from the jerry can. She brings the glass to her lips with gusto and makes a great show in drinking. But now, each time the glass touches her lips she takes in as little of the wine as she can get away with, disguising small sips behind elaborate gestures and spilling as much as possible. The guard is keeping up with her enthusiasm but emptying far more of the oversized bottle.

Eventually, Sarah draws a blank when searching for another toast to be mimed. She points to Niko—'*Niko tamada?*' He smiles shyly and refills their glasses before launching into a long monotone toast. Sarah does not understand a word, but she is grateful to have been relieved of the pressure to perform. Her head is starting to swoon, and she feels her balance shifting as the alcohol sinks in. She hopes she will not come to regret this exuberance, waking up in the morning tied to a cold pole with a cracking hangover. But she must try.

She spills from her cup down her chin or over the tray with energetic gestures. Niko keeps pace, drinking full glasses with each toast, draining and refilling his glass several times over as they continue their cell-bound *supra*. She watches as his gestures become looser and his menacing scar disappears into a deep dimple in his cheek. His elbow sways as he pours from the can and occasionally he misses the glass. His red face glows with the sweaty sheen of alcohol. So far so good.

As the last of the jerry can is emptied, Sarah stays close to the ground. She keeps her hands down now and her back against the pole, as it had been when she was bound, sitting back with the vacant grin of a contented drunk. She wants to give Niko the confidence that he can leave her, that she is happy where she is and will not try to escape.

He raises the final toast, eyes teary and shot with red. Picking up the empty bottle, he suddenly seems unsure. Sarah gives a shy smile. '*Didi madloba*,' she thanks him with a nod, keeping her hands down behind her. '*Arapris*,' he answers, beads of sweat forming at his temples. He bends down to pick up the tray. 'Good night,' Sarah whispers as he straightens up, swaying uncertainly. He looks around the room in slow motion, as if trying to remember what he's doing there. Then he gathers the glasses and the empty bottles on the tray, picks up the wire cutters and leaves.

Sarah sits as still as she can, her head spinning from the wine, but her pulse thumps with the thought of escape. She will not move until she is sure he is not coming back. She half expects him to stumble into the room at any moment with another industrial cable wrap. But time passes and she is still alone. She has no idea how long she has waited, listening for noises outside, anything that might tell her what is behind the door. But she hears only the thundering of her heart.

The moment has come. The wine might make her clumsier, but it also gives her courage. She walks slowly to the door and tries the handle. It swings open. She slips through, closing it behind her, suddenly fearful that she might find herself face-to-face with Skarparov's sadistic sidekick. As her eyes adjust to the gloom after the harsh fluorescent light of her cell, she can see a cement staircase leading out of the basement. She creeps up the stairs, pausing on each step to listen for movement in the house. All she can hear is a faint rumbling from above that sounds like snoring, a low-pitched repetitive vibration of one deeply asleep. At the top of the stairs, Niko is lying on a small sofa, limbs dangling over the edges, head thrust back in drunken oblivion.

Sarah edges gently past him and towards the door. She tries the handle, but the door remains shut tight. She looks around frantically, refusing to accept that she could get this far only to be met with another locked door.

She sees a bulge in Niko's pocket, a flash of silver. She creeps nearer, testing his reactions, testing her luck. He seems solidly asleep. She reaches for the keys, tentatively sliding her fingers into his pocket, trying not to press into his sleeping form. Her fingers curl around the warm metal, hook into the loop of the key chain, but as she tries to slide it out, he stirs. His whole body seems to swell as he catches his breath, his face grows purple, and he lets out an enormous snore as he rolls over. The bulk of his heavy form leans into her and then settles, crushing her arm beneath him, pinning her in place. She can't quite believe her luck that he didn't wake up, but she's stuck. He only needs to open his eyes, register for a moment the unfamiliar lump of her arm, and she's lost.

She hears noises, she thinks she hears voices but coming from where? Or is it just the sound of her blood frantically racing through her body mixed with Niko's unsettled snores? She remains in her awkward crouch; her face and ears are red hot, but her arm feels cold with the lack of circulation. She wiggles her fingers gently in the pocket, trying to keep her grasp on the keys. It's a huge bunch, she has no hope of sliding it out without waking him. Niko swells again, his chest rising, his face flushing as if he's about to expire. When once more he gasps for breath, his mouth and eyes flick open.

Sarah stares into his bleary red eyes, frozen in place, her breath caught in her throat. She holds his gaze for what feels an eternity. Then his eyelids droop back shut and he shifts away from her, allowing her to pull out her hand and the keys.

She's free, but how much time does she have before his drowsy brain registers the disturbance? She tries a key in the lock, but it doesn't turn. The next one doesn't fit either. It's a huge bunch and with each turn and twist the keys jangle together. The noise sounds deafening, loud enough to wake an army, but Niko snores on. More noises coming from somewhere far off, Sarah can't tell if it is in the building or outside. She has no time to wait.

There is a window, but it too is locked, or painted shut. She grabs a sweat-stained cushion from Niko's sofa and presses it against the glass. God this had better work. She punches against the thin cushion as hard as she dares. Her fist bounces off, knuckles smarting. She glances back at where Niko lies still snoring a deep reverberating rattle. Another punch, harder this time and her fist breaks through the glass. The noise is shockingly loud. So much for the dampening effect of the pillow. She spins around. Niko is staring at her, rubbing his eyes, his brain still lost in the fog. She climbs up onto the sill and picks her way amongst the shattered glass. The window frame is only just wide enough for her to squeeze through but at least that means Niko can't follow. She hears him behind her, his muffled tongue forming angry words, unintelligible shouts. The window is higher than she hoped but she has no choice now but to risk it. Still clutching the keys she jumps, landing with a heavy impact that shocks her joints, bare feet stinging on the gravel. She is free.

CHAPTER 49

Kc2 Rxf1

Sarah runs, pushed on by alcohol and adrenaline. Niko will be raising the alarm, even if he can't follow her immediately. But after an initial burst of speed, her legs falter. She is lost.

Nondescript houses line roads of pale gravel and dust. She searches in vain for a street name, anything familiar to root her in the city. She keeps moving, following her instinct towards a main road, all the while committing to memory the ground she covers. The streets are deserted and eerily still. The late-night world has gone to bed and even the birds are silent.

The main road, when it finally comes, offers little comfort. All the windows are dark, and shop fronts hide behind tightly drawn shutters. Only the occasional passing car gives reassurance that people are close. Ahead of her rises the forest of Soviet-era apartment buildings that mark the edges of the city, their brutalist lines like teeth guarding the river-cut gorge. Finally, something she recognises. She is a long way from anywhere she knows, but at least now she knows which way to run.

A light flickers above a money changing shop, the metal shutter rolled up half-way. Inside a small man in an apron is sweeping. Sarah pleads with him for his phone. Staring at her like an apparition from the dead, he hands it over without question. She must look as rough as she feels.

'*Batono?*' Vakho's voice is drowsy, dragged from sleep.

'Vakho, it's Sarah. I need your help.' The embassy driver was the first person she thought to call. She needs someone she knows will come immediately without too many questions. And his is the only number she knows by heart.

'Sarah, you're here!' He snaps awake. 'We've been worried, where are you?'

'I'm in Tbilisi. Sorry for waking you, I need you to pick me up. Can you come now?'

'Of course, don't worry. I'm coming.'

*

A dull light in the sky announces dawn. Sarah watches the road nervously, willing Vakho to hurry before Niko is able to summon help. Her escape was hardly subtle. The bewildered money changer offers his curious guest a cup of sweet tea then disappears into the back of his shop, returning with a pair of bright green plastic flipflops. Sarah is overcome with gratitude for this small gesture and slips the sandals onto her bruised and filthy feet.

With a squeal of brakes, an embassy Land Rover pulls up and Vakho flings open the back door. Sarah climbs in, comforted by the familiar smell of pine air freshener and leather upholstery.

Vakho looks horrified. 'Sarah, are you okay? You look—'

'Terrible,' a deep voice cuts in, 'but thank God we've found you.' Sarah had not noticed Elias in the passenger seat. He leans across and offers a clumsy hug, but she holds herself back, still wary. Is she really ready to trust him? How was he here again so soon?

'I'm fine,' she pulls away.

'Your top: is that blood?' Elias looks deeply shaken by the sight of her.

She instinctively folds her arms across her middle, flinching with the pain. 'I think it looks worse than it is. What are you doing here?

'What do you think I'm doing here? You vanished from my car in the middle of nowhere. No one saw a thing and I've been searching for you ever since. I asked Vakho to let me know if he heard from you, I didn't know what else to do.' Elias's eyes are rimmed with red, his hair sticks up in strange directions and he looks as if he hasn't slept in days.

'How do you know Vakho?' Sarah asks.

Vakho leans back, grinning. 'Everyone knows Vakho!'

'What happened to you?' Elias asks. He's trying to keep his voice gentle but there's an urgency to his questions. 'Where did you go? What are you doing out here?'

'What day is it? What have I missed? Has the state visit happened?'

'Slow down.' Elias places a comforting hand on her arm, but she draws it away. 'The main event is this afternoon. The US president flies in this morning, then he and Saakashvili are due to address their adoring crowds in Freedom Square later today.'

'We need to get to the American Embassy; we need to warn someone,' Sarah says.

'Why would you want to go there? I thought we were trying to escape?'

'But don't you see? This isn't over.' Sarah stares into Elias's red-rimmed eyes, trying to read his reactions. She wishes she could shake the snag of doubt scratched into her trust by Skarparov's sidekick, replace it with the unblemished confidence she had felt before. This is Elias, her Elias. Why would she believe the lies of that sadistic rat over his word? The fabric of her faith is frayed, the rodent's insinuations have revealed its fragility. But for now there's no time, he's here and she needs him. 'Why would Skarparov have me locked up if there wasn't more? Would he really have put the success of his whole attack in the hands of Irakli's men? There must be a Plan B.'

'Okay,' Elias rubs his eyes with the heels of his hands. 'If he's still planning something, I doubt he'll try again to attack the main event. The place will be crawling with security. They've installed metal detectors at every entrance to the square and there'll be a sniper on every rooftop.'

'What, then?'

'There's another event this evening, a reception hosted by the US embassy. Only the most important business contacts of the embassy and military top brass are invited. But it's a pre-screened event, so security on site will be much lighter. According to a friend of mine, Skarparov has managed to get himself on the invite list.'

'But even with an invitation, how is he going to smuggle a warlord's collection of weaponry into the American embassy? There was only one gun in Mother Georgia's warehouse. What about the rest of the kit?'

'That might have been it.'

'What? But there was a whole arsenal leaving Russia?'

'I forgot you've been out of it the last couple of days. Those weapons that you thought were going to Ibragimov? It looks like they are being shipped out through Crimea, so they are probably not coming to the Caucasus at all.'

'How do you know?' Were Elias's sources better than the British Government's or was she just behind the times?

'A drink with a Chechen mercenary can be very revealing. One of my bear hunting friends has been doing some logistics work for Skarparov.'

'But it *was* Skarparov moving the weapons, not Ibragimov?'

'Yes. He's definitely moving them out of Russia, but they're not coming here.'

'So Ibragimov—'

'Is starting to look pretty small fry.'

'Okay, but just because Skarparov hasn't got a small country's worth of weapons pointed at the American president, doesn't mean he hasn't got something planned.'

'You want to go home, Ms Sarah?' Vakho looks at her through the rear-view mirror with his solicitous eyes.

'No. Let's go to the American embassy,' Sarah says. 'We can't let him beat us.'

*

The American embassy, located in an old palazzo in a leafy square behind Rustaveli, is swarming with suits. Catering vans trying to squeeze through the heavy security cordon, a makeshift media centre set up in the foyer filled with journalists and reporters testing equipment and harassed looking embassy staff trying to coordinate the chaos.

'How do we get in?' Elias asks.

'Do you think you can carry me?'

'Of course.'

'Then go in search of first aid.' Sarah yanks up her sweatshirt with a painful tear, the fabric pulling away the newly formed scab.

Elias flinches at the sight of the fresh blood.

'Quick! Get help!' Sarah feigns a swoon.

Elias scoops her up in his arms and barrels towards the entrance. 'Coming through, coming through, this lady needs first aid attention, move aside please.'

Sarah buries her fingers into the wound and waves her blood-smeared fingers in the face of the security guard who is preparing to object, as Elias sweeps them both through the main entrance.

Once inside, Sarah accosts a woman at the entrance wearing a headset who seems to be in charge. 'We need to talk to whoever is responsible for the reception tonight.'

'Sorry, the event is strictly invitation only. The guest list is full and there will not be any changes. If you wouldn't mind moving away…' The woman casts a troubled glance at Sarah's bloodstained hand.

'I'm not looking for an invite; we've received a security threat—'

'Another one,' the official rolls her eyes. 'The security team are in the meeting room at the end, but they're on the wire so make it brief.'

Elias and Sarah press down the corridor. In one of the grand rooms of the embassy, a security war room has been set up. Rows of desks pushed together, elegant windows boarded up, a battery of television screens showing images from cameras all over the city and a map of Tbilisi pinned to an oversized cork board. The map is annotated with cryptic notes and highlights that remind Sarah of chess notation—each of the principal pieces named and coded descriptions used to describe their movements. King to e5, bishop to g3, POTUS to FS.

A sandy-haired man, armed with a tool-belt of walkie-talkies, pagers and a prominently displayed gun holster, is shouting into a mobile phone. 'Well get them to think of something. And quick. The principal can't address an empty square. Get the people in.' He looks up and spots Sarah and Elias in the doorway.

'Sorry, you can't be in here.' He pushes Elias in the chest back through the open door.

You can't let him beat you again. Never forget to watch the pawns. Sarah studies the virtual Tbilisi chess board, her father's parting advice replaying in her mind.

'You have a Viktor Skarparov on your list for this evening's event?' Elias raises his voice over the agent's efforts to shut him down.

'Wait,' Sarah shouts, grabbing Elias's arm. 'We've got this all wrong. He's a King's Indian player.'

'What?'

'Skarparov.'

'Chess?' Elias asks sceptically.

'Yes. The reception is the distraction. We should be watching the pawns. Think about it. Why would Skarparov put himself in such a vulnerable position? Why draw attention to himself getting on the guest-list if this was the event he is planning to attack? He must be positioning his people elsewhere, hoping we'll follow him—and take our eyes off the advancing pawn!'

'Which is who?' Elias asks. 'Who would he trust to carry out something like this for him? His sidekick will be here with him at the reception. Irakli would have been the obvious fall guy—but he must have pissed off the boss too soon.'

'You think Skarparov killed him?'

Elias looks at her incredulously. 'Of course Skarparov killed him. He knew too much.'

'Giorgi?'

'No. Giorgi is a good man. Anyway he's in the mountains.'

Sarah watches the images move on the wall of screens.

'Levon!' she shouts.

'Who's he?'

'Exactly! Levon must be the pawn. The greasy teenager I saw in the offices in the mountains. He was in Tbilisi too, the first time I was at the Skarparov Foundation. But no one knows him, nothing links him back to Skarparov if it goes wrong. Follow the pawns. It must be him.'

'Who says he's not just the IT guy?' Elias asks.

'The sequence of moves. It fits Skarparov's style perfectly. I'm sure of it. How do we find him?'

'Dato would know—he drives everyone up and down from the mountains. But I don't know—'

'Vakho will find him.'

*

With Vakho's help, Sarah and Elias soon catch up with Dato in a faceless street back in the crumbling suburbs. Sarah recognises him immediately: the cynic-faced driver she had last seen hanging unconscious over the wheel of a battered Niva in the mountains. She makes to jump out of the car, but Elias stops her.

'What are you doing?' he asks. 'You're supposed to be locked in a basement. If Dato recognises you, you'll be caught immediately. He knows me as a Skarparov employee, let me talk to him.'

Sarah slides out of sight as Elias approaches the van. Dato looks annoyed to have been disturbed. He slouches in the driver's seat, mumbling his responses without looking up. Elias grows increasingly insistent, thumping the flat of his hand on the roof of the car, but Dato continues to ignore him. Eventually, he turns to Elias, his thin top lip set in a careless sneer and says something with a malicious grin.

Something in Elias snaps. He drags Dato out of the car through the open window, pulls back his fist and smashes it into the bridge of Dato's nose. Vakho jumps out of the car and runs towards them. Dato tries to stand, blood pouring down his face as Elias kicks him to the ground. Sarah watches in mute silence as Elias lands another punch on Dato's skull. Dato's legs buckle and he slumps at Elias's feet. Elias raises his fist again, but Vakho grabs his arm to restrain him. Elias whips around, his eyes small and cruel. Sarah is horrified; surely he's not going to hit Vakho too? But he turns away, kneading the skin of his knuckles, leaving Vakho to continue the abuse in a stream of colourful Georgian.

Sarah feels nauseous, repulsed by the calculated control of the violence, the unrelenting thump of flesh on flesh. It is a side of Elias she has never seen, something darker unleashed that she wishes she could erase.

'What the hell was that?' she asks as Elias climbs back into the car.

'The bastard,' Elias mutters under his breath. 'The way he talked about you, Sarah. He said you were probably dead, and the way he said it, the look of glee… I don't know, perhaps he didn't deserve that, but the look on his face…'

'He wasn't the one that hurt me.'

'It doesn't matter. You have no idea what it's been like the last few days, not knowing where you were. Or what they might do to you. You were in *my* car. If I hadn't left you, they'd never have been able to get you. Have you any idea how that felt? And if I ever get my hands on Zaur...'

'Zaur?'

'Skarparov's ratty sidekick; it was him, wasn't it?'

Sarah falls silent. The change in Elias was brutal, his violent response unrestrained. But through the shock, there is also overwhelming relief. This animal act of male revenge was a visceral retaliation for her kidnapping, the release of days worth of worry and powerless frustration. With all of Elias's measured elegance swept away, she can see motive in its rawest form. She sees the poison that Zaur tried to feed her for what it is. The puckered run in the fabric of her trust is smoothed out. She knows that Elias is on her side.

Vakho returns to the car.

'Did you get anything?' Sarah asks.

'He pretended he didn't know what we were talking about. But after Elias's unique powers of persuasion...' Vakho raises an eyebrow at Sarah. 'He gave us an address.'

Elias stares out of the front window, still nursing the side of his hand.

'It's not far from here.' Vakho says. 'We go!'

*

They pull up at a small wooden house, lost in a forest of communist-era apartment blocks, tall towers separated by patches of dead grass and rusted leaking mains. It smells of wet concrete, and only a flash of red poppies growing stoically out of a drainpipe breaks the expanse of grey. Vakho stops the car at a distance from where they could watch the house without attracting attention.

'I'm going in,' Elias says.

'Wait.' Sarah stops him. 'We need a distraction; he's hardly going to invite us in for a cup of tea. Vakho, you go to the front door. I'll look for a way in round the back.'

Vakho rings the doorbell. The porch is on the verge of collapse, the windows webbed with ripped mosquito netting. Voices come from inside: an urgent male voice, followed by a female voice shushing and shuffling closer. A stout woman opens the door, hands on ample hips, upper arms folding over into creases at her elbows. The male voice shouts again.

Elias points towards a small basement window, propped open on its latch. 'Do you think you can climb in?'

'I should be able to squeeze through.'

'Make it quick. I know Vakho has the gift of the gab, but even he won't be able to distract them for long. You had better be right about this.'

The window is only just wide enough for Sarah's hips, and she has to lift her arms above her head to inch her shoulders through the frame. Elias takes her hands to lower her down. His touch sets off an electric shock of pheromones shooting through her skin, the tender grasp of hands freshly turned in rage.

She finds herself in a basement room, pale blue walls lit by a bright neon strip. Heart beating fiercely, she sucks the damp air into her lungs to focus her mind.

The room is immaculately organised. A set of shelves covers one wall with various hardware supplies: wires, nails, strips of metal, pieces of wood, bottles and several plastic jerry cans branded with the skull and crossbones of toxic materials. Each item is carefully arranged by size and use, labelled, neatly stacked. A pair of Samurai swords hang on the wall, blades gleaming, their cases mounted alongside in polished wood.

Sarah opens a large cupboard—what if she is wrong? What if they are wasting time in an IT geek's workshop? The cupboard is filled with tools—hammers, files, spanners, screwdrivers, miniature to mammoth. One shelf contains nothing but mercury thermometers. She wants to touch them, just to disturb the clinical precision of their arrangement. A work bench in the centre of the room is covered in pieces of fabric—small towels, sections of woollen scarves, cleaning cloths and a tartan handkerchief. She can hear voices upstairs, the male voice—presumably Levon—is raised in aggression. Vakho is reasoning with him, calming and smooth. Come on, Vakho, keep up that silver tongue.

As she lifts the tartan handkerchief, something thuds onto the table. Sarah jumps back, still clasping the cloth. A hand grenade. Should she touch it? Would pressure in the wrong place cause it to explode? The pin seems to be in, and the safety catch down.

Sarah thinks quickly, her pulse roaring. There is no time for careful planning. Her first instinct will have to do, far-fetched as it seems.

She scans the meticulous ordering system on the shelves—nails, tacks, split pins, electrical tape, duct tape, superglue. Picking up the duct tape, she considers binding the grenade but thinks better of it. The tampering would be too obvious. She examines the adhesives and picks the one that looks most potent.

She applies the glue around the safety lever, dripping generously into the hinge and the handle mechanism.

'Sarah, what are you doing in there?' Elias calls through the window. 'Hurry up! I think Vakho is running out of steam.'

'Hold on,' Sarah shouts back, liberally applying the glue, trying not to stick her fingers, 'I'm nearly finished.'

'Now! He's back inside the house!' Elias's usually cool monotone bristles with urgency.

Sarah adds a final gloop, replaces the tube in its slot on the shelf and wraps the grenade back in the handkerchief, hoping it looks about right.

'Sarah!' Elias hisses through the window. She finishes rearranging the cloth, then reaches up through the opening. As Elias grabs her wrists, the handle of the door begins to turn. He heaves her through the narrow gap in one swift action. The basement door opens, and Sarah hears movement inside. Without looking back, she runs towards the road where Vakho is waiting. Only when she reaches the car does she notice she is still holding Elias's hand.

Vakho pushes the car into gear and tears off.

'What did you find inside?' Elias asks.

'There was a grenade on the table.'

He lets her hand drop abruptly 'What did you do with it? Did you take it?'

'No, I didn't want to make it obvious that we had been there. He might have a back-up. I defused it.'

'How on earth do you know how to do that?'

Sarah grins. 'I improvised.'

'And were there any other weapons?'

'There were some samurai swords on the wall: but decorative, and huge, at least three feet long. Not something you could sneak into a crowded square. Otherwise, it was just a workshop. We're just going to have to hope the grenade is what he is planning to use.'

'I wish we had something more to go on.' Elias's face is taut, his jaw tightly clenched.

'Sorry, Sarah,' Vakho says, 'I did my best—the mother I could have kept at the door all morning, but her son was too keen to get rid of me.'

'Don't worry Vakho, you did brilliantly, I'm amazed we got in at all. God, I hope we've got the right guy.'

'He definitely had something to hide, he could not get rid of me quickly enough, even shouting at his mother to make her shut the door. What kind of a son shouts at his mother?' Vakho asks incredulously.

Sarah laughs. 'Even a Georgian boy might drop his manners when he has a hand grenade wrapped up in his basement.'

CHAPTER 50

INTRUDER

Was someone here? The Pawn peers through the open window. Surely no one could fit through that gap? He scans the back yard, the passage that runs along the side of the house. Nothing moves. He pulls the window shut and slams the lock into place.

He is sure he heard a noise. And that guy at the door? Someone must know he's here.

The Castle never reappeared, but another guy had finally turned up. Little guy, nasty ratty face. The Pawn didn't like dealing with someone new; definitely not now, with so little time. But what choice did he have? Rat Face had turned up at the house to check on all the details. Seemed to know about the plan. Wanted to check the weapons. The Pawn had felt like he was being tested, like he wasn't trusted to get it right. At least the guy talked about the money. Was he back for another check?

The Pawn stalks the room, footsteps silent, braced for attack. The space is still. He eyes up the storage cupboard, behind the worktable, the corner of the room under a pile of chairs, visualising every spot large enough to hide a human form. He grabs a Samurai sword from its mount on the wall and approaches each hiding place, waiting, stepping closer, hyper-alert for sounds of intrusion. The cupboard he leaves until last; raising the blade, he draws a deep breath before flinging open the door. No one. The room is empty. The sound of breathing must be his own.

Finally, he approaches the weapon. The wrapping is in place, where he'd left it. Edging forward, moving slowly but with a steady hand, he uses the sharp corner of the metal blade to lift away the folds of the handkerchief. He hasn't touched it since wrapping it. It feels wrong, as if he might jinx it by too much handling. Could fingerprints remain? He doesn't want it to feel like something that is his. He's been given it; he is simply moving it on. It isn't his plan. He can't take the blame; he doesn't even know where it came from. He rehearses the name Rat Face had given him. The name to say if the worst comes to the worse. Plea bargain for spilling on Ibragimov. Ibragimov. He stumbles on the unfamiliar syllables. It needs to come more naturally.

Beneath the folds of fabric, the weapon lies in the centre of the cloth. He checks the serial number on the bottom, lowering his face closer to the instrument, bracing both his hands on the table. The pin is in place, the handle looks correct. He sniffs. Is there something? Ethanol? Or Ballistol? He sniffs the handkerchief, it smells like his mother - sweet, clinging, inescapable. The edge of the sword shines, the metal freshly oiled.

He folds the cloth back in place and goes to check the back up.

CHAPTER 51

d6 Nc6

'Sarah, have you been drinking?'

Steve, the embassy spook, leans over the granite countertop in his kitchen, still wearing his dressing gown. The sleeves are too short and the greying flannel flaps above his knees.

'What sort of a question is that? I've just told you we've uncovered a plot to assassinate two presidents, and you're asking about my alcohol intake?'

'No, Sarah. You've just given me a far-fetched report of a teenager acting shifty. That's hardly enough to call off the state visit.' He wanders across the kitchen to switch on the kettle. 'And what are you wearing on your feet?'

'I can't go through all the details now, but you're going to have to trust me.' Sarah rakes her hands through her unwashed hair, feeling something sticky clumped at her temple. 'I am sure this guy is part of Skarparov's plot. He was the one who—'

'Would you like a coffee?' Steve reaches down the only clean mug from the shelf.

'There's no time for that. We've got to stop him. The US president is going to be in Freedom Square in a couple of hours and—'

'Sarah, slow down. You've just turned up on my doorstep at God-knows-what-time in the morning with a half-cooked story about a sulky teenager. You reek of booze and who knows what you've spilt down those clothes. Sure you don't want a coffee?' Steve opens his fridge, stares at the shelves for a moment before closing the door.

Sarah wants to shake him by his dressing gown lapels but it's unlikely to help her case. 'But what about the hand grenade?'

'What about it? What kind of hand grenade was it?'

'I don't know. I've never seen one before.'

'Great. You just saw a hand grenade for the first time and suddenly it's a plot to assassinate the leader of the free world. Have you any idea how many Georgians have weapons in their basement? We're only a few years out of full lawlessness and civil war. If we went around arresting everyone with military memorabilia in their cupboards…'

'Can't we put a tail on him?'

'I think you'd better go home and sleep. You've clearly been through a lot.'

'Can we at least warn the Americans?'

'Look I'll call them, if it makes you feel better. But I'm only telling you now what they'll say. Without something more concrete, there's not much they can do. The security level is already at high alert—they'll be looking out for this sort of thing.'

'But we *do* have concrete information.'

'At best circumstantial evidence and a hunch.'

'Oh forget it.'

'Look, they'll only ask the same questions—'

'Just forget it.' Sarah snaps before hurrying back to Vakho's waiting car.

CHAPTER 52

WAITING

He waits. As instructed. Rat Face told him to get close to the entrances and wait for the right moment. Try to be unobtrusive. Watch the security and look for weak points. There is no way they will be able to check everyone coming into the square, tens of thousands are expected. It is too big a job.

The crowd is growing impatient, bodies surge towards the metal cordon and hastily erected metal detectors. There is nowhere to hide, no safe place away from all the other carcasses pushing forward. He bolts his hand over the weapon like a protective claw.

Where the hell is The Castle? They are supposed to arrange a place to meet. He was going to reveal the pick-up point, tell him which way to run. The Pawn tries his number again—no answer. Nothing from Rat Face either.

The sun is above the rooftops now. There is no shade, but the pinched triangle cast by the peak of his baseball cap. His jacket feels three inches thick.

But the security officers are feeling it, too. Big-haired Americans, blowsy embassy staff, McDonalds-fat from desk jobs and SUVs and comfortable climate control. He watches them sweat, brine stinging their eyes, hair beginning to mat. Their cheery demeanour sagging like the elastic waistbands of their synthetic trousers. He can outlast them. Of this, he is sure.

He's been waiting years for this moment. He can wait a little longer.

CHAPTER 53

Kb2 Rf2+

Sarah slumps into the back seat.

Elias turns expectantly. 'Well? What did he say?'

'It was useless; I don't think he even believed me.'

'And what about the Americans?'

'He said he'd call.' Sarah beats her fist against the headrest of the passenger seat. 'What if I'm wrong? What if our teenager is the decoy and we're missing something bigger? What if he's just one of the pawns?'

Elias lets her finish. 'All of that is possible. And there's still time to properly alert the embassy before the reception. But this guy needs to be stopped now.'

Sarah stares out of the window. 'Steve said I looked like a wino,' she mumbles.

'Well I didn't want to say anything, but you do smell a little…'

'Oh shut up.'

'So where to next, Miss Sarah?' Vakho peers through the rear-view mirror.

'We're just going to have to go after him ourselves,' Sarah says. 'Vakho, you go back to the house and follow him. Elias and I will head for Freedom Square and see if we can spot him there. I wish we had a way of warning the security teams. No one is picking up their phones. Alistair's line is going straight through to voicemail. Even the duty officer's phone is ringing out.'

'You need to warn the President, Miss Sarah?' Vakho asks.

'Why, you have his number?'

'No, no.' Vakho laughs. 'Okay, so Vakho doesn't know everyone, but I know some people who might help. Don't worry, Miss Sarah, I'll make some calls.'

*

It is a blisteringly hot day for early May. Huge crowds have gathered in celebratory mood for a chance at a glimpse of the American president, flanked by his Georgian counterpart. Sarah and Elias are swamped in the throng, faces turning pink and foreheads glistening with sweat. As they push their way closer to the entrance of the square, they realise that the crowds are not moving. The square is still cordoned off and only a slow trickle are passing through the metal detectors at the entrance points. Sarah feels the surge of bodies behind her.

'We'll never make it through in time,' she shouts to Elias. 'Let's try the Embassy. We should be able to see what's going on from there.'

They fight their way towards the side of the square where two security guards are trying to control the entrance to the hotel underneath the Embassy.

'You can't come in here.' A black leather jacket blocks Sarah's progress.

'I work here. Please let me through.'

'No badge, no entry. You have to move away.' The security agent makes no eye contact with Sarah, not breaking his focus from the crowd.

'Come on, I work in the British Embassy. I need to get to my office. Please let me pass.'

The security agent looks down at her, snorting at her dishevelled appearance. 'And I'm a movie star. Move back please.'

Elias appears behind her. 'Do you want me to floor him?'

'I don't think that would help. Hold on. Sopho!' Sarah catches sight of Sopho watching from the door to the Embassy. 'Sopho? Can you get me in? It's urgent.'

A nod from Sopho and the mountain of a security man moves aside with a broad grin. 'You should have said you know Sopho. Please, go ahead.'

They hurry upstairs. 'I could have floored him, you know,' Elias mutters.

From the Embassy window, they have a perfect aerial view of the crowd gathering around the great golden statue of St George. Packs of people stretch back for miles down side streets, but the square is still half empty. Suddenly a wave of bodies surges forward and people flood in from all sides. At the entry points, hot and flustered American officials stand back and let the crowds pass through the barriers unchecked. The square is soon full, tens of thousands of people press against the temporary stage that has been erected at one end. It is a mass of red and white. Huge Georgian flags hang from windows and drape over balconies. Bleachers at the side of the square begin to fill with children in traditional dress, the colours of their clothes forming the crosses, stars and stripes of the Georgian and American flags.

Sarah scans the crowd for their suspect. She can see Secret Service and snipers positioned on all corners of the square, on every rooftop, at every entrance, flanking the stage from all sides. It seems unthinkable that anyone would be bold enough to mount an attack under such visible surveillance.

Suddenly, through the crowd, an odd movement catches her eye, like a rip current pushing against the waves.

'There,' she points. 'Is that him, moving towards the stage, in the black jacket?' Elias follows her finger to a man in a heavy leather jacket, sweating profusely, his right hand clutched to his chest.

'How should I know? You're the one who met him.'

'Only very briefly in an office, I wasn't really paying much attention. I think that's him; he definitely looks suspicious. What does he have in his hand?'

'A scarf maybe?'

'Oh God, I hope it's the right handkerchief.' Sarah tries to get a better look, but he keeps slipping behind other bodies in the crowd as he pushes towards the stage.

'Handkerchief?' Elias asks.

'The grenade was wrapped in a tartan hanky. At least it was when I left it.'

'And you're sure it's not going to go off? There will be complete carnage if he launches that onto the stage or the crowd.'

'Well, I hope not.' She tries to quash the mental image of a grenade ripping through the packed mass of bodies.

'How did you defuse it?'

'Superglue.'

'You did what?! You know the force with which those things explode? What makes you think some superglue is going to hold it?'

'It was the best I could do. I did a pretty thorough job, I'm fairly certain the safety handle won't release,' Sarah says, her confidence in her make-shift solution swiftly vanishing.

'Remind me why we didn't just bundle him into the boot of the car when we had the chance?'

'I thought we'd get some back-up. And if he disappeared, they might have activated Plan B.'

A tunnel of red and white has been created at the back of the stage so that the dignitaries can enter directly from their limousines parked in a side street. Even after hours of waiting in the blazing heat, the crowd is still in boisterous spirits. At the sound of the approaching motorcade, flags wave furiously, and the crowd starts chanting the President's name.

Secret Service agents sweep onto the stage, taking positions near the podium and the seats at the back. The crowd rises in a roar of welcome as the VIPs finally arrive. Saakashvili in navy blue suit, looking hot but delighted and beaming like a beacon. The US president unexpectedly small next to his Georgian counterpart, even with both arms raised towards the crowd still chanting his name. The two men link hands, arms high in victory, and survey the sea of people come to celebrate their alliance.

The American takes the podium. 'My wife and I were in the neighbourhood, and we thought we'd swing by and say *gamarjoba*.' The Georgian greeting, rolled out in a Texan drawl, is met with another roar of approval and applause.

Sarah can see their target edging closer to the stage. His hand still tightly clasped to the flash of tartan against his chest, his lips moving, muttering to himself. To Sarah, he sticks out like a black cloud in a clear sky. She watches the secret service agents scanning the crowd, trying to see if any of them have spotted him, but they remain inscrutable, their watchful gaze moving over the mass of faces.

CHAPTER 54

IN THE CROWD

Focus, Levon. You promised The Castle you could do this. It's just people. They can't see you. Their eyes are not on you. You are nothing to them. Levon wipes the sweat out of his eyes. Why is it so hot?

If they don't get him out, he has no chance. There is security everywhere. Levon watches the snipers on the roof surveying the crowd. There are agents on either side of the stage with guns across their chests. All this to protect the pig and his puppet master.

Don't look up, keep your head down, face shaded by the baseball cap: the instructions were clear. There are no cameras in the square, they can't trace you. It had all been clearly explained, but that was then. He had been thinking of CCTV and the all-seeing eye. But all these people. Everyone will see. He has no chance of escape.

Forget it, just get closer. There's a job to do. He moves with the swell of people who crowded through when the wilted security officer had finally given up, surging towards the stage.

Kill zone five metres. Damage zone fifteen metres. He has to be close. Much closer. He hadn't prepared for all the noise. People, he knew there would be people, but the waves of noise almost knock him sideways. Who are these morons anyway? Damage zone fifteen metres.

He pushes on, head down, elbow out, hand still clamped protectively over the weapon. Shit, bullet-proof glass, two-metre-high panels running across the length of the stage. Why hadn't he thought of that? His practice throws had all been straight. Why hadn't he thought? Why hadn't they said?

Maintain focus. One task, then freedom. One task. To set them all free.

CHAPTER 55

Ka1 Qh1+

'I've got to get closer; we've got to stop him.' Sarah runs out of the Embassy, hurtling down the stairs two at a time. Elias follows close behind. At the entrance, she grabs the mountain of a security guard who had tried to block their entry and drags him through the crowd towards the attacker. The guard looks dumbstruck. 'Just follow me,' she shouts over her shoulder and pulls him on.

'You gathered here with nothing but roses and the power of your convictions,' the President's voice booms around the square, 'and you claimed your liberty.' Sarah struggles to keep her eye on her target through the throng. Elias is shoving people aside while she ducks underneath shoulders, using her size to her advantage to navigate through the forest of legs. Sarah shouts for people to give way, but the crowds, stupefied by the heat, mostly ignore her—another nutter wanting attention.

She spots Levon, now right up against the stage. He shifts uncomfortably, tugging at his waist and his collar, wiping sweat from his forehead with his free left hand.

'Did you see that?' Elias asks. 'Has he got an explosive vest on under that jacket? Was there anything besides the grenade in the basement?'

'Quite a collection of hardware supplies, but no obvious signs of bomb-making.' Sarah realises that she does not really know what bomb-making would look like.

They are now just a few rows behind the attacker, Sarah can see the sweat glistening on the back of his neck. He turns away from the stage and his eyes meet hers, his face gripped with panic. 'Get him!' Sarah screams to the security agent.

The suspect wheels round, raises his right hand and throws the red-wrapped projectile towards the stage. He aims it high to clear the bullet-proof glass, but it seems to bounce off someone in front of him in the crowd, altering its course away from the podium. The handkerchief lands at the feet of the First Ladies, who look on in surprise.

Sarah holds her breath. Moments pass, long drawn-out seconds as she stares at the tartan package lying on the stage, waiting, hardly daring to move, blink, or swallow. Another roar from the crowd rips round the square and Sarah squeezes her eyes shut, bracing for the worst.

When she opens her eyes, a Georgian security agent on the stage, who looks suspiciously like Vakho, is hurrying towards the package—in one swift movement he bends down to pick it up and disappears.

'Was that…?' Sarah watches open-mouthed.

'His cousin, I think,' Elias says.

The First Ladies watch without response, maintaining their practised unruffled calm. At the podium, the President continues his speech, seemingly unaware of the danger that has just passed.

'You've got a solid friend in America,' he booms into the microphone to another eruption of delight.

Elias pulls Sarah into a tight embrace. 'You did it, you beautiful thing. I can't believe that worked, but you did it! Have you any idea what level of global chaos you have just managed to side swipe with that sticky grenade?'

'Where is he? We need to find him.'

Elias points to where the embassy security guard lies spread, his hefty body pinning the slight Armenian to the ground, calling into his radio for back-up. Suddenly the security guard rears up, clutching his hand to a spreading gash across his forehead. Blood is pouring down his face and he buckles forward, falling heavily to the ground.

Levon is behind him, brandishing a foot-long knife in one hand, and staring wildly. He runs for the stage, slashing his blade in violent frenzy. People around him scream; some throw themselves to the ground while others run from the stage in panic, piling into the crush of bodies trying to escape the square. His blade catches a girl's arm as she runs, her scream soaring above the noise of the crowd. He glares at her, knife held high, as if weighing up a follow-up hit, but turns back towards the stage, seeking out his target.

Sarah is torn. Her instinct is to run; what chance does she stand against Levon's blade? But she has come this far, she has to stop him. The tightly packed crowd push against her as people run to the exits, tripping over fallen bodies in their hurry to get away. She can see Levon's face, his eyes torn open in panic and fear and desperation. Had he thought he would get away? Had he thought he would escape? She wonders who he is most afraid of—the American snipers or facing Skarparov having failed in his task. He looks determined to go down fighting.

The security guard staggers back to his feet. Shouting into his walkie-talkie, he lurches towards Levon, the whites of his eyes like two half moons in his blood-soaked face.

Secret service agents swarm the stage to remove the Presidents and First Ladies. Sarah catches sight of the American's ashen features and the glowering look of fury on the face of President Saakashvili as they are bundled back into the tunnel to safety. With the stage now empty, Levon reels back, searching out his next victims. His eyes meet Sarah's, the terrified eyes of a drowning child, pleading, grasping. She sees the click of recognition, the accusation, and then he runs at her, both hands clutching the blade high above his head.

'Here!' Sarah screams, trying to call as much attention as she can. She runs deliberately towards the stage, away from safety, drawing Levon away from the crowd and back into open view. She leaps the fence at the front of the stage as he lunges towards her, blade drawn. She feels a sudden pressure in her ears and the world falls silent. Levon crashes to the ground, felled by a knee shot from a rooftop sniper. Slowly, the noises of the crowd return, the screaming, stamping, trembling hysteria rising to a painful pitch. Sarah sinks to the ground as the hive of secret service agents close in around Levon and secure his hands in cuffs.

Elias appears at her side and raises her gently from the ground. 'Sarah, you were amazing. Completely mad, but amazing.'

'But is that really it?' Sarah looks up into his eyes. 'Is it over?'

Elias draws her in. 'I think that's it. You did it.' He kisses her and she feels herself melt—days without sleep, the pain of her injuries, the tension and adrenaline of the past few hours all dissolve into his glorious embrace.

'We did it,' she whispers into his chest.

CHAPTER 56

Nb1 Bd4+

Sarah stares at the ceiling of the waiting room to the American holding cell in Istanbul, a fluorescent strip flickering in time with the throbbing in her head. The waiting room air tastes stale. Too many days without proper sleep and too much celebratory Georgian wine drunk has left her feeling ragged.

The door flies open. An American with military bearing and wide hips strides into the room, offering his hand.

'Ms Black?' He looks her up and down, his expression giving little away. 'Thank you for coming at such short notice. I'm gonna be straight with you, this is all highly irregular. But we are hoping you're gonna be able to help.' His smile looks forced, his face weary and harassed. 'I don't know how much was explained to you on the phone,' the officer begins.

'Very little, just that I was wanted for information on a question of global security.' Sarah grins at the sour-faced official. 'It's difficult to ignore that kind of summons.'

'Please sit,' he lowers his heavy frame into a chair, placing his fingertips on the table.

'There was a serious security incident during the visit of the President of the United States to Tbilisi.'

'Oh?' Sarah feigns ignorance.

'An attack was made on the lives of the President and the First Lady. Thank God, the weapon used in the attack malfunctioned and no one was hurt.'

'Thank God indeed,' Sarah focuses on the table to suppress a smile.

'But it remains a very serious attack and the perpetrators must be brought to justice.'

'Of course,' she nods solemnly, watching how the closely cropped hair on the side of his neck stands up as it pushes against his collar like the bristles of a hedgehog.

'We've got the guy who carried out the attack, but we suspect he was just a foot soldier in a bigger operation. He claims he worked for an Azeri citizen by the name of Iii-brag-iii-mov,' the officer labours each syllable in his heavy drawl, 'and our intelligence sources back that up. He was the mastermind and the money behind the attack. And we have him in custody. Here.'

'Ibragimov? He's here?' Sarah is stunned. After the sting in Baku she did not expect to see him again, and the mention of his name sends a hot rise of blood to her throat. She has not forgiven herself for how blindly she fell for his trap.

'I believe you know Mr Ibragimov, ma'am?'

'We've met once, not under the best of circumstances.' Sarah regrets her fragile state. She had come expecting to receive accolades for her help, not a reminder of her previous mistakes.

'He's asked to see you.'

'Me?' Sarah looks for the trap.

'We normally wouldn't go with something like this. It's not the way we work. But he is refusing to speak until you are here.' The officer clears his throat with a slight growl. 'He has proved quite determined on that point.' He holds Sarah's eye to the point of discomfort. 'Would you agree to speak to him, ma'am?'

Sarah wishes she had more time to prepare, that they had been less obtuse on the phone when summoning her to Istanbul. That they had warned her what she was coming to.

'He's in the interrogation room. As you know, Ms Black, he is a highly dangerous and unpredictable man and must remain under restraint. You're gonna have two officers from the Turkish Military police in there with you. My colleagues and I will be watching from next door.' Again the forced smile, his cheeks receding into deep creases under his eyes. 'Are you ready, ma'am?'

Sarah's head throbs. 'Yes,' she says. 'I'll come.'

*

A bare bulb hangs from the ceiling above the table where Sarah sits. The chair facing her is empty, the built-in shackles awaiting the prisoner. She searches the blank walls, but nothing gives away how the Americans would be watching.

Ibragimov enters, led by a Turkish soldier. He wears dark grey overalls, thick and coarse, his hands bound in cuffs. Sarah is surprised by how small he looks. The projection of power, the elegant grandeur he had exuded in Baku are gone. His eyes, rheumy and empty, appear sunken into his bruised and swollen face.

The guard pushes Ibragimov into the chair opposite Sarah, clamps shut his restraints and secures his feet to the floor. There is a resignation in his movements. He allows himself to be manhandled without resistance—a last effort at maintaining dignity, or has he lost the will to fight?

Sarah stares at him, her anger faltering at his diminished state. He meets her gaze, thick lips twitching.

Finally, he speaks. 'Thank you for coming, Sarah.'

'If I'd known it was for you, I might not have bothered.'

'Please accept my apologies for causing you any trouble in Baku. I hope you did not take it personally.' He speaks slowly, each word lingering on his lips.

'How could I not? You set me up.'

'I had nothing against you; it was your organisation I wanted to discredit.'

'But why? What was in it for you?'

'Disruption of the status quo. A chance to knock British Oil and Gas off their throne. A piece of the pie for some of us more deserving of our country's riches. Don't take it personally.'

'How did you know who I was? Did Skarparov give me away?'

'I bet he'd like to take credit for that. But I knew who you were before you even arrived in Baku.'

'Your thugs on the train?'

'You can never be too careful.' He narrows his eyes and gives a thin smile.

'And the silver car? You sent him to follow me?'

'He didn't do you any harm. Irakli warned me you were trouble. I just wanted to work you out for myself.'

'What do you want?' Sarah asks abruptly. 'Surely you didn't bring me here to crow.'

'I need you to help convince these thick-headed Americans,' he pauses to take a laboured breath, 'that I had nothing to do with their failed attack in Tbilisi.'

'And why me?'

'Because I trust that you know who was really behind it.' He watches her carefully.

'What gives you that impression?'

'Because it is your job to know, and I'm sure you are very good at your job.'

Sarah waits, watching Ibragimov, trying to sniff out whether it is fear or cunning that lies behind his enigmatic smile. His yellowish skin is even more jaundiced than before. A crust has formed around the prominent mole above his left eyebrow. His hands, the papery skin dotted with liver spots, lie palm-down on the table, a fortune teller preparing his cards.

'It is the job of the CIA to know, too, and they have good

reason to suspect it was you. Why would I think otherwise?'

'Because you have been following my dear nephew for some time. I suspect your interest is not purely personal.' A trace of his former self resurfaces as he speaks, his spirit is not entirely beaten.

'That still doesn't explain why the Americans have you sitting in a Turkish jail and not him,' Sarah says.

'I don't know what they have on me, but I have no doubt that whatever it is, has been passed to them by my nephew to cover his back.' Ibragimov keeps his voice controlled.

'Suppose you are right, and that I did know there is someone else behind the failed attack in Tbilisi.' Sarah holds his eye. 'Why would it be in my interest to help you? The last time we met you landed me in an Azeri jail. There is something rather enjoyable in seeing the tables turned, don't you think?' Sarah expected to take more pleasure in her vengeance. But Ibragimov's sorry state sours her enjoyment.

'Come now, Sarah, you whiled away a few hours in a Baku police station. I am being kept in solitary confinement and subjected to the enlightened interrogation techniques of our American friends.' He raises his voice and looks defiantly around the room. 'But I don't expect or deserve your kindness, or even your sympathy.' He watches her, his thick tongue separating heavy lips. When he speaks again, his voice is scarcely more than a whisper. 'I can help you get him.'

Sarah remains silent.

'You don't want him to get away with this, do you? Whatever you might think about me, I'm sure you feel no more affection for Viktor.' Ibragimov speaks so softly that Sarah has to lean right across the table into the cloud of his stale and putrid breath to hear him.

'What can you give me on him that I don't already know?' She pulls away.

'I can tell you who he was acting for.' He observes her closely. 'Think about it: why would my nephew, who enjoys his comfortable life in Tbilisi, want to blow up the Georgian president, and risk pulling Georgia into a war with the US in the process?'

'To create instability, panic, halt the changes that are bringing Georgia closer to the west?' Sarah lists the reasons that Skarparov himself had given her as motives for Ibragimov to mount a similar attack.

'No, you misunderstand him completely. Viktor loves the West; he makes full advantage of being able to live in both worlds. This little stunt in Tbilisi was not for his benefit. It was payment to a client, for services rendered. A client who is not going to be happy that he failed.'

Sarah considers her opponent, remembering their meeting in Baku. How callously he set her up, how little understanding she had at the time of what he was planning. How all the while she thought she was in control of the game. Even chained to a table, he retains something of that slippery charm she had failed to see through. Had Michael fallen for it too, or had someone set him up, eager to puncture his rise? 'So Skarparov is a gun for hire?' she asks. 'A paid assassin?'

'Among other things, I suppose you could put it like that.'

'And who is this client who wants to sow chaos in the Caucasus?'

'Who do you think?' Ibragimov's thick lips scarcely move. 'The Russians,' he hisses. 'Nobody else has such a vested interest in seeing Saakashvili and his great ambitious project fail. And if the American president had happened to go down in collateral damage, then I don't suppose they would have lost too much sleep over that either.'

'But why would Skarparov do it if it wasn't in his interest? Why not let the Russians do it themselves?'

'For what they could give him in return—weapons. Vast quantities of Russian-made arms and explosives, and the mercenaries and foot soldiers to use them.'

'What does Skarparov need an army for?'

Ibragimov straightens up. 'Have I not given you enough?' He examines the backs of his hands. 'Surely there are some things you can work out for yourself.' His lips curl into a self-satisfied smile.

'Why should I believe any of this? Skarparov fed me an equally convincing story that implicated you in an attack of this kind. Why should I believe you over him?'

'I can give you proof—a name, the KGB officer who organised the weapons sale. Given that Skarparov has just failed to keep up his end of the deal, they should be happy to sell him out to you.'

Sarah hesitates. She wants nothing more than to get to Skarparov—he can't possibly be allowed to get away with this. But trusting Ibragimov feels reckless.

'What about the train? You planned the crash to kill the agent who linked you with those weapons.'

'Who told you that? Another of Viktor's stories?'

'No, that one came from our intelligence sources.'

'Classic Viktor. You set up a fake mole, then you kill him to add to his credentials and remove the risk of him turning on you. Two birds with one stone. That agent was a friend of mine. Of course I knew he liked to talk, but if I had wanted him dead, there would have been much easier ways to do it.'

'The tickets of the bombers were traced to employees at one of your companies.'

'Were they? Then it must have been me.' He smiles laconically. 'You see how easily you British can be led? My poor dead friend was no angel. He was well known as a go-to for sourcing Russian armaments and ammunition. Maybe he knew too much about what Skarparov was up to and had to be removed? Three birds with one stone? I have to give it to him. Viktor is smarter than I gave him credit for.'

'And Vienna? I was shot at in the middle of a crowded cafe—was that you, too?'

'My apologies.' His voice is unapologetic. 'The bullet was meant for Dilara.'

'You mistook me for Dilara?'

'You don't think it was me pulling the trigger, do you? She killed one of my most trusted operatives, fed him to the pigs. Silly bitch boasted about it to a friend. But she didn't know, her friend was also my friend.'

Any pity Sarah felt for him is gone. 'Tell me the name. I will check it out and if it proves your story, I will talk to the Americans.' She is happy to leave Ibragimov to rot. But she can't refuse the chance to bring down Skarparov too. Ibragimov might be deserving of his lot, but Skarparov deserves much worse. Unless Sarah helps Ibragimov, Skarparov will get away with it all. He must be brought to justice.

'How do I know that you will keep up your side of the bargain?' he asks.

'You don't,' Sarah says coldly, 'but you don't look overwhelmed with options.'

Ibragimov hesitates. 'Very well, Sarah, but this is just for you. Come closer.'

She leans her ear towards Ibragimov's mouth. The Turkish guard moves suddenly to place himself behind them. Sarah is engulfed by the stench of stale bodily fluids.

He whispers a name, his hot foul breath brushing her ear—Nikolay Kuznetsov. The name that the banker in Tbilisi had written on the back of his business card. She leaves the room without looking back.

CHAPTER 57

Nb2 Rf1

Sarah finds Elias sitting at a corner table in a small cafe in Beyoglu, one of a crowd of colourful awnings that line the sloping alley. Brightly painted wooden beams hang over the tables, and Elvis croons gently in the background.

She sucks on a tall glass of lemon and mint, savouring the sour freshness, having run from the holding centre to escape the stale air and the Americans who wanted to sit her down for an interrogation of her own.

'And what do you think of the world's finest refreshment?' Elias asks, grinning at her like a happy lion, anticipating future pleasure.

'It's perfect; I thought I was going to be stuck with that smell all day.'

Elias lights a cigarette as he listens to her explanation of what Ibragimov offered. 'So?' He asks. 'What next?'

'It shouldn't be too difficult to follow up on the name, and if he's right then this is far from over.'

'What a shame. I thought we might be able to enjoy a little time off-duty.'

'There will be plenty of time for that. Besides, you're not even on duty. Or is this the moment you're going to tell me you actually work for Dutch intelligence? Or the CIA?'

Elias laughs. 'No, happily not. But you've dragged me into this now. I can hardly go back to being Skarparov's fix-it guy, can I? And besides, you make it look like fun.'

'Supposing Ibragimov is right and Skarparov is putting together an army of Russian weapons and mercenaries, I still don't understand what he would want it for.'

Elias unfolds a napkin in the centre of the table and takes out a pen. 'Let's start with what we have. How much do you know about Skarparov's connection outside the Caucasus?'

'There were the people he met in Dubai.' Sarah recalls the details Steve uncovered. 'A Cypriot shipping company—presumably if you're moving large quantities of illegal goods and weaponry around the world, you're going to need a friend who can help keep customs and transport authorities off your back. And that ties up with what your Chechen said about the weapons being shipped out through Crimea.'

Elias scribbles the word Crimea on the napkin. 'Any idea where the weapons could be heading?' He speaks in lowered tones, but his eyes are bright and inviting, as if discussing something far more romantic.

'He had another meeting with UN Logistics, so he must be operating somewhere with a significant UN presence. Post-conflict maybe? Or where they're providing disaster relief or humanitarian assistance?' Sarah assembles a mental map of possible destinations.

'Should have known that pumped-up gravy train would be involved: saving the world, one spoiled expat at a time.'

'I bet anything is for sale if you know the right person to ask. He also met someone from the African Union, so let's assume we can focus our search on Africa.' Sarah grabs the napkin and draws a crude outline of the continent below Elias's musings.

'African countries with a high UN presence? Rwanda? Congo? Liberia? Do you have anything else?'

'Nothing from the meetings in Dubai.' Sarah tries to remember any other details that could help. She can't look at Elias without wanting to be distracted from the task at hand so stares up at the turquoise painted beams for inspiration.

'It may be incredibly cheesy, but he does have the most beautiful voice,' Elias says in his deadpan tone.

'Skarparov?'

'No, although who knows, maybe he's a secret cabaret star. I meant Elvis.'

Sarah listens to the King slip gently through the melody of *Only Fools Rush In*.

'The nun! There was an Irish nun in Dubai who was looking for Skarparov.'

'What on earth did she want with him?'

'Money. She knew him from where she was working. She was a missionary, but I can't remember where she said she was based.'

'Any way to track her down?' Elias doodles a nun's habit over the map of Africa.

'I wasn't really paying much attention, I thought she was just a useful decoy produced by the Ambassador to distract the officious security guard. I hope Alistair can remember more than I can.'

She dials the Ambassador's number. 'Alistair, I need your help.'

'I do love it when you say that.'

'Do you remember that Irish nun we met in Dubai?'

'That sounds like the opening line to a rather good joke.' Alistair chuckles to himself. 'Yes, of course. Lovely lady, rather the worse for wear.'

'Can you remember where she said she was working?'

'Let me see, I think she said she was Sister Margaret from Kenema, it made me think you could write a good limerick about her. Would that sound about right? No idea where that is. Hold on a moment. Sopho!' Sarah moves the phone away from her ear. 'Where or what is Kenema?' A pause. 'Apparently it's in Sierra Leone! Funny sort of place for a nice lady like that to end up. The spiritual vocation knows no bounds.'

'Sierra Leone? That's it!'

'Is it? Well, happy to help. Will we see you here again soon?'

'I do hope so, thank you Alistair.' Sarah rings off.

'Sierra Leone?' Elias asks. 'That's blood diamond country.'

'It certainly fits the bill. And Sopho uncovered a diamond polishing business owned by Skarparov in Amsterdam. But what would Skarparov be doing exporting arms to Sierra Leone?'

'Weapons in return for preferential treatment—access to diamond concessions? Favourable terms? That amount of hardware could buy quite some influence.'

'Can you have another chat with your Chechen drinking buddy to see if it matches up?'

'Of course.' Elias reaches across the table for her hand. 'But for now, will you allow me to show you around the most romantic city in the world?'

He leads her out into the narrow street, holding her hand tightly in his and humming the Elvis song that had been playing in the cafe. Suddenly he spins her round in a pirouette, catching her as she lands in a deep swoon over his waiting arm.

'What are you doing?' Sarah collapses with laughter at being made to dance in a crowded tourist street.

'I'm rushing in,' Elias replies in his deep monotone.

'In the middle of the street?'

'Can you think of a better place to dance?'

Sarah looks into his laughing eyes and allows herself to be waltzed through the streets of Istanbul, secretly hoping the whole world is watching.

CHAPTER 58

0-1

Sarah is inspecting a pile of gnarled and twisted carrots when the smell of purple basil draws her back to the Caucasus. She looks around, half-expecting to see a hawk-eyed mountain man hoisting a tray overflowing with herbs and fat spring onions. But the traders and their calls are distinctly English, the scene unmistakably London.

Rain falls from heavy skies. Borough Market, usually packed and bustling on a Saturday morning, is almost deserted. Sarah finds the weather strangely comforting; it makes her happy to be home. Without the crowds, she has more time to browse and inspect the striking shapes and colours of the produce on display. As she follows her nose towards an array of fresh cheese, she becomes aware of someone strolling beside her, adjusting his pace to match hers.

'Michael?'

Since her return to London, she had thought endlessly of him. Every grey head startled her, she looked for him in every shadow.

But to see him again makes her breath stick in her throat.

'I'm so glad to see you back in one piece. I wanted to congratulate you on a job well done.' He holds out his oversized umbrella to shield her from the rain.

'Where the hell have you been?'

'Over at the organic butchers, they've got some excellent sausages on special.'

'Don't be funny. I haven't heard from you for weeks. What happened to you in Vienna?'

'I'm so sorry I lost you. I had another appointment, but as soon as I heard what had happened, I came straight back to find you. You vanished. I went to the hotel you were supposed to be staying at and even waited for you at the airport the next day, but you had gone without trace. You have no idea how worried I was when you didn't turn up in Kentucky. Steve told me what happened in Tbilisi, but I'm looking forward to hearing your version of accounts. You've certainly proved your worth.' He smiles at her, his blue eyes penetrating and warm. 'How did you link Ibragimov to the attack in Tbilisi?'

'Ibragimov didn't do it.'

'Oh?'

'Skarparov was behind all of it—the train derailment, the anti-aircraft gun, and the grenade attack in the square.' Sarah approaches a cheese stall, wheels of prize-winning Caerphilly stacked up against paper wrapped wedges.

'But Ibragimov's fingerprints were all over it?'

'Hold on, I want to try a bit of this.' Sarah asks the salesgirl, rosy face half-hidden in a blue tartan scarf, for one of the small slices stuck with a toothpick. Michael tries to move her on, but she is enjoying herself too much.

'Think about it,' Sarah says, having complimented the girl on her cheese, 'Skarparov wouldn't agree to carry out an attack like that unless he was one hundred percent confident he wouldn't get caught. What better way to avoid suspicion than to have all fingers point to your own flesh and blood?'

'But the anti-aircraft gun—'

'Wow, look at that one.' Sarah points at a towering wheel of Cheshire cheese, high as a hat box wrinkled with age. 'I bet that's good.'

'Wasn't it Irakli's goons with the anti-aircraft gun?'

'I bet even Irakli thought he was doing Ibragimov's bidding. And that's why Skarparov had to wipe him out—too much of a risk that he might unwittingly give the game away.'

'And the weapons—'

'Flawed intel, provided by a dead guy. Don't you see, Michael? You've been duped. You were so blinded by your desire for revenge against Ibragimov that you took your eye off the bigger picture.' Sarah is enjoying this immensely. 'Why didn't you tell me your motives for nailing Ibragimov were personal?'

The blood drains from Michael's face. 'It wasn't relevant.'

'Not relevant? I think it was crucial. What if Skarparov fed this to you, knowing you'd chase doggedly after his trail of clues to pin it on Ibragimov?'

Michael's lips are pinched. 'Skarparov didn't feed this to me.'

'So who did tip you off in the first place?

'The Russians brought it to us. An old colleague of mine, Nikolay Kuznetsov.'

Sarah laughs and shakes her head. 'Never trust an old fox. Goodbye Michael.' She turns to leave.

'Wait, Sarah.' He takes her arm and pulls her round to face him. 'I came here to congratulate you, not to scare you off. You did well. You prevented two attacks that would have changed the course of history; and if Ibragimov ended up in a US jail because of it, well I can't say he doesn't deserve it. But Skarparov got away. We're not finished yet.'

'No.' Sarah wrests her arm free and makes towards the exit. 'We are.' Michael is right that it is far from over, but she doesn't need his help to finish the game.

'But I would have thought—'

'I don't want anything more to do with your hush-hush

operation. You left me for dead. You sent me in completely unprepared on your own private revenge mission, and then you disappeared.'

'You're here, aren't you? What more did I need to give you that you didn't already have?'

Sarah continues to push through the market stalls, forcing Michael to trot to catch up.

'Of course you are free to go,' he keeps up his casual tone, but his composure sounds strained. 'But you do realise what you're giving up by leaving? I think it's best if—'

Sarah spins on her heels and stares him down over a pyramid of inky olives. 'You don't get to decide what's best for me, Michael. Your protection gave me nothing. I owe you nothing. I'm out.'

'You should think about this first.' The blue of his eyes is all the more startling against the grey skies. 'Take a few weeks rest and recuperation, look after yourself. I'm sure you have plenty to catch up on in London. Then we'll talk.'

'Goodbye, Michael.' Sarah strides out of the market and up towards the crowd of umbrellas on London Bridge. This time, he does not follow.

She gazes up at the sky where a beam of sunlight is struggling to pierce the heavy cloud. She feels alone and unsure, but tantalisingly free.

A message beeps on her phone.

Elias: Freetown confirmed as destination. What do you say to a holiday in Sierra Leone? I hear the beaches are fantastic.

Sarah pushes across the bridge, considering a return to the world of job applications and CV tweaking, Sunday lunches under her father's heavily-worn concern, trying to explain to her brothers why her promising career in the Civil Service had petered out so soon, evenings in the pub with friends listening to rehashed stories of drunken escapades or trying to avoid Jenny's more probing curiosity, all the while scanning the news for reports from Sierra Leone.

It is an impossible future—a world where she no longer belongs.

She types her reply: *I'm in*

HISTORICAL NOTE

On the 10th May 2005, an ethnically-Armenian Georgian national threw a live hand grenade at US President George W. Bush and Georgian President Mikheil Saakashvili as they addressed huge crowds in Freedom Square. The grenade, wrapped in a tartan handkerchief, landed close to the stage but failed to detonate. This much is true. Skarparov's plot and Sarah's involvement is complete fabrication, invented to try and fill in the gaps as to how and why this could have happened. Reports at the time suggested that the grenade failed because it was too tightly wrapped in the handkerchief, but that sounded just too far-fetched to be true…

Did You Enjoy This Book?

If so, you can make a HUGE difference.

For any author, the single most important way we have of getting our books noticed is a really simple one—and one which you can help with.

Yes, you.

Us indie authors and publishers don't have the financial muscle of the big guys to take out full-page ads in the newspaper or put posters on the subway.

But we do have something much more powerful and effective than that, and it's something that those big publishers would kill to get their hands on.

A committed and loyal bunch of readers.

Honest reviews of our books help bring them to the attention of other readers.

If you've enjoyed this book I would be really grateful if you could spend just a couple of minutes leaving a review (it can be as short as you like) on this book's page on your favourite store and website.

Acknowledgements

A great many people have helped me develop this story from a writing-prompt that got out of hand to a fully fleshed out novel and opening of a series. My first thanks to Laurence Daren King who held my hand through the early drafts when I had no idea what I was doing and the team at Jericho Writers for their enthusiasm and support.

Thank you to Jill Crawford who patiently read through early drafts—still deeply flawed—and wielded her red pen in a way only a most insightful editor (and dear friend) could do.

To my very first beta readers—Gianna Minton, Kim Geene, Hanako Brown and especially Pippa Brown for her no holds barred feedback—looking back I hate my main character as she was at that iteration too! Thank you for telling me what I needed to hear.

Thank you to my Georgian readers Gia Kvinakadze and Nino Gugunishvili and also to Lali Meskhi and Beka and Nino Gotsadze for their important roles in igniting my love affair with Georgia.

Thank you to Frederik Rengers for answering a question about betting in Dubai with a fully formed character and to all of the staff in the British Embassy in Tbilisi. Any similarities you may recognise in my characters are entirely coincidental.

Thank you to the Caledonia Novel Prize for long-listing an

early draft of this novel just at the point that I was about to consign it to a drawer. Your endorsement gave me the confidence to keep fighting for the story I wanted to tell.

Thank you to Curtis Brown Creative for another confidence boost and introducing me to a talented group of writers, including beta readers Sheena M and Daniel Aubrey—the world's best cheerleader and the one who brought me to the VWG, the most supportive and inspirational group of writers on Twitter. Writing can be lonely work and the journey to publication can be long and full of setbacks. I don't think I could have persisted without the community, encouragement and support of the team at @ virtwriting.

To Rebecca Millar whose astute editorial eye and thoughtful feedback helped me to make the jump that was needed to take it from 'almost' to 'yes'.

To my agent, Tom Cull. I knew he would understand what I was trying to write when I learned we had a shared love of Patrick Leigh-Fermor, Ian Fleming and classic espionage fiction. Thank you for believing in Sarah from the start and for sticking with us to find the right home.

To Simon and Pete from Burning Chair for their enthusiasm for the series and dedication to bringing books into the hands of readers. They have been a pleasure to work with and their inputs have only made the story stronger.

To my mother for giving me a life-long love of books and reading and making this something I've always wanted to do.

To my father for not quite managing to put me off a career in the civil service and the rich seam of copy it brought.

For my children—Freddie, Amalia and Marcus—who inspire me and make me laugh every day.

To everyone who has looked after my children giving me time to write—you are all heroes. Especially Caroline Malamba to whom the book is dedicated, gone much too soon. If you had not cared for my children with such big-hearted love, I would never have begun.

And finally to Daniel—spinner of stories, weaver of dreams, squeezer of juice, the best possible co-creator and collaborator without whom none of this would have been possible.

About The Author

For as long as she can remember, Lucy has always been in love with books – stories of adventure, of weird and wonderful places, and seeing the world through someone else's eyes. She always dreamed of writing, but there were other things to do first.

She studied languages and philosophy at Oxford and joined the Foreign Office straight out of university in search of adventure and new people and places. She quickly moved across to the Department for International Development (DFID), where she spent time in Georgia, Armenia and Azerbaijan, China and Sierra Leone. She left Sierra Leone to join her now husband in Jordan, taking the long way there across the Sahara, Europe, the Balkans, Turkey and Syria in a much-beloved Land Rover. In Jordan, she worked for Her Majesty Queen Rania while spending much time bumping around the phenomenal Jordanian desert.

After Jordan, she spent several years in a jungle camp in Gabon surrounded by elephants and humpback whales, which is where the Sarah Black books began. They took life as a way to record all the best bits of people she had met and places she had been, with a plot to make them much more exciting. Lucy has always plausibly denied being a spy – but the books were written to show what that life might have been like.

She spent three years in Brisbane, Australia, and another two experiencing deep culture-shock in the Netherlands during the weirdness of the pandemic, and is now enjoying the freedom of living at the end of the world in Lüderitz, Namibia, crafting stories and making films about the adventure of growing giant kelp.

She also wastes a considerable amount of time on Twitter @ HooftLucy

About Burning Chair

Burning Chair is an independent publishing company based in the UK, but covering readers and authors around the globe. We are passionate about both writing and reading books and, at our core, we just want to get great books out to the world.

Our aim is to offer something exciting; something innovative; something that puts the author and their book first. From first class editing to cutting edge marketing and promotion, we provide the care and attention that makes sure every book fulfils its potential.

We are:

- Different
- Passionate
- Nimble and cutting edge
- Invested in our authors' success

If you're an author and would like to know more about our submissions requirements and receive our free guide to book publishing, visit:

www.burningchairpublishing.com

If you're a reader and are interested in hearing more about our books, being the first to hear about our new releases or great offers, or becoming a beta reader for us, again please visit:

www.burningchairpublishing.com

More From Burning Chair Publishing

Your next favourite new read is waiting for you…!

The Other Side of Trust, by Neil Robinson

The Brodick Cold War Series, by John Fullerton
   Spy Game
   Spy Dragon
   Burning Bridges, by Matthew Ross

Killer in the Crowd, by P N Johnson

Push Back, by James Marx

The Casebook of Johnson & Boswell, by Andrew Neil Macleod
   The Fall of the House of Thomas Weir
   The Stone of Destiny

By Richard Ayre:
   Shadow of the Knife
   Point of Contact
   A Life Eternal

The Curse of Becton Manor, by Patricia Ayling

Near Death, by Richard Wall

Blue Bird, by Trish Finnegan

The Tom Novak series, by Neil Lancaster
  Going Dark
  Going Rogue
  Going Back

Love Is Dead(ly), by Gene Kendall

Burning, An Anthology of Short Thrillers, edited by Simon Finnie and Peter Oxley

The Infernal Aether series, by Peter Oxley
  The Infernal Aether
  A Christmas Aether
  The Demon Inside
  Beyond the Aether
  The Old Lady of the Skies: 1: Plague

The Haven Chronicles, by Fi Phillips
  Haven Wakes
  Magic Bound

Beyond, by Georgia Springate

10:59, by N R Baker

The Wedding Speech Manual: The Complete Guide to Preparing, Writing and Performing Your Wedding Speech, by Peter Oxley

www.burningchairpublishing.com

CPSIA information can be obtained
at www.ICGtesting.com
Printed in the USA
LVHW112026291022
731756LV00001B/1

23/1/23

9 781912 946303